27 rue Mortain

Michael Alty

Published 2016 by arima publishing

www.arimapublishing.com

ISBN 978 1 84549 686 9
© Michael Alty 2016

Printed and bound in the United Kingdom

Typeset in Garamond

Swirl is an imprint of arima publishing.

arima publishing
ASK House, Northgate Avenue
Bury St Edmunds, Suffolk IP32 6BB
t: (+44) 01284 700321

www.arimapublishing.com

Chapter One

My name is Gertrude, Alison Tomlinson, formerly, Partridge, a Bournemouth greengrocer's daughter and I reside in a prestigious North of England seaside town called Southport and for all my sins it is situated in the notorious district of Merseyside. My husband, Thomas, until 1992 was a doctor, a medical practitioner in the family-run Tomlinson's clinic in nearby Ainsdale but tragically he died of a heart attack eight years ago whilst taking Rufus, our Border Collie, out for his evening walk; sadly fourteen year-old Rufus died peacefully in his sleep last year and I miss him dearly.

I was until 1980 a nursing sister at Ormskirk General Hospital, Lancashire which was where I first met my lovely man, Thomas, during an extended coffee break which seemed to last for hours. I had previously been a nurse in the old draconian Kings Park Hospital, Bournemouth but because of over-staffing problems I was given the opportunity to be transferred to another hospital or by modern terminology made redundant.

Thomas departed this life leaving me comfortably well off, rattling around in a four bedroom Regency town house in Lords Street and a barrel load of money in the bank to keep the wolves away from my front and back door for many years.

Tomorrow is my birthday; Saturday the first of January 2000, the millennium when I will have reached the grand old age of eighty. Last evening, I phoned my nephew, Christopher Travis and his wife, Lynette, who live in a rural haven on the periphery of Bournemouth. There was only one purpose behind this, but as soon as I heard the phone ringing in their spacious nineteen-thirties semi-detached town house in Queens Park Avenue, I wondered why I had decided to get in touch with him; a man I'd never really taken to even when he'd been a child, but for my part, this sudden over indulgent out of character desire to make contact with what little family I had left overruled the wisdom of resurrecting part of my family history that would be far better relegated to a black hole in outer-space which was where it really belonged. People say I am a stubborn old woman, who complains a lot and almost invariably get things wrong and out of perspective; they are probably right, but that is my business. Christopher took a long time to answer the phone, making it a continuation of the aggravation which I'd had to tolerate yesterday afternoon, most of which was promulgated by my solicitor, Mr George Hesketh of Messrs Hesketh & Draper solicitors and notaries, when he failed to convince me he couldn't put together a simple Last Will and Testament, but he could however extract a large sum of money from me to ensure that part of the proceeds could be used to buy a new garage for his Porsche 911 sports car. I would have hung up, but only by sheer determination and, most importantly, the ability to hang on to my faculties and to try and maintain what little common sense I had left inside my brain, deterred me from doing so.

My fifty-one year old nephew, Christopher is the son of a younger sister, Agnes and brother-in-law, William Travis, who were tragically killed when a branch from a tree careered through the windscreen of their Austin Minor 1000 car somewhere between Salisbury, Wiltshire and Ringwood, Hampshire during a violent storm in 1987.

Sitting alone in front of an artificial electric log fire in the drawing room I am looking at the Christmas tree and all the decorations I so precariously fixed with Sellotape on to the ceiling and I am asking myself the question was it all worth the effort. My conclusion; maybe it was, although Christmas today does bring hypocrisy to its maximum but, however, knowing I had made arrangements earlier for my nephew and niece to inherit my estate and, together with the heat billowing out from the fire on to my arthritic ankles, was not entirely a comforting thought.

With only my twice-weekly visit from Joan Webster, the Social Services daily help, the regular delivery of 'Meals on Wheels' by Tommy Smith at midday and the gardener, Fred Barratt who can't wait for the Spring season to arrive so he can serve me with another contract to rip me off by another thousand pounds, I feel as though I'm being deprived of friends and neighbours.

I am glancing at the antique clock on the mantelpiece; it is about to chime midnight. My small Roberts transistor radio is switched on low to

Radio Merseyside and the Swedish group, 'ABBA' is singing sweetly "Happy New Year" making me feel sad and even lonelier; nobody wants you when you're old. The door bell is ringing and a large pepperoni pizza which I had ordered half an hour ago is about to make its grand entrance into my house, courtesy of a Southport Pronto Sprint Pizza Express.

'Will you join me in a small glass of homemade lemonade young man?'

'No thanks, Missus, I have a motorbike waiting for me outside.'

*

Mrs Tomlinson, Gertrude, Alison Partridge died on the 23rd February 2000 following a stroke, leaving her house, money and all her worldly goods to Travis and his family.

*

No 46 Queens Park Avenue, Bournemouth Tuesday 22nd August 2000

May I introduce myself? My name is Christopher Miles Travis and I am going to tell you a story which will hopefully remind everyone of the persecution and suffering of the Arabic and Jewish people throughout the ages, beginning with the Crusades, the Knights Templar; the Knights of Saint John of Jerusalem and more recently, the Nazi regime orchestrated by Adolf Hitler during The Second World War; the deportation of Jews to the death camps in Poland from their homes in occupied France beginning in October 1940 until August 1944 and, as with the *Koran*, the *Old* and *New Testaments* in the *Holy Bible* and the scriptures belonging to the *Dead Sea Scrolls*, I want this to be one of the greatest stories ever told...

I am a lecturer in medieval history at Royal London House, the University in Bournemouth and my wife, Lynette, has her own dress shop in Boscombe, specializing in garments for larger women. Our two bright teenage children, Barbara and Victoria are twins and are both studying for their Bachelor of Education degrees at the Westhill teacher training college in Selly Oak, Birmingham.

Lynette and I both belong to the Anglican Church and were married in St.Clements Church, Bournemouth on Wednesday 12th May 1982. We can remember that day all too well because it was the day the cruise liner,

QE2, sailed from Southampton to take the British Task Force to the Falkland Islands. I remember my mother and father seated in their favourite wooden pew in the front row of the church and little did we know that we would be on the same seats five years later by the side of two mahogany coffins. We can recall Aunt Gertrude not being able to attend the wedding because of Uncle Thomas's death during the same week and of feeling guilty because of not going up to the North of England to attend his funeral; Aunt Gertrude could never allow me to forget the time when I tried to explain to her in my younger days, it was a hot water bottle which made her brand new '*Slumberland*' mattress wet and not me.

I am now standing in front of the bar in Bournemouth's Premier Inn on Westover Road drinking my second large Scotch and soda and contemplating the incredibly strange and bizarre events which had happened since Lynette and I bought the *pied-á-terre*, our second home in Northern France less than three months ago.

This morning we returned home to Bournemouth by car from the French port of Cherbourg to nearby Poole in Dorset, travelling on a Brittany Ferries boat, having sold our house in *Méridon* to a Russian film producer, Boris Polyakov and his clarinet playing wife, Esmeralda.

It is very windy this evening and as I look over towards Lower Gardens and the Pavilion Theatre I can almost hear my Auntie Evelyn jokingly saying "does anyone want to buy a teddy bear?". At seventy-six years of age, Evelyn Partridge was a spinster, a 'Santa's little helper' working voluntarily for the 'Rotary Club of Great Britain' also part-time in the Samaritans shop in Holdenhurst Road; she became a celebrity, especially in the summer when she handed out cuddly toys to children who were seen to be down on their luck. Auntie Evelyn, the epitome of an eccentric charity do-gooder died in her council flat on Christmas morning in 1998 when her rather antiquated gas oven exploded whilst cooking the turkey and, apart from Lynette, the two girls and me, not one of her so called friends attended her funeral. She was well known by the local police constabulary too, because on moonlit nights she would soft pedal her bone-shaker bicycle along Undercliff Drive without lights and a bell that had ceased to function for many years. It was only after she had been cautioned for the hundredth time and the patrol car had disappeared around a corner to join in a Harry Ramsden's fish and chip extravaganza, Auntie Evelyn would get back on to her bike to cycle home.

Barbara and Victoria had already begun their summer recess from college and were delighted to see their mum and dad back for good on British soil.

It is five minutes past seven and I am waiting outside the Gala Casino for Lynette, Barbara and Vicky to arrive in the car; an old dark blue Volkswagen Polo Classic Estate which has been in the family since its launch in 1985 and we are about to replace it sooner than later with a vehicle manufactured in Britain; if you want to buy a tank you buy a tank and preferably one that doesn't have Adolf Hitler's name connected with it.

I can now see Lynette pulling up next to the bus stop alongside the Pavilion coach drop-off point and I am about to attempt to cross this busy road where most of the traffic seems to be making its way down towards The Square and Richmond Hill.

'Well, darling, this week we'll be able to see the Friday Family Fiesta fireworks display in the gardens, won't we?' my lovely wife is trying desperately to inform me.

'Yes dear,' shaking my head disapprovingly. 'I think we have seen enough fireworks during the last couple of months to last us an entire lifetime.'

'The Family Adventure Festival sounds good too, doesn't it Barbara? And that will be fun won't it dad?' Victoria has just said looking over at The Bournemouth Balloon securely tethered in the Lower Gardens.

'Don't even think about it!'

Vicky is now suggesting we all go to the BIC, Bournemouth International Centre on Friday to see 'The Stink Pots' Revival.

'Don't you mean 'The Ink Spots' Vicky?' says Lynette.

'I knew it was something that came out of a bottle.'

'We can always learn to surf, dad,' says Barbara who is now showing signs of life seated next to her sister on the back seat. 'They have lessons daily you know.'

'Are you the full box of matches, Barbara? I am nearly fifty-three years of age for God's sake, not a teenager.'

'Okay dad, point taken, we don't want you to clap out just yet do we?'

Vicky is now telling me, she and her went to a new wine bar in Winton called 'Stud in the Gob' and that it had been closed for several weeks because of a drugs raid.

'Thank you very much, Vicky I need this like a hole in the head; you are about as funny as a broken leg and what may I ask is that white thing resting on your tongue?'

'It's a POLO mint, dad.'

I am asking: 'Where would everyone like to go for a meal?'

Vicky is getting a little bit impatient and says she would like to go for a Chinese meal because she's starving.

'Well then, it's going to be The Mandarin Chinese restaurant in Old Christchurch Road; their beef in black bean sauce and Cantonese fried rice is wonderful, don't you remember, ladies?'

Barbara, who is going through a spate of bad luck having just split up with her Indian chef of a boyfriend, Raman Patel, and is perhaps going to tell me she has ruined her career by becoming pregnant to a man who drives a prestigious car; a three year-old, Mercedes Benz saloon and keeps an elephant and a tiger in his restaurant's back yard.

'As usual, dad, you are totally wrong and whatever gave you that idea.' Barbara now trying to put the record straight continues to inform me: 'Raman continually goes back to Bengal on business; that's in India, dad.'

'Yes, I do know where Bengal is Barbara and had it not been for me being in France I would have bought him the air ticket and, furthermore, this is the second time he has done this to you; he's the only man I know who should walk around with a mobile bidet in his back pocket.'

'Mum says Barbara is getting quite plump and has put on a lot of weight recently.' Vicky put in.

'Well, I am suggesting it must be all those beef and chicken noodles they keep feeding her on at college.'

'Dad, how many times do I have to remind you, I'm bloody well starving?'

'Vicky.'

'Yes dad.'

'Just shut up.'

'And what would you like to eat in the Chinese restaurant this evening, Barbara?'

'Noodles I think, dad.'

After parking the car in Glen Fern Multi Storey car park we all made our way along Glen Fern Road to the Mandarin Chinese restaurant in Old Christchurch Road; me as usual leading the way followed by Lynette and the two girls walking side-by-side, stuck together likened to Siamese twins.

The restaurant was pleasantly packed with an overspill of Bournemouth business people and office workers, turning themselves into party revellers who just can't wait to visit the '*Le Chic*' Lounge, Bar, Club a few doors away.

We were shown to a table by a waiter resembling a young Bruce Lee who gave me the impression he could without hesitation leap over tables and chop a person in half with just one single blow to the chest. The highly polished circular table featuring a round swivel centre-piece, to enable diners to rotate the food in their direction was novel, but it was later to become a hindrance when everyone wanted the *prawn balls* and the *sweet and sour chicken* at the same time.

The menus were offered to us by Mr Lee and immediately a huge plate of traditional *prawn crackers* arrived by a waiter who looked remarkably like a moustachioed Genghis Khan; a throw-back from Outer Mongolia.

It was time to order. I began by asking for some pre-dinner drinks, consisting of two glasses of Coca Cola for my two lovely daughters, a large gin and tonic for my equally lovely wife and a whiskey and dry ginger for my good self.

'Don't worry about driving back to Queen's Park tonight, mum.' Victoria said, crunching noisily on her third *prawn cracker*. 'Just settle down and relax and I will take care of the driving.' I could tell by the expression on Lynette's face she was relieved and very happy to do this.

I ordered the family favourite: *stir-fried beef in black bean sauce*, *Cantonese fried rice* and *prawn balls*; the *sweet and sour chicken* and just for Barbara, a portion of *deep-fried crispy noodles*.

'Tell me Barbara: where did you get that crucifix which is suspended from your pretty little neck and lights up in the dark?'

'I bought it from 'Bizarre Things' in Commercial Road.' she replied before making it disappear down her more than ample cleavage.

I don't suppose Jesus is complaining, I thought to myself.

'I like to wear unusual things.' Barbara told us, as if we didn't know already. 'I would much prefer to shake-off the shackles of the archetype, dad.' she added.

The next day I visited 'Buxom Books' bookshop in Winton Road because I had been told by one of my colleagues at the University it is a gold mine where there are lots of interesting books of historical importance on the shelves just crying out to be read.

I chose to peruse through a book called the Last Battle of The Crusades written by a Yorkshire man, Tim Pickles and it was whilst I was being taken back in time I realized it was by no means the end but the beginning of a new type of crusade; the horses had now been replaced by helicopter gunships and Chieftain tanks; the musket with a SA80 assault rifle.

*

My story begins in March 2000 when a letter from Mr George Hesketh of Messrs Hesketh & Draper, Solicitors arrived, asking me if I could visit their offices in Southport to discuss "The Last Will and Testament" relating to Mrs Tomlinson, my late-Aunt Gertrude. The thought of travelling two hundred and seventy-two miles to a coastal town somewhere between Manchester and Liverpool wasn't my idea of beginning the weekend with a smile, especially when Bournemouth were playing at home against Portsmouth in Bournemouth's AFC Goldsands Stadium, but then a game of soccer became insignificant knowing I was going to return from the North of England with a considerable amount of money.

Chapter Two

The date, I can recall, was Monday the 13th March 2000 when I ventured the two hundred and seventy-two mile sleigh ride to Southport, England's classic resort in a town situated somewhere in the northern hemisphere on the outskirts of Liverpool. It had taken me five and three quarter hours to reach my destination having stopped for a much needed cup of coffee in a Gloucestershire Service station on the M5 motorway where...

A pretty boy who was serving behind the counter and purporting to be a '*Michaelwood*' Service Station snack bar assistant was beginning to get up my nose when I instantly recognised he was one of those, and then, after I had attempted to ask him for what I thought would be a simple request for a cappuccino, he said:

'My name is Winston, what can I do you for, sir?'

'I'll castrate you, if you don't watch it.' I said to him angrily, staring up towards the ceiling to avoid looking into his dark penetrating eyes.

'You've no need to be unpleasant, sir; I'm only doing my job.'

'I would like a cappuccino.' I demanded assertively.

'We don't do cappuccinos, sir.' he replied, pointing in the direction to a board which endorsed his last statement.

'Well, in that case I'll have one of those *Skinny Lizzies.*'

'Don't you mean a *Skinny Latte*, sir, they come with fresh cream.' he said, gesticulating with a slack wrist.

'No, I do not! If I wanted one of those I wouldn't be standing here. I just want an ordinary cup of coffee with milk and sugar, if it isn't too much trouble.'

'Would you like a muffin, sir? They have lots of chocolaty things inside.' he added.

'Now you *are* winding me up.' I emphasised, tapping nervously on the counter with my car keys.

'Today's specialities are individual dishes of Gloucestershire hotpot served with red cabbage or, if you prefer, I recommend the homemade meat and potato pie with onions and gravy.'

'Could you please give me my cup of coffee, Winston; I want to arrive in Southport today and not tomorrow.'

'Just as you like, sir.' he said and then continued to ask me if I would fill in a customer satisfaction form. 'Have a pleasant journey to the turn-off at Knutsford.' Winston added.

'Well, you will know all about that, won't you?' I said, giving him *carte blanche* to increase my credit card balance by seven pounds and sixty-three pence.

The last remnants of snow, having just disappeared had now been replaced by the hides of March that could only be described as being bitterly cold with strong gale force winds transporting the fine golden sand and tumble weeds from the dunes of Merseyside into a bleak town that resembled a sleepy Las Vegas in the middle of the Arizona dessert.

It was just after three-thirty pm when I checked into the four star hotel in Lord Street, The Belvedere Hotel & Spa where I was to stay for two nights and returning to Bournemouth on the Wednesday morning once the business with George Hesketh had been finalized.

The hotel where they still have blackout drape curtains and part of the room amenities were probably left over from the aerial bombardments during The Second World War and I was to find they became essential during my stay for the in-room Central Heating control.

After I had parked the Volkswagen in a NCP car park which the brochure had stated was only five minutes away I trekked down a long and winding busy road back to the hotel.

The young lady behind the reception desk was called Abigail Rainford according to the badge pinned on to her white cotton blouse which didn't leave much to ones imagination. It was when Abigail turned round to find the access card to open my bedroom door I was confronted by her enormous rear confined within tight fitting black trousers which gave me the impression they were about to split open at any second.

'Breakfast is served from seven-thirty until ten o'clock, Mr Travis or, alternatively, you can have it in your room.' Abigail conveyed to me in her eloquent Liverpudlian accent.

'Have what it my room?' I asked, inquisitively trying to find out just what she meant.

'Breakfast, of course but there will be a charge for the extra services the hotel has to offer.' she explained, omitting to tell me what kind of extra services they were.

'Now, what is a beautiful lady like you doing working behind a hotel reception desk?' I asked.

'I used to work as a 'Blue Coat' for 'Pontins', in Pontins Southport Holiday Park just down the road but I had to leave when I tripped and fell off the stage during a performance of "The Sound of Music".'

'And which part did you play in all of this, Miss Rainford?'

'Maria Von Trapp, of course.' she said before coquettishly looking in a mirror behind the desk,

'I have been told by the management not to get too familiar with the guests, Mr Travis.' Abigail said, when she caught me glimpsing at a couple of buttons on the top of her blouse which were about to pop.

'Don't flatter yourself, young lady and I would suggest you stick to falling over dwarfs.'

'It was only a year ago I had the pleasure of meeting James Last at the Preston Guild Hall & Charter Theatre.' Abigail told my quietly.

'Blimey!' I said. 'Apart from Tony Blair you must be the most important person I've ever met.'

'And what line of business are you in?' Abigail asked.

I retreated to my room on the third floor post haste after telling her I was a taxi driver from Bournemouth and then looking inside the register she said: 'Oh that's funny, Mr Travis we have you down as being a doctor from the University; would it be possible to examine my chest?'

Following several attempts to gain access to my room using a flexible plastic card to activate a green light, I eventually moved in to find the most wonderful accommodation and my immediate reaction was to stretch out in a cosy armchair facing a flat screen TV. The remote control to activate the television, as I recall, was very complicated and one needed a degree in electronics to understand it. However, I managed to watch the end of an episode of 'Allo 'Allo!' where an officer in the German army was seen to be bumbling around in Rene's Café with a chicken impaled on a spike on top of his helmet. I can also remember watching David

13

Dickinson, the suave and handsome antiques wizard, presenting a new television series called "Bargain Hunt"; a very popular show which ran for four years. The highlight of this episode was when he dismissed a Japanese cup and saucer which later fetched millions at a Sotheby's auction.

The time was moving very quickly that afternoon and, after synchronising my old Westclox travel alarm clock which had been adjusted to read four minutes past five, I placed it on the small bedside table before going down in the lift to the hotel's Spa bath and Jacuzzi situated well below ground level. The kidney-shaped pool has a terrace where guests can sit and relax, perhaps with a cocktail underneath parasols advertising, *Martini* and *Becks bier*; a health, fitness, gymnasium, beauty centre and other sporting facilities can also be found in the adjoining rooms; these leisure pursuits seemed to be endless and cycle hire is available for those needing a quick get-away.

An unmanned bar at the back of the terrace became very handy when I developed a thirst and had to ask Abigail if someone could furnish me with a pint of beer which can be dispensed from a huge decorative Bavarian pump. Abigail, sounding as though she was speaking from inside a bucket suggested I should help myself because there was insufficient staff around to deal with my immediate requirement. She continued to say she would be finishing her shift at six and could possibly join me in the pool because there is hardly anyone around at that time of day.

'Familiarity all of a sudden seems to have flown out through the window, hasn't it Abigail?'

'Don't worry about the manager,' she sighed, 'he is a gay Frenchman who spends most of his time on the nearby golf course with his Belgium boyfriend.'

At that precise moment I experienced a vibration inside the pocket of my tight-fitting Bermuda shorts and at the same time hearing the tune, "Waltzing Matilda", it was Lynette phoning my mobile and fortuitously coming to my rescue. I then made another quick exit, going up to my room to take the call.

Lynette began to tell me the solicitor, Mr George Hesketh, had just phoned on her mobile and was looking forward to our meeting at ten o'clock the following morning to discuss the proceeds of Auntie Gertrude's Last Will and Testament and the sale of her house. I wasn't entirely convinced Hesketh was on the level because he chose to phone Lynette instead of me.

Auntie Gertrude's house, just a stone's throw away from the hotel was still for sale and the signboard depicting Estate Agents, Maynard & Bamber was swinging freely, blowing in a strong north-westerly wind, when I walked past the property in Lord Street earlier that afternoon.

It was time for me to have a drink in the cocktail bar before going into the hotel's own French restaurant. Picture yourself wandering down the world famous *Champs Elysées*, pausing at a window of a warm and inviting bistro, the aromas emerging from the kitchen draw you inside and before you know it you have spent an evening wining and dining Parisian style. It is this kind of relaxing experience the guests at The Belvedere Hotel & Spa, can experience in *Le Café Francais* which is next door to a coffee shop and breakfast room situated on the ground floor.

Abigail was still on duty and was about to finish her shift when I bravely ventured down into the reception area.

'It was a pity you had to dash off, Mr Travis because you could have relaxed in the Jacuzzi and then afterwards I could have given you one of those Swedish therapeutic massages.' she said, teasing me to the point of explosion. 'Well, being as you are staying here for two nights, there is always tomorrow.' she added.

Inga Petersen, the Scandinavian receptionist came on duty at six o'clock precisely and this was when Abigail the auburn-haired seductress said to me:

'If you want you can take me for dinner this evening. There is an Indian restaurant down the road that has a delicious *Bengali Scouse* curry on their menu; it's a vegetarian dish and is real toilet paper in the fridge kind of stuff.'

Miss Rainford made it blatantly obvious she was looking for a man and wanted my body to satisfy her abnormal sexual behaviour. I told her in no uncertain terms I was a happily married man with two grown up children and furthermore, I was not into *Bengali* curries which are usually hotter than a stoker's shovel. She discontentedly walked out of the hotel by way of a revolving door leaving me to consider my fate if Lynette had learned that I had been playing away.

I was about to enter the lounge bar when the blonde-haired Inga Petersen, smoothing down her short black pencil skirt, smiled in my direction and said: 'If there is anything you would like, Doctor Travis, you only have to ask.'

'Oh no, not another one' I muttered to myself.

The bar area was beginning to fill up with a multitude of pretend people including representatives from Health and Safety, Quality Control and Trade Union arsonists belonging to a nearby pharmaceutical company who just couldn't wait to vacate the conference room on the first floor to have a drink in the cocktail bar. The theme of the seminar was, ironically, alcohol awareness and abuse in the workplace. It was when I witnessed a woman falling off a stool after drinking a couple of 'Harvey Wall bangers' I realized why they were there.

The Portuguese barman whose name had a certain ring to it was called Miguel Columbus and after he had pulled me a perfect pint of Guinness I sat down at a table in the corner listening to highly paid tipplers talking about Britain's current non-caring 'put me down culture' and arguing over the price of fish'n chips; this was when I decided to go into the restaurant for my evening meal.

The Australian waitress was called Josephine Drummond and I could detect from her accent she came from a backwater somewhere between Alice Springs and Melbourne. I followed her to a table she had so kindly selected by a window where I could see heavy rainfall lashing against the Victorian shopping arcade across the road and adjacent to the main entrance to the hotel.

'Would you like an aperitif before you order your meal, sir?' Josephine asked, handing me a leather-bound menu politely explaining in English and in French what the restaurant had to offer.

After quickly perusing through the drinks section, I gave her instructions to bring me a whisky and dry ginger and to boomerang back in five minutes to take my order.

I ordered the *plat de jour* consisting of two courses; *soup à l'oignon*, French onion soup accompanied by *croutons* and shredded *Emmental cheese*, continuing with the *boeuf bourguignon*, huge chunks of braised steak served with *Penne*, a dreamy pasta enriched with *Crème frais* and *Stilton* cheese. For desert, I chose a platter of tasty *Lancashire, Cheddar, Camembert, Danish blue* cheeses and an assortment of pickles from the sweet trolley; Josephine then offered me savoury biscuits from a tin box which had a portrait of King George VI and Queen Elizabeth, The Queen mother, embossed on the lid. The wine, full bodied *Beaujolais*, was opened by a Parisian wine waiter called Laurent Duval who poured sufficient into a glass for me to taste before giving him my approval.

To add to the ambiance, I can recall a tape was playing accordion music in the background, "Under the Bridges of Paris", followed by "No Regrets" and I can also remember sitting at the table mesmerized, gazing at a nineteenth-century reproduction print depicting 'The Moulin Rouge' theatre in Paris and showing glamorous young ladies on the stage dressed in knickerbockers bending down to touch their toes; I was half expecting Edith Piaf to walk in through the door at any second.

'Would you like some fresh coffee, sir?' Josephine asked with a smile. 'I'm not interrupting anything, am I?' she added. 'Do you know,' she went on, 'one day that picture will make someone blind.'

'I would like a large bottle of mineral water to take to my room, if you don't mind?' I demanded.

Suddenly, I was being called Doctor Travis when a plastic bottle of chilled sparkling water was brought to the table along with the bill.

'Here you are Doctor Travis,' Josephine said, patting me slowly on my back. 'This should cool you down.'

On my way out of the restaurant I was confronted by the gay golfer, the hotel manager, who introduced himself as Raymond Gaultier, the brother of the owners, Stephan and Michelle.

'I trust everything is to your satisfaction, Doctor Travis. The hotel staff, including myself, will do almost anything to make your stay as comfortable as possible.'

'What do you mean by almost anything?' I curiously asked him.

'Well, Doctor, we have to draw the line somewhere.'

'I suppose you must, Mr Gaultier,' I said, tongue in cheek. 'And does this line begin at the reception desk and end up beside the pool?'

'Would you like a night cap before you retire to your room, Doctor Travis?' he asked, rolling his eyeballs similar to a whirly-circle thing going round on a laptop computer.

After I had witnessed a wet and somewhat bedraggled Abigail standing in the foyer I said to the manager: 'I think I will give this one a rain check.'

My bedroom, situated on the third floor, was conveniently positioned next to the fire escape and became a safe haven when I securely locked the door to keep out any would be predators with desires of lust and evil intentions.

I can remember hearing the wind howling in the street and seeing hailstones; small pellets of ice, noisily hitting the supposedly double-glazed window which I immediately covered by a drape curtain to keep out the cold.

The satellite television was repositioned to face my cosy double bed and when I was about to climb into it a smoke alarm went off and as I learned later in one of the bedrooms on the fourth floor. Everyone had to vacate the hotel and stand underneath a shop canopy directly across the road. It wasn't until the fire brigade had given the non-smoking establishment the all-clear three-quarters of an hour later we were allowed to go back inside.

Standing with me outside in the cold was Abigail, soaked to the skin, her dark wet and straggly hair falling down over her face and shivering like a frightened gazelle. I became the hero that night, having transformed myself into a Sir Walter Raleigh when I removed my coat in the pouring rain and placed it over her shoulders.

It was around midnight and I was sitting in the hotel's coffee shop with a blanket draped around my shoulders to keep warm, drinking a mug of hot Bovril and eating *croissants* which resembled well-burnt suitcase handles. Back in my room, I was in no mood to watch the late-night movie "Singing in the Rain" and as I attempted to turn out the light there was a knock on the door. 'Oh no it's that Abigail coming after me again.' I frantically muttered to myself, leaping out of bed for the second time. I opened the door slowly and standing in front of me was the night porter holding my umbrella which I had inadvertently left in the coffee shop.

'Good evening, sir,' Basil Goldsmith, the night porter said, staring at my brand new Marks and Spencer blue and white striped pyjamas.

'Good evening! Good evening, what is good about it, Basil? So far I've had a pretty shit evening!' I replied angrily.

*

I started the day by getting out of bed at seven-thirty and my first instinct after opening the huge drape blackout curtain was to turn on the television to see what the weather was going to be like for the next twenty-four hours. It was to be much of the same thing; strong winds and heavy rain heading down towards the South Coast, Bournemouth and the Bay of Biscay.

The solicitor's office, conveniently situated in a muse was just off Lord Street and within easy walking distance from the hotel and, apart from repositioning the car into a space directly below my bedroom window, there was no need for me to use it again that morning.

There was a spacious breakfast room adjoining the Conservatory Bar & Bistro and I was amazed at the continental style buffet the hotel had to offer; the fair consisting of a variety of ham, cheeses, cereals, individual fruits and yesterday's *croissants*. A full English breakfast was also available and served separately by 'Skippy the Kangaroo', the Aussie waitress, at extra cost.

'My goodness me, Josephine, do you never go to bed?' I asked, gazing into her innocent-looking brown eyes.

'Is that an enquiry or an offer, Doctor Travis?' she replied before jotting down my room number in order to charge me for a rather expensive fry-up.

It was when I heard the melodious tones of the French singer and

19

guitarist, Sacha Distel on the radio singing: "Raindrops keep falling on my head", I knew then, it wasn't going to be my lucky day.

'Will you be having lunch in the hotel, doctor?' Josephine asked. 'Today we have New Zealand lamb on the menu.' she added.

'Well, that should bring you a little closer to home,' I replied with an air of sarcasm, 'and from now on it is my intention to alter my eating habits by turning myself into a vegetarian.' I added, looking down at a ring of well burnt Cumberland sausages on my breakfast plate.

'I hope everything is to your liking, sir? she said repositioning the front of her bra to accentuate whatever was inside.

My mobile with its rather appropriate ringing tone, "Waltzing Matilda" sounded and, once again, it was Lynette coming to my rescue and to wish me the very best of luck when I visited the solicitor's office that morning.

*

It was when I was dashing along Lord Street to visit Messrs Hesketh & Draper solicitors and notaries in Bramley Court Yard, an eighteenth century cobbled muse in the centre of town, my recently acquired telescopic umbrella decided to invert, turning inside out rendering it completely useless and destined for the nearest dustbin.

I can recall arriving and standing at the bottom of the steps to the solicitor's office feeling somewhat miserable because the rain had penetrated my so-called waterproof raincoat. I can also recall looking at a silver-grey Porsche 911 sports car parked in the yard opposite to the offices of Hesketh & Draper and wondering who owned one of Germany's favourite modes of transport.

The Estate Agents, 'Maynard & Bamber' had their offices conveniently situated next door and I couldn't help but take a look at the properties they had for sale in their window giving prospective buyers an idea of the price and a snapshot of what they were like from the outside.

The details of Auntie Gertrude's four-bedroom Regency Town House commanded a good position in the centre of the window conveying to everyone that number 259 Lord Street, Southport was a freehold property and being sold for two hundred and fifty thousand pounds and it was with this information I was able to sit down in front of Hesketh to deal with his feeble attempt to lower the price.

The time was exactly ten o'clock when I entered the office of George Hesketh. I can remember seeing a sea of portfolios, files and law books scattered untidily on a long wooden banquet-type table and positioned to one side of a handsome mahogany desk which wouldn't have been out of place inside the Lord Chancellor's office in Westminster.

George Hesketh ushered me into the room gesturing to where I was to sit down at a disadvantage in front of his desk for the next half an hour before he silently closed the door. He started the proceedings by telling me the good news and the things I already knew and it was just like he was trying to teach his grandmother how to suck eggs. My immediate impressions were that the guy is definitely not on this planet because every time he spoke his nose began to twitch nervously, giving me the impression the infliction may have been caused by a serious accident. The bad news came after he had read my aunt's Last Will and Testament when he told me about the dilapidated state of the interior of the house and that it would cost me a substantial amount of money if I were to take the property prospectus out of Maynard & Bamber's window in order to carry out a renovation programme.

Hesketh made me an offer of one hundred and eighty-seven thousand pounds for a quick sale and asked me how that sounded. I said to him assertively that I wanted two hundred and twenty thousand pounds and how did *that* sound?

'Well, that sounds fairly good.' he said, continuing with his nervous twitching.

The Travis coffers had already been enhanced when Hesketh handed over to me a cheque for thirty-five thousand pounds being the residue of my late aunt's bank account; her possessions, what little were left, became less important as most of her valuable items including jewellery were sold to a bogus door-to-door antique dealer before she died.

It was ten forty-five when I walked out of the solicitor's office and into the muse a few pounds richer than when I went in. I made a point of looking in the estate agent's window once again to find my aunt's house had been sold subject to contract and this explained why George Hesketh had excused himself for five minutes during the proceedings.

The wind and rain had suddenly dissipated turning into a bright and sunny morning and because of the heat which had been generated by me in Hesketh's office I was now completely dry.

I walked along Lord Street heading for Southport's famous shopping arcade and feeling quite pleased with myself knowing I had managed to bring Hesketh down to size, who it would seem is one of the biggest crooks on Merseyside but, however, my victory over him was to be short-lived when some months later I realized he had dangerously set me up.

The Wayfarers Shopping Arcade has everything you need under one spectacular roof and walking down from the entrance I was captivated by this Grade II listed building. A pot of morning coffee was in great demand when I sat down at table in an enclosed area surrounded by the exclusive designer boutique shops of Broadbents & Boothroyds.

There was a certain ambiance to the entire place where shoppers can shop 'til they drop, sit and watch the world go by and enjoy listening to the music of Mantovani and his Sein Orchestra playing "Charmaine", "Some Enchanted Evening", "Moon River" and the hauntingly lovely Edith Piaf song, "La vie en rose". For some strange reason, I didn't want the morning to end and it was when Lynette phoned me on her mobile to enquire how things were progressing and how much she loved me I began to relax drinking my freshly-made Brazilian coffee and munching my way through a breakfast bacon, lettuce and tomato wrap.

It was getting close to lunchtime and the café had begun filling up with shoppers who had difficulty finding places to sit. I was at a table with an empty seat next to the aisle where I could command an excellent view of the wrought-iron balconies over the shops. Suddenly, I was approached by a glamorous middle-aged lady who I thought was desperate to sit down at my table surrounded by tropical palm plants.

'May I sit down at your table, sir,' she asked with a pleasant smile. 'The café is getting a little crowded now, isn't it?' she added.

I could tell by her accent she was foreign and, removing her red blazer to place it on the back of her chair, she said she was French and qualified this by saying she came from France.

The lady then introduced herself as *Mademoiselle* Brigitte-Helen Boullard, a Property Consultant for the *Immobilier*, 'Circa Habitat', an estate agents in Paris and it was of no surprise to me several months later just why she wanted to sit down at my table.

I introduced myself as Christopher Miles Travis, a lecturer in medieval studies at the University of Bournemouth and a citizen of the world.

It will be of no surprise to hear Brigitte Boullard knew already I was a happily married man and what a fool I was to fall for her charm when I was lured into her spider's web.

'Are you married Mr Travis?' she asked pretending not to look at my eighteen carat gold wedding ring glinting in the sunlight which was now shining and penetrating the stunning glass-domed roof.

'Well I was just a few minutes ago when I was on the phone to my wife.' I replied thinking this was extremely funny. 'And what, if I may ask, is a French lady doing in Southport?'

'I am visiting Janet one of my English friends who has a cottage in Churchtown, on the northern fringe of Southport.' she replied knowing this to be a pack of lies. 'And why are you here in Southport, Mr Travis?'

At this point, a waitress came to the table to take Brigitte's order consisting of coffee, a salad baguette comprising: salami, ham, sliced boiled egg and *Emmental cheese*; I can recall, the captivating jazz singer, Ella Fitzgerald singing "April in Paris" as if it were only yesterday.

'It's a bit early for April in Paris.' I said to her pointing towards one of the loudspeakers suspended from a balcony.

'We will have to wait a couple of weeks then, won't we?' she so confidently replied. 'Have you got a car?' she went on to ask me.

'I had one at eight o'clock this morning, but things have a tendency to disappear without trace around here so I'm told.' thinking my car could be in danger of being stolen by a stray scrap metal merchant from nearby Kirkby.

'Well then, I will pick you up at your hotel at seven-thirty.' Boullard said, taking another bite out of her sandwich which by this time resembled a squashed-up mouth organ. 'I will entertain you by taking you out for dinner.' she added, but little did I know that during the course of the evening I was going to be introduced to the French property market.

It was just after seven when I drew the drape curtain to obscure the last remnants of light from entering my room and after I had verified that my car was still parked in the street with a full set of wheels I went down to the reception area to meet Brigitte-Helen Boullard.

Abigail Rainford was on duty behind the desk reminding everyone she had the body likened to a Greek goddess; her undulating cleavage pulsating out of control when she continually hitched up her skirt to make it look shorter.

'Good evening, doctor.' Abigail said before taking out a lipstick and a powder compact from her soft leather handbag to recreate her face.

'Good evening, Abigail, I didn't think you would be here today, especially after last night.' I replied, praying that Brigitte would arrive quickly in order to rescue me.

My prayers were indeed answered when she elegantly walked in through the swing door.

'Hello, Christopher, we meet again.' Brigitte said, before kissing me four times on both cheeks, I was to learn later that all this kissing and shaking of hands was a total waste of time.

It was when we had stepped out into the street I saw her car; a 1997 silver-grey, 2.5 litre. Porsche 911 sports car, the very same one I had seen in the muse earlier that morning.

'Tell me Brigitte, is this your car?' I asked beginning to question my sanity.

'Of course it belongs to me, jump in.' she replied, having no idea what I was going to ask next.

'If you are only here on a flying visit to see your friend, why is your car a right-hand drive and has a British private personal number plate HSK151X, and for a person who doesn't smoke the ashtray seems to be full.

Chapter Three

The day began without a hitch in sight; it was Abigail's day off and I had the pleasure of meeting the blonde-haired Swedish receptionist, Inga Petersen, for the last time.

'Have a pleasant journey back to your home and, may *Odin* blow the sails of your boat into safe and calmer waters.' she said, leaning over the reception desk especially to show me her bosoms.

'You mean the M6 motorway?' I asked, not quite knowing what the doe-eyed Viking tart was referring to, until I aquaplaned through a lake on the outskirts of Warrington.

Josephine Drummond was standing at ease in front of the buffet waiting for guests to arrive when I walked into the breakfast room at seven-thirty that morning. Josephine made a point of suggesting to me that if I were to visit Crocodile Springs, a town situated some one-hundred and fifty miles north of Ayres Rock in the Northern Territory of Australia she would lay on a barbecue. I said to her: 'Wouldn't you find it a little hot?'

'Oh, Doctor Travis, you crease me up, you do!' she replied, nudging me in the chest with a lethal elbow and grinning like a Cheshire cat. 'I can cook for you the biggest Aussie burger in the world, cobber; much better than the ones you get down the road from here; they taste like shit but you can live on them. And if there is anything I can do for you, Doctor Travis before you leave, just let me know.' she added.

'Not tonight Josephine.' I replied, emulating Napoleon Bonaparte before his disastrous departure to Waterloo.

After I had discarded another well-burnt Cumberland sausage on the side of my breakfast plate, I made my way out of the room to have the unpleasant experience of bumping into Raymond, the frog, who asked:

'I believe you are checking-out of the hotel this morning, Mister Travis?'

I replied by saying: 'Well, yes I am,' 'and not before time, Mister Gaultier.' I muttered to myself.

'It's a great pity we couldn't have got to know each other better.' he insisted on telling me, placing one of his dainty hands on the sleeve of my jacket before continuing to say: 'We could have played a round of golf at Royal Birkdale and had some nibbles at the nineteenth hole; the fairway is pretty quiet at this time of year.'

'I don't play golf.' I emphatically pointed out to him making things clear I wasn't going to fall for his advances.

'Well, that's a shame; anyway, have a safe and pleasant journey back to Bournemouth.' he genuinely said.

I went up to my room to collect my suit-carrier and bag and this was when I noticed an envelope which had been positioned against the mirror on top of the dressing-table directly in front of the bedroom door. The envelope had the smell of expensive perfume, reminiscent of the toiletry department in Debenhams of Bournemouth and I couldn't help but wonder who it was from as I placed it underneath my nose to enjoy the fragrance. I carefully opened the envelope with its delicate gothic-type handwriting to find it was from the cool and collected seductive actress, *Mademoiselle* Brigitte-Helen Boullard; strange but surprisingly not so strange because it was a couple of weeks later I learned she was called Helen Hesketh, formerly Braithwaite and came from Bolton in Greater Manchester and the wife of George Hesketh; International crook and *notaire* of extreme notoriety.

The personal letter was to wish my wife, Lynette and myself the very best of luck and, after penetrating my heart which I thought was my least vulnerable spot she continued to turn me into a rank sentimentalist, persuading me to buy a property in France. Brigitte-Helen explained that house prices were low due to more and more foreigners having to sell their houses because of habitation taxes being imposed on them.

Looking out from the bedroom window I could see Brigitte-Helen extricating her car from a parking space directly in front of the arcade; it was of little consequence to me to see she had just been presented with a ticket placed rather ominously behind the front windscreen wiper.

I began to reminisce about what happened the previous evening when I was taken to Portofino's, the Italian pizza pasta and pizzeria restaurant in Lord Street, by Boullard. I can remember sitting in her expensive sports car mesmerized as I looked at a multitude of LED illuminated dials on the dashboard and listening to Shirley Bassey, singing: "Big Spender" in loud quadraphonic sound bass booming in my ears; the tune still going round inside my head.

Brigitte-Helen circumnavigated Southport a couple of times before pulling up outside the small ten-table restaurant which, incidentally, was only a few doors down from the Hotel, Belvedere & Spa. I couldn't quite work out just who she was trying to impress, was it me or the local populace who preferred to watch classy women driving around in flashy sports cars.

This 2.5 litre symphony on wheels was something else; automatic windows, automatic aerial, automatic seat adjustment and an automatic rear-view mirror essential for her to check her bright red lipstick before moving off. I can recall, sitting uncomfortably in what looked like a Martin Baker rocket assisted ejection seat capable of getting me to Bournemouth sooner than expected.

"You're So Vain", written and performed by Carly Simon, became the next song to penetrate my eardrums as she skilfully drove the car along Marine Drive for the second time, heading towards the sand hills in nearby Ainsdale.

Boullard stopped the car in a lay-by across the road from a backdrop of scenic sandy dunes, popular with bathers during the summer and lovers in winter. My heart began to pound as she unfastened her seat belt from around her voluptuous body to reach over and kiss me passionately on the lips. It was when I was about to pull on the ejection seat handle I saw a slight figure of a man walking his dog along the pavement; it was George Hesketh.

'Would you like to take a walk with me?' she asked, putting a hand on the inside of my thigh.'

'You seem to know this area pretty well.' I said to her as I looked over to an expanse of beach not dissimilar to the wrapper on a 'Bounty Bar'. 'I think, Brigitte-Helen, we had better go for that meal, don't you think?'

'Yes, maybe you are right, Christopher,' she said before clunk-clicking the cumbersome seat belt back into its original position and parting two mounds of cleavage.

*

We were greeted by Tuscan born, Tony Zeffirelli and his wife Francesca, the husband and wife dream team in one of Southport's most fashionable Italian restaurants, Portofino's. The waitress, Flamina Bianchetti, the sister of Francesca, showed us to a cosy table for two in an alcove underneath a wrought-iron staircase leading up to the first floor and overlooking the street. An array of freshly cut daffodils had previously been placed in the centre of the table and when we sat down they were taken away by Flamina and replaced by a red slow-burning candle.

I ordered the aperitifs; two 'Godfather Slap on the Backs' consisting of *Cointreau*, orange juice, *Bombay Sapphire*, *Chartreuse*, *Blue Cacao*, *Crème de Menthe* and lime juice which after the ingredients had been shaken to death formed a prismatic spectrum inside tall glasses.

'You don't know what you missed back there.' Brigitte-Helen said slowly, shaking her head disapprovingly.

I wasn't sure what she was referring to; her body or George Hesketh, however, whatever it was I had missed, I had seen enough and my immediate thoughts were: If she scratches my conscience, I will most certainly drive her Porsche into Southport's Marine Lake, the largest man-made leisure lake in the United Kingdom.

Flamina opened the wine at the table, a full bottle of Tuscan *Chianti Melini*; only the very best for Mrs Helen Hesketh I discovered when the first course arrived; a bubbling dish of mushrooms baked in a creamy *mascarpone*, spinach and garlic sauce and crispy yet perfectly tender *calamari*. The main course was a red pesto-based pizza, loaded with roasted red and yellow peppers, olives, cherry tomatoes, red onion and *mozzarella* cheese. The dessert, being a mountainous creation of chocolate fudge brownie, vanilla and strawberry ice cream covered with a generous helping of gooey chocolate.

I can recall Dean Martin singing in the background "Everybody loves somebody sometime" as I looked at Brigitte-Helen through the haze of candlelight.

We drank our coffee in silence looking into each other's eyes and when the silence was broken by me trying to explain to her the friendly relationship had gone too far and it would be a crazy idea to continue, she picked up her handbag from the floor and taking out a sequined purse tossed enough money down on the table to pay for the bill before leaving the premises and for me to walk back to the hotel alone.

I crept out of the Hotel Belvedere & Spa at eight-thirty precisely knowing Brigitte-Helen Boullard's conscience could never be scratched and she also had the brass neck to deposit an envelope in my room when I was taking breakfast.

The horrendous journey back to Bournemouth began after the car had developed a flat tyre. This unfortunate incident became even worse because when I was placing my luggage inside the boot I discovered the spare wheel had gone through a similar fate and waiting impatiently for over an hour for the AA man to arrive, I eventually made my way to the M6 Motorway via Saint Helens.

Driving in the fast lane through Warrington in Cheshire, I aquaplaned through a pool of water; the weather at this point was atrocious and the torrential rain was forcibly hitting the windscreen of my car similar to sitting at the wheel while going through a car wash. I managed to control stop the car on the grass verge by the side of the barrier and it was at this point I made God my best friend and becoming mates for life because I was so lucky that day to be alive.

Suffering from acute and severe backlash I called in to the *'Michaelwood'* Motorway Service Station in Gloucestershire some seventy-two miles north of Bristol.

'Hello again, sir,' Winston Clarke said excitedly. 'I thought I saw you.' he added.

'Don't start on me, Winston,' I replied, nervously. 'I've had enough these last couple of days to last me a lifetime.'

'Enough of what?' he asked looking at me with a cheeky grin on his face.

'People coming out with silly remarks,' I said, looking at a glass-fronted display cabinet. 'Just give me a cup of coffee and one of those chocolate muffins before I collapse.'

'Would you like Demerara, granulated, brown or caster sugar, sir?' Failing that, sir, we have saccharine sweeteners, if you prefer.'

'Just give me the coffee and then I can sit down and take a well deserved rest.'

'Will you be staying for lunch, sir? we have...'

'I can see what you've got, Winston; I can read you know.' I strongly emphasised.

'One cup of coffee and a chocolate muffin coming up, as ordered.' he said, handing me a square plastic tray with a heap of paper sachets containing different types of sugar.

Taking my tray over to a table I plonked myself down on a red leatherette seat and I had already estimated it was going to be around four pm that afternoon when I would eventually arrive home in Queens Park Avenue, Bournemouth.

I said goodbye to Winston and thanked him for his warm and friendly attitude towards me and wished him every success serving '*Michaelwood*' customers from behind his counter.

The M5 motorway was busy with lots of articulated trucks and slow-moving traffic heading towards an arc of colourful light; a rainbow had suddenly appeared overhead. I turned on the radio to listen to a local FM radio station and ironically it was James Last and his band playing: "Go away little girl"; there was an instant feel-good factor knowing I wouldn't have to meet any of those people in Southport ever again.

The afternoon became sunny and pleasantly warm as I travelled through Salisbury, Wiltshire on the A338 to join the turn-off to Ringwood and Bournemouth. This particular stretch of complicated circuitry has always been an enigma to me and I have a theory; if one doesn't have one's wits about them on this stretch of road, you could end up travelling back where you came from or, even worse, on Salisbury Plain with the barrel of a Chieftain tank poking you in the backside.

As I had estimated I arrived back at No 46 Queens Park Avenue at exactly four pm, having taken my life into my hands travelling along three of Britain's busiest highways; the M6, M5 and M4 motorways. Lynette had taken the afternoon off away from the dress shop to greet my safe arrival, emerging from the front door of the house.

I was so glad to be home and after Lynette and I had embraced for a while, kissing on the lips as if we hadn't seen each other for years, she took hold of my bag and suit carrier and led the way into the house through the vestibule door.

When I followed her in to the house I remarked: 'that was a nice kiss, Lynette.'

'It will give the neighbours something to talk about, won't it, Chris.' she replied.

'Are you going back to the shop this afternoon, Lynette because I have a lot of things I would like to discuss with you?' I asked, settling down to relax in my favourite armchair.

'Tell me, Christopher how did you fare in Southport?'

'Southport has a fair,' I replied, giving her the benefit of my wealth of geographical knowledge. 'Well, they had, but that was until half of it was found in New Brighton on Tuesday night.'

'Not that kind of fair,' Lynette said, calling me a silly arse which was totally uncalled for. 'I mean, how did you get on? she continued.

'The helter-skelter and the carousel were a little difficult but the dodgem-cars I thought were relatively easy.' I said, jokingly.

'I hope we are not going to go on talking like this for the rest of the afternoon because I will certainly go back to work.' Lynette said, now becoming irritated by my sense of humour. 'I want to know how you made out in the hotel and, more importantly what was the final outcome in the solicitor's office? she asked, inquisitively.

In response to her first question, my answer was: 'I didn't' and in answer to her second question was: 'we are richer by two hundred and fifty thousand pounds and fifty five pence, to be precise.'

'And where, if I may ask, does the fifty-five pence come from?' she anxiously wanted to know.

When I told her it was the change from a packet of POLO mints she said, 'That's done it, I'm going back to the shop because at least I can get a modicum of sense from my assistant.'

'Well in that case you will have to wait until later to unwrap your present I bought you in the Wayfarers Shopping Arcade in Southport.'

'Okay, you win Chris, hand it over.'

I gave her a small decorative carrier bag with the name and address of the jewellers shop printed on the side. Lynette excitedly untied the ribbon before opening the gift-wrapped box which contained a Saint Christopher pendant suspended from a delicate-looking nine carat gold chain.

'Oh, Chris, you do spoil me.' she said turning around for me to fasten the clasp. 'It must have cost you a lot of money.' she added giving me another big kiss.

I told her she was worth every penny and there would be more to come after I had banked all the cheques and we had received the last pieces of Auntie Gertrude's jewellery from George Hesketh.

'When the girls come home for the weekend on Friday we can all go to the Pavilion and see the 'The Moscow State Circus' and that will be fun, won't it.' Lynette suggested, still looking at her recently acquired necklace in a mirror on the wall. 'And, perhaps we can have a meal afterwards.' she said, adding to my excitement.

For some peculiar reason I didn't tell Lynette about the incident on the motorway or indeed the events which took place in Southport and I was giving her the impression I had been squeaky clean but that was until she found the envelope containing Brigitte-Helen Boullard's letter concealed inside my coat pocket.

I had to explain to Lynette in a round-about sort of way the sequence of events that led up to me receiving the letter; a handkerchief smeared with bright red lipstick didn't help to defuse the situation either and when I discovered Saint Christopher lying on the floor in the bathroom suffering an indentation caused by a kick from a size six and a half inch high-heel shoe, I knew my days living at number 46 Queens Park Avenue would soon be over.

Lynette stormed out from the house in a fit of temper. She had taken the Ford transit van parked next to the Volkswagen back to her shop, 'Lynette Travis Ladies Fashion' in Boscombe High Street, Christchurch

Road and I thought this would be an ideal time to pull the emergency handle and go down to the pub, the Queens Park Hotel.

Chapter Four

The lounge bar in the Queens Park Pub was beginning to fill up with late afternoon customers who had either finished work for the day or just escaped from their repetitive and tedious domestic lifestyles. Sitting on a stool propping up the bar was seventy-nine year old Bill Cartwright, an ex Pilot Officer with 41 Squadron, Royal Air Force based at Manston and as usual letting everyone know, he could drink bottles of '*Shepherd Neame Spitfire Premium Ale*' faster than anyone else.

Standing in front of the bar was Frederick Bennett, a local councillor for Bournemouth East, doing his best to impress everyone with another expensive project; namely, to clean up the pavements in Springbourne after putting his foot into something nasty outside the Conservative Club in Holdenhurst Road.

It is quite common on Sunday evenings to have a sing-along with Roy Vatcher, the pianist, tinkling away on the ebony and ivories of an upright piano; "Roll out the Barrel", "We'll Meet Again" and "The White Cliffs of Dover" have become very popular tunes in the pub during the past sixty years and it is only recently they have been drowned out by Oasis' Noel Gallagher, Hot Chocolate and West Life bellowing out from the juke box.

It was similar to a Smokey Joes Bar when I walked into the pub; the foggy atmosphere caused by cigarette smoke and pipe tobacco was wafting everywhere and I could just imagine what it must have been like during the war years when everyone possessed a respirator gas mask in order to survive.

'Good evening Bill,' I said creeping up behind him. 'How many Fokker's have you shot down this afternoon?' I added.

'Bandits coming in at six o'clock old boy.' he said looking inside his pocket watch to check on the hour.

'Well, in that case I shall be leaving at five forty-five.' I hastily replied.

'Good afternoon, Chris,' Councillor Bennett said, regally holding a large glass of whisky in one hand and a lighted cigar in the other; the bevelled mirror behind the bar having alerted him to turn around.

'Good afternoon, Frederick.' I replied disdainfully, knowing he was going to start boring the pants off me. 'Stepped into any dog pooh recently?' I asked wrinkling my nose.

'Well, now you come to mention it, Christopher, I ...'

'Don't even mention it.' I said to him having heard it all before from Christine Crow, the gossiping grave digger's wife from Ashley Road in Boscombe.

After I had declined his offer to buy me a pint and to sell me one of his Saint John's Ambulance raffle tickets I quickly moved into the corner of the bar where I could seek some kind of well deserved solace.

The grave digger, Denzel Crow had somehow managed to find his way back from the toilet having downed several pints of Taunton's best Cider, his ashen and gaunt face, brown curly hair peppered with dust and deep sunken red eyes that looked similar to a road map, epitomized his profession giving one the impression he was related to Count Dracula and had just emerged from six feet under the ground.

I greeted the *Costa del Dorset* bumpkin with disdain knowing him to be always drunk. 'Good afternoon Wurzel, seen any ghosts lately in that graveyard of yours?'

'Oh aagh, Oh aagh, I can remember seeing one yesterday.' he seriously replied, wiping some of his spillage from the top of his dungaree overalls.

'I think you should drink less *Scrumpy* because it may be affecting your eyesight.' I said and before continuing to tell him one of my little jokes.

'Did you hear the one about the hearse going up a steep hill and then suddenly the back door opens and a box shoots out from the back? The man inside who incidentally had died from asthma walked into a chemist and asked the assistant if she had anything to stop his coffin.'

'I suppose you're thinking that was funny.' Denzel said, sorrowfully. 'One day you will be in one of those boxes yourself.' he added, trying successfully to impersonate Christopher Lee.

At that precise moment Lynette walked into the pub and I thought to myself, Denzel was probably right in what he had just said because my days on this earth were indeed numbered.

'I knew you would be in here.' Lynette said sauntering over towards

35

me. 'Now, how did I know that?' she added.

'From years of experience, I suppose.' I replied, sighing.

'I have just been to the bank to deposit the two cheques you brought back from Southport.' she said, frowning. 'The interest rate in our savings account is absolutely pathetic at the moment, Chris; Auntie Gertrude's money would be far better invested in property.' Lynette went on, sounding more like a finance consultant by the minute.

'I agree, Lynette.' I replied, agreeing with every word she said and hoping she wouldn't come out with the obvious line...

'Tell me Christopher, who was that woman you were with in Southport? And did you go to bed with her?'

'No, I bloody well didn't and I am ashamed of you for asking me that question.' I said, feeling somewhat pissed-off by being accused of bad matrimonial behaviour.

I took the last swig of my whisky and then made a beeline for the door. Lynette swiftly followed me out into the car park and grabbing my coat from the back stopped me from running across the busy road.

'I'm really sorry, Chris.' she said, resting her head on my shoulder and weeping at the same time. 'I had to know, Chris.'

I safely drove the transit van back to Queens Park Avenue because Lynette, emotionally, wasn't fit to drive and it was possible I could well have been involved in two accidents in one day.

Lynette removed the somewhat distorted Saint Christopher necklace which I had draped over the rear view mirror and clutched it in her hand. She said to me, I was her Saint Christopher and then I thought to myself, if only that were true.

'You seem to have done a lot this week, Christopher,' she said opening the door to the house and then continuing to say: 'The highlight of my week, Chris, apart from having you home was to buy a new frying pan from Debenhams.'

The significance of her buying a new Tefal frying pan and my home-coming were by no means related; the thought of having a large diameter cast-iron cooking appliance forcibly placed on the top of my head brought tears to my eyes.

'Where would you like to eat this evening?' Lynette asked with a loving smile. 'I wanted to try out our new frying pan but I'm not in the mood for making dinner tonight.' she added.

I wanted to say to Lynette, I wish she would stop talking about bloody frying pans because they were doing my head in and enough to bring a tear to a glass eye.

'Why don't we go to Raman Patel's Indian restaurant 'The Bay of Bengal' in Old Christchurch Road?' I suggested, now beginning to find my lost appetite. 'Apparently, they have an extensive menu, serving extremely hot curries.'

'I thought you didn't like curry, Chris?' Lynette said, obviously confused by me turning my culinary preferences in a direction towards the Far East.

'Well, I do now,' I replied assertively, and adding 'the hotter the better.'

'We can relax and enjoy our food, Chris, and then you can tell me all about your trip to Southport; what you did and most importantly what you didn't do in that hotel.'

I was now really looking forward to my evening out on the town with my tender loving wife, Lynette.

'Go and get yourself ready, Chris, and then I will phone for a taxi to take us into Bournemouth.' she insisted. 'And by the way, why is the front number plate on the Volkswagen tied up with string?' Lynette added and now sounding melodiously like Julie Andrews in the feature film "The Sound of Music".

I explained that the car had been vandalised and damaged by Liverpudlian hooligans in Southport and to make matters worse there is a hub cap missing from one of the wheels.

'It's a wonder you got back home in one piece having gone through all of this.' she said without knowing what I had been through that morning.

'Yes, it is indeed a miracle, an absolute miracle.'

*

The United taxi, conveying Lynette and myself to 'The Bay of Bengal' Indian restaurant pulled up directly outside the front door. It was when I was rummaging in my purse to find some suitable coins to tip the driver I saw Raman Patel's, shiny black, three year-old Mercedes Benz motorcar parked across the road. This I thought was very strange because Patel had told Barbara he was going to garage his car until he returned from India in the summer and the whole idea of him being in two places at once became puzzling.

We entered the restaurant to the sounds of a *vina sitar*, a type of mandolin, *tabla* drums and a female Indian singer; her vocal techniques screeching in the background, as though she was suffering from acute belly-ache. Once our coats were taken away from us we were immediately shown to a communal table by the restaurant manager, a Mister Mohandas Maharashtra dressed in a long brown frock-coat and a green fluorescent designer turban just in case the management began cutting costs and turned down the lights. I can remember my line of vision towards the kitchen being cleverly obscured by the luminous glow of a fish tank; the Paraná happily swimming around, ripping apart pieces of chicken *tikka masala* and *tandoori* left-over's.

'You don't like it here, do you Chris?' Lynette asked, as I perused through the menu to find something worthwhile to eat. 'I knew we should have gone to 'Hare Rama's' this evening to have their Indian fish'n chip experience; a pianist plays a medley of Gershwin tunes when the fillet of haddock, chips, mushy peas and gravy arrive at your table.'

'Do you know, Lynette, for the first time today you are right and no, I don't like this place.' I replied, trying to penetrate her bullet-proof facade.

It was at this point I manoeuvred my body over to one side to see who was behind the door which was being constantly opened by a waiter, Ray Robinson, an Indian imposter from Sandbank Road in Parkstone; his green mock turban precariously placed on the side of his head gave the impression it was about to fall off and together with the roving restaurant manager and fellow waiter they could have easily been taken for brothers had it not been for the difference in complexion and regional accents.

Hovering in the background was a Bengali half-caste waiter called, Baldric Chatterji, Ray Robinson's counterpart and looking every inch like the Indian servant depicted on the label of a Camp Coffee bottle. He told us his great-grandfather was an Indian belly dancer who came from Scotland and his great grandmother, a kilt-maker for the British Army; this was when I renamed him, Baldric McChutney, the great grandson of a Bengal Lancer.

As I suspected, Raman Patel was in the kitchen wearing a chef's uniform and a white side-cap which made him look like Jawaharlal Nehru, himself. I immediately rose to my feet and barged into the steamy kitchen looking for trouble.

'You shouldn't be in here, Mr Travis;' Patel said, waving a number three cook's knife in front of my face. 'You really shouldn't be in here.' he added.

'It is you who shouldn't be here and, according to my daughter, Barbara, she tells me you should be in India.'

'Well, I had a problem at the airport; my passport expired a month ago and so I had to cancel my visit.' he replied, moving his head from side-to-side similar to a tormented punkah wallah.

'I have heard some stories in my time but, this has taken the biscuit.' I said to him angrily, increasing the temperature to boiling point. 'I thought you and Barbara had an understanding, and if you upset my daughter again, I will thread your nuts on to one of your kebab skewers and watch them sizzle on top of a stove.'

I walked slowly back into the restaurant knowing I had achieved something special on Barbara's behalf; the entire meal, including the wine, beer, stilled water and a gift-wrapped red rose for my daughter were all on the house.

The Spanish Inquisition had begun with Lynette bouncing back to continue with her serious questioning.

'Tell me, Chris, who is the woman you met in Southport?' she asked, momentarily glancing up from a huge plateful of turkey *Korma* and *Pilau* rice.

I explained to her that she was called Brigitte-Helen Boullard, a Parisian lady who was staying with her long-established English pen friend in nearby Churchtown, close to Southport. Lynette then asked:

'And what does this Brigitte-Helen what's-her-name do for a living?'

she anxiously wanted to know.

Lynette was surprised to hear she was an estate agent in Paris and not one of those floozies who frequent the bars and cafés of *Montmartre*.

'And, if I may ask this question, under what circumstances did you meet her?'

'It was yesterday morning when she sat down at my table in The Wayfarers Shopping Arcade, shortly after I phoned you; Brigitte couldn't find a seat because the coffee shop was so busy.' I tried to explain, in between taking crackling bites out of an exploding *Poppadom*.

'Oh, its Brigitte now, is it?' she said, smiling nervously. 'The next thing you will be telling me is you took her out for dinner last night.'

'No, I did not; it was she who took me out for dinner.' I truthfully explained.

'And why did she do that,' Lynette asked, filling her wine glass with more *Merlot* from a small carafe. 'There must have been an ulterior motive for her to do that, mustn't there, and now you are going to tell me she wanted to sell you a house.'

'As a matter of fact *Mademoiselle* Boullard was telling me all about properties in France and how cheap they are to buy at the moment.' I explained, trying to bring the subject to a close.

'It is *Mademoiselle* now, is it? Your French language has improved enormously during the last few days, hasn't it; she sounds like a real Madam to me.'

'Do you know, Lynette, ever since I arrived home this afternoon you have been a pain in the proverbial backside and personally, I don't know what to do about it.' I told her emphatically. 'And when I was staying in Southport, I was like a fish out of water, a duck without a pond and a nose without a bleed.' I said, adding to the rhetoric.

'Oh, you poor thing,' she said, looking at a reproduction print on one of the walls. 'Who is that man in the picture?' Lynette asked and at last beginning to change the subject.

'It is an artist's impression of Rudyard Kipling.' I quickly replied.

'Oh, he's the guy who bakes exceedingly good cakes, isn't he?' she said.

'When I go back to University on Monday I am going to tell that one to professor Stevens; I'm sure his students will appreciate him joking about one of England's finest writers and poets.'

'Christopher, I wasn't aware I was joking.' she said, trying to disguise her academic ignorance to a satirical level.

I quoted "The Ballad of the King's Jest" by Rudyard Kipling to Lynette:

"Four things greater than all things are –

Women and Horses and Power and War"

'What are you talking about, Chris? No wonder his work has been reappraised and has received considerable critical acclaim.' she said, allowing me to be surprised. 'You don't always have the monopoly in trying to be clever, Chris.' she added.

'And what happened in the kitchen, I take it Raman Patel is still alive?' Lynette asked when I resumed eating my now cold chicken *Madras* curry and *Pilau* rice.

'He is still alive, but only just.' I replied, looking at the bill which was brought to the table somewhat prematurely by Mister Maharashtra with a zero balance after I had given Ralph McTell in the kitchen an ultimatum to stay away from my daughter and not to upset her in any way.

'Curry, my mum used to say is muck.' I told Lynette as I munched away on the last *Poppadom* smeared with onion and mango chutney.

'Well, like you, Chris she probably didn't like it.' she replied, nodding her head like a donkey. 'It is only right and proper to tell Barbara before her birthday on Saturday, that Raman is still in Bournemouth, and not washing his feet in the muddy waters of the river Ganges.' Lynette seriously suggested.

'I will inform her on Friday when she comes home for the weekend.' I said, momentarily and volunteering to be a Good Samaritan. 'You know, Lynette, these Indians can be dropped from a dizzy height and almost invariably they land on their feet.'

'Why don't we visit the 'Ideal Home' Show in the Bournemouth International Centre tomorrow?' she suggested. 'It will give us some ideas as to how we are going to invest in our new-found wealth.' she added.

'That's an excellent idea, Lynette, and then perhaps we can have lunch in Harry Ramsden's.' I enthusiastically suggested.

'Tell me, Chris, what is your idea of an ideal home?' Lynette asked.

'I would much prefer to live next to a Waitrose supermarket, my general practitioner, a hospital and a cemetery at the end of the road.'

'Those two young ladies, Victoria and Barbara, will be nineteen on Saturday; it is amazing and where does the time go?' Lynette said, placing a hand on my arm just to confirm I was still there.

'I don't know, Lynette,' I replied with a sigh. 'But what I do know is; human beings are a collection of people who come and they go and, we are all in an almighty long queue, but some of us get to the front quicker than others.'

'Christopher, will you please stop joking with me.' she said, now looking up towards the nicotine-stained ceiling.

'I'm not joking, Lynette.' I replied.

'I'm an optimist, Chris.' she would insist on telling me, adjusting her spectacles.

'Not bad for a woman who has a problem with her eyesight.' I replied.

Chapter Five

No 46 Queens Park Avenue, Bournemouth Thursday 16th March 2000

The day began with Lynette and I having a rather pleasant morning sitting at the breakfast table eating our traditional bowls of fortifying Kellogg's cornflakes and I had no idea the day would start so peacefully without a repetition of a third-degree interrogation, reminiscent to the one I had been subjected to the day before.

'At what time do you think the 'Ideal Home Show' opens this morning, Chris?' Lynette asked, pouring more steaming hot coffee into my favourite bone-china cup.

'At ten o'clock, I should imagine.' I replied and giving her the impression I wasn't in any hurry to go there. 'You know what they are like at the BIC, Lynette, they open when they feel like opening the doors.'

'Well then, we don't want to miss the grand opening, do we.' she said, allowing me to end my mediocre breakfast in peace when she got up from the table to feed Hannibal our Siamese cat and afterwards picked up 'The Times' from behind the front door.

'You know, once I phoned the box office in the BIC because we wanted to go and see The Ken Dodd Happiness Show. I asked, what time did the performance start and they told me at what time can you turn up. And, what is it you particularly want to see in the exhibition hall, Lynette?'

'Well, for starters we need to replace our existing double-glazing and to find a new cooker, suitable to go with the frying pan,' she quickly replied.

'Oh, we are back to frying pans again, are we?' I said, jokingly.

'Anyone would think we don't have two pennies to rub together, Chris,' she said, clearing up the debris I had created at the table. 'I hope you are not going to turn into a regular Mister Scrooge now that we have come into all this money.' she added before I told her:

'If you look after your pennies, the pounds will take care of themselves.'

'Yes, I can understand that, Christopher, providing you don't die in the meantime.'

'Well, in that case *you* can always enquire at the box office.' I put in, laughing at my own sense of humour.

'You know, Chris you haven't been the same since you came back from Southport; what's with that place; and, do you know something that I don't?'

'Don't start on me again, Lynette, because I shall certainly walk out through the front door and never come back.' I insisted on saying.

'Sorry, Chris, but you will have your little jokes, won't you?' Lynette replied, giving me the impression she wasn't sorry at all after she said: 'will you be staying for tea before you leave me?'

I said to her, it is possible I could reconsider only if she offers me some of her rich and delicious home-made fruit cake.

Time was getting on rapidly that morning and it was exactly ten o'clock when I managed to open the up-and-over garage door at the top of the driveway. The Volkswagen, still suffering from minor injuries attributed to reckless motorway driving the previous morning needed to be fixed and this was when I suggested to Lynette we should go into town in her van. She was anxious to know when I was going to take the initiative to buy another car and after mentioning we were not made of money, Lynette angrily stormed back into the house through the side entrance door.

'Come on, Lynette, lighten up, I was only joking,' I said, putting an arm around her shoulder. 'I will have a look round The 'Westover' used car salesroom this afternoon and that will keep you happy, won't it?' I added with a smile.

'No, it will not,' Lynette replied, shrugging me away. 'And whatever happened to reputable car showrooms where one can buy a brand-new Skoda without getting ripped-off.'

'Well, Lynette, since we are contemplating buying one of these rather expensive Eastern Bloc vehicles, why don't we go the whole hog and buy a silver-grey Porsche 911 sports car, they seem to be in vogue at the moment.'

'You what?' Lynette said, looking at me somewhat strangely in the mirror. 'You're not going funny on me again, are you?' she added.

'Well, I might.'

Lynette and I climbed into the van and set off down Queens Park Avenue with me volunteering as usual to do the driving. It was whilst I was driving along Exeter Road towards the Bournemouth International Centre I noticed Boullard's silver-grey Porsche 911 sports car parked outside The Royal Exeter Hotel and the adjoining multi-award winning Lounge Bar & Restaurant.

I thought to myself, how is this possible and then all kinds of ideas were beginning to swirl around in my head like; has Brigitte-Helen Boullard followed me back to Bournemouth and to crudely quote Humphrey Bogart: 'In all the gin joints and towns in the world, why did she land up in mine?'

'You are driving the van rather erratically, Chris, is there something on your mind?' Lynette asked, obviously feeling rather nervous sitting next to a potential escapee.

'You don't seem to realize, Lynette, the town is extremely busy with traffic and to add to it all, the Dagenham Girl Pipers; the female bagpipe marching band are going to appear soon making a Hinge and Bracket.'

'What on earth is a Hinge and Bracket, Chris? They were two female impersonators who used to be on television, weren't they? Lynette asked, looking out from the nearside window to see a tartan-clad girl banging on a drum the size of a gasometer.

'A Hinge and Bracket, my dear, in London cockney slang is a racket; an ear-shattering noise.' I replied and instinctively knowing what she was going to say next.

'Yes, I do know what a racket is, Chris, I'm not stupid you know.' reminding me once again she wasn't and continuing to tell me: 'I still have my old tennis racket, Chris; it is somewhere amongst all the junk you keep promising to chuck out in the garage.'

I wasn't going to tell her I had previously backed into it and is now looking in a sorrowful state hiding among a hockey stick, boxing gloves and ancient gymnastic equipment.

'I can smell something wonderful wafting in from somewhere nearby.' Lynette said, momentarily looking like a '*Bisto kid*', pointing her sharp nose upwards and towards the bonnet of the van.

'Now, you are beginning to hallucinate, Lynette.' I replied, thinking it must be Harry Ramsden who was responsible.

Lynette and I walked up the steps into the BIC's main entrance hall showing our on-line ticket to a man standing by the door. From there we could initially observe the vast number of displays and demonstration stalls along the main thoroughfare as we shuffled our way through the centre of the exhibition hall. I can remember holding her hand and reminiscing back to the time when we were first married, looking for various items of kitchen equipment for our ideas of the perfect dream and ideal home. The smell of fresh homemade bread, doughnuts, waffles and popcorn interacting with fragrant air freshener as I can recall, was permeating all around the place interfering with my taste buds.

We looked at the cookers, fridges and appliances which needed to be replaced in our home and it was when we were watching carrots being sliced into two by a Turkish kebab demonstrator wielding an extremely large bowie knife I saw the intrepid George Hesketh standing to attention at a double-glazing stall.

'Bloody hell, what's he doing here?' I said to Lynette, who was now happily witnessing cucumbers being decapitated with a kitchen utensil resembling a miniature madam guillotine.

'Who is he, and where?' she asked, staring at the beetroot-stained bandage on the demonstrator's finger.

'It's George Hesketh, Auntie Gertrude's solicitor from Southport.' I replied, wondering whether it was me who was hallucinating. 'Has he by some kind of strange metamorphosis, changed into a double-glazing salesman overnight?' I said, adding to the ongoing confusion.

'Well, he's probably got two jobs; many people have these days to make ends meet.' she said, mesmerised by more carrot heads falling into a basket.

'Make ends meet, making ends meet; he's got more money than Richard Branson.' I told her, in no uncertain terms.

It was then I realized that the car, parked outside the Royal Exeter Hotel belonged to George Hesketh and how stupid it was of me to believe the vehicle was owned by Brigitte-Helen Boullard.

'Those hotdogs are enormous, aren't they Chris, *Titanic*, in fact.' Lynette pointed out, as we pushed and shoved our way down the central walkway of the exhibition.

'Yes, and like Ruby Wax's mega rich father, they will go on, and on, and on.' I put in, not wanting those over-indulgent *'Weenies'* to spoil our visit to Harry Ramsden's.

'You are joking with me again, Christopher, just stop it.' Lynette said, poking me in the ribs with her elbow.

'Just stand back and wait for the flak.' I said to her, wanting desperately to know why Hesketh should be selling replacement windows and doors.

'I wouldn't advise you to go over and speak to him because he could stop the cheque from going through the bank into our account.' she immediately pointed out.

Lynette, as usual was right and I came to the conclusion that there was nothing of interest to satisfy our requirements and after I had walked into a fake red brick wall which fell over on to a settee we decided it was time to leave. When we were about to venture into the foyer the smoke detector bell rang and almost at once the sprinklers were activated. She said to me quite calmly: 'It was a good thing I brought my umbrella.'

We managed to escape to the top of the steps where I saw a Dagenham Girl Piper at the bottom squeezing the hell out of a tartan-clad bag trying to make it work. And standing by her side was another, simultaneously twirling two drumsticks around in the air likened to a Chinook helicopter.

Harry Ramsden's Fish & Chip Restaurant, formerly the Anchor Bar, is only a stone's throw away from the BIC and just a short distance down the hill towards Bournemouth's Pier Approach.

At ten minutes past twelve, Lynette and I were shown to a table by a waitress called Veronica who immediately took our order for a meal we had waited since breakfast to die for; consisting of: battered cod, chips and mushy peas, or alternatively; steak and kidney pudding accompanied by bread, butter and a pot of tea. The pianist, who had just arrived looking every inch like Max Wall, wearing a penguin suit, flipped up the back of his coat and proceeded to park his botty on a stool. He began to play, surprisingly enough, Stevie Wonder's *"Isn't She Lovely"* to the diners who were fortunate to listen to his music as most of them appeared to be deaf.

I can recall, an ankle-biter, an unruly child crawling around underneath the table but that was soon remedied by me when I gave it a swift kick from one of my size seven and a half inch brown leather shoes.

It was after this unfortunate experience occurred and having to put up with constant screaming and hollering in the background, I decided to make a quick exit from the restaurant under the pretence I was going to visit the gents.

With the speed of a thousand gazelles I dashed up Exeter Road towards the hotel where the Porsche 911 was parked and then walked into the reception lobby with one aim in mind; just who the hell owns that bloody car? I asked the receptionist, who looked vaguely familiar and extremely like a victim from one of my many broken-down relationships, if she had a Mr George Hesketh staying in the hotel. She looked inside the register and told me there was a Mr and Mrs George Hesketh from Southport staying at the hotel and this was when I saw Brigitte-Helen Boullard opening the door to the sports car.

I had instinctively known Brigitte-Helen was in town and now also how Colombo must have felt when he solved his first crime.

The receptionist, who was called Patricia Price, said to me: 'we meet again, Christopher Travis; after all these years.'

Nervously, I said to her: 'What is the time? I must be going.' and that was when I made a dashing exit from the hotel before hot-footing back to the Fish & Chip Restaurant.

On re-entry into Harry Ramsden's I could hear George Gershwin's, "*Rhapsody in Blue*" being beautifully played by Cole Boardman, our versatile resident pianist for the afternoon.

'Makes a change from Stevie Wonder,' I said, creeping up behind Lynette to stop her from falling asleep.

'But I like Stevie Wonder, Chris.' Lynette said, taking me back in time when we used to watch 'Spitting Image' on her mum and dad's black and white television set.

The next of Cole Boardman's piano renditions to hit the keyboard was:

'*Ebony and Ivory*'; this unfortunately had been requested by Lynette, whilst I was supposedly parking my arse in the gents.

'You were away a long time, Chris.' she said, looking down at her watch.

'It must have been the mushy peas which caused the delay.' I hastily replied, and before asking her: 'Do you know who the Patron Saint of Bournemouth is?'

'This is not going to be another one of your silly little jokes again, is it?' she asked, momentarily glancing up towards the ceiling.

'It is Sir Walter Raleigh.' I said to her, enhancing her somewhat limited historical knowledge and then continuing with my informative albeit, geographical short story. 'If it wasn't for Sir Walter Raleigh introducing the potato to Britain from the Americas, Bournemouth wouldn't have its fish and chips.'

'And, is he responsible for all those cigarette ends on the pavement outside?' Lynette then asked.

'It is possible; it is possible,' I replied, failing miserably to get the better of her stupid insinuations.

'I wonder what the man from the 'Coal Board' is going to play next' she then asked, looking at a poem on the wall which read:

'Symphony in Suet'

"A pastry construction made with some flour
Carefully rounded and built like 'The Tower'
Inside this sculpture lay mouth-watering savoury
Braised Steak and Kidney in a rich tasting gravy
Serve it with chips and big mushy peas
The Queen serves them daily when having high teas
Charles eats them in *Claridges*
They're not quite the same
Southern Fried Chicken, they are to blame
A Beefeater looking up is on to a Good'n
When a tourist goes down for stealing his *Pudd'n*"

'I don't honestly know, Lynette, maybe something from Cole-Porter.' I frustratingly replied.

'Did you know, Chris that just before Sir Walter Raleigh had his head chopped off in Westminster is said to have remarked, on feeling the edge of the axe before his execution: "Tis a sharp remedy, but a sure one for all ills".'

'Yes, I do know this, Lynette, and the executioner also said he hoped he wasn't going to be called out again because it looked as though it was going to rain.'

Lynette and I having just taken out a second mortgage to buy two fish and chip lunches made are way to the car park to collect the van.

'I am in no mood to go looking at cars this afternoon.' Lynette said, as she scrutinised the restaurant bill which was presented to us at a till by the door. 'Why don't we pay a visit to Barclays Bank in Boscombe to find out what the rate of exchange is between the French Franc and the Pound Sterling?'

'And why, if I may ask, do you want to do this?' I was anxious to know.

'It is because we have all this money, Chris and I think now is a good time to buy a property in France.'

We entered the bank with gusto with the idea a knowledgeable banker would be in a position to tell us the current rate of exchange.

'I can tell you what it was yesterday, but I can't tell you what it is today; alright? If you want to know what it is tomorrow, you'll have to speak to Mirabelle but she's off sick today, alright?'

We later looked inside the travel pages of Bournemouth's '*Daily Echo*' where the tourist rate of exchange was shown and this gave us some idea roughly as to what it was. I was thinking about the Heskeths, and their possible plan to plough back some of the money from Auntie Gertrude's estate.

"Step into my parlour said the spider to the fly and don't forget your cheque book".

Chapter Six

The following morning...

It was Friday again and I couldn't believe our two daughters, Victoria and Barbara, would be arriving at 16.25, travelling on the 13.04 train from Birmingham New Street that afternoon; time had passed so quickly since Lynette and I said our goodbyes to them on the platform of Bournemouth's railway station the previous Sunday.

We were both sitting down at the breakfast table, Lynette continuing to read through the travel pages of yesterday's '*Daily Echo*' and me perusing through the 'Leisure, International Venues & Events' brochure before booking on-line, the tickets for The Moscow State Circus in the Bournemouth Pavilion that evening.

'Why don't we take the girls for a pre-show meal in the '*eighteen twelve*' restaurant next to the Royal Exeter?' Lynette suggested, and me abruptly replying with:

'No, I don't think it would be a good idea.'

'For Pete's sake, Christopher, why don't you want to go there?' she asked, looking through into the kitchen to find the whereabouts of the frying pan. 'We, if you can remember, enjoyed going to the 'Royal Exeter' before we became engaged to be married and you always ordered the same thing, a large tee-bone steak. Tell me, Chris, are you hiding something?'

After I had gone through the motions of checking my pockets to find nothing in particular that would interest her except for some loose change, I said no there wasn't.

'Well, in that case we shall go; the show doesn't start until seven-thirty pm and that will give you enough time to polish off a huge tee-bone steak to die for as you used to say, but that was when you were in a better frame of mind.'

'Okay, you win, Lynette, you always do.' I put in, making a sort of irritating clanging noise with a teaspoon as I stirred it around violently inside my favourite 'Kiss me quick' coffee mug which she bought from a souvenir shop in front of Boscombe Pier.

'Do you have to make that hinge and bracket, Chris; the noise you are making is getting on my nerves.'

'Can you remember, Lynette when the waiter asked how I would like my steak and I told him, preferably on a plate; just remove the horns and dust it down, I said.'

'Yes, I can remember it all too well,' she sighed. 'It was your birthday and the waiter brought you a steak resembling well-burnt chamois leather and I couldn't help but notice how squidgy it was around the edges.' she added.

'Did I tell you, Lynette, that one Christmas my mum and dad gave me a pair of boxing gloves as a present?' I asked, knowing full well I hadn't. 'She became the only woman in Bournemouth who cooked the Xmas dinner with a black eye!'

'I suppose you think that was funny.' Lynette said, and then went on to say: 'I can see it's going to be another one of those days.'

Lynette, having read the print off the travel pages of the newspaper proceeded to get up from the table to cook a fried breakfast for both of us. I momentarily glanced inside the *'Daily Echo'* to find she had high-lighted and ringed a couple of French properties with a red colour pencil and this was when I knew she was serious about us buying a *pied-à-terre*; a second home and becoming owners abroad. The characteristic aromatic smell of bacon and eggs, fried bread, mushrooms, tomatoes and black pudding was wafting into the small breakfast alcove leading from the kitchen. Lynette's apron which she tied around a waist wider than a broadband radio has a poem that reads: "Alfred and his Cakes".

'Alfred and his Cakes'

Alfred whilst eating his Kellogg's Corn Flakes
Decided to bake one or two of his cakes
With some syrup and sugar, nutmeg and flour
He set the timer to read half-an-hour
The alarm went off without any hassle
The cakes came out burnt to a 'frazzle'

'What is on the itinerary for tomorrow, Lynette?' I asked, looking at the two little girls in the family photo frame on the sideboard.

'Well, first of all you and one of the girls will have to go to Sainsbury's in Boscombe to get some booze for the party whilst I will be working in the kitchen slaving my guts out over a stove.' she so enthusiastically replied.

'It should give me time to look in the Winton car salesrooms; they have the latest Alpha Romeo models in their forecourt window and if you buy now they will give you the opportunity to dangerously drive at speed around the motor racing circuit at Silverstone.'

'I've got a better idea, Chris,' she quickly put in. 'why don't you visit Tinker Bell in Barclays Bank so we can continue with our enquiries about the current rates of exchange, that is, if she's back to work and not on the 'Moby Dick."

'Apart from Moby Dick being an enormous whale, characterized by, Hermann Melville, the mid-19th century American writer and novelist, what exactly are you talking about, Lynette?'

'It means, sick, my dear Christopher, sick.' she so eloquently said in her melodious Charminster accent.

I was trying to make up my mind just who it was on the sick list, Tinker Bell or Lynette when the front door bell rang. It was DHL carriers asking me to sign for a large cardboard carton containing Auntie Gertrude's effects which Hesketh & Draper, Solicitor's and Notaries had so kindly managed to release.

Lynette and I similar to the nineteen-sixties television host, Michael Miles, who created the Game Show, Take Your Pick! slowly, albeit, apprehensively opened the box to see what was inside. However, using an extremely sharp kitchen knife wasn't part of *his* performance.

'It's a bit like opening 'Pandora's Box' isn't it Chris?' Lynette said removing pieces of Sellotape from one of the corners.

'When I was at school I knew a girl called Dora, I never did get to see *her* box though.' I replied, emulating a classic line by the character Spike in the classic film, *Notting Hill*, starring, Hugh Grant and Julia Roberts.

'You didn't tell me you knew a girl called Dora, Chris, because if you had it may have put a different light on our marriage.' she said, this time waving a pair of extremely large dressmaking scissors in front of my face.

'Point taken.' I cautiously replied, giving in to her threats of violent behaviour.

There was a huge pile of brown paper packaging, bubble-wrap and to add to the debris, pellets of white polystyrene scattered untidily on the floor. 'Will we ever get to find out just what is inside the box because I'm supposed to be back to work on Monday.' I said to myself as Lynette and I delved deeply to find at least one item of value below a canteen of electro plated EPNS cutlery and a bone-china tea service.

Most of Auntie Gertrude's valuables had been sold prior to her departing this world but then there were several items lying at the bottom of the box which later realized a small fortune at a Stanley Gibbon's auction in London; my uncle Thomas's coveted and prized collection of rare stamps which fetched more than the house, the estate and what was left of their effects.

'What are all these black and blue things slipped inside Auntie Gertrude's family photograph album?' Lynette asked, not knowing the meaning of the word philately and what the famous Victorian 'Penny Black' and 'Two-penny Blue' were.

'Those, my dear, are postage stamps produced in 1840 and they are in mint condition.' I said, excitedly and highly delighted with my find.

'Do they come in a flavour other than mint?' she then asked.

'Don't joke with me, Lynette; it's pay day.'

'Tell me Chris, why do we have to buy another car?' Lynette asked. 'The Volkswagen has still a lot of mileage left in her and we can easily replace the things which are missing.' she seriously added.

'You're not becoming a regular Missus McScrooge are you Lynette?' getting my own back because of what she said to me the previous day.

'Well, after all it was you Christopher who said, if you look after your pennies, the pounds will take care of themselves.'

'It would be a good idea Lynette, if we could give the girls a special birthday present tomorrow,' I said, browsing through the automobile pages of the *Daily Echo*; 'A brand new shiny black Toyota Corolla for Vicky and a bronze metallic Mazda MX5 sports car for Barbara, and that would really get up Raman Patel's over-sized Bengali nose, wouldn't it?'

'You do realize, all of this vindictiveness is going to cost you a great deal of money,' she strongly emphasised. 'and on several occasions you said to me Chris, you didn't like Japanese cars.'

'Ah, that was because my first car was a Honda Civic which blew up on me half-way between Eastleigh and Southampton, but I suppose it does help to put water in the radiator.' I said, cowering down behind the newspaper and failing miserably to make myself disappear.

'Come on, Chris, you cannot be serious.' Lynette said, sounding like a female John McEnroe. 'It would be a good idea to buy them a sensible car so that they can use it at the weekends to travel down from Birmingham and this will mean they won't have to pay for exorbitant and excessive railway tickets.'

'And when are we supposed to do this, Lynette?' I asked, glaring at her from over the top of the paper.

'Next weekend, when they return home to Bournemouth.' she suggested. 'We have far too much to do this weekend, especially tomorrow, haven't we Christopher?'

'Can you tell me, Lynette, at precisely what time is kick-off tomorrow?'

'Do you mean at what time is the birthday party due to begin,' she replied, rendering another one of her smart arse attitudes. 'The party will start when I am ready which will be after I have spruced myself up having worked all morning in that bloody kitchen baking cakes, sausage rolls, mini quiches in between preparing bowls of Mediterranean salad.'

'The only reason why I wanted to know, Lynette is because I may have time to go down to the pub after doing all of the weekly shopping in Sainsburys.'

'Now, you really are joking, Chris,' she said, punching one of her fists through the sports page.

I thought to myself: What did the Bournemouth *'Daily Echo'* do to deserve this? And the road to hell is paved with good intentions but some of us get lost along the way. Lynette, by attacking me in this way had raised the level on my *crap ohmmeter* into the danger zone, almost reading one hundred percent.

*

Bournemouth Railway Station around four pm that afternoon.

Lynette and I, having walked over the railway bridge inside the station, stepped on to the platform and waited for the train to arrive from Birmingham New Street and, given its previous track record, the locomotive I can tell you pulled in on time.

The train was of the old type with separate second and first-class compartments, assessable only by way of a sliding door in a long narrow corridor.

Victoria and Barbara, I could see, were standing inside one of these compartments reaching up towards the luggage rack in order to retrieve their small weekend trolley bags and this was when I swung into action, boarding the train to help them with their luggage.

Lynette was busy too, applying more gloss to an extensive liposuction operation with the aid of a mother-of-pearl compact I gave her as a Christmas present.

'Hi dad.' Victoria said, followed by Barbara sounding like her echo.

I reciprocated by making the Hi's and Hello's into an ensemble helping Vicky and Babs to put their identical pieces of luggage on to the platform.

The door to the carriage was loudly banged shut by the guard before blowing his whistle to allow the train to slowly pull out from the station and to go back to wherever it came from.

'Do you think the door is closed, dad?' Barbara said, turning around to watch and say goodbye to the rather antiquated mode of conveyance moving away from the platform.

'I think so, Barbara.' I replied, as we trudged our way through into the station hall. 'Oh by the way, your ex-boyfriend, Raman Patel gave me a red rose in the Bay of Bengal restaurant on Wednesday evening.' I also put in.

'You should be so lucky, dad.' Barbara said, smirking.

'It wasn't for me, silly, it was for you.' I told her as I led the way into the car park.

'I know, dad, and Raman is coming to my birthday party tomorrow with the other six.'

'So does this mean you are both back together again?' I asked, momentarily stopping to wait for an answer.

'Well you could say that, dad.' she replied as I gathered up speed wheeling two trolley bags up to the boot of the car.

'You're minus a hub cap, dad.' Victoria said, noticing one was missing. 'And what is all that string doing holding up the front number plate.' she was anxious to find out.

'The car is beginning to look like a heap of old rubbish,' Barbara said, quickly putting her five eggs into the basket. 'Why don't you and mum buy a new car; it's not that you can't afford something better than this.' she added.

Lynette, having endorsed what Barbara had said remarked that next weekend would be the ideal time for buying a new car.

'At what time this evening does the Ring Master at The Moscow State Circus start to crack his whip?' Vicky asked, looking down closely at her tiny *Timex* wristwatch.

'At seven-thirty prompt.' I replied, sliding into the driver's seat after I had secured the doors next to the passenger seats.

'But first we are going for a meal in the *'eighteen twelve'*, 1812 Lounge Bar & Restaurant, next to the Royal Exeter Hotel.' Lynette excitedly said to the two hungry young ladies.

'That's good, dad because, I'm bloody well starving.' Vicky said, looking at Barbara chewing away on a couple of *Twix* bars, enthusiastically licking the sticky caramel and chocolate from her fingers.

'I hope we are not going to the Royal Exeter Hotel in this car.' Vicky said, putting her snobby hat back on again habitually gesticulating in inverted commas with her fingers.

'You're not turning into an Easter Bunny are you, Victoria.' I said, looking at her in the rear view mirror.

'Raman is changing his car next week, dad,' Barbara said, trying to emulate Victoria's stuck up type of attitude. 'He told me he is going to buy a brand new top of the range, 1999 318i E46 BMW in British Racing

Green before we tour around Longleat Safari Park.' she added smugly.

'Well, I hope the weather will be fine for you both but, be careful, I believe there are lots of monkeys hanging about in the grounds just waiting to pinch a bottom or your shoulder bag.' I replied, thinking I too, can be smug. 'And who are you inviting to the party, Victoria?' I asked, hoping Lynette wouldn't have to change the menu to please another member of an ethnic group.

'I am inviting Simon Bennett, Frederick Bennett's son.' she replied on the approach to Queens Park Avenue. 'You always said you wanted to be a councillor, dad, so here's your chance.'

My little daughter, Vicky, has turned into a creature of nepotism, whatever next, I thought to myself, visualizing me standing for the next mayor of Bournemouth and momentarily nodding-off outside the front door to the house; in my dreams was all I could achieve but then, one can always live in hope.

*

The '*eighteen twelve*', 1812, Lounge Bar & Restaurant, Bournemouth

It was exactly six o'clock when the four of us, having taken a taxi into the town, marched into the restaurant to find a table conveniently situated next to an escape hatch close to the door of the kitchen.

'Oh, no.' I said to myself, seeing Patricia Price entering into the restaurant with a notepad in her hand.

'You've gone a funny colour, dad!' Victoria said, before I relished in the pleasure of saying to her: 'it's not going to be as funny as tomorrow when Ralph MacTell shows up with his bunch of clapped-out flowers, but I don't think for one moment it is his fault he comes from the far reaches of the outer Hebrides.

'Your geography leaves a great deal to be desired.' she put in, looking at the extensive range of cocktails in the restaurant's menu.

My geography was I had an excellent view into the car park when I looked out from one of the windows from where I was sitting, and as I had envisaged, Brigitte-Helen Boullard and George Hesketh were to make an appearance. Brigitte, walking alongside George was carrying two boxes of Kentucky Fried Chicken; the paper napkins flapping up and down on the top in time to a gentle sea breeze. It was what I had suspected about her; no culture, no finesse, no knickers and no brains and I breathed a sigh of relief, knowing they were heading for the hotel and not the restaurant.

Chapter Seven

The Moscow State Circus which came direct from Russia's cultural and perfect backdrop, Park Gorkogo (Gorky Park) was a complete success. We watched a hula-hoop act suspended from a revolving ring above the stage, high speed juggling acts, mass skipping as you have never seen before; the performers changing their costumes in seconds and leaping acrobats.

The show was in two parts, flying, back flipping, juggling and roller skating, trapeze artists, clowns, Cossacks and the famous clown Popov. The circus didn't include any animals and the emphasis was on the spectacle and the theme; a Russian legend consisting of twelve chairs. The music typically was "March of the Elephants" however, there were no elephants to be seen in this circus, but then I thought, perhaps one could arrive in Queens Park Avenue tomorrow; all of this reminded me of the poem called, 'The Circus Clown', which goes:

'The Circus Clown'

When the circus came to town
We were entertained by a clown
With a big red nose and wearing a frown
He was the star when the circus came to town
His tears were controlled but they could not stop
Falling on to the ground of the 'Big Top'
The audience laughed when he fell about
Inside the sawdust ring
Every day he does the same old thing
To make people happy for a while
In his own make-believe style
And when the show has ended
For him there's always a tomorrow
To continue with his sorrow

Lynette, Victoria, Barbara and myself, were all seated around the table having breakfast as we usually do on Saturday mornings and me, of course trying my best to read the *Times* in peace and quiet instead of listening to pathetic jokes coming from our resident comedian, Victoria Travis.

'Thanks mummy and daddy for the birthday card, it's great.' Barbara said, gazing at a comical sports car with headlights posing as big ears on the front cover.

'Thanks, dad for the musical card,' Victoria said, reaching over the table to give me a big kiss before playing the tune: "Daisy Bell (Bicycle Built for Two)", composed by the English composer, Harry Dacre in 1892.

'I know another version to this song, dad,' Vicky anxiously wanted to tell me: "and you'll look sweet upon the seat of a toilet seat made for two".

'Victoria, I think that was uncalled for.' I remarked looking at Lynette who was doing her best trying not to laugh. 'Your mum and I spent a lot of time trying to find an appropriate birthday card for you, Victoria and if that's what they are teaching you at Birmingham University, I want my money back.' I added.

'What do you call Irish pasta?' she asked, applying more black pepper on to her egg-in-a cup breakfast.

After we had all held up our hands to inform her we had no idea, she replied by giving us the answer:

'*McNamara Carbonara*.' she said, laughing at a joke which was not in the least bit funny.

'Did you hear about the one…?' Victoria would insist on telling us.

'Vicky, just shut up will you, I'm trying to read the newspaper.' I said, smiling when I saw a picture of William Hague on the front page; his head looking like a miss-shaped monkey nut.

'It's a good thing newspapers cannot talk, isn't it, dad.' Vicky said, noisily munching away on a piece of burnt toast heavily smeared with marmalade.

'What do you mean by that, Victoria?' I asked, inquisitively.

'Well, dad, he speaks with a posh Yorkshire accent that no one outside the House of Commons can understand.' she replied, applying more butter on another slice of bread resembling a doorstep.

It was then I heard the postman delivering the mail through our letter box and for some inexplicable reason there were more envelopes piled up on the mat behind the door than usual. The post was mainly for Vicky and Babs; their birthday cards and presents, the remainder consisting of harrowing energy bills; gas, electricity and water charges.

Seconds later, Mrs (Frau) Maria von Strudel arrived from Frederick Strauss's Austrian Patisserie in Boscombe delivering a huge birthday cake, complementary multi-coloured candles and a book of matches depicting the name of the firm responsible for setting fire to our home. She had come direct from her Tyrolean outpost situated at the top of Sea Road and with a metaphorical jingling of cow bells, moos and unexpected rude noises, I was half expecting her to start yodelling or to break out into song at any moment: "brown paper packages tied up with string, these are a few of my favourite things", or something equally ridiculous.

The well-rounded, Maria, looking every inch a plumpish, Delia Smith, brought the cake into kitchen via the side entrance and after taking it out from the well-advertised box placed it carefully down on top of Lynette's work table.

It was when the two young ladies were occupied; happily opening their cards and presents I couldn't help but go into the kitchen to prematurely snaffle a tiny piece of pink and lemon royal icing from the top of the cake.

Walking back into the lounge I approached the girls who were now sitting cross-legged on the carpet in front of the fireplace and after I had opened a bottle of *Café de Paris*, Lynette gave them their presents, two gift-wrapped boxes containing eighteen carat gold earrings and it was then I began to sing: "Happy Birthday to you, squashed tomatoes and stew, bread and butter in the gutter, Happy Birthday to you"

'What's that stuff around your mouth, dad?' Barbara asked, looking up from where she was sitting on the floor.

'Oh, it's a tiny rosette from the top of your birthday cake.' I explained to her.

'You know that's not royal icing, don't you, dad?' Vicky said.

'What do you mean; of course it's royal icing.' I replied, not knowing whether it was or it wasn't.

'Sorry to disillusion you, dad, but what you've just eaten was wax; all part of the decoration.'

'Now, you really are joking, Victoria.'

*

Sainsburys Supermarket, Boscombe High Street, Bournemouth

At ten thirty that morning Victoria and I began our shopping expedition to Sainsburys in Boscombe leaving Lynette and Barbara to prepare the buffet for the party. Somehow I managed to park the Volkswagen around the back to avoid paying the obligatory car parking fees and if anyone had designs on stealing it they would be doing us a great favour.

Sainsburys, surprisingly enough, wasn't too over-populated when we arrived and after pulling out one of those trolleys that give you an electric shock when you begin to exceed the speed limit, I took on the role of the champion Formula One racing driver, Michael Schumacher.

The shopping list which Lynette had knocked up earlier that morning was to hand and I was finding her handwriting somewhat difficult to read because I had left my spectacles in the car. I asked Victoria if she would mind going back to the car to retrieve them as her mother's script left much to be desired and I didn't want us to leave the shop with boxes of 'Coca-Cola' thinking they were tins of 'Carlsberg Export' lager beers or a bottle of 'After Shock' purporting to be 'Jack Daniels' bourbon whiskey.

I handed over the keys to her and five minutes later Victoria rushed back into the shop saying loudly:

'You've been wheel clamped, dad.'

'Bloody hell, no.' I said, looking out into the street from the doorway.

'There is a yellow piece of paper behind the windscreen wiper, dad, and it's going to cost you fifty quid for the authorities to come out and remove the clamp.' she said, adding more fuel on to the chip pan fire.

'Come on, let's go and phone them up before they decide to take the car away, which could under the circumstances solve one of my problems

63

and every mistake helps.' I said to her, feeling a little less depressed.

'That was a big contradiction in terms, dad; what are your other problems?' she asked as we walked along Harwood Road to where the car was parked in a no-go area.

'I will tell you after your birthday party and a bottle of 'After Shock' may not be a bad idea after all.' I said, jokingly.

It had taken us one hour and ten minutes for one of Bournemouth's wheel clampers and take-away merchants to arrive to relieve me of fifty pounds so I could retrieve my much treasured car. At this point I remembered a poem from my days at Oxford which was called "Aliens" and goes something like this:

'Aliens'

"A Martian came to watch some cricket
And after the match he received a ticket
He said I'm not really into cars
And then he flew off back to Mars"

Victoria and I found a car park in Centenary Way and after feeding a metre with a load of dross we hot-footed back to the supermarket in an attempt to resume the weekly shopping.

I began filling up the trolley with beers, wines and spirits, paying more attention to the items Vicky was selecting from the bottle department.

'Why don't we buy a bottle of 'Baileys'?' Victoria said, looking at the extensive range of liqueurs on the shelf.

'Does that come with cream?' I replied, joining her before gently placing a bottle of Jack Daniels inside the trolley.

'You know how mummy enjoys a small glass of 'Bailey's Irish Cream' with a splash of whisky.' she said, reminding me of the time Lynette became tipsy at a New Year's Eve party having drunk several measures of this lethal concoction. 'Giving that stuff to your mother Vicky, is just like giving strawberries to a donkey.'

'I shall put it back on the shelf then, dad.' she said, somewhat sorrowfully.

'No, don't do that, Vicky, it might just help brighten my day up when your mother falls into the fish pond.'

'Da...d, you're joking with me, aren't you?' Victoria said as we trundled along the aisle towards the crisps and nibbles section.

'Well, she can keep the Paraná fish company this afternoon while I'm drinking my Jack Daniels whiskey.'

The bill which was presented to me at the checkout came to a lot more than I had expected and I thought to myself, it was a good thing Victoria and Barbara were not born at Christmas because it would mean me having to take out a loan.

It was on our way back to Queens Park Avenue when Vicky said to me:

'Mummy tells me you are thinking about buying a property in France and she is very enthusiastic about it all.'

'Now, let's get the record straight here, Victoria, I am not going to buy a property in France and that is final.' I emphatically said to her.

'But, she said...'

'Vicky, just shut up, the subject is closed.'

'How are you going to tell mum we were wheel clamped, dad.'

'It's quite simple, Vicky, we are not going to tell her.'

*

Meanwhile, back at the ranch, No 46 Queens Park Avenue

Lynette and Barbara, having just taken the sausage rolls and mini quiches out from the oven, began to decoratively arrange the triangular egg and watercress sandwiches on to a couple of plates. The wonderful smell of freshly baked pastry was permeating all around the house when Vicky and I walked into the kitchen from the driveway.

'Where the hell have you two been, do you realize it is nearly half-past one and the guests will be arriving soon?' Lynette said, in her usual loving way.

The first person to arrive and darken my doorstep was the intrepid Ralph MacTell, carrying a bunch of red roses and a bottle of orange squash.

'Where have you parked your elephant, Raman?' I said to him knowing he was showing off as I'd already seen his shiny black Mercedes Benz driving along the road towards the nearby golf course.

'In the car park next door to the clubhouse.' he replied cheekily.

'In his dreams,' I said chuntering to myself as we walked into the house through the porch, 'Nice car, Raman, shame about the driver.' giving him my views on him seeing my daughter. 'Will you be staying long? I see you have brought a bottle of jungle juice with you and don't tell me it is against your religion to drink alcohol because I saw a half pint glass of beer inside your kitchen on Wednesday evening.'

'It's a nice afternoon, isn't it?' Raman said, instantaneously changing the conversation into a more temperate one.

'Are those roses for me, Raman? I said, holding my arms out to receive them.

'If you want.' he replied.

The next person to arrive on my doorstep was Simon Bennett, carrying an arrangement of daffodils and tulips which were not dissimilar to the ones growing in the park across the road.

Simon had parked his brand new Skoda Octavia far enough away from the Mercedes to save being embarrassed lest Patel passed comment about its unmentionable predecessors, and this was to be the second contradiction in terms Vicky and I made that day.

'Czechoslovakia has a reputation of exporting shoddy goods on to the European market,' Patel imparted to me later, shaking his head from side to side like a demented Chogi Wallah. 'And apart from *Skoda* motor cars and *Semtex* explosives the country hasn't got much going for it.' he added.

'Is that a fact, you don't say.' I knowingly replied giving the impression I hadn't the faintest idea of what he was talking about.

Meanwhile, Victoria had taken it upon herself to dispense the drinks inside the conservatory.

'What would you like to drink, Simon? Whisky or a beer perhaps,' Vicky asked, pretending she didn't know his favourite beverage.

'I would like a glass of Carlsberg lager.' he replied, looking at Lynette and Barbara, carrying platefuls of food into the dining room from the kitchen.

'I just knew you would say that, Simon.' Vicky said, making advances towards him by placing her hand on his forearm. 'We have plenty more tins in the garage should we run out.' she added.

'I have no intention of running anywhere.' he said, picking up a piping-hot curried to death Campbell's meatball which was really meant for Ralph MacTell's gullet.

'Mummy is trying to cater for everyone at this party.' Vicky implied when she observed Patel tucking into a thing-on-a-stick resembling a bent Sainsburys cocktail sausage. 'There is also five-minute paella on the menu made from a packet; it's okay, but it takes one over an hour to eat it.' she described.

'So you have invited someone from Spain.' Simon asked, and was surprised to hear that Margarita Santana, Vicky's friend from junior school and now a waitress in the Spanish restaurant *'Tao Pep pies'* in Old Christchurch Road would be arriving in just a few moments.

The doorbell rang again and I, being the resident, congenial host, concierge, doorman and bellboy for the afternoon, duly answered it. It was Margarita looking as lovely as ever, her long dark wavy hair glistening in the sunlight giving me the impression it had just been doused with a couple of bottles of brilliantine and combed with a wire brush.

'Hello, Chris,' Margarita said sounding completely out of breath, 'but I'm sorry to arrive so late but I got held up in the traffic in the town centre, and to add to all of this, there was an accident involving a sports car.'

'Good afternoon, Senorita Margarita Sultana.'

'It's Miss Santana, if you don't mind, Christopher; you do remember, don't you?' she said before reminding me of the time I helped her to change a beer keg down in the cellar of *'Tao Pep pies'* restaurant.

'I wasn't into current affairs then, you know, Margarita.' I said, finally giving her the 'subject closed' on matters of no historical importance.

'It wasn't a silver-grey Porsche 911 sports car was it by any chance?' I asked, taking Margarita by the hand into the conservatory to offer her a well deserved glass of bubbly.

'I think it was, Chris, and I can recall the front number plate hanging down as it collided with a set of the traffic lights on Richmond Hill.'

The music was 'BOYZONE' singing "No Matter What" as I showed Margarita the geography of the house, beginning with what I have always described as the ladies powder room.

Our friendly neighbours began to arrive from their houses next to ours; the Hutchinson's, Steven and Dorothy, who are the co-directors of "Bliss", an International marriage bureau and a dating agency based in Bournemouth and Mr and Mrs Rodriguez, Joseph and Grace, the wealthy couple from Manila in the Philippines who own the Oakdale Nursing Home next door. It was whilst we were enjoying our Christmas festivities the previous year I had to draw the line when a ninety-five year-old woman wearing a dressing gown began to blow air kisses in my direction from over the back fence and after telling her to go back to bed lest she caught a chill she suggested I went with her; all good fun, I suppose along with the trials and tribulations of being married to Lynette and living at number 46 Queens Park Avenue.

The ever popular 'SPICE GIRLS' were now singing "We're going to make it happen" which followed a raucous song called "Wannabe". Barbara and Vicky, in between eating egg and cress sandwiches, were gyrating together in the middle of the dining room floor when the birthday cake was brought into the lounge; the candles illuminating the entire area.

By this time I had drunk at least three large measures of 'Jack Daniels' and I decided to give everyone a rendition of the 'Meatball' song, sung to the tune of: "On top of Old Smokey".

> "On top of Spaghetti all covered with cheese
> I lost my poor meatball when somebody sneezed
> It rolled off the table and on to the floor
> And then my poor meatball rolled out of the door".

Having been told to shut up by Lynette in a failed attempt to disgrace myself by singing 'Costa del Dorset for me' she told me to put my eyes back into their sockets when I observed Basque separatist movements revolving around Margarita's shapely bottom.

I asked Raman if he'd had sufficient to eat when I looked at him cramming enough *Bombay mix* into his mouth to feed the entire Indian army.

'Yes Mr Travis,' was his answer. 'I am Ram-jam full.' he sarcastically added.

Chapter Eight

The following morning in St Clements Church, Boscombe, Bournemouth

The service began with everyone singing the hymn, "Fight the good Fight" with Lynette, Vicky, Barbara and my good self standing huddled together in song, joining in with others to try and quell a raucous noise coming from the pew in front. The woman, Mrs Gwyneth Bryce, a resident of Springbourne and a one-time member of the highly acclaimed, Cardiff Symphony and Orchestral choir, later got her comeuppance and just deserts when the vicar, the Reverend, David Thomas, inadvertently spilt the bright red communion wine down the front of her white silk blouse when one of the stained-glass windows was blown out of the Grade One listed building into the gardens when someone in the congregation sneezed. Mr Gareth Bryce had witnessed it all before when he and Gwyneth were sitting outside on a pub terrace in Bournemouth's town centre. She was forced to buy a new summer outfit from Debenhams because the table they were sitting at collapsed and tomato juice from a 'Bloody Mary' she was drinking ended up running down the front of her pink and cream floral dress. I learned all of this through Gareth Price, our family butcher in Boscombe, when I tried to knock him down in *price* when purchasing a leg of Welsh lamb.

After falling asleep listening to Thomas prattling on about how we could try a little harder to become better persons and then having to put my hand in my pocket to find some suitable change to put in the offertory box we headed for the open door to the melodious sounds of the organist and choir master playing "Handel's Messiah". I have always maintained that fifty pence put into the non-obligatory collection could ensure you a whole week in heaven.

The Reverend Thomas dressed in traditional ecclesiastical attire; a surplus, cassock and dog-collar was waiting at the door to shake hands with the congregation and to ask them if they would be coming back next Sunday for a repeat performance.

'It was a bit chilly in there, dad.' Barbara said, as we headed for the car which was parked in Cleveland Road.

'It was because one of the windows was open,' Vicky pointed out to us all. 'I was bloody well freezing in there.' she added, rubbing her hands together to improve her blood circulation.

'Victoria, how many times have I told you not to swear, especially on a Sunday?' I said to her in no uncertain terms.

As we were clambering into the heavily fortified Volkswagen Estate the alarm went off and this was when Lynette asked:

'What is that which has just fallen out of your overcoat pocket?'

'It's a piece of paper, Lynette.' I replied, breaking out in a cold sweat.

'Yes, I can see that,' she said and holding out her hand to receive it. 'Come on, Christopher, hand it over, I know what it is because Vicky told me this morning.'

'Bloody hell, this is all I need before I return to work tomorrow.' I said, banging my fist down on top of the car roof in an attempt to silence the alarm.

Lynette, because of the hard work she had done in the kitchen the previous day, had suggested earlier we all go to the Queens Park Hotel - Pub for a Sunday Roast lunch. This was indeed a good idea until I discovered when I reached the bar to pay for the drinks my wallet was missing and that I had left it in the pew in church. Needless to say, it was returned to me that evening by the verger who said his job was to labour and not to ask for any reward, however, he was more than happy for me to donate five pounds into the church coffers towards replacing the stained-glass window and I knew then my best church was by my bedside because it was less expensive.

It had been a lovely sunny morning and just after midday we walked through the triple- arched doorway into the pub where I managed to find a table for four in an alcove by one of the front windows. As usual, flying officer kite, Bill Cartwright was sitting on his favourite stool at the bar reading *'The Sunday Times'* newspaper, it was if he had no home to go to and had been sitting there since the previous evening.

'Good afternoon, sir,' I said to him after creeping up behind him just to satisfy myself that he really wasn't a cardboard cut-out.

'Good afternoon, Christopher,' he replied, looking over the top of his bifocal spectacles. 'I see you have brought with you the trouble and strife.' he added.

'Yes, it makes quite a pleasant change, doesn't it, Bill.' applying a happy medium into the somewhat dull conversation.

'I can see you've brought your two daughters as well; you really are pushing the boat out.'

When I had finished determining that there was nothing wrong with his eyesight, I ordered the drinks; a pint of beer for myself, a *Desperado* for Vicky and two glasses of Coca Cola with ice and lemon for Lynette and Barbara.

It was then as I was about to pay I discovered my wallet was missing and realized that I must have left it behind in the church. Lynette wasn't overjoyed at this when she reminded me of the fifty quid we had to fork out the previous day to unclamp the wheel on the car and now having to give me a loan to pay for the drinks and our Sunday lunch.

'Chock's away, bandits at four-o'clock.' I said, before walking unsteadily back to the table holding their drinks.

'What are we going to have for our lunch, dad because I'm bloody well starving.' Vicky asked, probably knowing what I was going to say to her next.

'Victoria, how many more times have I got to insist on telling you about swearing?' I said, and this time wondering what I had brought into this world.

'The roast beef and Yorkshire pudding looks good, dad.' Barbara said as she clocked Effie, the buxom waitress, delivering a huge mound of piping-hot food over to the next table.

'I have a joke to tell you dad.' Vicky enthusiastically said to me knowing she was going to get the last laugh in a pub devoid of any humour or ambiance.

'Okay, Vicky, let's go for it, and if it's anything like the other jokes you have cared to bestow upon us in the past, forget it.' I said, wondering just what she was going to come out with next.

'Why do the Russians have zips on their underpants dad?' she asked, smiling in anticipation to our reaction.

'I haven't a bloody clue, Vicky.' I replied, prompted by Lynette to curtail my usual Sunday afternoon language.

'It is because Chernobyl fall-out.' Vicky said, laughing at the reaction to the punch line of what I thought to be a rather pathetic little joke.

'Victoria, instead of becoming a school teacher, have you ever thought about becoming a comedienne; you would go down very well at the Pavilion in Bournemouth.' I said when we all fell about laughing at the table.

'Don't worry dad, I have thought about it,' she replied, adding more humour to liven the place up.

Effie Winters, the waitress and female weight lifter in her spare time, brought our meals to the table; three plates of roast beef, Yorkshire puddings, roast potatoes; two vegetables, consisting of carrots, peas, accompanied by a delicious *Bisto* type of gravy. Lynette, always being different and quick to point out her culinary expertise, had made up her mind earlier to have the roast turkey with stuffing and this was when I reminded myself she really did deserve it.

I asked Effie politely where her name derived from, to which she replied:

'You what?'

'I mean, what exactly is it short for?'

'Effervescent and bubbly.' she replied, bending over the table to arrange the plates.

'Stupid cow.' Lynette said when Effie, the heifer, departed the area to bring over her turkey roast laced with venom.

'Effie is the diminutive Greek name for 'Euphemia'.' Barbara said studiously. 'And the word 'euphoria' is also a derivative of the same name.' she added, giving Lynette and I a lesson in Greek mythology.

'I bet they are.' Lynette said when she ignorantly looked up towards the ceiling. 'I always knew there was something funny about that woman ever since one of her top buttons flew into your beer, Chris.'

We began tucking into our succulent lunch as if we hadn't eaten for days and Barbara being a fully paid-up member of the Diplomatic Corps, asked:

'I heard you and mummy are thinking about buying a house in France.'

'Whoever put that crazy idea into your head?' I said to her knowing who it was; 'It was you Vicky, wasn't it?'

'Well, it seems like a good idea, dad, and then Barbara and I can visit you during our sabbatical.' Vicky said, pouring more horseradish sauce on to her plate.

'I'm glad everyone is in agreement; I knew you would all rally round in the end.' Lynette said, sounding so confident and laid back.

It was a miracle we didn't fall off of our seats when we saw Denzel and Christine Crow sitting in a corner like two love birds on a washing line waiting for their fish fingers to arrive at their table.

There was to be no show without Punch when we saw Councillor and Mrs Bennett, and of course Simon, making a grand entrance into the lounge bar, heavily armed with newspapers as if they were walking into Bournemouth Town Hall on business. They immediately walked over to our table with the aim of letting us know they had arrived and, just in case we had forgotten, who they were.

'Good afternoon Councillor Bennett, Mrs Bennett, Simon,' I said to them before they reciprocated the greetings.

'At what time does your train depart for Birmingham New Street, Victoria?' Simon asked, giving me the impression he had designs on seeing them off leaving Lynette and me standing in the background to watch a display of passion.

'The train departs from Bournemouth at half-past three and arrives in Birmingham New Street at approximately nine minutes past six.' she replied, and then suggesting they could transfer their trolley bags from our car into his and go straight to the station.

I soon put the dampers on that one when I took her to one side and told her it was to be a family's only departure that afternoon and I didn't want anyone else to be there.

At that precise moment, Raman Patel walked into the pub wearing a golfing hat with the Queens Park Golf Club logo depicted on it.

'Don't tell me, you've come to post your red spot, Raman?' I said.

'Good afternoon, ladies, gentlemen, just thought I'd drop in for a gin and tonic before going to the golf club.' he said, looking round to see if there were any local dignitaries in evidence to enhance his social climbing activities. 'Where have you parked your sleigh, Mr Travis?' he so impertinently asked.

'It's in cold storage.' I replied, knowing the car was parked around the back of the pub.

He suggested that after playing eighteen-holes and having another gin and tonic at the nineteenth he could take Barbara to the railway station in the Mercedes; this was when I really had to put my foot down saying:

'I thought your lot, didn't drink.' I said, and now beginning to think he was an out and out liar.

'Only on Sundays.' he replied.

'And, how can you possibly play an eighteen-hole round of golf, go to the clubhouse for another gin and tonic and still have time to take Barbara to the railway station,' I politely asked him.

'Well, I don't hang about on the golf course, especially when the buggy is into overdrive and I put my foot down.'

'That's it; no you can't take my daughter to the station.' I insisted on telling him. 'I can just imagine seeing a turban flying straight down the middle of the fairway after you have teed-off.' I added, trying to imitate Bing Crosby.

'What about next week, then?' he said, and was now on the periphery of being stabbed to death with an extremely sharp cutlery knife.

*

Bournemouth Railway Station the same afternoon

When Vicky and Barbara were about to board the train to Birmingham New Street, Vicky turned round with a cheeky grin on her face.

'Dad,' she said, one last joke before we leave!'

'Alright, Vicky, I'm listening.'

'What did the top hat say to the bra?'

'I don't know, Vicky what did the top hat say to the bra.' becoming exasperated by this time.

'I'll go on a head,' Vicky said laughing like a hyena. 'And you hold those two up.'

At that, I drew the line and said to Lynette I think I will buy myself a bar of chocolate because I needed some *polydocterranates*.

She asked somewhat inquisitively, 'What are Polly what's their names?' to which I replied that they are parrots that go to the 'Quack' three times a week.

'Well, I suppose they will make a change from *sodden glutamates*, won't they?' she remarked.

When the train was about to leave I gave Vicky two bars of chocolate and said: 'Have it in front of the television.' She said, 'I've never had it in front of a television, dad, because you never know who is watching.'

Chapter Nine

It all happens at the checkout

Lynette and I started Monday earlier than usual with me superficially glossing over 'The Times' newspaper at the breakfast table and her being somewhat occupied in the kitchen cooking sausages, eggs and bacon.

Time, it would seem, had passed slowly since I was last at the university and I suppose it was because there had been a multitude of things Lynette and I had to attend to the previous week, my visit to Southport being the main cause and, of course, our daughters' birthday party at the weekend.

I can recall we were listening to 'Wake up to Wogan' on Radio 2 and having to put up with the dulcet tones of ABBA, singing "Dancing Queen", interspersed by renditions of blarney being presented to us by Terry, the likeable Irish man who seems to have been around forever. The next song to be placed on "His Master's Voice" record deck was, "Avalon", sung by the unmistakable voice of Brian Ferry when my fried breakfast was delivered with great reverence to the table by Lynette.

'I hate Mondays.' I said to her before asking for another pot of coffee.

'If you don't like Mondays, you're in the wrong job Doctor Travis.' Lynette said, wearing her sarcastic hat again.

'You never let up, do you darling.' I remarked, applying more HP Sauce to the Bury black pudding artistically placed in the centre of the breakfast plate. 'And, if you do like Mondays, you're an extremely sad person.'

We continued to be entertained by Terry Wogan reading a poem that one of his listeners had sent in and went something like this:

'Roxy Music'

'In the eighties he was the saviour
Away from 'Punks' and bad behaviour
From Newcastle in to Scandinavia
He charmed the 'Yuppies' in Belgravia
He wears a Tuxedo and is into Brylcreem
Within a strange voice he is every girls dream
A likeable fellow with charming tones

He looks the part behind microphones
Now that the parties are over he hasn't gone
Still singing his song called: 'Avalon'.'

Wogan, continuing with his entertainment programme asked his listeners to join in with him to answer one of his County Limericks: 'What kind of antiseptic cream does Brian Ferry use when he cuts his finger?' the rather obvious answer to this joke was 'Savalon'.

'You don't half hear some garbage on the radio, don't you, Chris.' Lynette said as she poured the freshly-made Brazilian coffee into my favourite 'Kiss me quick' coffee mug.

'The poem isn't as bad as the one you have on the front of your apron.' I replied, munching away on pieces of toast and marmalade.

'Don't talk with your mouth full.' she said, looking at a tablecloth peppered with crumbs.

Hannibal, our Siamese cat, was sitting regally on the floor staring at a half-eaten Cumberland sausage I had left on my plate. I was immediately instructed by Lynette not to feed the cat with the leftovers as it could become a habit and that Hannibal would expect to breakfast with us every morning.

'Tell me, Chris, when are we going to make in-roads to fix the car and if possible to buy a new one?' she asked inquisitively and pensively frowning.

'Tomorrow.' was my reply, not knowing what was going to happen that morning to completely destroy my intentions.

'Would you like me to wrap up some egg and cress sandwiches for your lunch? We have loads of them left over from the party on Saturday.' Lynette suggested, showing me a roll of tin foil as if it had just been invented and I didn't know what it was.

'No, don't go out of your way, Lynnette,' I replied and then suggesting I would pop into Sainsbury's in Boscombe and buy one of their delicious triple bacon, lettuce and tomato sandwiches to go.

'As you wish, Chris.' she said, fastening the belt of her Burberry raincoat. 'Have a nice day.' she added as she walked through the lounge towards the front door.

'And you dear.' I said, peeping out through one of the windows to see her driving off in the van.

*

Sainsburys Supermarket, Christchurch Road, Boscombe, Bournemouth
It was a bitter pill to swallow during the weekend when I was relieved of fifty quid to have a wheel clamp removed from my car, and this time I parked the Volkswagen far enough away from any would-be predators whose sole aim in life is to stuff drivers for illegal parking.

After selecting a sandwich from the cool section and gone through the procedure of checking the sell-by date I headed towards one of the checkout ladies. It was quite common to see me whizzing around the supermarket with a triangular plastic box containing an egg and cress sandwich but that morning I had changed my culinary preferences to buying a BLT.

The checkout lady pointed out to me that the sandwich I was about to buy had a special offer; buy one and get one free. It was when I returned with a corned beef, tomato and onion sandwich, she said: 'the offer applied only to sandwiches of the same kind.' When I told her the bacon, lettuce and tomato sandwich was the last one, she said: 'we have lots of fresh egg and cress sandwiches left over from Saturday. I knew then, it wasn't going to be my lucky day and as I was making my way to the door I slipped on a banana skin and fell to the floor.

I was to wake up after being in a deep coma for several days in Southampton General Hospital, Hampshire; Lynette, the girls and an Indian doctor Vanessa Tilak, were at my bedside when I eventually returned to the land of the living during the evening of Friday 24th March and this was when I realized I was indeed lucky to have my family all around me. Apparently, it was Victoria who brought me out of the long sleep by singing Patsy Klein's song "Crazy" ever so sweetly into my ears and I knew then my lovely daughter had no designs on becoming a school teacher.

It was whilst I was in the coma I was dreaming, experiencing a flurry of adventures, overseeing characters that may or may not have existed. My first recollections from the bizarre dreams I had been having began in Northern France during the Second World War and at the end of them all, for me the war was far from over.

*

A medieval town somewhere in Normandy, Northern France - Tuesday 7th December 1943

The Vichy regime, a puppet Nazi government that was put into place in France until August 1940 and together with the German occupying forces affirmed a plot against the country which led to its fall. They believed "the Jew, the Protestant, the Mason and the Foreigner" were to blame and their involvement with the French Resistance or Jewish origins. Following a series of 'Roundups' organised by the Gestapo, thousands of deportees were murdered inside the gas chambers of Auschwitz Concentration Camp.

Jacques Mayer, an eighteen year-old horologer, a watchmaker and clockmaker from Cherbourg and nineteen year-old, James Cohen, an apprentice diamond cutter from Antwerp in Belgium were inside a railway boxcar full of helpless French Jews being transported to The Drancy internment camp situated in a north-eastern suburb of Paris. The transit camp at Drancy, France was an assembly and detention camp specially designed for confining Jews who were later deported, transported to Auschwitz-Birkenau, the notorious Nazi extermination camp in Poland. It was here in December 1941, forty prisoners from Drancy were executed by the Nazis in retaliation for a French attack on German police officers.

The train from Cherbourg on-route to Saint Lazare, Paris pulled into a village railway siding; the sound of the wheels screeching as they rolled along the track was likened to a blunt bacon slicer. Both Jacques and James were sitting, huddled together on a floor strewn with urine saturated straw and next to two sliding doors secured by a latch from the outside; this became their only means of escape when they saw that it could be levered opened from the inside with the aid of a wooden stick.

During the hours of darkness on Tuesday 7th December 1943 the word evening, which in normal circumstances is used to describe a relaxation period between afternoon and midnight had suddenly disappeared for ever from the deportees dictionaries.

At around eleven-thirty, the train screeched to a halt by a rusty corrugated railway shed; the steam from the engine having just been released hissed and billowed out with force from the side, wafting down the track; the electric lights illuminating the entire area shining brightly on to the snow.

Max Weisman, a sixty-three year-old antiquities dealer from Cherbourg, his wife of some forty two years and Yvette, a sixty-two year-old housewife, were also huddled together in the boxcar, and around their shoulders they shared the same course-looking mohair overcoat he had worn for years. They, along with one hundred others, were crammed together like sardines inside a tin, shivering from the extreme weather conditions and the cries from children in the next freight car became louder as the night progressed.

The train had stopped at the sidings away from the station to take on board relief troops from the *Wehrmacht*, who were destined for Paris; German shepherd war dogs could be heard barking angrily in the background thinking it could have been dinner time.

It had begun to snow again, drifting quickly on to the expanse of overgrown stretches of no man's land in between the tracks. Jacques Mayer and James Cohen took the chance to lever the door open and to jump out from a height on to the side of the track. More lights were being switched on and the sounds of police whistles began to blow loudly; the deafening sound of a siren became progressively louder and hand-held torches were being directed on to them from every angle of the goods yard.

James, after attempting to escape in the opposite direction to Jacques was immediately shot in the back by one of the soldiers pursuing him. This courageous young man had fallen on to a mound of shiny black coal piled high by the side of a ramshackle shed; the snow on the top resembling a miniature *Monte Blanc* and it was here he died of severe gunshot wounds.

81

Jacques, however, ran for his life, managing to escape from under a powerful searchlight and soldiers handling Alsatian tracker dogs attached to extended leads running wildly in pursuit. This brave young man made his way towards the periphery of a strange and bizarre medieval town called, *Méridon* in order to seek sanctuary.

Max Weisman had slipped several documents of historical importance into the deep pockets of Jacques Mayer's long woollen overcoat before he jumped out from the train; it was when he was fumbling around inside them to find his tobacco tin they were discovered.

The documents, written in Hebrew were rolled up into two bundles and contained valuable information together with badly drawn maps dating back to the First Crusades in the eleventh and twelfth centuries.

Jacques was fortunate to have been taken into hiding by the righteous owner of an antiquarian bookshop in the centre of the town and kept in a secret attic where he stayed for nine months, witnessing a mass retreat by German troops in *Méridon* which was the beginning of the end of the German Occupation in France. A section commander from the 21st Panzer division looked up to the skylight of the bookshop from the turret of his so-called impenetrable Tiger tank as it raced along the main road of *Méridon*. He pointed up to Jacques black beret, giving him the impression it was a Nazi salute, and then radioing down to the crew inside his tank said: *"Was ist deis, unt was ist das, ich glaube meine gross mutter Hut ist"*; translated: "What is this, and what is that, I do believe it's my grandmother's hat. Lieutenant Kurt Richter encountered extensive resistance when he and his tank came up against what looked like a giant bar of *Toblerone* blocking his way, however, this was to be remedied later when sappers from the British Royal Engineers filled in the gaps with sand to allow the American First army to go over the top; Lieutenant Kurt Richter survived the war and was able to tell the story to his grandchildren.

Monsieur and Madame, Mr and Mrs Weisman from Cherbourg, Brittany, died in Auschwitz-Birkenau Concentration Camp, Poland three weeks later on the 1st January 1944.

Southampton General Hospital – evening of Monday 27th March 2000

'You know something, Lynette?'

'What Chris?'

'You're different; more like the girl I first met, softer somehow.'

'Oh! Chris.'

'What's the matter; why are you crying, I'm on the mend now.' seeing the tears flowing unchecked down her cheeks; his tough wife who hardly ever wept.

'I thought I was going to lose you, Chris,' she sobbed, 'when I was sitting by your bedside in the hospital.

'Don't worry, Lynette; as you know I'm made of strong stuff.' I told her.

'Oh by the way, Chris, I took your car in for repair on Tuesday and collected it this morning, it looks as good as new.' she said, with a loving smile. 'Also, I made some enquiries about selling the postage stamps Auntie Gertrude so generously bequeathed to us.' Lynette added.

'My goodness, Lynette, you have been busy, haven't you.' I said, squeezing her hand gently.

'When you get out of here, Chris, you will need some kind of convalescence.' Lynette said giving me the impression it was she who needed the convalescence and not me.

'Yes, perhaps we can go to Torquay and stay at Faulty Towers or visit sunny Southport to have the car or your bottom pinched by an unruly *Scouser*; alternatively, we could sit in front of the band stand and listen to a number of Arthur Scargills blowing cornets, but then, we could just stay in Queens Park Avenue, and that will be fun and far less expensive, wouldn't it, Lynette.'

'This morning, I took the initiative to buy Victoria and Barbara, a brand new Volkswagen 1.9 litre Passat; I thought it was a bargain at twenty-four thousand pounds.' Lynette said, and was probably wondering what my reaction was going to be.

'Let me out of bed before I have a relapse.' I said, just before the bell rang out to signal the visiting hours chucking-out time.

'Don't worry, Chris, I was only joking.' Lynette said and began to laugh uncontrollably. 'Meanwhile, I have brought you a bottle of *Lucozade* and a beautiful bunch of ripe bananas; I will bring you some more tomorrow.' she added.

It was then I poignantly remembered Harry Belafonte's song "Day-O (The Banana Boat Song)"; the lyrics of which, I couldn't remember but went something like this: "Bring me a bunch o' ripe bananas, when daylight comes I'll want to go home".

*

The dreams continued to haunt me whilst I was asleep, lying unconscious in a semi-comatose state in Southampton General Hospital after taking in daily dosages of morphine which had been injected into my body. It was at nine o'clock the following morning that one of my dreams came true. Doctor Vanessa Tilak, complete with a bright red spot on her forehead giving everyone the impression she had been shot, told me I could go home and to stay well clear of supermarkets, bananas and their discarded skins.

I telephoned Lynette on the mobile to tell her an ambulance was waiting on the forecourt to take me home and also to put the kettle on. Lynette told me she had just arrived for work at the shop and would have to leave Audrey Wright, her assistant, in charge of the business whilst she was in Queens Park Avenue making pots of tea and furnishing me with endless pieces of delicious fruit cake which had Sainsbury's quality written all over them.

'You know, Christopher, sometimes you are not safe to be let out.' Lynette said, as I was escorted into the house by a paramedic.

'Well, in that case I will phone the hospital to see if there are any beds available.'

It was when I was relaxing, sitting on our cosy black leather settee in front of the television watching Loyd Grossman doing his 'Master Chef' impersonation, I realized just how lucky we all were as I continued to munch away on a squidgy banana sandwich.

'Oh, by the way, Lynette, who owns that Volkswagen Polo which is blocking the drive?'

'You mean the canary yellow one which has been here since you got back from hospital; it's ours Chris; your much cherished automobile has had a new coat of paint.'

'My goodness, it's a good thing, there are no bees flying around in Queens Park Avenue.'

Chapter Ten

'I really must be going back to the shop, Chris; it doesn't seem right and proper to leave Audrey all on her own because there is a tendency for it to become busy at this time in the afternoon.' Lynette said when our anniversary clock on the mantelpiece chimed softly at two o'clock.

'At what time will you be coming home, Lynette?'

'Around half past six, Chris, just in time to adjust the cushions on the settee and to prepare this evening's dinner.' she replied, patting me on the shoulder to reassure me that she was not going to interfere in any way with my convalescence.

'Should you be feeling hungry during the afternoon, there is some mushroom soup on top of the stove; you have only got to turn on a switch, give the soup a quick stir and then pour it into a dish, I think you can manage that, can't you?' she said sarcastically.

'Yes, I think I can just about manage to do that, and have a nice day at the office, dear and give my love to Audrey.' I replied in retaliation.

Lynette walked quickly out of the house as if there was a deadline she had to meet. The gears inside the van began to crunch loudly before she drove off at speed along the avenue towards Springbourne.

I continued to watch the television; it was Robert Lindsay and Zoe Wanamaker starring in the ever popular television sitcom "My Family"; the next batches of celluloid images to appear on the screen were Sir David Frost OBE and the former "MasterChef" presenter, Loyd Grossman, taking up cohabitation together in the not so popular television show called: "Through the Keyhole". The programme, silly as it may seem, reminded me of a poem, "Through the Peephole" which was sent to us inside a Christmas card and was penned by one of our friends; the verse began with:

> "Well Hello, Good evening and God help us
> Find the person who lives in this gaff
> You may find it good for a laugh
> And if you want a haemorrhoid
> Then it's over to you Loyd

Now I wonder who lives in a tip like this
We should really have given it a miss
Obviously not into washing up
He or she is a real mucky pup and has a poodle
With no finesse and eats 'Pot Noodle'
There are empty cartons and takeaway tins
They have probably never heard of garbage bins
In the kitchen which is a kind of pink
There are dirty dishes still in the sink
On the table lie a pile of books
And they are obviously into TV cooks
Before I proliferate outside this dive
Let us now deliberate and conjugate before we go
It's over to you David in the studio"

I turned off the television because Grossman had succeeded in giving me a headache, continuing with his conjugating, prevaricating, deliberating and proliferating, and combined with the noise screaming loudly from a high-pitched food processor in someone's kitchen, I came to the conclusion that he and David Frost should mind their own business and concentrate on presenting early morning breakfast shows instead of spying through keyholes.

As you may have already noticed, I don't suffer fools gladly and I am not afraid to say that Loyd Grossman is about as funny as a broken leg, dry as dust and possesses as much charm and charisma as a soggy chip; what's more to the point, where on earth did he get that stupid accent; hanging around the grounds of Buckingham Palace with an electric guitar trying to find a soul mate, I have no doubt; Grossman is a big man but a small coat fits him.

The glow from our artificial gas fire was making me feel drowsy and it wasn't long before I drifted off into a deep sleep, dreaming of historical events which happened hundreds of years ago. I can recall my dreams being similar to my lectures in medieval studies at Bournemouth University and in particular the one I was supposed to have given to my students on the Monday afternoon of the previous week. They began with Richard I of England, the great-great grandson of William the Conqueror in the late twelfth century; his involvement during the Third Crusade to Jerusalem and ending with the story of the Last Crusade, the Great Siege of Malta in 1565. The dreams, mostly of fictitious characters and events, had been conjured up and stored in my brain and were similar to a film shown in four parts, they were unbelievably credible, another contradiction in terms.

The Crusades sparked by zeal to rid the Holy Lands of "infidels", meaning Muslims primarily, was completely unjustified and the Crusades are in many ways Europe's "Lost weekend"; in the name of Jesus of Nazareth, the Road to Jerusalem was supposed to be the Road to Paradise, but, it was a way to enhance one's wealth, plundering gold, silver and precious jewels in the Near East and the Mediterranean. The Crusaders opened up and maintained trade routes in the Mediterranean and built more Masonic Grand lodges throughout Europe; the road to hell was paved with bad intentions. After the suppression of the Knights Templar on the islands of Malta and in Rhodes, there were many Jesuit knights infiltrating aristocratic families, marrying into royalty throughout Europe when the Last Crusade ended; Prince Rainier of Monaco was known to have said: "Where would one be without the 'Red Cross'?" The Order of St John of Jerusalem, however, transformed Hospitaller into warrior, wearing a 'White Cross' that became tarnished with blood. The Order of the Temple was military but also created the first International Banking System, and with the *"Elders of Zion"*, the Jewish money lenders of Amsterdam, established a bank of England. This made the Order extremely rich, and eventually it was wiped out by King Philip IV the Fair of France, who wanted to get his hands on its money.

Richard *Coeur de Lion* or mainly Richard the Lionheart, Duke of Normandy, succeeded his father, King Henry II; his accession to the throne was on the 3rd September 1189. He was born on the 8th September 1157 at Beaumont Palace, Oxford, England; his religion was Catholicism and he spoke with a French dialect and no English. A well known Anglican hymn was to sum it all up: "Onward Christian soldiers marching on to war with the cross of Jesus going on before"; the irony of it all was that during the Third Crusade, with the exception of the Muslims, the Crusaders, Freemasons and Jews were all singing from the same hymn sheet.

The Muslims called him *Melek-Ric* (King Richard) or *Malek al-Inkitar* – King of England and he became the central Christian commander during the Third Crusade; *Gesta Regis Ricardi*, scoring considerable victories against his Muslim counterpart Saladin.

By the age of sixteen, Richard the Lionheart, a great military leader and warrior and an iconic figure in England and France, had taken command of his own army, putting down rebellions in Poitou against his father, King Henry II.

When he was crowned, Richard barred all Jews and women from the ceremony, but some Jewish leaders arrived to present gifts for the new king. Richard's courtiers stripped and flogged the Jews, then flung them out of court.

When a rumour spread that Richard had ordered all Jews to be killed, the people of London began a massacre and a multitude of Jews were beaten to death, robbed, and burned alive. Many Jewish homes were burned to the ground, and several Jews were forcibly baptised. Some sought sanctuary in the Tower of London, and others managed to escape. The Archbishop of Canterbury, Baldwin of Forde, reacted by remarking: "If the King is not God's man, he had better be the devil's". Richard's ambition was that of a mere warrior; he would fight for anything whatever, but he would sell everything that was worth fighting for. When Richard was raising funds for his Crusade, he was said to declare, "I would have sold London if I could find a buyer."

On the 21st January 1188 after receiving news of the fall of Jerusalem to Saladin, King Richard I of England and King Philip II Augustus of France agreed to go on the Third Crusade to the Holy Land.

King Philip II Augustus of France and like Richard had an equally passionate flair for anti-Semitism and was responsible for the persecution of the Jews throughout his reign, beginning when he held Jews hostage for a heavy ransom and used the ransom money for his financial situation, which was dire. He also released all Christians from paying the debt they had from loans given to them by Jews in exchange for twenty-percent of the debt owed. On one Sabbath day, he had the synagogues raided and looted. He shortly afterwards expelled the Jews from France, seizing all buildings and other assets owned by the Jews for his own use.

In September 1190 Richard and Philip arrived in Sicily and in April 1191 Richard, with a large fleet, left Messina in order to reach Acre, 130 km from Jerusalem on the shores of the east Mediterranean and where the Order of St John of Jerusalem, together with the Knights Templar, the mercenary aristocrats of St John, established themselves for nearly one hundred years.

The knights, subsequently, went into battle wearing their distinctive tunics of a white cross emblazoned against a scarlet background; the ruse being, 'the white cross of peace in the bloodstained field of war'.

Richard the Lionheart landed at Acre on the 8th June 1191 and by the time *Acre* surrendered on the 12th July, Philip became seriously ill with dysentery, which reduced his zeal, and ties with Richard were strained, acting in a haughty manner after *Acre* had fallen. When word reached Philip that Richard had finished crusading and had been captured on his way back from the Holy Land, he promptly invaded *Vexin*, a medieval county in Northwest France, twenty kilometres from Rouen. In November of the same year, following the fall of *Jaffa*, the Crusader army advanced inland towards Jerusalem. In June 1192, following two unsuccessful attacks on the city, King Richard I and Saladin, the Muslim leader knew that their positions were growing untenable and the Crusaders were forced to retreat back to the coast. In the same year Richard sold the island of Cyprus to the 'Knights Templar'.

King Philip II Augustus went on the Third Crusade with King Richard I of England with the aim of easily taking the Holy Land, occupied by the Muslim leader, Saladin, however when the Saints tried to go marching into Jerusalem the Knights were met with heavy resistance and came up against what seemed to have been impregnable walls and fortifications.

On the 6th April 1199, King Richard I of England, died, aged 41 in *Chalus*, Duchy of *Aquitaine*, France and his burial was at *Fontevraud* Abbey,

Anjou, France. Richard was deliberately shot in the shoulder near the neck by a boy standing on the walls of the castle of *Chalus-Chabrol*, crossbow in one hand, the other clutching a frying pan; however, frying pans can be dangerous, especially when they are used for aggressive purposes inside and outside of a kitchen.

On the 14th July 1223, King Philip II Augustus, died, aged 57 in *Mantes-la-Jolie*, located in the western suburbs of Paris, France and is buried in *Saint Denis* Basilica.

King Philip III the Bold so called because of his abilities in combat and on horseback and not his character. He was pious but not cultivated and followed the dictates of others. He died of Dysentery on the 5th October 1285, aged 40 in *Perpignan* on the island of Mallorca

*

The suppression of 'The Knights Templar' and it's expulsion from France.

King Philip IV the fair, preceded by his father, King Philip III the Bold, was substantially in debt to the 'Knights Templar' and on 13th October 1307, hundreds of Templars were rounded up and simultaneously arrested, to be later tortured into admitting heresy in the Order; the forced confessions to have many Templars burned at the stake. Philip IV arrested Jews so that he could seize their assets and in 1306 expelled the Jews from France.

In the same year, Philip was condemned by his arch enemy, Pope Boniface VIII in the Catholic Church for his spendthrift lifestyle when he levied taxes on the French clergy. This was the excuse that his successor, Pope Clement V, needed to plunder the spoils of war from King Philip IV, who constantly stole from the Knights Templar; the treasure; gold, silver and precious gems stripped from the uniforms, weapons, ornaments and jewel-encrusted copies of the *Koran* which had belonged to Muslim officers.

A caravan of tired, bedraggled and worn out Christian soldiers travelling on horseback to the medieval port of *Touques*, in the Forest of *Saint-Gatien* en route to *Temple Ewell* in England. With their weary heads facing towards the ground they were attacked by agents of King Philip IV as they approached the coast, however, eight months later King Philip IV of France died at the early age of forty-six and Philip's death was spoken of as a retribution for his destruction of the Templars in France, "Glory, Glory, Hallelujah", however, in the twenty-first century the Order of the Knights Templar still exist as a powerful Masonic sect.

The Knights had to take vows of poverty, chastity and obedience, "Faith, Hope and Charity", however, this undertaking was forgotten during the Crusades when most of them became extremely rich, contracted syphilis and behaved inhumanely towards their fellow man.

Brother's *Roger de Charney, Edwin of Charnock, Charles Blanche* of Burgundy and one hundred mercenaries of the 'Order of the Knights Templar', following a brief struggle to save the lives of their men were all put to the sword; their blood flowing down into the Channel from the River *la Touques, Pays d'Auge* and the Knight's treasure of unimaginable size and proportion was confiscated. The Knights were buried with dignity in the catacombs of Saint Agatha in *Méridon* and little did Lynette and I know we were going to end up one day living in the same town.

My dreams continued witnessing the last battle of the Crusades; the great siege of Malta in 1565.

The date of 21st June is the feast of Corpus Christi which the Knights celebrate every year and because of the numerous battles that were taking place in and around the Grand Harbour; 1565 was no exception when I watched the colourful display of fireworks by courtesy of Mustapha Pasha, the Turkish Ottoman Empire leader.

It was the morning of the 23rd June, two days later and the eve of the feast of St. John, I was standing on top of the bastion wall of the fortress of St Elmo in *Valletta*, Malta observing an attack by Ottoman officers, elite Turkish Janissaries and various other assault troops. The Knight's garrison knew their final hour had arrived when the Turks rushed through a breach in a wall when it collapsed. The garrison at Fort St Elmo over a period of thirty-one days of remorseless bombardment had lost fifteen hundred Christian lives, nine knights were captured, eighty-nine were killed and twenty-seven wounded by the Muslims, beheading Knights, flaying or impaling their bodies and using them for target practice; the blood running down the white cross of the Order emblazoned on their red robes. A Jewish paymaster escaped the onslaught that day by jumping from the rocks and swimming across the waters of Grand Harbour to Fort St Angelo and safety, taking with him the bounty which was meant to be given to the soldiers. The silver coins that were contained in a wooden treasure chest went down to the bottom of one of the world's deepest natural harbours.

Jean Parisot de la Valette, during the Great Siege of Malta was the Grand Master of the Order of St. John of Jerusalem, of Rhodes and Malta. He was a Frenchman from Provence and Sir Oliver Starkey, his English friend and secretary were the last of the Crusader Knights to fight in the siege. In my wildest of dreams, I witnessed the crushing defeat of the Ottoman Empire's mixed forces, the Turks, Arabs, North Africans, Balkan Muslims and others; the final retreat and the evacuation of their armies. I can recall buying a choc-ice from a Turkish belly dancing usherette who, complete with an illuminated tray just happened to be in attendance that morning. Dreams are supposed to be bizarre and this one most certainly was.

Finally on 21st August 1568, La Valette, the Grand Master, died of a stroke and when the cathedral of St. John was completed his body was laid to rest in the crypt and in due time that of Sir Oliver.

The English sovereign then was the arch protestant Elizabeth I, Queen of England and on hearing the news of Sir Oliver Starkey's death she ordered the Archbishop of Canterbury to give thanks in special services over a period of six weeks .

Lynette woke me up soon after the clock on the mantelpiece had chimed half-past six. She asked me if I had been asleep for a long time to which I replied: 'Yes, about eight hundred and fifty years.'

'What on earth have you been dreaming about now?' she asked, continuing to empty the contents of her Sainsbury's shopping bag.

'I was dreaming about The Last Battle of The Crusades in Malta.' I replied, rummaging around behind the cushions to find the television handset.

'Oh, you want a glass of Lucozade.' Lynette said in a raised voice which bellowed out from the kitchen, 'there are more bananas and bottles of Lucozade in this kitchen to supply Sainsburys for several weeks.'

'When one slips on a banana skin the natural reaction is to laugh, but you know, Lynette, I'm not laughing.'

'Christopher, it may have escaped your notice, but I'm not laughing either.'

Chapter Eleven

Sitting at the dining room table the same evening

It was bangers and mash, fresh garden peas and my favourite Bisto onion gravy for dinner that evening and as I can recall, Lynette asked if I had enjoyed the meals in Southampton General Hospital to which I replied: 'the food tasted like shit but you could live on it,' quoting the Aussie waitress, Josephine Drummond in Southport's Hotel Belvedere & Spa; 'the roast beef, mashed potato and spinach, followed by the everyday speciality of rice pudding and a dollop of raspberry jam was the easiest dish on the hospital's repetitive menu to digest.' I added.

'I have made a Sainsbury's rice pudding for our dessert, and that will make a change, won't it?' Lynette said, failing miserably to whet my appetite.

I devoured the Walls pork sausages as if I hadn't eaten for weeks and I couldn't help but notice a kitchen window that was deliberately left open by Lynette to allow the Bisto gravy smells to waft into the Rodriguez's garden next door.

The rubbish skip which stands next to the compost heap and is only moved into the drive on special occasions like when the dustbin men decide to make an appearance would have been the best way of disposing of my wife's culinary expertise until she said: 'Just don't think about it!'

'Well, Lynette, it was impossible for me to escape through one of the hospital windows in order to find a Chinese take-away because I was on the fourth floor, and I wouldn't be sitting here next to you this evening if I had jumped out on to the concourse; no aluminium cartons of Cantonese fried rice are worth that.'

'You are right, as usual, Chris, let's not have any more arguments.' she said cheerfully. 'There are still plenty of bananas in the kitchen; I could always make you a deep fried banana fritter.'

'Tell me, Lynette, did you find it difficult opening that tin of rice pudding?'

'You've always got to have the last word, haven't you?'

'I should be back to normal by the weekend, Lynette,' I said with total

Michael Alty

confidence, 'perhaps when Victoria and Barbara are back on Friday we can visit a car showroom, and that will be fun, won't it?'

'And what if I may ask, are we going to do about the one which is parked outside?' she asked.

'You mean our Volkswagen Polo Estate that should be parked in Canary Wharf.' I replied giving her the benefit of listening to my endless bouts of priceless sarcasm.

'I thought you would like the colour, Chris, it will bring a little brightness into our dismal lives.'

'If you're not happy being married to me, Lynette, you can always visit our next door neighbours, Steven and Dorothy to arrange a swap.'

'Now, Christopher you are being extreme, and to go down that road would be a total disaster for all of us.' Lynette said, looking at the lonely hearts column in the 'Daily Echo'; I would have thought the lost and found column would have been more appropriate in her quest to find a better standard of living.

'When the girls come home we can have a meal at the Bistro on the Beach,' Lynette suggested. 'It is situated right on the beach, with stunning sea views of just about everywhere in Bournemouth. It's open all year round as well, but opening times may vary and we may have to book.' she added.

'I will check on their website, tomorrow, Lynette; that will give me something to do whilst you're at work.'

'Don't go out of your way, Chris; just put your feet up in front of the television and relax.' she insisted with a view to a speedy recovery.

'Oh, by the way there was an advertisement in the travel section of the newspaper, Lynette; two weeks holiday in Trinidad and Tabasco for nine hundred pounds per person.'

'Don't you mean, Trinidad and Tobago, Chris?'

'Yes, but Tabasco is hotter, similar to the bottle we have in the kitchen cupboard.' I said laughing like a demented hyena.

'Yes well, very funny, Christopher, very funny indeed.'

'What's that noise I can hear coming in from our back garden?' I asked.

'It's one of the elderly residents from next door trying to impersonate

96

Dame Vera Lynn.' Lynette said, tapping on the table in time with the melodious rendition of: "We'll Meet Again".

'I would have thought, "Don't Fence Me In" would be more appropriate.' I said to Lynette before going into the kitchen to close the window.

'Have you no compassion for the elderly and age concern, Chris,' Lynette said, on my way back to sit at the table, 'those bleak war years must have been pretty awful; ration books, gas masks, air raid shelters and blackouts.'

'Age is timeless, Lynette, and from what I've seen of Mrs Hutchinson, next door, she's never wanted for anything and has never had a blackout in her life.' I put in.

'Well, some people were more fortunate than others during the war and we were fortunate to have missed all of that.' Lynette said, failing miserably to emulate the Pope.

Another poem which landed on our doorstep last year was from our family friend and Poet Lauriat, Robert Bingham, reminding me I had been on this planet for half a century managing somehow to escape being locked up inside a sanatorium.

Lynette, having purchased a suitable red, white and blue picture frame from Woolworths, displayed it on the sideboard next to a photograph of her father. The poem was called "The Royal British Legion" (The Last Bastion of an Empire) and reads:

The Royal British Legion
(The Last Bastion of an Empire)

From dark ages past one sees the light
To defend our country against foreign might
To those past and present we cannot forget
And we will be forever in their debt
It is important that we all must pray
To keep our sacred 'Remembrance Day'

'Tell me, Lynette, are you still thinking of us going to live in France, because there is another advertisement in the newspaper giving the name and address of an estate agent in Paris; they have their own website, speak English and promise to send details of properties every week.'

'Yes, I am, we need something like this to invest in, it will be a challenge for all of us.' she said, getting up from the table to give me an ineffectual kiss on the top of my head.

'Tomorrow afternoon, on your way home, why don't you pop into Thomas Cook in Boscombe High Street and ask them for a Brittany Ferries brochure and short breaks in Paris.' I said to her, knowing she was going to give me her seal of approval.

'That's a good idea, Chris, now you are beginning to recover.' she said, sighing with relief.

'Yes, I feel better already.' I replied.

'Also, I will visit Jarvis & Hayes, postage stamp Auctioneers and Valuers in Old Christchurch Road during my lunch break to see if they have made any headway into selling Uncle Thomas's stamp collection.' Lynette said excitedly, rubbing her hands together like a female Ebenezer Scrooge.

'That is another good idea,' I replied, giving her the impression I wasn't as enthusiastic as her but, underneath that facade, I couldn't wait to realize the extent of their worth.

'I should be in a position to go out tomorrow.' I said to her with a view to going to the Queens Park for a liquid lunch.

'Whatever you do, Chris, just stay away from Sainsbury's, and if it's not possible for you to restrain yourself from going to the pub, I won't interfere my dearest.' she said, with another loving smile.

'I just knew you would say that, Lynette; as always my darling, you are so perceptive and understanding.'

'Well, you haven't had an alcoholic drink for well over a week now, Christopher, just don't make up for lost time by overstaying your welcome.'

'It is your birthday in two weeks' time, it falls on a Saturday this year Chris,' Lynette said, reminding me as if I was suffering from a complete loss of memory. 'And, what would you like me to give you for a birthday present, dear?'

'Preferably, a football season ticket so I can go to Goldsands Stadium to support AFC Bournemouth on Saturday afternoons.'

'Do you know how much a season ticket would cost, Chris?' she said, not knowing I was succeeding in trying to wind her up. 'I used to work for Marks and Spencer, I didn't own the store.' she added.

'I'm only joking, Lynette; where's your sense of humour?'

'Well don't joke with me, Christopher, and as for my sense of humour, I think it was left some time ago in St. Clements church when you came on with a nose bleed in front of the vicar.' Lynette was quick to answer.

'It was all that excitement, Lynette; the musty and damp smells emanating from the stone walls of the crypt didn't help the situation either.'

'You've always got an answer to everything, haven't you Chris, the truth of the matter is you got yourself pie-eyed the night before our wedding in the Queens Park.'

Tomorrow morning, I will phone Professor Stevens to ask for a twelve month sabbatical I decided assertively when she rummaged around inside a cabinet to find a suitable DVD for us both to watch that evening.

'What about Alf Garnet?' Lynette suggested.

'What about Alf Garnet?' I replied, knowing we were going to see "Till death do us part" for the hundredth time.

'He was very funny, especially when he arrives home drunk having been to Wembley Stadium to see England v Germany in the 1966 World Cup.' Lynette, ever so patriotically, pointed out.

'I once used to tell a joke, Lynette which went something like this: There was a British prisoner of war camp in Berwick on Tweed. When the Germans were about to play a game of football, the British referee, having tossed a coin said: 'the first one to touch the ball will be shot, Germans kick off.' I told another one that goes: There was a German prisoner of war camp in Hamburg. The camp commandant said one morning: 'today we have received your 'Red Cross' parcels; thank you, we are most grateful.'

'That wasn't very funny,' she said looking at another one of our wartime DVDs, "The Longest Day".

'I've got a good idea, Lynette,' when I came up with a final solution to our celluloid image-watching dilemma. 'Why don't we go upstairs to the study, pull up two chairs in front of the desktop computer and search the website for a suitable estate agent in Paris; the one mentioned in the '*Daily Echo*', '*Circa Habitat*' Paris sounds okay.' I added.

'And why not, it will be like going to the movies, Chris,' she said, while contemplating an hour and a half suffering the constant fluttering of Hugh Grant's eye lashes in the box office favourite, "Four Weddings and a Funeral". 'We could have a couple of choc-ices and a bucket of popcorn, and that will also be fun, won't it?' she added.

It was when Lynette and I were climbing the stairs I couldn't help wondering where I had heard the name '*Circa Habitat*', the estate agents in Paris, then, suddenly it occurred to me, it was Bridgette Helen Boullard who said she was an *immobilier*, an estate agent working for that company.

I couldn't wait to access the internet, forward slash, back slashing my way through to get into her website with a view to finding out Boullard's real name.

'Would you like some orange juice or Pepsi Cola during the intermission,' Lynnette asked, cuddling up close to me as my fingers danced quickly over the keyboard.

'A large glass of whisky will do fine.' I said, instantly accessing *Circa Habitat's* website with great enthusiasm.

I searched for the name of an estate agent called Bridgette-Helen Boullard to no avail, but then I saw there was a Helen Hesketh working for them in their offices in *Boulevard Haussmann* in Paris.

This was what I wanted to know, this woman had been stringing me along in Southport, and all the time she is married to that crook, George Hesketh, who was using her to steal our money.

'I don't like the look of '*Circa Habitat*' estate agents, Lynette; they sound like a bunch of crooks to me, also, they're into finance in a very big way and at very high interest rates.'

'Well, we will have to look at another one, Chris, Paris is quite a large city; I went there once on a school day trip from Southampton, it took us five minutes to get up to the top of the *Eiffel* Tower and three quarters of a bloody hour to get down and then we nearly missed the coach.'

'You should have gone on one of those glass-roofed tourist river boats, Lynette; you know when the water level is high because of serious flooding, you can damage your head as you pass underneath a bridge; if one doesn't get you, the other twelve will.'

'I can remember it was a beautiful sunny day in August when we all queued up outside the *Louvre* and the *Tuileries* in the *Place du Carrousel*, waiting to go inside.' Lynette explained, 'I can also recall a cool breeze emanating from the air conditioning as we strolled around the magnificent art galleries. It was when I was about to buy the biggest ice cream cornet in the world in the public gardens, Miss Hargreaves told us girls to lower our skirts a fraction because she had just seen Sacha Distel whizzing round the corner in the *Place de la Concorde* in an open-top sports car. The picture in the hall downstairs, Chris, was bought in the museum's fine art souvenir shop; it is a portrait of the famous Mona Lisa by Leonardo da Vinci.'

'Do you know, Lynette, I always thought it was one of your ancestors.'

'It's only a print, Chris; I had to bring it home rolled up inside a discarded paper towel tube.' she would insist on telling me, as if I thought it was an old photograph of her Auntie Mabel from Southbourne.

I began to yawn when Lynette and I saw a multitude of estate agents windows passing by in front of our eyes. My advice to her was to pick up where we left off tomorrow and then perhaps we may have gathered up sufficient enthusiasm to search the web for the ideal French property; preferably one, very Provence with louvered shutters and a Mediterranean blue door.

'That seems a good idea, Chris,' she said, putting a hand over her mouth to camouflage her own yawning.

'Let's go back downstairs and watch Hugh Grant; he's enough to send anyone to sleep and I could do with an early night.' I quickly suggested.

'You've been asleep for most of the afternoon, Chris; you're beginning to act like Rip Van Winkle.'

The following day

During the night I had been subjected to an awful nightmare when I dreamt about climbing into bed with Brigitte-Helen Boullard after she had blackmailed me, threatening to tell Lynette of our harmless relationship in Southport.

Lynette painfully poked me in the ribs with her elbow when I had supposedly shouted out: "You can leave your hat on", emulating the ever popular, Joe Cocker on one of his bad nights when he sounds as if he is singing from the bottom of a metal bucket.

After Lynette had ordered me to go back to sleep, preferably for a long time, I got out of bed to make myself a cup of 'Twinings' Earl Grey tea.

At breakfast Lynette said: 'There's a thin red line between kinkiness and eroticism you know, Chris, and if you want me to wear a hat in bed, to look like a Dame Van Winkle, the sour tempered woman who beats men up twice a week for neglecting the farm and being idle, I will be more than happy to do so.'

'You can do both, I don't care.' I said to her, negotiating the possibility of me completing *The Times* General Knowledge crossword before switching on the television to watch Delia Smith in action...

'Delia Smith's keep on cooking'

"Now wash your hands before we start
To make the perfect Bakewell Tart
And don't forget to switch on the oven
Before putting on a nice clean apron
The one I am wearing has had its day
The lace around the edge is beginning to fray
On the front it says: 'Cook of the Year'
But you can't see this it's not very clear
Now wash your hands before we begin
These are called Baked Beans in a tin
And now I would like to show you these
They are called tins of Peas

A perfect standby for all you housewives
Watching television and leading busy lives
And now wash your hands before we try
To make the perfect Apple Pie
Here's one I baked earlier its very hot
Sorry about the apples I forgot
To find my books keep on looking
They're called Delia Smith's, "Keep on Cooking"."

I phoned Professor Paul Stevens at ten o'clock to ask him for a twelve-month sabbatical, the much needed period of convalescence promulgated by a Sainsbury's banana. This wasn't a problem because he had already taken steps to find a temporary replacement and of course, when I was feeling much better, I would call into the university to speak with him.

It was when Lynette was about to leave the house to go to work she turned round and said:

'If you feel hungry during the course of the day, Chris, help yourself to a banana.'

'One of my lady students was from British Guiana.' I jokingly told her

And then after saying, she once knew a gentleman who was the manager for the British Home Stores branch in Bournemouth, Lynette told me, in no uncertain terms, to go and visit a clinic to have my ears syringed.

'That's funny, Lynette; all of a sudden I can hear a pin drop.'

'Sorry, what did you say, Chris?'

Lynette had rubbed shoulders with the postman on her way out of the house via the front door. A letter was being delivered by courtesy of 'Royal Mail' from the head office of Sainsburys, informing me of compensation being upheld for an immediate payment. They had come up with the goods in just over a week offering me an out of court settlement for twenty thousand pounds, with the proviso I stayed away from bananas in their chain of supermarkets for a very long time. This was really music to my ears and I couldn't wait to tell Lynette about the additions to our family fortunes on her return home.

103

'I have something to tell you, Chris.'

'Is it good news or bad news, Lynette?'

'It is positively good news, Chris, those postage stamps that belonged to your Uncle Thomas have been realized by Stanley Gibbons, the stamp dealers and auctioneers in London, to be worth at least one-point two million pounds. Also,' she added excitedly, Jarvis & Hayes have told me they're destined for the philately section in the British Museum.'

'Bloody hell.' was my clear reaction. 'And this makes my compensation from Sainsburys a drop in the ocean.'

Chapter Twelve

Suddenly, it was Friday once again when Victoria and Barbara were due to come home from Birmingham.

I can recall sitting on a stool next to Councillor Bennett in the lounge bar of the Queens Park, waiting for Lynette to walk into the pub through the open door before we both made our way home in the van. I can also remember it was a beautiful sunny afternoon with lots of blue skies to brighten up my day after receiving begging letters from the Water Board in Bristol, threatening to cut my supply off should I not pay them within the next seven days; I suppose it wasn't their fault when I kept forgetting to sign the cheques.

'You seem to be very pensive, Christopher; is something on your mind?' Frederick Bennett asked me, concernedly. 'Come on, open up, you know you can share your problems with me.' he added.

'It's the Southern Water Board again; they're really getting up my nose this time.' I replied with caution knowing he and his Freemason mates would do something underhand to alleviate my problem.

'Just give me some names, Chris, and I will stitch them up good and proper.'

I can recall listening to him, offering to resolve one of my problems by systematically dismembering a member of the Water Board with a two-edged broad sword, and Denzel Crow explaining to his wife, Christine, that when he was filling in a hole in the ground, a mobile went off.

It was when I was waiting impatiently for Lynette to arrive bringing with her some unexpected news, I heard Christine Crow say to her husband: 'But you don't have a mobile, Denzel.'

I came to the conclusion the undertaker must have carelessly left his phone inside the coffin before he screwed the lid down and was searching Bournemouth cemetery in an attempt to find it.

I jokingly said to Frederick, that when I was a boy I ran inside George Scott's Funeral Parlour in Somerset Road, Boscombe and after jumping on to the counter asked whether they had any empty boxes.

'I always thought George Scott was dead?' Frederick said with a peculiar look on his face.

'He is;' I replied. 'that's why he hovers around inside Bournemouth cemetery.'

We were both laughing uncontrollably at what seemed to be two jokes of the year when they were later circulated around the pub and me becoming an instant celebrity after I had convinced some of the regulars that I was their local comedian.

'It's wasn't funny you know, Chris.' Denzel said to me seriously at the bar.

'What's not funny?' I asked, inquisitively. 'Was it my little witticism or you hearing a mobile phone go off from inside a grave?'

'Who the hell is Witty, if you don't mind me asking?' Denzel said, with his usual bouts of stammering.

'Watty?' I replied, imitating, Ian Smith, a former Prime Minister of Rhodesia.

The time on the clock behind the bar was reading three forty-five when Lynette walked into the lounge looking like the cat that got the cream.

'You seem very happy, Lynette; run over a black cat today, have you?' I sarcastically asked.

'A little drop of poison may do you good later, Chris,' Lynette replied, sounding like the wicked witch in a pantomime. 'Don't forget we are picking Victoria and Barbara up from the railway station at twenty-five minutes past four, but now we must go home in the van to collect the car.' she said, looking at her watch. 'I have got some interesting news to tell you, Chris, but unfortunately I can't tell you in here because there are a lot of people standing around with big ears.'

'I hope that remark doesn't include me, Mrs Travis?' Frederick Bennett asked frowning.

'No, whatever gave you that idea, Councillor Bennett,' Lynette remarked and then continuing to say: 'And besides, you are sitting down.'

'Let's get the hell out of here.' I said, wondering what Lynette was going to come out with next.

As we were travelling along Queens Park Avenue, Lynette took her left hand off the steering wheel to change down a gear; she then glanced at me momentarily and said:

'I received a telephone call from Jarvis & Hayes, the Stamp Dealers and Auctioneers in Old Christchurch Road, who informed me that Stanley Gibbons, the Stamp Auctioneers and Valuers in the Strand, London, had just sold Uncle Thomas's stamp collection for a record one point three million pounds, and with a minus of a ten and a five per cent commission fee totalling, one-hundred and ninety-five thousand, we should be receiving a cheque for one million one hundred and five thousand pounds.

'Lynette, just stop the car will you, please, I feel a sudden urge to go to the toilet.'

'Don't be so dramatic, Chris, we will be home in less than a minute.' she said, reminding me where we live.

'I too, have some interesting news for you, Lynette; it came in the post this morning at the same time you left the house to go into Boscombe.

'Don't tell me, it's a brown envelope from the Inland Revenue in Post Office Road.' she asked, nervously.

'No, nothing like that, Lynette.' I pointed out with a smile. 'You will just have to wait and see; I have placed them both in front of the mantelpiece clock.'

'Both? I thought you said there was only one letter.' Lynette said, looking puzzled and no doubt now beginning to wonder what the other one could possibly be.

'It's a letter from Southern Water Board threatening to cut our water supply off if we don't pay our water bill in less than seven days.'

'What do you mean, we; how many times do I have to remind you, Chris, that it is important *you* sign bloody cheques when *you* pay the bills.'

Lynette soon recovered from her over reactions concerning the Water Board and was now concentrating her efforts and energies on the letter from Sainsbury's head office.

'I suppose, that's not bad considering the distance I had to travel almost every other day from Bournemouth to Southampton.' Lynette said, trying to impersonate the television presenter, Carol Vorderman, Britain's number one human calculator.

'Did you pop into Thomas Cook, Lynette?' I asked.

'Yes, Brittany Ferries and P & O, have some marvellous City Breaks to Paris at the moment and we can sail over to France from either Portsmouth, Southampton or Poole,' Lynette told me with great enthusiasm. 'Also, I went into Barclays Bank to enquire about the rate of exchange between the French Franc and the Pound sterling.'

'Blimey, you have been busy, haven't you, Lynette,' I said, taking pity on Audrey Wright, our trusty sales assistant who had to be in charge of the business in her absence.

On our way to the railway station, Lynette asked what I ate for lunch. I told her I had a cheese and pickle sandwich in the Queens and that I was now beginning to feel rather hungry. She then enquired about me finding 'The Bistro on the Beach' on the web, to which I replied: 'Yes, but they're fully booked for that evening because of a party of full-time Trade Union Officials from Huddersfield taking up residence by the sea complete with 'Kiss me Quick' hats and buckets and spades. I suggested we all go to an Italian restaurant called the Villa Marie, located at The Triangle in Bournemouth; they have an interesting Pizza Pasta menu and it doesn't cost an arm and a leg.

I had just enough time to buy myself a bar of fruit and nut from the buffet bar before the train arrived from Birmingham New Street.

'Hi dad,' Victoria said, going through the same routine as the previous week. 'I could murder a pizza, dad because I'm bloody well starving.' she added, as if she had suddenly read my mind.

'Hi dad,' Barbara said after giving me two big kisses on both sides of my cheeks. 'Vicky and I have just purchased two new students rail cards; they last for three months and we can come home as many times as we like now.'

'Tell me, Barbara, how much did you and Vicky have to pay for these replacement student rail cards?' I impatiently asked.

'They cost four hundred and fifty pounds.' Vicky attempted to explain.

'I suppose, that's quite reasonable given to understand the distance between Bournemouth and Birmingham New Street.'

'That's only for one, dad.' Barbara said alarmingly.

'What I can see is, we will be eating banana sandwiches tonight at this rate of expenditure.' I pointed out to Vicky in no uncertain terms.

'Oh, don't be a Mr McMeany, Christopher,' Lynette said, before coming out with the most obvious of lines. 'And as for bananas; you know all about those.'

'Dad, can I ask you a question?'

'Yes, Vicky.' I replied walking towards Bournemouth's Station Premium Car Park, wheeling a huge red trolley bag in order to find our bright yellow Volkswagen Polo Estate.' 'Why is the car painted bright yellow?'

This was when I said to Lynette: '*A vous,* Lynette'; and now, it's over to you.' I continued to say, practicing my schoolboy French very badly.

'It is the same car, isn't it mummy?' Barbara asked, running her fingers down the paintwork to ascertain that it wasn't still wet.

'Yes, Barbara, it is,' Lynette replied, not knowing how to eventually explain the change of colour to the Vehicle Licensing Authorities in Swansea. 'I just thought a lick of paint would brighten up our lives a little, but as usual, I can't do right for doing wrong, can I?' she added.

'I suppose I will get used to the colour in time.' Barbara sighed deeply.

'Well, you know all about that, don't you Barbara?' I said to her, hoping Raman Patel's ears could be burning in his kitchen.

'You are horrible to me, dad, and what has Raman done to deserve all of this?' she, so hastily enquired.

'It's not what he's done, it's what he is about to do,' I immediately said to her. 'and to think that less than two weeks ago he was drinking my orange juice and munching his way through huge portions of your birthday cake; it was a pity he wasn't standing in front of it when the candles were blown out.'

'That's it, dad, I'm going home by bus.' Barbara said, searching for a handkerchief from inside a pocket of her windproof jacket.

'I will come with you, Barbara.' Vicky insisted, before they made their way to Holdenhurst Road to grab some fish and chips and then catch the next bus to Queens Park.

'You really are a pig, Christopher Travis; you really are.' Lynette would insist on telling me. 'Apologise to Barbara and Victoria, Chris and then perhaps we can drive home without any more unpleasant incidents.'

'That's if I can catch up with them in time.' I said slowly.

'No wonder your Auntie Gertrude didn't like you very much, Christopher.' Lynette hastily replied.

'Well then, can you explain, how come, she left me all of her money and the house?'

'Auntie Gertrude must have been having one of those days when she made out her 'Last Will and Testament'. And now, suddenly, everything belongs to you, does it?' Lynette went on, continuing to answer some of my enigmatic questions.

It was when I turned left into Holdenhurst Road, Lynette and I saw Barbara and Victoria sitting on a wall eating fish and chips from what seemed to be a copy of *The Daily Mail* newspaper. After Lynette had wound down the window on the passenger side, I leaned over and said to Vicky:

'Why are you both sitting on the Hampshire Regiment Drill Hall wall eating fish and chips? Do you intend to join the Territorial Army?'

'It is because we are starving, dad, and the bloody bus driver wouldn't allow us to get on to his bus while we were eating our food.' Victoria explained, in her usual lady-like manner.

'Come on you two, get in the car and then we can all look forward to having a decent meal at the Villa Marie Italian Restaurant this evening.' I said, trying to lower the tone of the conversation to a more sensible pitch.

'Would you like a chip, dad? They sure beat the hell out of McDonald's potato sticks.' Victoria said when I saw traces of tomato sauce being wiped away from the side of her mouth in the rear view mirror.

'No thank you, Vicky,' I replied when I glanced at her again in the mirror. 'I have just eaten a Cadbury's fruit and nut chocolate bar, and much that I would like one of your soggy chips, I'm afraid I shall have to decline your offer.' I was forced to say.

'I wouldn't mind having a quick bite.' Lynette said, showing two perfectly formed incisors inside her mouth, and this was when I remembered being introduced to a rattlesnake when I was trekking in the desert wastes of Arizona.

On the approach to the Golf Club I said to Barbara that there was once a competition in *The Daily Mail*; the first person to find one centimetre of news in their paper would receive two free fish and chip luncheon vouchers to be spent in any Harry Ramsden's restaurant.

'That was very funny dad; have you got any more jokes like that one?' Vicky said, picking up on my newly found celebrity status.

'It's funny you should say that, Vicky, but have you heard the one about...'

'Don't even think about it!' Lynette said, nudging my rib cage with her right elbow. 'I don't want to hear anymore about empty boxes and funeral parlours, thank you.' she added.

'I was only going to tell Victoria and Barbara about Sir Walter Raleigh being the Patron Saint of Bournemouth.'

'And we don't want to listen to anymore jokes about fish and chips.' Lynette said, determined to shut me up.

The pungent smell of salt and vinegar was now beginning to get up my nose and this was when I said to Vicky and Barbara: 'It's like driving inside a fish and chip shop.'

'Don't be so bloody stupid, dad,' Vicky put in. 'You can't drive a car inside a fish and chip shop.'

'Don't be too sure about that,' I said to her, knowing I was about to win the argument, 'Have you seen the standard of driving along Holdenhurst Road, Vicky, especially, on Saturday nights when the revellers leave The Lion's Head Pub?'

*

The 'Villa Marie', Italian Restaurant, the evening of the same day

We arrived at the Villa Marie by taxi at eight-thirty precisely having booked a table for four during the afternoon. For all who dine here, one visit leads to many more, and over the years it has become our favourite Italian restaurant in Bournemouth's bustling and vibrant seaside town.

The extensive menus were handed to us by the owner's wife, Gabriella who immediately asked us if we would like an aperitif before ordering our food. I kicked off with a large whisky and dry ginger while, Lynette preferred to drink vodka and orange; Barbara opted for a Martini Bianco with lemon on ice and the unpredictable, Victoria volunteering to drink After Shock.

The proceedings developed with Tony, the waiter, placing a wine list in the centre of the table. I asked him if he could bring my usual flagon of Chianti Melini red wine, the one wrapped in colourful raffia around its base; the empty bottle one can take home and transform into a decorative table lamp reminding you of another memorable visit to the Villa Marie.

Tasty red pesto thin-based pizzas, loaded with roasted red and yellow peppers, creamy *mozzarella*, aubergine and plum tomatoes were the order of the day, but first the starters, consisting of mouth watering crispy deep fried calamari. The dessert; an Italian version of a 'Knickerbocker Glory', consisting of several flavours of ice cream and a chocolate topping has for a long time been our favourite weight watchers nightmare.

'Nice in here, in it,' Vicky said to us all spontaneously, trying miserably to imitate Lorraine Chase in the *Cinzano Bianco* television advert shown shortly after the war.

'Well, you should know, Vicky,' I said, glancing at her empty plate which looked as though it had metaphorically been through a dishwasher. 'And, taking into account the number of *Chianti Melini* basket bottles we have stored in the garage, this is an indication as to how many times you've been here.' I added.

'Mummy told me yesterday, dad, that you are about to buy Victoria and me, two brand new motor cars to add to our birthday presents.' Barbara would insist on telling me after waiting until I had finished another large whisky and dry ginger.

'That was until you both decided to buy two expensive Student Rail Cards today.' I said to her, thinking unnecessarily about our financial position and at the same time giving Lynette a discreet ankle-kicking session underneath the table.

'But, we didn't buy them today, dad, we bought the bloody things on Wednesday.' Victoria had to say as she shovelled more ice cream into her delectable little mouth that resembles a clown every time she speaks.

'I wouldn't mind an Alpha Romeo, dad.' Barbara put in and then continuing to say: 'That would really get up Raman's nose, wouldn't it?'

'The subject is closed, Barbara, Victoria,' I said to them both and to Lynette who was now suffering minor bruising to the lower part of her leg. 'I will review this situation in three months' time.'

'Would you like some fish and chips, dad, on the way home?' Vicky asked, laughing.

'You're joking, Vicky.' I said, beginning to feel I was somewhat responsible for her gluttonous passion for fish and chips.

'Yes, I'm only joking, dad.' glancing at her watch to check on the hour.

'Oh no, she isn't,' Barbara quickly put in. 'Umberto Zaveroni, the owner's son of 'Something Fishy' looks awfully sweet, especially when he is standing behind a large jar of pickled eggs.'

'Is this person someone else belonging to another ethnic community I will have to contend with at my birthday party?' I said to Vicky and Barbara.

'No I don't think so, dad, he will be far too busy working, watching the traffic inside his fathers fish'n chip shop.' Vicky said, sarcastically.

Chapter Thirteen

Breakfast at Tiffany's – No 46 Queen's Park Avenue, Bournemouth the following morning

'Hi, you guys.' Vicky said melodiously, skipping down the stairs like a bandy legged ballerina and saying at the top of her voice: 'I'm bloody well starving.'

And, following on several steps behind was Barbara, the beauty who is capable of sleeping on a clothes line.

'Good morning everyone,' Barbara said meaningfully, rushing down the stairs and giving me the impression she couldn't wait to claw deep down inside the Kellogg's Cornflake packet with her long scratchy fingernails.

'I trust everyone had a good night's sleep after eating your way through mounds of food in the 'Villa Marie'. I said, reminding them I was still on medication and to keep the noise down to an acceptable level of decibels.

'I had this weird dream, dad,' Barbara said, looking over the top of her reading glasses which she finds necessary to wear when reading her mail at the table. 'I dreamt I was sleeping on the clothes line in the garden and then suddenly I fell off into the compost heap.' she added, knowing the clothes line bit was one of my favourite tales I tell out of school.

'What's that thing sparkling in your ear, Barbara.' I asked, inquisitively.

'It's an earring, dad,' she replied touching it with her index finger. 'Raman gave it to me for my birthday; it's from Calcutta.' she added.

'Our coalman had one like that years ago; his ear went septic and he was unable to deliver a sack of nutty slack.' reminding Barbara of the time she was a little girl and when we all sat in front of the fire toasting Warburton's crumpets for our afternoon tea.

'Is it a real diamond?' Vicky asked, knowing it to be an imitation fake zircon.

'Of course it is, Raman says it weighs one-carat.' she seriously remarked.

'We have plenty of carrots in our kitchen, Barbara, but it doesn't necessarily follow they are diamonds.' I said to her emphatically.

'I'll turn on the television, dad, so we can watch the breakfast show while we are eating our food.' Vicky suggested, fumbling with a handset which had been contaminated with Robertson's Golden Shred Marmalade. 'Oh, No, it's Sir Paul McCartney being interviewed by Nick Owen and he is about to sing "Yesterday".'

'Who is about to sing, "Yesterday" Nick Owen or Paul McCartney?' I asked Vicky who was now devouring what seemed to be the last remnants from inside our once full breadbin. 'I particularly like the poem penned by our close family friend, describing Sir Paul McCartney as a musical genius which goes:'

Musical Genius

It doesn't seem so far away
When he walked on stage to sing his favourite song
"Yesterday"
The man with extraordinary hair
Wears a suit with a flair
He plays a guitar, piano and sings
Went on to do better things
When he formed a band called 'Wings'
He composes songs and then lets them be
Then breaks off for a cup of tea
I can remember this guy when I was at school
A musical genius from Liverpool

'I would much prefer to watch Delia Smith, chef, author and TV personality on BBC1.' Barbara suggested, 'you can learn a lot from Delia; Raman does.' she added.

'Delia Smith goes Bombay'

"First of all do you see the Sari?
You know I look like Mata Hari
And now I'm going to make a curry
So I hope you are not in any hurry
To dash out today to your favourite

115

Indian take-away
Now wash your hands before we commence
You know it makes a lot of sense
The curries I make are very hot
Sorry about the onions I forgot
The sauce I have prepared comes out of a jar
You can get this from your local Spar
One can make this dish in a trice
With lots and lots of Pilau rice
And if you want to know where
I am coming from
This is called a Popadom
They start off all round and kinda flat
I like those and so does the cat
You will find this recipe somewhere in my book
So it's goodbye for now from Delia
And lots of good luck"

'Alternatively we could listen to Sara Cox, the new Radio One presenter and the show is aptly named: 'Cox's Breakfast Show; she only began yesterday having taken over from Zoe Ball on Thursday.' Lynette said, recommending a little light entertainment, concentrating on listening to poetry for a change. I can still hear, Sara, reading the lines of the poem as if it were only yesterday.

'A Poem at Breakfast Time'

When you lose your crackle and pop
And life is becoming a complete full stop
Through the letter box comes another bill
As the toast burns underneath the grill
When everything costs an 'arm and a leg'
And the wife puts an end to your bacon and egg
Into the bin you feel there is no hope
It is only another envelope

And when it goes to the bottom of the pile
Just sit back and give her a smile

'Everything is important,
But nothing is that important.'

'I used to like listening to Pam Ayres, the poetess, broadcasting on Radio Four a long time ago.' Lynette put in again. 'Pam was an RAF fighter pilot during the war you know.'

'She was good she was, especially on Sunday evenings after I had consumed a gallon of Taunton Best Somerset Cider in the Queens and sang to my mother and father a few lines of 'Sing something Simple' when I came home, I was then ready to fall asleep sitting on the settee.' I nostalgically explained to the girls. 'Jean Metcalf had a lot to do with it as well.' I added.

'Who the bloody hell is Jean Metcalf?' Vicky asked, inquisitively.

'Oh, she was just one of my many girlfriends in those days.' I replied, looking at a signed photograph of Doris Day on the sideboard.

'Hey, has anyone seen the cat this morning?' Barbara asked with a worried look on her face.

I replied by saying: 'He has gone out.'

'What do you mean, Christopher, he's gone out?' Lynette asked, looking at me as if looks could kill.

'When I came down for breakfast, Hannibal attacked me on the stairs, making a bee-line for my ankles; as luck would have it, the banister window was wide open at the time.' I so eloquently explained. 'And, did you know if an Indian falls from a great height he always lands on his feet?'

'What has Raman got to do with Hannibal jumping out through the banister window?' Barbara asked, continuing to stir her coffee with a personalised silver spoon.

'Ah, Hannibal is Siamese, and is much smarter than Raman because he knows his life expectancy is longer than his.'

'Well, how come, dad, Hannibal has just limped into the house through the cat flap with a bandage around his leg?' Barbara said, making a move forward to turn herself into a veterinary nurse.

'I suppose the whole situation is like one of your medieval dwarf tossing competitions, dad,' Victoria put in. 'and, apparently they use their arms and legs to land on their feet.' she added.

I explained to Victoria in no uncertain terms it wasn't politically correct to use dwarfs as human projectiles these days and that sort of thing should be confined to the past.

'And what is on the itinerary for today?' I asked the ladies, knowing Lynette would have to be in attendance in the shop for most of the day.

'Raman will be picking me up this morning at ten-thirty in his brand new British Racing Green 318ci E46 BMW before he takes me on a tour around Longleat Safari Park.' Barbara explained to us all in extensive graphic detail.

'Well, don't bank on it, Barbara and let's not beat about the bush, if you pardon the pun; there are lots of lion, Bengal tigers and monkeys hanging around in Longleat Safari Park; Raman will be at home there, and furthermore, I hope you're not thinking of buying any long-playing Bollywood records.' I said to her, hoping he would be parking the car in range of a catapult which was capable of projecting a brick through the windscreen of his over-priced shag mobile.

'Do you remember the one about the monkey?' I said to Barbara, Victoria and Lynette who was now somewhat preoccupied and mesmerized following David Attenborough, the famous naturalist through an Amazonian rain forest trying his best to contract malaria.

'I can remember Richard Attenborough,' Lynette said, reminding me again she was showing signs of acute memory loss. 'He was the actor who rode a motorcycle in the epic movie, "The Great Escape".' she finally added.

After reminding her it was Steve McQueen who rode the motorbike and not Richard Attenborough, David's brother, I then proceeded with my poem:

'The Monkey'

A Monkey went to Longleat Park
And ate his lunch in the dark
He phoned his mate in British Guiana
With a look-a-like plastic banana
I cannot take anymore of this crap
It's just another tourist trap

'You never bloody well let up, do you, dad; always having a go at someone.' Vicky said to me in her melodious Dorset accent which she frequently changes to suit the occasion.

'Did you hear the one about the Lion? I don't think you have, I fear.'

'Chris, just shut up and eat your breakfast.' Lynette said assertively.

'I haven't heard that one.' Vicky said with caution, believing it to be another one of my spears being thrown metaphorically at Ralph MacTell.

'The Lion'

A lion escaped from Blackpool Zoo
And said to-day what shall I do
Maybe a stroll along the Promenade
And then stop off to buy a postcard
Maybe I'll go to 'Yates' for a drink and some coke
Then take in a show for a laugh and a joke
He had a chat with a legless Buffoon
And said it was quiet for a Saturday afternoon

'And, Vicky, how are you going to spend your day?' I asked, confidently knowing we would all, with the exception of, Lynette, end up in the Queens for lunch.

'I promised to meet Simon in the pub for lunch, dad, and by that time I shall be looking forward to tucking into my favourite snack, chicken in a basket.' she replied, giving me the impression I have a daughter who has a gastronomic problem on a par with Loyd Grossman.

'Before I go to the shop, I will show you all how to switch on the dishwasher.' Lynette said, getting up from her chair to remind us where the kitchen is situated.

Lynette, having just found her forte by turning herself into a kitchen appliance demonstration expert, said her goodbyes as she made her way out of the house through the front door.

'I will see you both in the Queens at one o'clock,' Lynette said to Vicky and me as we waited for the clock on the mantelpiece to strike ten-thirty to herald Patel's arrival. 'Have a nice day at Longleat, Barbara, and contrary to what your father says I'm sure you will have a good time.'

It was now ten forty-five and there was no sign of Raman Patel making an appearance.

'He's blown you out again, Barbara, how many more times have I got to impress on you that he's only good at one thing.'

'And what's that, dad?' Barbara curiously asked, tapping nervously on the table with her fingers and vacantly looking up towards the ceiling.

'Well, you know Barbara, pulling strings and shining shoes, that's all he's fit for.' I said, thinking about the over-stretched punkah wallah in the popular nineteen-eighty television series "It Ain't Half Hot Mum".

'That's two things, dad.' Victoria so cleverly pointed out to me.

'He's good at something else as well.' I said to Barbara, not knowing what her reaction was going to be.

'And what may I ask is that, dad? Is this something else I don't know?' she replied.

'From what I have heard from Councillor Bennett, he's got a keen eye for finding stray golf balls in the rough and getting his feet wet in the burns, the narrow streams that run through the finest of golf courses in Scotland.'

'That's it, dad, I've had enough of you prevaricating, and what is more, I'm going back to bed.' she said, angrily.

'Be careful not to fall off the washing line into the compost heap, dear.'

A few minutes later I poked my head around the door to Barbara's bedroom to see her sitting at the dressing table applying purple gloss to her guppy lips.

'Will you be joining us for lunch in the Queens, Babs? because I have just phoned 'The Bay of Bengal' Restaurant and the manager, Mister Mohandas Maharashtra informs me that your long-suffering boyfriend, Raman departed from Heathrow on a bucket-shop flight bound for Calcutta last evening, and unless you have four bums on fire, Barbara, you will never be able to catch up with him.'

Vicky shouted from down stairs: 'Raman has just arrived in a Winton Garage courtesy car, a Volkswagen Polo, and is just about to ring our front door bell.'

'Bloody hell, this is all I need to start the weekend.' I said to myself as I watched Barbara applying the last remnants of plaster to her face with a trowel.

I raced down the banister like a bat out of hell to open the door and I couldn't wait to find out why Patel was driving a courtesy car around the shores of Great Britain.

'How many more times do I have to tell you, Raman, the tradesman's entrance is at the side of the house?' I said, pointing towards the drive.

'Sorry, sorry Mr Travis, such a lack of general direction, and I grovel in mortification.' he replied, waving his head from side to side similar to a pendulum clock.

'Mister Mohandas Maharashtra told me this morning you were on your way to India, Raman, and why are you driving a Winton Garage courtesy car?'

'Such complication at the airport, Mr Travis, I had my passport confiscated by the authorities at Heathrow because they said my face wasn't brown enough on the photograph, but, I suppose it was partly my fault because I had been visiting a solarium for the past six months.'

'And why, if you don't mind me asking, is there a courtesy car parked directly in front of my house.'

'It was during the early hours of this morning, my BMW which was being driven to Heathrow by my best friend, Lino Chatterji, was in collision with a lamp post in Hounslow.'

'Oh, what terribly bad luck Raman, what terribly bad luck.'

Chapter Fourteen

Sitting in front of the fireplace the same morning

'Tell me, Raman why do you call your best friend, Lino?' I asked as he sipped a cup of our *Twinings* Earl Grey tea which had been appointed by Her Majesty, Queen Elizabeth II; his little finger raised high above the handle to show his native Rajasthan poshness.

'It is because when, Śrila, (Lino) Chatterji takes his girlfriend to the ice rink on Saturday mornings, he spends more time on the floor than he does skating.'

'Oh, that's very funny.' I said, reminding him it is very difficult to keep ones balance on the ice rink, especially if one is used to being on *terra firma.*'

'Who's talking about the ice rink,' Raman replied as he nicked another finger of Walkers Scottish Highlander shortbread from a crumbly packet which had been lying around since last Christmas. 'I am referring to the park around the back.' he added.

'Wouldn't you prefer to eat a *Crawford* Cream Cracker with *Patak's* mango chutney?' I asked, after seeing a packet of shortbread biscuits being depleted in front of my eyes.

'No thank you, Mr Travis, you see I have always had an affinity with Scotland and their traditions.' Raman said convincingly.

'It is a good thing you are not wearing a sporran, Raman, because rumour has it, Scottish people keep more than their loose change in them.'

At this point in the proceedings I asked Raman, if he knew of the British Airways' cabin cleaner's worst nightmare? When he emphatically said, he didn't know, I explained that on a flight between Prestwick and New York they have to contend with brushing up pieces of discarded shortbread and handing in bottles of Famous Grouse whisky to lost property which passengers had inadvertently left in the overhead luggage compartments.

'The passengers were fortunate to be able to buy most of their bloody stuff on board the aeroplane, Mr Travis,' Raman said with tears beginning to appear in his eyes. 'Before I had the chance to walk through into the departure lounge this morning, I had my passport revoked; a full bottle of Boss after-shave confiscated and a giant tube of *Smarties* resembling a cosh which may have concealed multi-coloured amphetamine; the ironic part of it all was, Mr Travis, with the exception of the odd flick knife, machine gun and an exploding James Bond *007* Parker propelling pencil, you can buy most things in the airport shops.

'I just knew you would turn up, Raman.' Barbara said, giving him gentle pecks on his brown pot-marked cheeks that resembled the rugged craters on the moon.

'You mean like 'Haley's Comet,' I said to Barbara, broadening her astronomical knowledge. 'And we won't be having any of that in here; your mother has just washed the cushion covers.' I emphatically told her.

'Why don't we all go to the Queens?' Raman suggested with gusto. 'After all it is lunchtime and I am feeling rather hungry because of not having anything to eat since last evening.'

'That's a good idea, Raman; you have just become my favourite guru.' I said before making inroads to collect my jacket from the hat and coat stand. 'The Queens Park Pub and Restaurant are having a run on curries this week, Raman, and they should keep you on the go for several days, especially, if you decide to eat their exceptionally hot chicken Madras; this is why the pub always keep their toilet paper in the fridge.'

'I am fed up with curries, Mr Travis,' Raman sorrowfully said to me. 'I have had enough of that shit to have me sat on the toilet for a lifetime.'

'You don't have to tell me, Raman, I know the feeling.' I replied, sighing.

'When I was a small boy, living in a Bengali village,' Raman began to tell me in confidence. 'We used to wrap snow around onion bargees and throw them to the tigers.'

'Is that one of the reasons why you won't be taking Barbara to Longleat Safari Park today, Raman, lest a reincarnation of a Bengal tiger decides to jump up on the roof of your Winton Garage courtesy car, and' I added, 'why this sudden urge to go back to India for six months, Raman?'

'It is because my mother has arthritis in her hands and my father is suffering from elephant's foot having been well and truly trodden on by one; they both need some spiritual and moral support.' Raman seriously replied.

'Who needs the spiritual and moral support, your mother's hands or your father's feet; I would have thought, you were the last person to be asked for some spiritual and moral support and you do seem to be having a great deal of trouble with your passports, don't you Raman?'

'I only have one passport, Mr Travis.'

'That's not what I have heard.' I took great pleasure in telling him.

We all piled out from the house as if we were on a mission to get to the pub in record-breaking time. Vicky took it upon herself to drive the Volkswagen because she says it reminded her of the canary yellow car in the popular kiddies television programme: 'Magic Roundabout'.

'I hope you are not going to take me to the Queens in a Winton Garage courtesy car, Raman; what will the regulars in the pub think?' Barbara said to His Royal Pushiness with her hands firmly resting on her hips. 'It is a far cry from a brand new 318ci E46 British Racing Green BMW, isn't it?' she added.

'Well, if you want to arrive at the Queens in a car that looks like "Thomas the Tank Engine" Barbara that will be fine by me.' Raman said, knowing he was going to save a few quid on petrol.

It was just after midday when we walked in through the door into the lounge bar, and the first person we were to bump into was Denzel Crow.

'Have you fallen over any foreign bodies today, Denzel?' I asked, looking over towards the bar to see Raman deliberately stalling at the back of a queue.

'No, I can't say that I have my dear friend.' Denzel replied, clutching a pint pot with hands that look similar to his mechanical digger.

'Well, just hang around at three o'clock this afternoon because there is a possibility you might.'

Standing at the bar, alongside Frederick and Simon Bennett, was Doctor Hadrian Watson, a local General Practitioner based in Boscombe.

'What do you recommend for elephant's foot?' Raman asked, seizing the opportunity to give the baggage handlers at Heathrow more credence to go out on strike.

'Extremely large shoes, Mr Patel.' Dr Watson advised as the glass mirror behind the bar became splattered with salted peanuts.

'Oh, I never thought of that,' Raman replied, giving Watson the impression he was quite serious. 'Do they have jingle bells around the ankles as well?' he added.

'If you want.' Watson quickly suggested.

'Elementary, my dear Watson, nice one,' I said to Hadrian, sounding like a modern day Sherlock Holmes as Raman departed solemnly from the bar holding a tray of drinks.

'There's no need to thank me, Chris,' Dr Watson replied. 'after all, I am only doing my job.'

'Are you going to stand up here all afternoon, Simon, or are you going to sit down with me in the corner?' Victoria said giving people the impression her boyfriend was rapidly going off her for some inexplicable reason.

'Yes, in a minute, Vicky, I just want to know who's running in the three-thirty at Bath.'

'Hopefully, a horse, Simon and not Raman Patel.' she replied. 'And, I hope mummy will be arriving shortly because I'm bloody starving, Simon, and I bet that toilet paper can't wait to jump out of the fridge.'

'But, I thought you and your mum usually have the chicken in a basket; I suppose now you will be having the hot Madras curry, Vicky,' Simon asked with caution. 'Rumour has it that Mahatma Ghandi called into the Queens once for a Chicken Tikka Masala and hasn't been seen since.' he explained.

'But, Mahatma Ghandi is dead.' Vicky quickly put in.

'Well, that will explain everything then.' Simon confidently replied.

On Vicky's return to the table she asked Barbara what her preference for lunch was to be; to which she replied:

'I think I will have the Ploughman's lunch on a wooden board,' reading from the menu, 'they have Melton Mowbray Pork Pie, Cheddar Cheese, salad and an assortment of pickles; all served with freshly baked crusty bread.'

'And what are you going to have, Raman?' Barbara asked, knowing he wasn't going to change his culinary preferences.

'I think I much prefer to have the hot beef Madras curry with *Pilau Rice*.' Raman emphasized having transferred the print from the menu into his brain at least twice.

I, meanwhile, had already decided to have the steak and kidney pudding, chips and mushy peas served with the pub's delicious onion gravy.

At this point, Lynette walked into the lounge clutching a bunch of P&O and Brittany Ferries travel brochures and this was when I knew the topic of conversation for most of the afternoon would be about sailing the high seas to that green and pleasant land they call France.

Simon, after selecting his favourite horse, 'Bombay Safire' to win the three-thirty at Bath, came over to the table to plonk himself down next to Vicky and Barbara.

'I think I will be on the safe side today and have the steak and kidney pie and chips,' Simon said to Vicky after he had put up with her talking about Umberto Zaveroni, Bournemouth's number one Italian fish and chip shop gigolo.

'I see you have had a couple of Jack Daniels already, Chris,' Lynette said after she had so cleverly pointed to two small engraved glasses on the table.

'And what would you like for your lunch, Lynette; roast iguana, a hot rattlesnake sandwich or the buffalo grill?'

'What is a buffalo grill?' Lynette asked perusing through the menu in an attempt to find a platter of dismembered frogs cut off from the waist.

'A Buffalo Grill, my dear is a cow, and after removing its horns, one dusts it down and rotates it on top of a fire.'

'Excuse me, Mr Travis,' Raman said, leaning forward next to Lynette, to give me a lecture in Infallible Justice. 'in India the cow is a sacred animal and is not for eating.'

'Well, how come, you are just about to order the hot beef Madras curry; double-standards if you ask me, however, my sacred cow, Raman, has just turned up.'

'I can always have the basket thing, Mr Travis.' Raman said, in a failed attempt to curry favour.

'You will know all about those, won't you Raman?'

'All about what?' he replied, trying to give me the impression he had no idea what I was talking about.

'Come on, Raman, you are renowned International Master Chef and a Citizen of the World and you should know what the definition of a basket is.'

'I know the definition of a barstool,' Raman was quick to retaliate. 'but, that doesn't necessarily mean that I have sat on one.'

'Why don't you call me Christopher, Raman,' I said to Patel after he had imparted his wisdom in my direction on more than one occasion that afternoon; I had the idea that the sudden change to over-familiarity wouldn't last for long. 'Would you like a pork scratching, Raman?' I said when my generosity began to run away with me.

'Thank you, Chris, I would love one of those; they go down very well with a pint of '*Shepherd Neame Spitfire Premium Ale*'.'

'What can I say but, chocks away, Raman.' I said, lifting my barrel glass to toast the latest addition to his dossier of double-standard achievements.

'You know, Chris, it's your bloody foreigners who are spoiling this country at the moment; you have only got to look outside the bloody window.' Raman pointed out to me with a sense of pride and half expecting him to break out into song, singing: "Rule Britannia".

Effie Winters, the pub waitress appeared ready to take our order.

'Can I do you now, sir?' Effie said as she nudged her way alongside the narrow gap at the end of the table.

'I just knew that was coming.' Lynette said, prodding me in the ribs with her elbow. 'Does she never let up?' she added.

'Well, you know what she's like, Lynette; she is anyone's for a sherbet dip.' I replied, whispering and covering up my mouth at the same time.

'She should be so lucky; I haven't had a sherbet dip since our wedding night.' Lynette said, speaking from the side of her mouth reminding me of one of the happier times in my life. 'But that was when you were flavour of the month.' she added.

'Will you be staying here for long dear?' I asked before giving the wrong impression that we were a happily married couple with two lovely daughters.

'Anyone would think you don't want me here, Chris, I can take a hint,' Lynette replied as she witnessed the hem of Effie's skirt gliding over the top of the table, in time to the American country singer, Patti Page, singing: "Tennessee Waltz".

'And, I didn't hear what you are going to have for your lunch, Lynette?'

'Oh, I think I'll just have the 'Hot Rattlesnake Sandwich' if you don't mind, Chris, it will make a change from 'Toad in the bloody Hole'; microscopic Cumberland sausage concealed in batter.'

After Patti Page had prematurely finished her song because of someone putting his foot through the juke box and Effie had stopped making a draught I proceeded to order the food, beginning with Lynette's culinary preference; steak and ale pie, mash potatoes, garden peas and gravy.

Effie went away satisfied she had taken the order for our food without having to suffer an ear-bashing from Lynette. However, it transcribed that our over-friendly waitress from the depths of the New Forest had given up her job two weeks later after being given a black eye by Christine Crow when she caught Denzel having extra maritals in the back of his Landover.

Little did I know, it would be several weeks later I was to discover that Lynette was partially responsible for the demise of Effie Winters. Lynette, apparently, had joined forces with Doreen Stables, the landlady of the Queens Pub and Restaurant, and together with Councillor Frederick Bennett they successfully got rid of a roving embarrassment that would be more suitable stretched out and filling in the personal columns of the 'Daily Sport' newspaper.

Meanwhile, Ralph MacTell, my recently acquired man servant brought another round of drinks over to the table.

'Do I not get any change, Raman?' I asked after parting with another twenty pound note.

'But, of course, Chris, unquestionably.' he replied, looking down towards the deep lined pockets inside his trousers.

'What's that noise I can hear, Raman? And, I thought I told you my Christian name was Christopher.'

'No need to worry, Chris, it is only my loose change rattling inside my sporran.'

'It didn't sound like your loose change to me, Raman, and even if it was, it's my loose change, if you don't mind.'

'Such complication, such complication, indubitably.' Raman sufficiently emphasized to convince me not.

This was when Vicky said to us all, I know a good joke to tell you all:

'An Indian illegal immigrant was seen rowing in Shotley Marina, off the coast of Suffolk. He was spotted by the captain of a Royal Navy mine sweeper, who immediately asked him where he was going.

'Is this the shores of Bradford?' the Indian asked.

'No, it is the Ganges.' The captain bellowed out to him from his megaphone.

'My goodness me,' the Indian replied. 'I must have been going around in circles for months.'

'I don't think that was very funny,' Raman said to Vicky, horrified with her sense of humour; 'the joke was totally uncalled for, unquestionably.' he added.

'Well, I'm only trying to liven up the place; there was more life in the rue morgue when Barbara and I went to Paris.' Vicky replied.

'We all seem to be going around in circles these days and losing our sense of direction.' Barbara put in, as if the end of the world was nigh.

'And does that include falling off washing lines into compost heaps, Barbara,' I couldn't help but mention. 'Perhaps, this evening, you could attach yourself to the whirligig and be projected over to the Isle of Wight.' I added

'One has to look at things laterally these days and deal with situations all on one level.' Simon said, giving me a lesson in Japanese working practices.

'What the hell are you talking about, Simon?' I replied before giving him a descriptive answer to his statement. 'Does that mean when one goes to the toilet things begin to go sideways instead of straight down the middle?'

'I wouldn't go as far as to say that, Mr Travis,' Simon said, continuing to talk in his Bournemouth upper middle-class civil service accent. 'And, do you mind, Mr Travis, you are beginning to get my gander up, my steak and kidney pie is just about to arrive at the table.' he added.

'Please call me, Chris, Simon, everyone else seems to be doing so around here, and if I'm going to be a candidate for Bournemouth Borough Council, it is the least I can offer.' I emphasized.

'Oh, by the way,' Lynette said to me looking down at her shopping bag on the floor. 'we have an appointment at three-thirty to see one of the travel agents of Thomas Cook in Boscombe; I don't want you going into their offices smelling of alcohol, Chris, do you understand?'

'Loud and clear, my dear; loud and clear and here's me thinking I was going to watch a good game of football; Bournemouth are playing Sheffield Wednesday.'

'You, Chris, you are just one lazy idle git!'

Chapter Fifteen

Thomas Cook Travel Agents, Christchurch Road, Boscombe, Bournemouth

'Is this the place you keep threatening to visit every time you want to leave me, Lynette? I can just imagine you turning into another Shirley Valentine; Lynette Valentine, it has a certain ring to it, hasn't it?'

'Just shut up, Christopher, and adjust your King's College Oxford tie, the Windsor knot has somehow managed to disappear down inside the front of your shirt; you are getting to look like a real scruffy bugger and I don't want the manageress to get the wrong impression.'

'I didn't realize we were going to a banquet this afternoon, otherwise I would have worn my red silk cummerbund, tuxedo and a bow tie.'

'Listen, Chris, you either want to join me inside the travel agents or you don't; we may be in France the week after next and that will be exciting, won't it?'

'That's what the Germans said in nineteen-forty, just before they goose-stepped into Paris.' I told her as we entered into an office of mass migration and deportation.

'Will you stop going on about the bloody war, you are beginning to give me a headache,' Lynette emphasised in no uncertain terms. 'I wouldn't mind, Chris, but you weren't old enough to be in the bleeding war, and you were lucky to be of an age not to be called up for National Service too.' she added.

'And if it wasn't for bad luck, I wouldn't have any good luck at all; had I been old enough to have been called up for National Service, I would have been in an exempt occupation, namely, a University lecturer and that, as you know very well, Lynette means being clever and not having to go down the coal mines because of one's conscientious beliefs.'

'Beliefs, beliefs, the only belief you are concerned about is the next visit to the Queens.' Lynette so kindly said before reminding me it was time for me to take another Polo Mint to take the alcohol away from my breath.

'Haven't you got any work to do, this afternoon, Lynette?'

'I have taken a sabbatical this afternoon; time off,' she gratefully replied. 'Audrey is looking after the shop and will close at six-thirty after the last customer has managed to walk out of the shop without becoming stuck half-way through the front door.'

From where we were sitting in Thomas Cook, I could see Audrey Wright in the street polishing the window of Lynette's shop giving me the impression the boutique wasn't busy; the precinct was quiet for a Saturday afternoon, strange but, maybe not so strange because AFC Bournemouth were playing Sheffield Wednesday in the third round of the Premier League at Bournemouth's Goldsands Stadium.

'Tell me Chris, why do they call a football club Sheffield Wednesday?'

'It is because, if it was Tuesday and the manager said it was Wednesday, it is Tuesday.' I replied feeling pleased with myself when I agreed to give her the wrong answer.

'But, they play football on a Saturday.' Lynette so kindly reminded me.

'Oh, I thought it was Friday,' I quickly put in. 'How forgetful of me for not noticing.'

'Do come into my office, Mr and Mrs Travis,' the manageress, Patricia Whitaker, said to Lynette and me as soon as we had taken five minutes to wander around the world gazing at the posters depicting the famous, Taj Mahal in Agra, Uttar Pradesh, India, the Empire State Building in New York and a picture of the Eifel Tower in Paris taken just before the outbreak of The Second World War.

'Please take a seat; I will be with you in just a few moments.' Patricia added, before going back into the main office to obtain more reams of recycled paper which had previously been manufactured from wood stripped from the trees of the Amazonian rain forests of South America.

'That looks nice,' I said to Lynette, looking up towards another poster. 'I have always wanted to go to the Seychelles and laze underneath a palm tree on a sun-kissed stretch of beach waiting for a *peno colada* to arrive.' I continued to say to Lynette, sitting by my side in front of a desk complete with a monitor to show me just where I was supposed to be going.

'You can do that at home, Chris when you stretch out on the sofa dreaming of far distant places with strange sounding names,' Lynette geographically explained. 'Mind you it may not be a bad thing after all, if you were to be hit on the head by a coconut and you were not able to board the next *peno colada*.' she added with a girlish giggle.

'I suppose you think that was very funny, Lynette?' I said, glancing at the clock on the wall. 'Things do seem to be going by very quickly this afternoon, Lynette; where is this manageress? It's a good thing there isn't a war on because no one would be able to buy a ticket to get away, and at the speed she is working, it will be nearly time to go back to the pub for happy hour.'

'You know, Chris, you really are the pits, you really are, and what is that white thing you keep swirling round in your mouth?' she added.

'It's a Polo Mint, Lynette; you know the mint with a hole.'

'Oh, thank God for that; for one moment I thought you were turning into a Black & White Minstrel.'

'I can see Messrs Thomas Cook is short-staffed this afternoon and the manageress has to deal with at least three people all at the same time.' I said to Lynette as I looked through into what seemed to be an extremely busy outer office.

'Well, the travel business usually gets busy at this time of the year,' she replied making excuses for Mrs Whitaker's absence. 'We are coming up to Easter and the Spring Bank holiday and this is when people pack a small bag and get away.'

'I was led to believe, don't leave the pub until after the tide has gone out.' I said with a view to my getting away from the travel agents as soon as possible.

'That's what drunkards used to say in the eighteenth century when they were three sheets to the wind and press-ganged into joining the Royal Navy.' Lynette smugly replied.

'How much stuff are you thinking of taking to Paris, Lynette? I don't want to go down with another hernia similar to the one I had when we were on our honeymoon in Torquay.'

'You would insist on buying three pieces of luggage, designed especially to snugly fit one inside the other.' she said, reminding me again I should be making inroads to clear the rubbish away from the back of the garage.

'Yes, but how was I to know I would end up humping two of them like a bloody pack-horse, and then there was you prancing down Bournemouth's platform 'B' wearing a pair of high-heeled shoes and carrying a stupid red wet-look vanity case. I can also remember saying to a merchant seaman who was carrying a more user-friendly bag on his shoulder that he had missed the boat because it had sailed from Southampton to the Ascension Island at midday.

'Those were the days; those were the days.' Lynette said, nodding her head like a deranged donkey, determined to wind me up even further.

I looked up to see yet another framed poster advertising holidays to Ceylon. In the picture there was a woman wearing a rather provocative dress and what looked to me like diamond studded safety pins protruding through her nose and midriff.

'Don't be taken in by the sari,' Lynette said, quickly putting my eyeballs back into their original position. 'Some of them are belly dancers in their spare time, but then the odd one can be seen on BBC1 making *chapattis*.' she added.

'The lady in the picture has something in her mouth as well.' I said, still mesmerized by her extraordinary beauty in this colourful and breathtaking print.

'Perhaps it's another one of your Polo Mints.' Lynette sarcastically put in.

Patricia Whittaker came back into her office carrying the same Brittany Ferries brochures that Lynette had been given earlier that day.

'We do seem to have a great deal of superfluous paperwork around here, don't we, Lynette, how many times are you planning on going to France?'

Lynette and I decided it was time for us to leave having wasted the best part of an afternoon waiting for a service that was apparently non-existent; we would have been far better sitting outside Bournemouth's Arts Festival by the Sea drooling over copies of Andy Warhol's famous surrealistic picture of an empty can of Coca Cola, and Salvador Dali's most famous work of art, depicting an African lady eating a Cadbury's Flake; both of which were gazed upon by Frans Hals's famous portrait of the "Laughing Cavalier".

'He who fights and runs away, lives to fight another day.' I said to Lynette after she had finished talking to Mrs Whittaker about her precious time schedule and that we would be calling in first thing on Monday morning just before the rush begins.

'Will you need any more brochures?' Mrs Whittaker asked, occasionally glancing into the outer office to see if there was anyone else she could pile her rubbish on to.

'I think we have enough reading material here, Mrs Whitaker, to keep us occupied for the next six months.' I said, without giving her the impression I had recently found a row of garbage bins at the back of Sainsbury's supermarket.

A lady with a bronzed complexion was looking at a poster of the cruise liner, the 'Ocean Princess', pulling away from the quayside in Tenerife. I asked her, if it was her first cruise? To which she replied that it was her twenty-second. I then asked: 'Did you sail with Captain Cook?' 'No, Thomas Cook.' she replied with seriousness combined with absolute naivety.

On our way out of the office Patricia Whittaker said her goodbyes and hoped that we would have a pleasant weekend soaking up the sun in sunny Bournemouth and hoping we would throw ourselves off from the top of Branksome Cliffs or Hengitsbury Head.

It was just after five when we arrived back inside the pub to begin the happy hour which was between the hours of five o'clock and seven. Amazingly, everyone, with the exception of Denzel Crow, who had positioned himself by the darts scoreboard were in the same places we had left them earlier, and it was as if, Lynette and I, hadn't been away at all.

Effie Winters made an appearance, having changed from her waitressing gear into something more adventurous, namely a pink Lycra micro dress, fishnet stockings and red patent-leather stiletto shoes to begin the afternoon's late entertainment programme.

'Would you like to join us in the pub quiz?' she asked, giving me a wink and a smile. 'There is a crate of Taunton's Best Cider for the winner.' she added.

'Well, that's provided Denzel Crow hasn't drunk it all,' I said to her putting my hand on her leg to feel something that felt like an expanse of elastic. 'And, if he carries on shouting one hundred and eighty, I will personally position him directly in the firing line in front of a set of darts.'

'It stops him from getting into mischief and falling down into holes, Chris.' she replied.

Percy Stables, the landlord of the Queens was ready to fire the twenty general knowledge questions in the direction of the thick as a plank local intelligentsia, most of whom were either standing or sitting around the bar like lambs to the slaughter; 'Let the battle commence.'

'Question number one.' following a loud cough from Percy into the microphone was: 'What did the Montgolfier brothers invent?'

Vicky reached over to me and whispered: 'Bournemouth's highest attraction; the hot-air balloon.'

'Don't be so silly, Vicky, it is the Crazy Golf Course in Lower Gardens.' I said to her so confidently.

'Okay, dad, you are so knowledgeable you are going to end up dying of thirst.'

Question number nineteen was more appropriate to Raman's culture when Percy asked: 'For which country does Sachin Tendulkar play cricket?' Raman's winning answer was, India.

And, the last question was: 'What is the maximum number of clubs a golfer is allowed in his or her bag for a round of golf?' the answer was given as fourteen.

It was after I realized my biro had run out of ink and I had omitted a four, Raman reached over to shake my hand and said:

'Hard luck, old chap, better luck next time.

Chapter Sixteen

My 52nd birthday – Saturday 8th April 2000

Saturday began with the usual ritual of sitting around the breakfast table joining in with the exchanges of rhetorical slanging matches which Vicky seemed to enjoy tremendously when she said: 'If you can't stand the heat you stay away from the bloody kitchen.' However, I try to avoid going into the kitchen because that could mean Lynette could transform her loving husband into a human dishwasher or similar to the launderette supervisor Dot Cotton in the intolerable television soap opera "East Enders". It may be interesting to note that after I had purposely gone berserk with a pair of garden shears and cut down a perfectly good laburnum bush when I was attacked by Hannibal for disturbing his toilet, I was banned from working in the garden indefinitely by Lynette when the cat became the recipient of a size eight and a half-inch Wellington boot.

'Would you like more coffee, my dear.' Lynette asked, reminding me it was my birthday and giving the impression it could be my Last Supper consisting of Kenco coffee and a bowl of Kellogg's Rice Krispies. 'Here you are, Chris, it is your birthday card, I designed it myself and it is especially for you, hopefully there will be another one for you next year.' she added, raising her eyebrows.

'Well, I can't see anyone else in here with the same birthday as me, can you Lynette? The card must be quite unique and exclusive to me.' I said, opening the top of the envelope with a table knife.

'It has taken mummy a long time to design your birthday card on the desktop and you should be more appreciative, dad.' Barbara said, snatching the envelope away from my hands in order to remove some of the marmalade oozing out from the top.

Having received several important documents that morning, this one really made my day when Lynette had pasted a banana with two black eyes and a pair of spectacles on the front cover of the card and printed on the top were the words: 'Stay away from Sainsbury's today.'

I had already decided I was going to go to the pub before the show was about to begin and that would give me the opportunity to avoid Ralph MacTell for a while before he gets the chance to bestow more additives to my given name.

'At what time is Raman due to arrive this afternoon?' I asked Barbara, pre-empting my essential getaway from the house.

'Around three o'clock.' Barbara replied. 'Raman has a special present for your birthday; he says it will keep you occupied for a long time.'

Little did I know that it was going to be a small green box, similar to 'After Eight Mints', containing cards in an after-dinner quiz called: 'Trivia Shit'. Here was I thinking he was going to present me with a trolley, half a dozen balls and a bag containing a set of fourteen golf clubs; some people may say I'm off my trolley, having to put up with all of this shit.

'And at what time is his Lordship Simon Bennett due to arrive, Victoria?' I asked her, not wanting to interfere with his gander in any way.

'At the same time as Raman,' Vicky said, unenthusiastically. 'He comes and goes these days. I'm beginning to think he's gay.' she added.

'Well, if he comes and goes, Vicky, how can he be gay?' I applied with caution.

'It's not what you're thinking, dad,' she so blatantly remarked. 'Simon just breathes heavy, turns up and then pisses off whenever he feels like it these days and I don't have to remind you I belong to the twenty-first century.'

'Have you renewed your membership card, Vicky?' I jokingly asked. 'And why, do you still go out with him?'

'The first thing we have to do, dad, is to secure you a seat on the council, and secondly, without Simon knowing, I will keep on buying the best fish and chips in Bournemouth.

Hannibal, who was sitting inside his basket listening to all of this stuff reminded me of a poem which had been delivered that morning inside a birthday card. The verse penned by our family friend who lives in Folkestone, Kent went something like this:

Pussy Cat

"Pussy cat Pussy cat where have you been?"

'I have been to London to see the Queen'
'And what did you do when you were there?'
'I saw Tony Blair underneath a chair'
'And what did you do when you got back?'
'I had a word with Jacques Chirac'
He said 'did you really have to bow?'
I said 'no, just miaou..."'

Patrick Marshall, the postman, arrived that morning knocking melodiously on the door giving me the impression he may have doubled up at the weekends as a percussion instrumentalist with the Bournemouth Philharmonic Orchestra. 'Post-it-Pat' Patrick handed over my birthday cards with great reverence as if he had been specially assigned by the Post Office to deliver the mail by him. He then asked me to sign for a registered letter which had the City of London stamped all over it. Having dismissed the idea it was a telegram from the Queen I saw printed on the back of the envelope that it was from Stanley Gibbons Stamp Auctioneers & Valuers, 399, The Strand, Covent Garden, London.

I was in no hurry to open the letter as Lynette would have taken umbrage if I was to do so in her absence.

There was a multitude of birthday cards, most of which were due to my advertising in 'The Times' newspaper and the local press. A special card which was sent to me by one of the old boys from my Oxford University days, Robert Bingham wrote the words:

"Happy Birthday to you,
Squashed tomatoes and stew
Bread and butter in the gutter
Happy Birthday to you"

'Well, thank you very much for that, Robert; that verse was fit to line the underpants of an incontinent monkey.' I thought.

Robert used to say he was related to 'lucky' Lord Lucan, the aristocrat who managed to disappear and has never been seen since. I thought this could have been a load of eyewash fabricated by Robert because of his passion for gambling, but, this was until I read an article in *The Sunday Times* supplement giving Lucan an entirely different name, which was: John Bingham. However, over the years, several sightings have been reported, especially on Saturday evenings when Percy, the landlord of the Queens, rings a bell and calls: 'time ladies and gentlemen please.'

'Did you receive our cards, dad?' Vicky asked as I sat down next to Lynette to begin opening the remainder of the mail.

'No, I haven't.' I replied, knowing they were about to be presented to me at any second by Barbara.

'That is because we haven't given them to you yet.' Vicky added, looking around to see where Barbara had gone.

'Well, I wish you would both hurry up, the suspense is killing me.'

Barbara came down from her bedroom waving two large envelopes in her hand; one from Victoria and the other from herself. They instantaneously broke out into song by singing "Happy Birthday" after Stevie Wonder had joined in noisily with a harmonica when I pressed around the hole in his belly button.

I thought this wasn't going to be my lucky day until, with Lynette anxiously watching me, I opened the important looking envelope from Stanley Gibbons. The letter contained details of the sale of the stamps which had realized for one point three million pounds and that it was vital we attend a meeting at their offices in The Strand, London to collect the cheque for one million, one hundred and five thousand pounds and to witness the auction fees being handed over to the representatives of the two companies, Stanley Gibbons and Jarvis & Hayes, philatelic postage stamp dealers, who were involved in the sale.

'You seem to be in a very happy mood, dad,' Vicky said when I happily clenched my fists and banged them down on the table to allow a Sainsbury's pork and beef sausage to jump from my breakfast plate on to Lynette's lap. 'You are acting like a cat that has just got the cream.'

'Yes, Vicky, I have just received an apologetic letter from Southern Water board offering me the chance to pay our bills by standing order.'

The letter from the water board seemed totally insignificant to the correspondence I had just received from Stanley Gibbons asking me to visit their offices at eleven on Tuesday morning. There was no doubt in my mind Frederick Bennett had been busy-bodying around the annals of Southern Water Board and eventually I would somehow have to pay him back; Scratch Balls, a common Rumanian monkey-see monkey-do euphemism, meaning: if you scratch my back, I will scratch yours, which would I have no doubt been lurking at the back of his mind; what a person's vernacular region has in common with one's torso, is way beyond me.

'When we're in London we will be able to go and see the stage production of *"The Mouse trap"*' Lynette said, enthusiastically. 'Saint Martin's theatre is only five minutes away from The Strand, and before we go and see the afternoon show, we can have lunch in the Savoy.' she added.

'Come on Lynette, we are not exactly made of money.' I pointed out when I gave Sidney Martindale my last one pound coin to pay for my Littlewoods football coupon. 'I know of a delightful pub, called, 'The Lord Moon of the Mall' and it's just around the corner from Trafalgar Square.'

'Oh, we're back to fish and chips again, are we?' she said, folding her arms and looking nonchalantly around the room.

'Certainly not, Lynette, they do a good steak and kidney pudding with mash potato, mushy peas and a small jug of delicious gravy, or if you want, you can have a beefburger with French fries.' I replied, trying to get her taste buds going by introducing her to some really decent food.

'That's it, I'm going back into the kitchen to knock-up something for your birthday party this afternoon and don't expect anything special because we've run out of chips.'

'No worries, I can solve that problem, I will nip along to Sainsbury's before I go to the pub.' I jokingly said.

'Don't even think about it, Chris, I want you in one piece when we go up to London next Tuesday.'

I can remember a faint knock on the door when Maria Strauss von Strudel, as I prefer to call her, delivered my birthday cake from her family

141

concern, the Austrian Patisserie in Boscombe.

'Good morning, Frau Strauss, we have got a state of the art bell attached to the door, you know.' I said, pointing to a light which had obviously gone out.

'It does help to put the batteries in correctly, Chris,' Lynette interrupted. 'When I ask you to replace one my dear, I don't mean you should put it in upside down!'

I made it quite clear to her that I am still a lecturer at the University, and not a bloody electronics expert.

'We have got a tradesman's entrance you know.' I said to Lynette, reminding her where the kitchen is situated in relation to the side door.

'I just wanted the neighbours to know how old you are, Chris, when they saw a huge birthday cake together with fifty-two candles and a rocket contained in a box being delivered to our front door and take your time when you blow them out, my dearest, because I don't want you to have a heart attack, well not until Wednesday anyway.'

'Well, that's nice, isn't it, Lynette, and just you wait until it's your fifty-second birthday, I may just tie you on to the back of a rocket.'

We said our goodbyes to Maria after she had positioned my birthday cake on top of the tumble dryer which had recently developed a vibration when it was switched on. I was singing to the "Sound of Music" when I watched Maria Strauss von Strudel, disappearing down the drive to go back to the 'Eagles Lair' in sunny Boscombe.

'I shall now attempt to start the baking; mini sausage rolls, *Quiche Lorraine*, individual apple pies and pizzas.' Lynette said with extreme furtiveness as she walked into the kitchen through the lounge.

A few moments later, Lynette screamed and called out from the kitchen: 'Oh, no, bloody hell, Chris; your birthday cake is splattered all over my recently cleaned floor.'

'Sod your clean floor, Lynette, what about my birthday cake.' I said, disgusted at her disgraceful and insufferable manner. 'There's no need to cry over spilt milk, Lynette,' I said, picking pieces of cake up from the floor in order to reshape it and place it back inside the box. 'No worries, I said to her adding to my ongoing benevolence. 'Raman will eat it and he can even take some home to his friend, Lino, he is good at eating things from the floor.'

'What are you giving Dad for his birthday, mummy?' Barbara asked.

'I'm taking him up to London on Tuesday on the train; we're going to take in a show.'

'Do you know, Lynette, apart from my much treasured Andy Stuart record which your mother sat on one New Year's Eve after listening to him singing: "When Donald drops his trousers", it is the best birthday present you have given me.'

'You are taking the proverbial urine again, Chris, just watch it because your birthday may just turn out to be your last one.' Lynette, so lovingly said to me.

'Everyone seems to think that 'Billy Elliot' is a good production in the West End,' Vicky said, as if she knew what I was going to say next. 'It's about...'

'There's no need to explain, Vicky, I do know what it's about, and we are not going to sit for two hours and watch a canny lad from the North East of England turn himself into a ballerina.'

'Well, you can always go to St Martin's Theatre in West Street, Soho and see 'The Mousetrap', 'Vicky then suggested. 'The stage production has been running for at least four hundred and fifty years, I think William Shakespeare had something to do with it?' she added.

'It was Agatha Christie who wrote the play, "*The Mousetrap*" and not William Shakespeare.' I insisted on telling her.

'Oh, dad where is your sense of humour.' Vicky then said, raising her eyebrows at Barbara as if I was some kind of dumb cluck that didn't know the works of William Shakespeare.

'I can remember visiting the old theatre in Stratford upon Avon when I was a scholar at Salisbury Grammar School; William wasn't in at the time but I did manage to get his E-mail address and Fax number.'

'I know a good joke, dad,' Vicky was anxious to tell me. 'Did you hear about the guy who knocked on the Russian Embassy and asked if Len was in?'

'Did you know an Eskimo won the Eurovision Song Contest this year, dad?' Barbara asked when she began to lighten up for the first time that morning. 'And do you know what he sang?' she continued to ask.

'Probably, it was "Something Simple".' I said.

"No dad, it was "Baby its cold outside".

On my way up to the bathroom to throw up and find five minutes of much needed sanctuary I began to sing softly, Andy Stuart's song: "Donald where's your Trousers", in a language no one three hundred and fifty miles north from Bournemouth could understand.'

> "Let the wind blow high let the wind blow low
> Up the street in ma kilt I'll go
> All the lassies will shout hello!
> When Donald drops his trousers"

On my return I felt so much lighter, knowing I had virtually read the print from the theatre and entertainment pages of *The Times* supplement.

'And, how do you propose to replace the birthday cake, dad.' Barbara asked, returning from the kitchen with bits of icing sugar surrounding her bright-red lipstick.

'All is not lost,' Lynette said, enthusiastically. 'I know a man who is the manager for Marks & Spencer in Bournemouth, I will phone him now and he may be able to help us.'

'Is this the same guy who worked for British Home Stores?' I asked, inquisitively.

'Yes, as a matter of fact, Isaac Green did work for British Home Stores, but that was a long time ago; elephants never forget do they, Chris.' she replied nervously.

'He gets about a bit, doesn't he, Lynette.'

'Tell me, dad,' Vicky asked,' how did you and mummy get on at the travel agents on Monday?'

'We leave for Paris on Good Friday, the twenty-first April and return Saturday the twenty-ninth, the following week.'

'Oh, that will be nice for you both,' Barbara enviously put in.' "April in Paris, Chestnuts in Blossom", and all that jazz.'

144

I wanted that day to be my best birthday ever because I could see in my mind's eye a brand new car standing resplendently in one of Bournemouth's show rooms waiting for me to test drive but, that was until I heard the sound of the front door bell ringing in my ears and the cuckoo in the Bavarian clock trying to annoy me at midday.

It was a man looking every inch like the American detective, Sam Spade, wearing a dark grey trench coat and a brown trilby hat, giving me the impression he had just visited the library because he was carrying a copy of the greatest story ever told.

'I am Jehovah's Witness,' he said, standing right in front of me with one foot resting firmly inside the door. 'I am here to save your soul.' he said, punching away at a bible which looked as if it had seen better days.

'You are not from Southport?' I asked nervously, knowing they had their headquarters next door to the Hotel Belvedere & Spa in Lords Street. I soon got shot of him after telling him I was a doctor, specializing in homeopathy and was used to seeing the sight of the odd blood transfusion in Sainsbury's.

'I'm off, down the pub, Lynette, and I will see you all around two.' I said to her with tongue in cheek knowing it would be sometime around three.

'Don't come home drunk Christopher, because if you do I won't speak to you ever again.' Lynette quietly pointed out.

'Is that a promise or a threat, Lynette?'

Chapter Seventeen

On entering the public lounge bar I became aware that the Queens Park Pub was becoming my second home because it seemed no time at all since I last visited the establishment which now resembled a waxwork museum; the regulars sitting in front of the bar like crows on a washing line waiting to bore the pants off me within the first few minutes of my arrival.

Sitting all alone in the far corner of the room was Jehovah Bill, the witness who had tried to save my soul without success earlier that morning. He was clutching what seemed to be a large glass of brandy, probably to calm his nerves after visiting a number of residences in Queens Park Avenue. I can recall an incident in the nineteen eighties when a multitude of skin-headed 'Bovver Boys' attacked a train load of bible punchers on Bournemouth Pier; the theory of safety in numbers collapsed when several Jehovah's Witnesses were seen jumping into the sea heading for the Isle of Wight.

The busty waitress, Effie Winters, made a special point of welcoming me that day because I had previously told her that on Saturday it was my birthday and I wanted it to be a special day to remember. Effie became highly noticeable when she appeared wearing next to nothing and then after she had tantalizingly licked the end of my nose with her tongue she continued to serve two generous portions of Steak and Ale pie to Christine and Denzel Crow who were sitting at a table in the centre of the room waiting impatiently for their huge meal to arrive.

'I will make it a special day for you to remember, Chris.' Effie said, licking the rouge coloured gloss of her lipstick in a way that could only be achieved by a woman enjoying the sufferings of a translucent clad nymphomaniac. Her tight black micro dress hugging her hour-glass figure left nothing to the imagination, and it was like the poem: "when it was up, it was up and when it was down it was down and when the dress was only half-way up it was neither up nor down".

I told her in no uncertain terms, that I am a happily married man with two lovely daughters and it would be folly to give all that up for a five minute quickie in the salubrious grounds of the pub car park.

'You don't know what you will have missed, Chris, until you have had the chance to go through it.' Effie said with an element of confusion which I am still trying to understand with the aid of a copy of the Kama Sutra. It was because I had left the Volkswagen at home and the thought of having it off inside a bright yellow Fiat Punto the size of a matchbox with extended sunroof and squeaky shock absorbers was enough to bring tears to a glass eye.

Percy and Doreen Stables were busy serving drinks behind the bar when I made an attempt to catch their attention to order a pint of best bitter and a whisky chaser.

Doctor Hadrian Watson was hovering next to the dartboard with a view to increasing his list of patients when he became concerned when the projectiles were not heading in the right direction.

Frederick Bennett and his son Simon were in evidence sitting in front of the bar laughing and joking together.

'Good afternoon, Christopher, and happy birthday.' Councillor Bennett said to me cautiously, giving me the impression he was going to come out with something sarcastic because of him not being invited to my party. 'It won't be long before you retire which is hard luck, Christopher, because I was thinking about putting your name forward as a candidate for Bournemouth Borough Council.' he added.

'Now, come on Frederick, I quickly replied. 'I am fifty-two today, not sixty-two, and as for not inviting you to the party, your name must have been overlooked when Lynette sent the invitation card to Simon.' I so cleverly put in.

'What time does the fun start, Christopher, because Bournemouth are playing Nottingham Forrest in the Premier League this afternoon and I don't want to miss the match?' Frederick was keen to tell me, knowing I would have loved to have been a spectator at the AFC Bournemouth Goldsands Stadium.

'Well, I will give you both a big piece of my birthday cake so you can both enjoy the culinary delights of the Austrian Tyrol together whilst celebrating your victory over Nottingham Forrest.

'That wouldn't be the scrapings from the kitchen floor by any chance, would it?' Simon said, turning his head away in embarrassment.

I explained to Simon, a replacement had arrived from Boscombe and that he had no need to worry about health and safety and then I immediately asked him how he got to know about the cake.

'Vicky told me on the mobile; she was laughing hysterically and said a replacement was going to arrive late this afternoon from Marks and Spencer.'

'You know, news travels like wild fire around here, and most of it starts from my own home.' I said to Simon beginning to play the whole thing down when I asked if they would like replenishment to their now empty glasses.

When Jehovah Bill made an attempt to leave the establishment I said to him, 'Have a nice day and don't forget to take your briefcase with you.'

'Arthur Withers, who by the way is a keen football fan, comes in here with his briefcase every Saturday afternoon.' Frederick informed me, lest I was somewhat confused about his vocation, Effie tells me his briefcase contains cheese and pickle sandwiches to eat at half-time at the stadium.'

It was then I told them one of my favourite jokes: 'A Liverpudlian security man at AFC Bournemouth football stadium asked a spectator what he had in his carrier bag because he said it was ticking. The man replied by saying: they are not chicken, they are turkey; they are my sandwiches for half-time.'

'I will tell that one to the mayor.' Councillor Bennett enthusiastically said, 'He likes jokes after telling me at the Christmas party about his wife's laughter lines. He said he wouldn't mind but she's not that funny.'

Denzel Crow having eaten his way through the steak and ale pie had somehow managed to extricate himself from the table to order two sticky puddings at the bar for him and his wife.

"Them bones, them bones; them dry bones".' I began to sing, winding Denzel up in my usual way after he had dug up half of Bournemouth that morning.

'Okay, you're the doctor of medieval studies and natural history and know a lot about artefacts of days of yore,' Denzel said to me as he waited for Doreen to give him his change. 'Tell me, Chris,' he continued, 'what do you make of this I found in a grave? I think it is one of those fossils from way back.' he was sure to tell me.

'I am sorry to disappoint you, Denzel, but it is a bit of tarmac from the road.' I was quick to point out when I saw the impregnation of a matchstick that looked like a bent tadpole buried in the middle.

It was when Denzel was walking back to his table looking rather disgruntled I felt something poking me in the centre of my back. I turned around to see Raman Patel standing there in his party gear looking every inch like Engelburt Humperdinck, wearing a dark blue velvet jacket, white trousers, black bow tie and a pair of patent leather shoes.

'I have come here especially to escort you home in the car.' Raman said, moving his head from side to side in a habitual way which seemed to be catching.

'I hope it isn't that awful courtesy car from Winton garage, Raman, because if it is I will surely walk home. And by the way, Raman, did you hear about the Indian lady who was dressed as Father Christmas? Someone asked her what was hanging down around her ankles. She replied by saying: 'they are "Jingle Bells".'

'And, did you hear about the guy who was so unlucky, Mister Travis, sorry, Chris?' Raman was so clever to ask me. 'He bought himself a box of 'After Eight Mints' and he died at half past seven.'

I said to myself, later that afternoon, he deserves to be deported for his insubordination but, seeing as he was born in Bradford to a Bengali mother and father who buggered off back to India after making a fortune selling shower caps and plastic curtains, this could prove to be a complete impossibility. I suppose, that's what happens when you stay clear of the Inland Revenue and make rupees, stashing pound notes underneath your mattress for a number of years hoping they will increase in value.

'I had the pleasure of having this year's, 318ci E46 BMW executive model returned to me this morning,' Raman said grinning like a Calcutta cat. 'It is in pristine condition and looks as though it has just left the car showroom.'

'Well, does this mean you will have to sell more golf balls to pay for the additional insurance premium?' I asked him with an air of sarcasm when I saw two of them bulging out from the front of his tight fitting trousers.

Pilot officer, Bill Cartwright, who was standing at the end of the bar, was allowing his eyes to be transfixed on the television; he was attentively watching the RAF's famous 'Red Arrows' aerobatic display team flying dangerously over Weymouth.

I gave him my rendition of the "Dam busters" theme tune and I could see he wasn't amused when he gradually lost interest in the television and turned around to face his Spitfire waiting to be taken-off from the beer mat on the bar.

'Would it be possible to give me a lift to Christopher's house, Raman?' Simon asked, wanting desperately to have a ride in his car.

'I'm not a bloody taxi driver, you know, Mister Bennett; I am a citizen of the world and a gentleman of historical refinement whose rather cramped circumstances, living in a two up and two down terrace house in Bradford compelled me to move in an entirely different direction.' Raman said with what seemed to be violins playing in the background.

Raman was giving me the impression he was going to drink orange juice that afternoon because of the police constantly patrolling the streets looking for drunken drivers who eventually lose their licences permitting them to drive. And if he were to be breathalysed, the strong smell of garlic from a plate of extremely hot Madras curry would certainly bang him up for years.

The smoky atmosphere was now beginning to get up my nose; the distinct aromatic smell of American black cherry tobacco emanating from a meerschaum pipe was permeating around the bar similar to a bonfire.

'Would you like a glass of brandy for your birthday, Christopher, before you leave?' Councillor Bennett asked, waving a twenty pound note high above his head with the aim of being attended to quicker than anyone else. 'And judging by the floorshow standing in front of me,' he continued, 'you most certainly will need it.'

'Well, in that case I will have a large one, Frederick.' I appreciatively said to him. 'And did you know,' I added, 'when the British Army was in India the Redcoats didn't shoot until they saw the white in their eyes.'

'What's that got to do with me offering you a brandy for your birthday, Christopher?' Bennett asked.

'It was Indian brandy that caused the mutiny in the first place.' I explained, giving him a history lesson which has long since been forgotten.

'Ah, get your drift, old boy; get your Rorke's Drift.' Councillor Bennett said, sounding as though he was about to give me a military history lesson about fuzzy-wuzzies, namely: the South African Zulu.

'Will you please stop this prejudice towards the African and Indian people; we are all God's children and not novelties, you know.' Raman said so righteously.

'Well, how come you worship Harry What's-his-name.'

'Harry Ramsden, I think he is called; he's got a fish and chip restaurant by the sea in Bournemouth.' Simon said, adding more fat to the chip pan fire.

'I think it is time we all go before the Queens Park Militia get here, namely, Lynette, to throw us out.' I suggested before Raman took it upon himself to begin charging us for the ride home and Michael Jackson stopped singing his song: "Happy Birthday" blaring out from the pub's jukebox.

Ralph MacTell, Simon Bennett and I arrived safely outside No 46. Queens Park Avenue much to the admiration coming from the neighbours not having seen a box of Black Magic on wheels before. There they were, standing at the door to my dwelling place, the Hutchinsons, Steven and Dorothy, looking as though they had just arranged to marry half the 'Gooks 'in Dorset; the Rodriguezs, Joseph and Grace, the nursing home proprietors accompanied by the glamorous Amanda Russell, the matron they use for window-dressing.

In my mind I was to charge my neighbours a hefty entrance fee to gain access into our house and then after they had all consumed great quantities of Lynette's curried to death deep fried samosas we were to put an 'Out of Order' sign on the bathroom door so they could go back home to their homes sooner than expected. It is not unusual to find that after a party the bathroom becomes a sanitary inspector's nightmare.

I had the presence of mind not to say, 'Just follow Ralph MacTell, he is familiar with the geography of the house and knows exactly where the tradesman's entrance is and don't block the drive on your way down because I need to park the car.' if I had not permitted them access via the front door.

Sitting in my favourite armchair was Professor Paul Stevens from Bournemouth University who was trying to figure out how a ship was put inside a bottle and how a cuckoo clock could possibly render one of our guests semi unconscious on his way in.

Victoria's Spanish friend, Senorita Margarita Santana, and my two teenage daughters were already helping themselves to a punch bowl containing a lethal concoction of sangria when Raman came over to give me my birthday present.

'It's a hat,' Raman said, 'you don't have to wear it or anything.' he added.

'Will you be staying long?' I said to him when he kissed Barbara passionately on the lips. 'I have some rat poison in the garden shed which could possibly pass for birthday cake.' I muttered to myself.

At that precise moment the door bell rang. It was Isaac Green, the manager from Marks & Spencer holding the biggest and most prestigious birthday cake I had ever seen complete with fifty-two candles just waiting to be lit. There was a gold motif in the centre divulging my age and another in blue saying: "Happy Birthday to Christopher" as if one had forgotten who the celebration was for.

'It's the guy from Pizza Pronto at the door, Lynette, you'd better see to it as you seem to know him already.'

'Come in, Is, and don't pay any attention to my husband, he is trying to give everyone the impression he is very happy.' she said, reminding me once again it was my birthday.

'Oh, it's *Is* now and not Isaac, is it?' I said to Lynette as I looked at a label dangling from the collar at the back of his brand-new black Barathea blazer. 'Are you is, or are you isn't?' I asked looking at a man who had obviously been put together inside a gentleman's fitting room in Marks & Spencer. 'I would suggest, Isaac, you use a pair of Lynette's dressmaking scissors before attempting to gain access to your sewn-up pockets.' I said, tempted to pull a length of white cotton which was coming away from the side of his trousers.

'Don't worry, Christopher,' Isaac said, putting my mind at rest when I thought he wasn't going to charge me for the cake.

'The bill for the birthday cake is already in the post and the candles will be extra.'

'That's really strange, Isaac,' I replied, inquisitively, 'because I thought the Post Offices in Bournemouth always closed at twelve-thirty on a Saturday.'

'Hi, Margarita,' I said to Senorita Santana, the young grease mama from '*Tao Pep pies*' restaurant in Old Christchurch Road. 'I see you have brought me a present.' I said as my eyes zoomed down on to a two-hundred millilitre bottle of BRUT aftershave lotion which was professionally wrapped in Superdrug paper. After I had inspected the contents of the box I kissed her in gratitude on her forehead to avoid being contaminated by the speckles of black mascara that had rained down from her eyelashes on to her Andalucía rosy cheeks. I truly thanked her for her generosity and said I would only use it on special occasions; freshening up the loo and the compost heap were just two of my ideas.

'BRUT makes you strut.' Margarita said, reminding me of the time when I used it regularly in my teens to attract the birds, but had to discontinue its use when a dog followed me all the way home from a cinema.

My birthday presents consisted of a Swatch wristwatch, an AFC Bournemouth football club sweater, a Parker pen, a box of fire-damaged handkerchiefs, a Braun battery shaver and a silly round the table after-dinner quiz purporting to be a box of 'After Eight Mints'; the latter, called 'Trivia Shit' became destined for the dustbin when I scored the least number of points against Raman that afternoon.

Victoria had taken it upon herself to be the resident disc jockey for the afternoon boring everyone to the point of collapse starting with: "The Spice Girls", "West Life" and an embarrassing Tom Jones singing "Sex Bomb".

The birthday cake was duly lit and steadily brought in by the man from Pizza Pronto and after I had pulled a length of white cotton dangling from the seat of his trousers, the gay Professor, Paul Stevens said: 'Oh, my God, this must be my lucky day'

Chapter Eighteen

It was Tuesday at long last. Our speaking alarm clock began its spiel by telling me it was six-thirty precisely, continually repeating: "Good Morning, Christopher, time to get out of bed, time to get out of bed, time to get out of bed..." until I silenced it by banging my fist down heavily on top of the snooze button in order to shut her up. The speaking clock voice was reminiscent of the time when I used to take the number ninety-one red bus to the London School of Economics in Houghton Street, Aldwych from Russell Square. I can recall it was an irritating woman sounding like the "Fawlty Towers" Re-mastered DVD presenter informing the passengers of the next stop and to stay clear of the door.

Lynette and I put our best foot forward out of the warm cosy bed to face the next couple of days in London; we hadn't moved so quickly since the fire bell sounded in the Oakdale Nursing Home next door and our garden became full of raving geriatrics.

Having packed our trolley bag the previous evening and made arrangements with matron next door to feed the cat; the only thing we had to do was to have breakfast and to make our way to Bournemouth railway station just a short distance away to catch the train leaving at eight minutes past ten. The two hours and thirteen minute journey to London Waterloo was destined to arrive at ten twenty-three which allowed us time to travel on the Underground to Covent Garden's Stanley Gibbon's offices in the Strand.

By using the Internet I had been able to select a hotel which I had used on so many occasions whilst I was doing my academic thing in London; the Royal National Hotel in Bedford Way, Bloomsbury, was to be our home for the next couple of days. One of the largest hotels in London, The Royal National, part of the Imperial group of hotels, is just a stone's throw away from Russell Square and boasts over fifteen hundred rooms. It has catering facilities for travellers from all over the world and specializes in different cuisines: Chinese, Indonesian, Malaysian, Indian, Italian and of course the typical British carvery, with daily choices of either roast beef and Yorkshire pudding, lamb or pork, always accompanied by a variety of vegetables and scrumptious gravy. They also have a traditional English pub on the way out from the hotel called the 'London Pub' where one can eat and drink at remarkably low prices.

My favourite chocolate bar dispenser on platform 'A' had recently been made redundant due to European health and safety regulations. I was pointed in the direction of the station buffet bar by a platform sweeper where I could buy the same product contained in a sealed wrapper, designed to protect it from serious contamination; amazingly, however, I discovered the chocolate bar had been considerably reduced in size and the price ridiculously inflated.

'At the end of the day, you will be able to buy as many chocolate bars as you like, Chris.' Lynette said giving me the impression she couldn't wait to get her claw-like hands on what turned out to be a Lloyds Bank Cox's & Kings banker's draft.

I had the presence of mind, appropriately, to buy Lynette a large box of 'Black Magic' chocolates to keep her quiet during our journey to London but then I decided against this because they brought back memories of when I was a child and my mother always gave me the hard caramels, nougat and butterscotch tablets from both layers which I wouldn't have given to a rabid dog.

It was halfway between Southampton and Eastleigh when I thought perhaps it hadn't been such a bad idea after all when she kept on talking about going to the theatre to see the *"The Mousetrap"* and how I could buy her a traditional box of milk chocolates from the kiosk. She suggested we could hire a pair of binoculars located in front of our seats to see the cast.

'Are you blind or something,' I said, 'I am not paying for your ophthalmic deficiencies and I don't need to remind you that I am employed by Bournemouth University and I don't own it.'

'You know those bananas they were selling in the buffet bar on Bournemouth station, Chris,' Lynette asked with a quirky smile. 'I could have bought you a couple and perhaps you could have turned into a monkey and leapt off the train.'

'Thank you, Lynette, you are so generous and when we're in London I may just introduce you to the front of a number ninety-one bus.'

'Would that be the number ninety-one bus to Crouch End?' Lynette confidently asked.

'How do you know that, Lynette?'

'Because one of my ex-boyfriends was a bouncer who stood in doorways of sleazy strip joints in Soho; Sinbad (Punch bag) Jaffrey, lived in Holborn for a while but that was until the police force became interested in his size ten and a half inch hobnail boots.'

'You mean to say he joined the police force and may still be hanging around?' I asked with caution.

'Got it in one, Chris.' she said, nodding her head similar to a seaside donkey. 'His patch may be right on our doorstep in Bloomsbury.' she added. 'And there's more, Chris, he is an Indian.'

'You are joking and cannot be serious, Lynette, and I need this like a hole in the head.'

Lynette began to laugh uncontrollably until another passenger who was sitting across from us took it upon herself to use a few choice words to tell her to shut up. Having relieved me of this task, the refined lady got up from her seat to sit down somewhere else where there was less interference.

'Yes, I was only joking, Chris, but you should have seen your face.'

'We have already got one comedienne in our family, namely, Victoria, Lynette; we have no room for another.' I said, as I snuggled down by the side of the window opposite to her to try and catch up on some sleep.

'Did, I tell you; Christopher, Victoria told me she wants to change her vocation into being a comedienne.'

'Not if I can help it, Lynette.' I emphatically pointed out to her. 'We have spent a great deal of money on her university education and for her to throw it all away on a whimsical stage-struck idea is ludicrous, if not outrageous.' I said before looking out through the window where I could see a cow in a field chewing cud; I was so tired I could have sworn it put two fingers up to me as the train raced along the track heading towards Winchester.

'She says she wants to team up with the guy from 'Something Fishy', the Italian fish and chip shop in Holdenhurst Road and call their act

'Vicky & Umberto'.' Lynette went on to tell me.

'You are joking with me again, aren't you? Lynette.'

'This time, no, Chris, Victoria and I are absolutely serious.'

'Bloody hell, just where are we going?' I said, trying for the umpteenth time to get some well deserved sleep.

I must have nodded off because I can recall sitting in the director's seat in front of the stage in the Bournemouth Pavilion, orchestrating the choreography at a rehearsal for Vicky & Umberto, the most famous man and wife comedy act in the country. I can also remember giving them a standing ovation at the end of their first night after they had both turned to face the Royal box to bow to Her Royal Highness Queen Elizabeth II and Prince Philip, Duke of Edinburgh.

'Would you like some fish and chips your majesty,' I asked, looking at a lady who had just been thoroughly entertained for over two and a half hours by my daughter and son-in-law, Umberto Zaveroni. 'Their family fish and chip shop 'Something Fishy' is only around the corner, maam; I could give you a lift in the Volkswagen.'

Meanwhile, standing at the door to the theatre was Lynette, wearing an usherette's uniform covered in chocolate ice cream and Sinbad (the sailor), Sergeant Sinbad (Punch bag) Jaffrey, the Indian policeman from High Holborn Police Station in London, showing their majesties to the door after visiting my talented Vicky and Umberto back stage.

During their act, Umberto said to Vicky: 'An Italian went to London for his holidays and when he was walking along the Mall he heard a rude noise, and standing by the side of a policeman he asked who that was? And the policeman said: 'oh, it was the Queen' and the Italian replied to him saying: 'Well, she blows a lovely trumpet.'

I woke up from the depths of sleep just before the train pulled into Woking, the last stop before we arrived at London's Waterloo Station. Lynette was occupied powdering her nose in preparation for the morning's events which had been organised by a Mr John Claridge of Stanley Gibbons Stamp Auctioneers and Valuers in the Strand. There had been arrangements made for representatives from Jarvis & Hayes, the stamp dealers in Bournemouth and an ancient relic from the British

Museum called, Mr Omar Temmam, an Egyptian gentleman who had removed his bandages especially for the photo call when the banker's draft was finally handed over to us. I was against the idea of having my photograph taken for everybody and his dog in London to scrutinise and to know that my bank account had just been enhanced by over a million quid, however, having seen the impressive picture taken by a photographer from the '*Evening Standard*', I quickly changed my mind because of his natural ability to portray a recently sculptured salt and pepper beard.

It was shortly after all the handshakes and pleasantries had been carried out by a number of obsessive philatelic people who were hell bent in displaying my collection of postage stamps behind a glass case in the British Museum, Lynette and I were asked by Mr Claridge, if we would like to have lunch with him that day.

'Where can we leave our trolley bag, Mr Claridge?' Lynette asked, as he flipped open his pocket watch to check on the hour and giving us the impression he wasn't interested in our left luggage.

'Oh, just throw it into the back of the Jaguar; you can retrieve it later at your hotel,' Mr Claridge suggested. 'And please, my name is John; it will be so embarrassing when we're inside the Savoy Hotel if you don't call me by my given name.'

'And please call me Doctor Travis, as it will be equally embarrassing for us all, if you don't use *my* given name.' I said to him knowing I now had enough money in my inside pocket to pay-off his mortgage on a two-bedroom apartment in Swiss Cottage.

Lynette clearly stated I had to behave myself and be pleasant in his company because if I showed any signs of sarcasm she would be on the next train back to Bournemouth.

'You will have to collect the trolley bag first, and if you are quick enough to retrieve it, perhaps John could drive you to the railway station.'

'You never let up, do you, Chris.' Lynette said, as we followed Claridge in through the front door of the hotel. 'You always have to have the last word.'

'And, by the way, Lynette, the train tickets are in the side pocket of the trolley bag.' I respectfully added.

The Savoy Grill is situated next to the piano lounge and American Bar where most of the tables are of the art deco period; booths, made from highly polished dark wood contrasting with chrome and silver hardware.

The lunch consisted of a starter; smoked salmon with roasted beetroot and vinaigrette dressing, the main course was a whole lemon sole with garlic and parsley butter, new potatoes and spinach and for desert; warm chocolate cake with white chocolate and strawberry ice cream. A generous serving of after-lunch drinks came in handy when Cointreau, Drambuie and Grand Marnier were brought to our table on a silver tray by the Portuguese waiter. I particularly wanted to know how much money to give our friendly waiter as a tip. John Claridge jokingly pointed out he used to leave a ten bob note and a guinea at Christmas, and when I said that we all went through a course of decimalization years ago, he said: 'Well in that case give him a tenner.'

I suppose, maybe I asked for that because he began to get bored with my company after telling him the only stamps I ever collected were Green Shield Stamps from my local garage. John gave Lynette and me a lift to The Royal National hotel, albeit dropping us off surreptitiously two miles away from the entrance to the forecourt and front door.

Lynette and I, after checking-in at the busy reception desk which seemed to be highly congested with foreign visitors, came to the conclusion they were from the uppermost regions of Outer Mongolia because of their winter attire.

The large double bedroom on the fourth floor was more than adequate to satisfy our requirements, but the tea and coffee facility left much to be desired with me having to purchase a packet of my favourite custard cream biscuits and a bottle of *Camp* coffee in *Gunga Din's* Indian souvenir emporium next door. We made a point of calling in to the booking office outside the hotel to arrange and pay for the tickets to see '*The Mousetrap*' that evening and to enquire into the possibility of having a refund on the proviso we don't fall asleep or be bored out of our minds. I also asked the friendly Frenchman, Patrice Beret who was kind enough to give Lynette one of his headache tablets: 'at what time does the performance begin?'

he replied, saying: 'at what time can you turn up?'

The London production of Agatha Christie's play, *'The Mousetrap'* was near to the end of its forty-seventh year, still maintaining "the atmosphere of shuddering suspense", according to one of *The Daily Express* reviews.

I said to Lynette, after the plot was finally uncovered: 'If I wanted to know who did it, I'd come back as a mind reader.'

Lynette was in the bathroom when I witnessed a couple having it off in one of the bedrooms directly across the quadrangle from our room. You would have thought they would have had the decency to close the curtains and to turn off the light before venturing down the road of extra marital bliss.

'Tell me, Chris, what is so interesting out there?' Lynette asked, sitting on the bed drying her hair with a hotel blow lamp. 'And what is that bulge I can see in your trousers?' she added.

'It's a large packet of Crawford's custard cream biscuits.' I replied, before going into the bathroom to cool down underneath a much-needed cold shower.

'You had better take more care where you put things, Christopher, because things have a tendency to melt.'

'Do they really, Lynette?'

'Where are we going to eat tonight, Chris? ignoring my facetiousness; 'I thought we might go for a meal in China Town which is near Leicester Square.' she asked, looking at a discarded copy of a *'Time Out'* magazine she had picked up in the lobby.

'Chucking-out time in the theatre isn't until nine o'clock, Lynette;' I clearly emphasised. 'I thought perhaps we could go to a Japanese Restaurant in Wardour Street; it is called: *'SUSHI SUES'* and, it was one of my favourite eating places in London.' I continued.

'Honestly, Chris, your choice of words is appalling, chucking-out time is not grammatically correct and you of all people should know that.'

'Well, it is the time when everyone seems to get up from their seats to bugger-off from the auditorium.' I went on to tell her.

'I hope you are not going to talk like this when we go over to France, Chris, because the French people can understand every word you say.'

'Well, how come, Lynette, when I asked a French waitress in Weymouth for a condiment at breakfast, she immediately slapped me around the head?'

'It was probably the way you pronounced it, Christopher; she probably thought you wanted a preservative.' Lynette explained, giggling like a demented schoolgirl.

'But, I didn't want any jam.' I said to Lynette before she told me I wasn't safe to be let out.

'Was that the time you gave the barman in the Four Seasons Hotel six of your Sainsbury's premium Melton Mowbray pork and apple pies to put in the fridge overnight and they ended up in the restaurant on someone's plate the following day.' she asked, rummaging around inside a *Gunga Din* plastic bag to find a litre bottle of water, *Camp* coffee and a packet of custard creams in pristine condition.

Lynette was looking the part; very pink, and I thought it amazing how a copy of *'Time Out'* could transform my wife's appearance with just a make-up bag, pill box hat and her mother's moth-eaten boa constrictor.

'Grab a paint brush, Lynette; we are going to paint the town red.' I said, positively.

Suddenly, it was time to have a drink in the London Pub where the manager, a pretty boy from New Zealand carried enough keys suspended from what seemed to be a studded dog lead wrapped decoratively around his waist to secure all the doors in the tower of London, and he possessed about as much charm and charisma as a sheep dip laced with disinfectant.

Lynette and I discussed the manager's sexuality in great detail having witnessed a small rubber penus being violently sucked on the end of a HB pencil, and judging by an Australian barman who was more concerned about things down under than serving me a pint of, *'Carlsberg Cold'* lager, I began to get seriously worried when he kept on repeating: 'No worries.'

When the price of drinks began to fluctuate, going up and down more times than a bride's night dress, I thought it best we should leave the establishment having just taken out a second mortgage to buy a packet of cheese and onion crisps.

On our way out, a pint-sized barmaid with hair like a pig-tailed Lucy Locket and another Australian wan-a-be English person poked her head up from down-under the bar to say: 'Good day'; my reaction to this was to think it could very well be.

It was six-thirty when Lynette and I made our way to the taxi rank situated in the forecourt of the hotel. A not so typical pink, albeit, appropriate London cab pulled up to take our fare; and we must have looked like two characters from the children's popular television series, "Thunderbirds", Brains and Lady Penelope, on their way to the theatre.

After paying the taxi driver a large sum of money to convey us to the theatre in the West End, Lynette and I settled down to enjoy the evening's entertainment.

'Would you like a box of chocolates, Lynette, preferably the ones without butterscotch, nougat and caramels?' I asked, feeling rather generous at the box office check-in.

'I suppose you would like them to be dark as well, Chris, because when the lights go down I won't be able to see you helping yourself to the good ones wrapped in silver paper.' she replied and before adding 'Maybe, it would have been far better all round if we had bought a bar of cut-price Cadbury's fruit and nut chocolate from TESCO in Trafalgar Square.'

'Yes, that sounds okay, I will just nip out and buy a bar before the lights go down and the curtain goes up.' I seriously suggested.

'Just stay where you are.' Lynette said, replying to my generosity. 'I don't want you walking into the auditorium half-way through act one upsetting the audience when you try to find your seat.'

'Point taken.' I said to her, knowing that a quick visit to a strip club was now well and truly out of the question. 'Would you prefer if I bought you a half-kilo box of Cadbury's Milk Tray; they should keep you quiet for five minutes, Lynette?'

It was when I was rummaging around on the floor to try and find a rare cherry brandy liqueur chocolate which I had inadvertently dropped when Detective Sergeant Trotter arrived on the scene during an unexpected snow blizzard and questioned the proprietors and guests of Monkswell Manor.

The binoculars were not exactly of the ten by eight prismatic type, most commonly used by twitters and snipers on military field-firing ranges, and they had a tendency to steam up with condensation emanating from the audience rushing back to their seats after visiting the theatre's bar during the short intermission; even the boxer, Henry Cooper had more time to take a swig from a bottle before the bell rang out to herald round two, and I thought Chuck Berry in the booking office had done me a great favour finding us two seats in front of a loudspeaker that had a problem with its volume.

It was because of this I fell asleep and dreamt of walking by 'Mad Harry's' Strip Club' in Wardour Street, Soho with two huge Cadbury's chocolate flakes and found myself gazing at black and white photographs of semi-naked women outrageously displaying themselves in the illuminated window. Whilst inspecting the goods I was approached by Sinbad (Punch bag) Jaffrey, Lynette's big-footed Indian boyfriend, who had been standing inside the doorway for several minutes watching my rear as I bent down. Sinbad offered to loan me his spectacles to focus more clearly on what lay in front of my eyes and to give me a free membership card if I were to buy a small bottle of *Moet* Champagne for forty pounds. After I had told Sinbad to go and piss up one of his ropes I was woken up at the end of the play by way of Lynette's right elbow. She said: 'Do you know, Chris, I knew all along who did it.'

'Yes, Lynette, I did too.'

The next port of call was 'Sushi Sues', a Japanese restaurant situated in Old Crompton Street, Soho and just a short hop, skip and a pleasurable jump away in London's theatre land, Leicester Square where a more than friendly waitress called Alice Entwistle lived in a tiny flat facing a cinema. It was here, in this family-run restaurant in the heart of Soho, I experienced authentic flavours of the Orient and Far East including Alice Entwistle, the beautiful Geisha girl from Luton in Essex. Alice, who wore a red silk kimono, tight-fitting sandals and white ankle socks, had what looked like two knitting needles sticking out from an artificial bun stuck to the back of her heavily greased black hair, however, this memorable experience had been a couple of years previously and the chances of her still working as a waitress in 'Sushi Sues' was only a remote possibility until.........

Chapter Nineteen

....a complete surprise had been achieved by Alice when she appeared from behind a strikingly red Japanese drape curtain after her coffee break which she shared with the restaurant's not so subservient English-born, Susan Yamamura, the wife of the proprietor, a Japanese businessman from Tokyo.

Lynette and I were tucking into our delicious starters consisting of: *Kono Mono*, mixed Japanese pickled vegetable and *Sashimi Mori*, two pieces of lean tuna, three pieces of salmon, white fish and mackerel. The drape curtain hanging in front of the kitchen door could have possibly been used as a flag during The Second World War to wave the code-word, *Tora! Tora! Tora!* Attack! Attack! Attack! In front of the Japanese *Mitsubishi* A6M Zero fighter pilots when they took-off from the aircraft carrier, *AKAGI*, to begin the aerial bombardment on Pearl Harbour, Hawaii. I can remember in 1991 reciting a poem to Lynette which our family friend, Robert had sent us inside another one of his bizarre Christmas cards to mark the fiftieth anniversary of the attack on Pearl Harbour on Sunday the seventh December 1941. The poem was penned to remember all the men and women who lost their lives during those times and the numerous men and women who were held captive in Japanese prisoner of war camps in the Far East. It goes something like this:

'Victory V's'

'There's a Gal that gets up with the Larks
In a tracksuit and trainers is seen jogging in the parks
Of grand appearance she's looking fine
Doing a few laps around the 'Serpentine'
After a swig of Sport Lucozade
She takes the salute from the 'Household Brigade'
A Japanese sniper takes a shot at the ducks
With a camera he is hoping to make a few bucks
Up with two fingers or maybe the one
She swallows a lozenge and is glad he has gone
Back to his country with something in mind

That thousands of people have an axe to grind
She sprints to the palace in time for the cards
Specially delivered by the Grenadier Guards"

'Why, may I ask, did you deem 'Sushi Sues' to be your favourite restaurant in London when you are so anti-Japanese, Chris?' asked Lynette curiously.

'It is because Alice, the waitress who worked in this establishment, told me that Susan, the owner's wife, said to her that when the Japanese Stock Market crashes and after Toshio, her husband, has thrown himself off from the top of Mount Fuji she will donate a large sum of money to 'The Burma Star Association', a group belonging to 'The Royal British Legion'.

The background music, sounding like someone hitting the spokes of a bicycle wheel with a spanner, blared out from a loudspeaker that was parked up by the side of a machine which dispensed cigarettes at extortionately high prices.

'You seem to know the waitress very well, Christopher; is she another one of your 'Have it away day' participants when you are absent from home?'

'I was just passing through, just passing through, Lynette; we are all just passing through, just ships that pass in the night.'

'Oh, we are back to Pearl Harbour again, are we?' Lynette said as she spotted a Japanese *Samurai* sword placed high on one of the walls well out of arms reach of an ankle biter who could use it to cut up a kiddies' menu.

'I'm just hoping Portsmouth will be better protected when we sail over to France, Lynette; we don't want to be caught with our trousers down, do we?'

'Well, you know all about that, Chris, I have caught you out on more than one occasion. And, if I may ask, how did you get to know about this place?'

'Sushi Sue was recommended to me by an American World War Two air force veteran; a B52 bomber pilot who was staying in the Royal National Hotel.' I so aptly tried to explain.

'I bet she was, Chris, I bet she was.'

'Did you know, Lynette, a Japanese *Yamamoto* motorcycle was completely taken to pieces at Donington Park Racing circuit in Derby and then went on to win the main event of the day?' I asked, knowing she had plenty of experience keeping a member of the 'Hells Angels' company in the nineteen-sixties, by riding on the back of his 'Harley Davidson'. 'The motorbike, when reassembled, had several bits missing and enthusiasts are still wondering how it was able to start up.' I said, continuing with my incredible story.

'It was probably something to do with the bike's powerful automatic ignition system; the magneto surrounding the induction coil feeding from the battery.' Lynette quickly pointed out before giving me a lesson in motor mechanics.

I suppose Lynette would say something like that knowing she had a previous track record, careering dangerously around the streets of Brighton, straggling a machine which had more mirrors on the handlebars than the Portland Bill lighthouse. And now, she has to carry the stigma of having to hide a spider's web tattooed on her backside, but that is a story belonging to another hideous Chapter in her life.

For several minutes I gazed up at the cleverly painted clouds on the ceiling and was hoping a Japanese *kamikaze* head case of a pilot driving an *Aichi* D3A Type 99 *Kanbaku* would appear and dive-bomb our table just in time for the second course to arrive: the breaded chicken *katsu* with *tomkatsu* sauce; I later called it, *Sushitsu*es, *Kitty Cat* in a tomato-based sauce after perusing the menu and convincing myself I was not suffering from chronic dyslexia. My thoughts immediately went back to Boscombe in Bournemouth when I used to hear Hughie, the cobbler, singing: "Suzie, Suzie, sitting in a shoe shine shop, all day long she sits and shines, all day long she shines and sits"; well, some of the words weren't quite right when he speeded up the tempo in time with his lathe.

The manageress once told me that Julia Roberts and Hugh Grant frequented 'Sushi Sues' Restaurant regularly, and after they had told everyone the food was really good and they had dicks the size of peanuts they left giving the staff a handsome tip and her a headache.

A miniature *Bonsai* tree planted in the centre of the table was the perfect cover when Alice Entwistle made her grand entrance into the restaurant, her eyelashes nervously fluttering up and down like butterflies happily playing in front of a rotating cool air fan.

'Oh no, bloody hell,' I muttered to myself, trying without success to hide behind the jungle of flora and fauna conveniently positioned in the centre of the table next to an ignited plate warmer.

'What on earth is wrong with you now, Chris? You are acting as if you have ants in your pants; your head keeps darting from side-to-side like a hyper-active parrot.' Lynette was kind enough to ask and to parrot phrase.

'Hello, Chris,' Alice said, when she brought the cat food to our table on a tray. 'This is so embarrassing,' she remarked in an accent that should be confined to Essex and Luton Airport.

'Hello, Alice,' I replied, fiddling nervously with the wooden cutlery the restaurant call chopsticks. 'Nice here innit.' I went on to say trying my best to defuse the situation by imitating her.

'You seem to know my husband very well, Miss,' Lynette said to her assertively, pointing two recycled chopsticks in front of her red flushed cheeks. 'but, you don't know him as well as I do.' she added.

'Oh, this must be your wife, Chris.' Alice said, dithering like your regular eternal gook.

'I have been relegated to this now, have I Christopher?' Lynette said to me angrily. 'This morning in Stanley Gibbons I was called an 'It' and now I am being called 'This'; I'm beginning to wonder when I will be called 'That' or indeed just one of those.'

'Now, if there is anything else you require, sir, just clap your hands twice, chop chop, and I will be here in a jiff, all right?' Alice said, making in-roads to make a quick exit. 'Have one of them, they're really nice.' she added, recommending a salmon roe parcel which looked like a multi-coloured rubber brick in the shape of a cube.

'And by the way, Yoko,' Lynette, delightfully said to Alice. 'My husband is called Christopher and not Chris but, recently I have been calling him something else, namely, a big shit.'

'The waitress is certainly getting her priorities right, Lynette, she is now calling me sir!'

'Do you know, Chris, you really are the pits.' Lynette said, looking once again at the lethal Japanese *Samurai* sword on the wall.

'Don't even think about it, Lynette,' I replied, and before going on to say: 'I can't wait until we get home so you can give me my regular good thrashing with a broom handle.'

'Anymore of this stupidity, Christopher and I will go back to Bournemouth right this minute!'

I told her calmly there were no trains running from Waterloo to Bournemouth at that time of night and she would have to make alternative arrangements like going to Heathrow and hopping on an *Aeroflot* flight to Moscow, making sure it is the Antonov AN-225 MRIYA 1988 transporter; undisputedly the largest aircraft in the world and big enough to take her weight.

For some unknown reason the restaurant manageress was called Jessica Lipmann, a Jewish woman from Chigwell in Essex, wearing a Japanese fancy dress; a midnight blue kimono with what seemed to be a pack on her back similar to a parachute. She brought our just desserts to the table, consisting of: a half-baked pineapple each served with ginger and a honey glazed cherry.

'If there is anything else you require, sir, just clap your hands three times and I'll be with you in a jiff.' Jessica said, looking precocious and giving Lynette the impression she had been playing second fiddle to Alice.

'Here we go again,' Lynette said, not so surprisingly. 'Chigwell, in the Epping Forest hey; a town that likes to flash it's cash, she sounds like a song which was quite popular way back in the seventies and sung by Tony Orlando & Dawn, which went something like this: "Hey man, what are you doing down there? Sitting alone while I'm standing above you; Oh, my darling, knock three times on the table if you want me, or twice on the pipes if the answer is no. Oh, my darling, once means you can bang me in the doorway or six times means you're not going to show".'

'The Driftwoods' are performing at the BIC next week, Lynette; it is a pity we won't be in Bournemouth to go and see them.' I jokingly said to her.

'Don't you mean 'The Drifters' Christopher?'

'Blimey, Lynette, you've got a good memory and here's me thinking you were thick.' I said, reminding her of a recent bout of amnesia when she purposely couldn't find one of their records. 'I can also remember your father not having a problem when I sat on one your mother's "Black & White Minstrel Show" albums one Sunday after we had all returned from the pub and I can also recall my mother and father taking me to the Pavilion in Bournemouth to see one of their shows,' I said to Lynette, trying to enthuse her brain with a degree of light entertainment. 'And, when the lights went out, due to a power-cut,' I added, 'nobody could see a bloody thing except for twenty pairs of white gloves moving about on the stage.'

'What have you done with those pink artificial wax flowers that were expertly arranged around your plate?' Lynette curiously asked, adroitly changing the subject.

'Oh, no, I've bloody well eaten them.'

It wasn't long after the manageress had departed from our table, the owner's wife, Susan Yamamua; a rather stout Jewish woman from Battersea made a courtly appearance and asked:

'Aren't you the couple who had their photographs depicted on the front page of todays, '*Evening Standard*'? And would you like to make a donation to the dog's home?'

After I had been forced by Lynette to put five pounds into a tin showing a picture of a well-fed Labrador pasted around the side, we made inroads to leave the establishment forever.

On my way out I couldn't help but feel we had been hoodwinked because the two complementary glasses of *Saki* included on our bill had been deliberately disguised as *Jack Daniels* whiskey.

In the street I began to sing to myself the song sung by Lou Bega, "MAMBO NUMBER 5" which goes:

"A little bit of Monica in my life,
A little bit of Erica by my side
A little bit of Rita is all I need,

A little bit of Tina is what I see
A little bit of Sandra in the sun,
A little bit of Mary all night long
A little bit of Jessica here I am,
A little bit of you makes me your man
Jump up and down and move it all around
Shake your head to the sound put your hand on the ground
Take one step left and one step right
One to the front and one to the side
Clap your hands once and clap your hands twice
And if it looks like this then you are doing it right"

Lynette and I walked into the breakfast room by way of a corridor which led from a small souvenir shop selling everything from plastic police helmets to postcards showing portraits of Princess Diana and Sir Winston Churchill, both putting two fingers up.

I must have resembled the Right Hon. Sir Neville Chamberlain when I waved a piece of paper in front of a Malaysian bouncer who had positioned himself just inside the door to allow the hotel guests to gain access to the cereals one could use to thatch roofs in the New Forest and muesli which could have been mistaken for pet food.

We found a table some miles away down inside the restaurant where a tape was bellowing out, Ludwig van Beethoven's, "Symphony No.3 in E-flat major", and together with the cacophony of noise which emanated from a woman from north of Watford who somehow managed to fall backwards in her chair while eating a bacon and egg sandwich, we began to enjoy our breakfast in a relatively safe environment. In my opinion there was so much noise and so much choice.

It was time to depart from the restaurant when 'The Berliner Philharmonic Orchestra' began to play Peter Tschaikowsky's Overture Eighteen-Twelve, especially when the canon began to fire-up sounding like Heinz baked-beans exploding in the background; this reminded me of two poems I used to recite to my fellow students at college which went:

'Heinz Beans'

We went to a gang-bang party my brother Tom and me
We met this girl called Freda and took her home for tea
We sat her on the sofa and then removed her jeans
We then pulled down her knickers and filled them full of beans
We did something else really, but it doesn't rhyme and...

'Baked Beans'

'Baked beans, the musical fruit, the more you eat the more you tute'

Anyway, the Russian guests who were staying in the hotel seemed to enjoy the music seeing as it was they who composed the Royal National's Number-one breakfast show tune in the first place.

We made our way out of the hotel after retrieving our luggage from the locker room where for a measly fifty pence one can easily deposit an explosive device capable of destroying the entire building. A number ninety-one bus, destined for Trafalgar Square arrived at the bus stop across the road and as Lynette and I were about to alight the typically red London Transport people mover, two policemen walked by the shelter. One of them, according to Lynette was, Sinbad (Punch bag) Jaffrey, dressed in the uniform of a sergeant and she then went on to explain as we gazed out of the widow that this must be his patch.

Following in the footsteps of Bonny and Clyde we decided to buy ourselves a pair of cheap dark glasses in Boots the Chemist because we thought it wouldn't be long before we were spotted and the Metropolitan Police station, based in New Scotland Yard, Whitehall was but a stone's throw away from the pub, 'The Lord Moon of the Mall'.

It was exactly twelve noon when we heard the chimes of 'Big Ben' as we entered the giant Wetherspoon hostelry in Whitehall.

'The Lord Moon of the Mall' stands out from any other pub in London in that it has a traditional lounge bar keeping a good stock of real ales, while the wine list is geared to suit palate and pocket alike. Behind the bar you'll find an extensive range of lagers and beers from around the world and my preference was to choose the Carlsberg Export because of its unique flavour and Lynette was quite happy to sample a large glass of Tuscany white wine.

I enthusiastically ordered the food separately at the bar consisting of two traditional steak and kidney puddings, chips, mushy peas and a small jug of Bisto gravy to table number twenty-four.

'The steak and kidney pudding had better be good, Chris,' Lynette said as we waited impatiently for our food to arrive. 'I was hoping to have the rack of spare ribs as described in the pub's magazine; don't they look fabulous and absolutely delicious served up in a special barbeque sauce.'

'They look like Peruvian flutes on a bed of mash potato, Lynette.' I said, looking at my glass which was crying out to be refilled.

'Why don't you take those stupid glasses off, Chris? You are not seeing things in their proper perspective.'

'Would you like a top-up, dear? Your glass is looking empty.' I said, before removing the darkened spectacles from my face.

'Can't you wait a minute, Chris; I have only just started to drink this one.' she so desperately asked. 'And we don't want to miss the train back to Bournemouth do we?'

The train departed from Waterloo on time at exactly ten-minutes past two. It was when the inspector punched our tickets at Farnborough he asked: 'Aren't you the couple who were in the newspaper last evening?'

My reaction to this was to remove my sunglasses once again and say: 'It is possible'.

'And would you be so kind as to give me your autographs?' he asked, giving me the impression it was another additive to his checking tickets.

'If you insist; if you want.' I said, rummaging around inside my leather briefcase to find a biro.

Chapter Twenty

Good Friday – Easter 21st April 2000

'It's Good Friday, Chris, Happy Easter.' Lynette was so enthusiastic to remind me when she shoved a Cadbury's chocolate bunny against the side of my face.

'It's good any day, Lynette, can we not have another hour in bed because I don't think we'll be getting much sleep on the ferry tonight.' I emphasised, reminiscing of the time I sailed over to Le Havre from Southampton by P&O ferries and just as we were about to enter the port I fell out of an extremely high bunk bed and hit my head on a stool. Lynette was obviously feeling journey-proud and couldn't wait to walk up the ship's gangway to mingle amongst other Anglo British prospective home-buyers standing around the bar explaining to fellow passengers as to why they want to leave Britain and how they can enjoy a better standard of living in a country where the majority of the population are hell-bent in ripping everyone off.

'Thieves, takers and piss takers.' I heard one disgruntled passenger calling the French when Lynette and I came home the following week. His wife's banker's card was snatched away from her hand by someone inside a Champion supermarket after she had keyed in the essential pin number; the thief immediately went straight to a *Credit Lyonnais* Bank and stole a considerable amount of money. Further to this, the man lost his wallet inside a public convenience at the Brittany Ferries Terminal in Caen and only managed to retrieve it several days later when a policeman knocked on the front door to his house and handed it back minus twenty pounds and another one of their credit cards. And, if that wasn't enough, this poor chap was later fined by the Driving License Authorities for not revealing his correct address and then, adding more insults to injury, he was cautioned by the police for possessing an invalid green insurance card whilst travelling abroad. However, he got away with the trauma of having to explain to his insurance company why he and his wife were careering around the South of France with a bogus piece of paper because they couldn't legally prove the driver and his vehicle had been away in the first place. His wife became furious the following morning at breakfast when she realized her leather jacket had been inadvertently left on the back of a chair in front of the bar. The purser had somehow managed to retrieve it before confining it to the boson's locker room and after a third degree exercise trying to persuade him that the garment belonged to her, it was eventually handed over at the Ferry Terminal in Portsmouth.

'Come on, Chris, jump to it.' Lynette said before the much-battered speaking alarm clock penetrated my ears patronisingly informing me it was seven-thirty and time to get up.

'We are not sailing until eleven o'clock this evening, my dear, and what on earth are we going to do until then, Lynette, watch a film perhaps, maybe "Titanic", or a couple of episodes of "The Love Boat". I said, looking at a plastic model of the German World War Two battleship Bismarck precariously anchored on top of the chest of drawers; on Saturdays it has a habit of turning round and pointing its twenty-five pounder guns in my direction when the washing machine in the kitchen goes into spin.

'Well, first of all I have to go into the shop and see that everything is okay before we leave for Portsmouth, and secondly, to ascertain whether or not you will be able to join the ship after visiting the Queens at lunchtime.' she said helping to pull the bed covers over to one side to allow me to put my best foot forward on to the pink deep-pile shag carpet.

'I suppose after reading the newspaper I could possibly watch Victoria's VHS video of "Fantasy Island", that was where she got all her ideas from.' I said to Lynette listening to Hannibal scratching underneath the bed alerting me that it was time for me to get up to make his gourmet breakfast.

'The ship has a cinema, duty-free shops, a bar with entertainment and two restaurants; one main and another self-service.' she so knowledgably pointed out.

'It will be a bit late to do all of that, Lynette, especially when we will have to put our watches forward one hour to fall in line with French time.'

'Oh, don't be such a bloody skinflint Chris; I need another bottle of *CHANEL No 5* Perfume and a new *Revlon* lipstick before we go ashore, and why can't you put your hand in your pocket and buy me something nice.' she asked, giving me a quick kiss on my forehead.

It was when Lynette and I were sailing the high seas much later that day I visited the Duty Free shop and bought her the said perfume and a lipstick. I had the unfortunate experience to have given the Brittany Ferries sales assistant the wrong impression when she thought I was one of the ship's entertainers looking for some replacement make-up. It was only until after she had said I could receive a staff discount and a free pair of tights, I realized the time had come to hastily disappear out of the shop.

I gave Lynette the surprise of her life when I said to her I had visited the Main Duty Free shop and bought a giant bar of *Toblerone*, similar to a chocolate Second World War tank trap, she said to me: 'I hope you are joking because if you are not I will take great delight in throwing you overboard.'

Lynette carefully inspected the goods which I had purchased in the '*La Boutique Parfums*', the Duty Free shop situated on Deck seven and was quick to point out, after removing the thin cellophane wrapper from a cardboard box, its contents contained a refill for a decorative empty *CHANEL No 5* bottle which had been standing on top of the dressing table for at least six months. 'And as for the lipstick', Lynette said when she embarrassingly perused its phallic type shape 'I was never into deep purple, but, at least you got the *Revlon* correct; I could easily have ended up with a tube of *Savlon.*'

When I told Lynette the lady in the shop had forgotten to give me the batteries, she asked: 'batteries; what batteries?'

'The batteries for the gold-plated lipstick that looks like...'

'Chris, anymore of this and I am going home.' she said, preparing to go to the Duty Free shop to exchange the non-returnable goods. 'Little boys with shiny toys; give them an inch and they take a mile.' Lynette remarked, adding to the confusion.

'You should be so lucky,' I said, wishing I had brought a slide-rule to calculate her words. 'We are now twenty miles out to sea sailing in severe weather conditions and I don't think you will be able to make it back to Bournemouth tonight, Lynette.' I said after perusing a small flashing light resembling the ship, "Normandie" after it had sailed past the Isle of Wight, portrayed on the illuminated GPS chart attached to one of the bulkheads on Deck number nine.

'Just watch me,' she said assertively, 'I will see you later, Chris; hopefully I will be back with what I wanted in the first place, a real bottle of perfume and a lipstick that doesn't seem to have been tested. 'Oh, and, by the way, now we are on the subject of batteries, why do you insist on putting them into our door bell the wrong way?'

'It is because, my dear, there is a method in my madness and I just want a quiet life without any interruptions.'

The entertainment in 'Le Derby', the ship's bar on Deck number nine, continued with Gloria Fontana, real name Arthur Wooten, the ship's drag act from Tipton in Staffordshire, appearing from behind a blue drape curtain at the back of a highly polished dance floor. He hovered around with a roaming microphone fluttering his false eyelashes which were heavily brushed with mascara and occasionally pushing up an artificial boob into a much safer position lest it fell out. Gloria was singing, "Hey Big Spender" when he, she, decided to pick on me to be her, his man of distinction, a real big spender, and I was the star turn for the evening when I was presented, with a collapsible beer trolley by the resident disc jockey from Preston in Lancashire who had been having some trouble trying to sell his raffle tickets earlier that evening.

'I don't usually have to beg, but can someone please buy at least one of my raffle tickets.' Peter Harmony called out, pointing to one of his trolleys he had difficulty in trying to get rid of, 'People may say I'm off my trolley for being here, but that's another story.' he added as the ship rolled from side to side in a gale-force wind. 'Well that was fun wasn't it?' he said, saying goodbye to another one of his collapsible trolleys which when extended looked like a geriatrics Zimmer-frame.

When Lynette eventually returned from her walk-about she asked me why a trolley was parked up against my seat. I told her I had won it in a raffle and it was for transporting cases of duty free beer from ship to shore.

'Don't even think about it, Chris, we have enough luggage to cart around without us having to turn ourselves into a mobile 'cash-and-carry'.'

Meanwhile, back at the ranch, I turned on the radio to listen to the BBC world news and the weather forecast just in case there was any likelihood of us not being able to go. There was a severe gale warning for that night in the English Channel and to alert anyone who was planning to venture over to France in a canoe, kayak or rowing boat.

On the first page of the '*The Times*' newspaper that morning was an article about an over-loaded car ferry capsizing in the Philippines, the passengers apparently having a great time swimming back to Manila chased by Paraná fish and great-white sharks with dentures the size of Margaret Thatcher's.

'Did you take out adequate travel insurance for us both, Lynette?' I seriously asked, thinking about when all the lights went out on the 'Titanic' just before it sank to the bottom of the Atlantic Ocean.

'We're only going over to France, for God's sake, not to the Americas,' she said softly, taking the trouble to point out to me where it was we were supposed to be going.

'Try telling that to Admiral Lord Horatio Nelson when he was fatally wounded at sea in the 'Battle of Trafalgar.' I replied, giving her a fictitious maritime chart reference as to where it took place.

'As always you have to have the last word, don't you, Christopher, but I must say you're very knowledgeable, however, Nelson is dead and I would find it impossible to talk with him, wouldn't I?' Lynette was so kind to remind me that morning.

'Yes, Lynette, I became knowledgeable by reading history books and I don't know how I do it for the money.' I replied, looking at an eye-level portrait in the lounge of me wearing an Oxford University cap and gown.

'Do what for the money.' she asked, inferring that my academic vocation and career had been in vain and a complete and utter waste of time.

'Can you remember, Lynette, that soon after I had graduated from Oxford University and got myself a steady job working all hours that God sent in that horrible glue factory in Salisbury, I was able to take you to the cinema in Bournemouth to see the block-buster movie, "ZULU", starring Michael Caine and Stanley Baker; we hardly had two pennies to rub together until then.'

'Yes, I do remember, Christopher, you were so stuck up in those days, you had to leave, and don't you mean the block-buster film, "Doctor Chivago", starring Omar Sheriff and Julie Christie?' Lynette asked, frowningly.

'Yes, that one as well; especially when the Zulu's did a runner when it began to snow.'

'And, I am still waiting for a choc-ice,' Lynette said, poking me in the ribs.

'Well, not only had we to sit in freezing cold temperatures when the fire door was opened during the interval to extract the cigarette smoke and having to watch a film where icicles were seen to be hanging down all over the place, I thought ice cream would have been superfluous and just far too much.'

'I can also recall your runny nose, Chris; it looked similar to a lime-green Popsicle.'

'Do you remember the weaving job I had to take for six months at Stilton, Lynette? And metaphorically speaking, it was if by magic, there were more carpets flying out through the back door than a flea market in Bagdad; more to the point, there was more theft than warp.'

'Don't you mean the carpet manufacturers in Wilton, near Salisbury, Chris?' Lynette said, sounding even more confused.

'No, Lynette, it was definitely Stilton because there was a creamery down the road which made and sold the cheese.'

I suddenly remembered that it was Patricia Price, one of my ex girlfriends who I had the pleasure to escort to the cinema to see "Zulu", and I don't suppose the back row of the Palais will ever be the same again now they have turned it into a supermarket.

It was just after nine when I heard the distinctive noise of someone trying to push something through our letter box; it was Patrick Marshall, the postman, one of the most important men in Bournemouth.

The statement on the side of the brown A4 envelope read: "Please do not bend" which came as no surprise as it fell on to stony ground; this, along with a few bogus begging letters, junk mail and a rather belated millennium calendar from the milkman, was sent from the photographer of the '*Evening Standard*' and contained photographs of Lynette and I standing like the happy couple who had just won the Littlewoods Pools. The pictures were not very good because my spectacles were steamed up looking at a secretary who was sitting at her desk filing her long scratchy finger nails, and Lynette who was grinning and looking like the cat that had just got the cream. Following a rather lengthy discussion between Lynette and me, we both came to the conclusion that they would be far better accompanying Guy Fawkes on top of a bonfire.

'The next couple of weeks will be strange, not being able to be with Victoria and Barbara.' I said to Lynette concernedly.

'I have no doubt in my mind, Chris they'll be more than happy staying with my mum and dad in Brighton for their Easter break.' she replied, putting a brave face on it all. 'Their granddad, as always, will spoil them rotten by giving them Easter eggs, sweets, and of course money.'

'Yes, I know and it is sad my mum and dad are not here with us to do the same.' I said, somewhat emotionally.

'Did you know Effie Winters has just been sacked, dismissed by the landlady of the Queens? Lynette asked, as if she knew her job was on the line.

'No, this has come as a complete and utter shock, my darling.' I replied, giving Lynette the impression I didn't know about Denzel Crow having extra maritals in the pub car park.

'I bet it has, Chris; I bet it has. Apparently, Denzel Crow is sporting a black eye and it was given to him by Christine.' she went on to tell me as if I didn't know already.

'Effie has been replaced by an attractive young lady called Pauline.' I unwittingly said to her.

'Well, Christopher, if you didn't know Effie Winters had been sacked, how is it that you know, she has been replaced.'

'Do you know Lynette, it is absolutely amazing how one gets to know all about what goes on in the Queens when one sits alone at home watching 'East Enders' or playing that mindless game called *Sudoku*.' I said, puzzlingly.

'It is quite simple, my dearest, if you look over to the occasional table you will see what is commonly known as a telephone and that is what I use to find out what is going on down at the pub.'

I knew then that it was only a matter of time before I could have been nursing a sore eye.

'The truth of the matter is, Chris, she's a Hampshire slut and is possibly one of those crazy wood nymphs that lurk around inside the New Forest. Effie Winters has probably had more prickles rubbed up against her backside than a second-hand wire brush.' Lynette went on to say.

'Anyway, Pauline Hodge, will I am sure do a good job.' I said to Lynette confidently.

'What sort of job?' she asked, looking at me as if I was about to be sliced into two by a sharp bread knife.

'I am so glad we are not taking the car over to France, Lynette,' I quickly changed the subject. 'It will give us more freedom to relax, especially when we visit the live cabaret at the 'Lido' on the *Champs-Elysées* in Paris, and me having the pleasure of seeing semi-naked women prancing around on the stage.'

'Well, Chris, I wouldn't have thought the cabaret consisted of dead people and besides we are not going all that way just to see women hitching up their skirts and screaming their heads off; it is "eroticism" at its worst, that's what I call it.' she said, doing her best to destroy what little sex life I had left. 'And, if you want that sort of thing you can always go down to the Queens.' she unashamedly added.

'If I can, you can, and then we can all do the *"Can Can"*!' I muttered to myself trying to enjoy what time I had remaining in "England's Green and Pleasant Land".

'We can discover Paris by sailing underneath the thirteen bridges along the River Seine in one of those glass-top river boats and that will be fun, won't it?' she happily suggested.

'Don't forget to take a steel helmet with you, Lynette, because the water level may rise as soon as you step on-board.'

Chapter Twenty-one

International Ferry Terminal Portsmouth Friday 21st April 2000

"April in Paris, Chestnuts in Blossom", I was singing to myself having spruced myself up in the gentleman's public convenience at Portsmouth's International Ferry Port, and little did I know that later on during the following week, the black jazz singer, Ella Fitzgerald, would have a lot to answer for.

Lynette, sitting at one of the tables by the bar had been guarding our luggage, consisting of two Marks & Spencer expandable trolley bags, each designed to carry an additional shoulder bag or vanity case, to create and enhance genuine freedom of movement in foreign countries.

It was approximately nine-thirty when we checked in at the Brittany Ferries desk to show our passports to the French maritime authorities and to convince them that Lynette and I weren't illegal immigrants trying to get into their country. After the formalities had been finalized and our boarding cards were handed to us, the young woman in a strikingly red uniform enhanced by a blue, white and red silk scarf, informed us: "At ten-thirty you will be asked to board at gate number one where a bus will be waiting to transport you to the ferry".

I can remember also singing softly "Many Rivers to Cross" by the Jamaican Rastafarian reggae singer Jimmy Smith when Lynette and I tried to exchange some of our money into French Francs at the *Bureaux de Change* only to find a cardboard sign behind the window saying: "We are Closed". She corrected me by saying that's Jimmy Cliff's song; he's a good singer, he's not called Smith, but perhaps this could have had something to do with the local radio station's presenter having a rather pronounced lisp.

'Don't worry, Chris;' Lynette said as I began to wonder if things were going to get better. 'We can exchange our money on the boat and still use our pounds.' she added.

Meanwhile, Lynette and I decided to have a couple of quick drinks at the bar before boarding. My immediate reaction when I received the bill from the barman who possessed a brain the size of a French *petit pois*, a microscopic garden pea, and a Portsmouth accent likened to a pneumatic drill and a shooting of crows, was to tell him that his prices were far too high and similar to the Savoy in London. He then had the cheek to ask me how I knew, and if I did how I got past the flunky at the door.

The next incident was when a gang of unruly school kids who had arrived by coach from Birkenhead, Merseyside near Liverpool and couldn't wait to step on-board to relieve the coffee shop, '*Le Pays d'Auge*' of its entire stock of Coca Cola, Pastries, *pain au raisin*, *croissants* and packets of Tyrell's cheese and chive flavoured crisps.

I later witnessed a young adenoidal Liverpudlian Scouse git bumping and nudging a gaming machine on Deck nine; the synthesized noises blaring out from its insides were similar to listening to a dalek screaming its head off frantically in the popular television series "Dr Who", especially when the jackpot had been forced to drop by him bending the glass to slow the wheels down. Ironically, apart from dozens of whisky bottles in the Duty Free Shop on Deck seven, there were no teachers in sight to sedate and control these half-pint passengers from hell.

It was only until, Peter Harmony; the ship's English resident disc jockey had switched off his colourful discotheque lights, turned on the main ones and given away dozens of *Brittany Ferries* tee shirts to the moronic head-dipping school kids, we were allowed to relax and enjoy what was left of the evening.

As if all of this wasn't enough to contend with, Lynette and I already had a rather unpleasant experience when we boarded the ship by trudging up a gangway similar to a one-in-seven helter-skelter and managing to convince a Brittany Ferries crew member what I really meant to say was *bonsoir*, Good Evening, and not *au revoir*, By bye, when I tripped and fell over a riveted steel step as we walked into the Reception and the *Bureau d'information* situated on Deck seven.

Our bedroom for the night, quite rightly was of the Commodore Class, '*Les Suites Commodore de Luxe*', situated at the stern of the ship on Deck seven and it comprised of a double bed, television, mini-bar, balcony and special services in the cabin. An all too familiar French steward with looks that could melt ice at the North Pole, was waiting to brighten up my day even further by offering to take Lynette on to the balcony to show her the coloured lights surrounding the fairground in Portsmouth Southsea while I freshened up and nursed a small head wound in an ultra modern bathroom especially designed for a couple of Hampshire dwarfs. Marcel Godard, the ship's white *ouchie-couchie* rubber band man and steward, assigned to Deck seven, was standing close to Lynette by the rail giving me the impression they were both about to throw up over the side similar to the actor and actress, Leonardo DiCaprio and Kate Winslet in the 1998 epic film, "Titanic", written and produced by James Cameron. I wasn't wrong in my assumption because when I saw Lynette's famous pink boa constrictor looking every inch like a feather duster or a snake stretched out on the bed waiting to go walk-about, I knew she was going to emulate the film's character Rose when we eventually went to eat in the "*Le Deauville*", the Main Restaurant and Bar on Deck eight.

For a second, I thought I was hallucinating when I glimpsed a rogue iceberg steadily floating by as I gazed at the distant mist obscuring Portsmouth's coastline, and then when I spotted a set of numbers painted in black on its side I realized it was a Royal Navy minesweeper from nearby Gosport.

Lynette, later, after opening a plastic bottle, disguised as *Champagne*, said:

'Would you like one of these 'Celebration' chocolates; they are delicious, especially the 'Twix' bars, and, it is amazing what one can buy in the confectionary section of the Main Duty Free shop. There are tins of Arbroath sardines, Scotch smoked salmon, haggis and packets of Walker's Highland shortbread biscuits.' she went on to explain in great detail.

'Do you know, Lynette?' I quickly put in. 'We can buy all this bloody stuff in Sainsbury's and we've not come all this way to sort out Scotland's failing economy and tourist industry.'

'I wouldn't like the SNP, the Scottish Nationalist Party to hear you say that,' Lynette said, and genuinely sounding concerned about my welfare. 'They would certainly tether you to a caber at the *Braemar* Highland Games and toss you over Hadrian's Wall.' she so lovingly added.

185

'Unless they have a speed boat or an inflatable capable of keeping up with a Brittany Ferry in gale-force winds, I don't think I've any immediate cause for concern.'

'You always have an answer to everything, don't you, Chris?'

'Well, I try.' I said, bringing the subject to an abrupt close.

It was time to eat in *"Le Deauville"*; we had the *plat de jour*, consisting of a starter, French onion soup, served with *croutons* and a generous bowl of shredded *emmental* cheese or alternatively a dessert with *crème frais*; the white stuff that disappears in front of your eyes. The main course was delicious *Filet de Beuf*, fillet of beef, served with roast potatoes, French beans and a dark *Madeira* sauce.

Lynette and I had decided in metaphor, to literally push the boat out by ordering a full bottle of *Chardonnay* from our friendly pretty-boy waiter from Paris, Jean-Pierre Emery, who, believe it or not, told us he is a distant cousin of King Louis the fourteenth of France. Emery quickly changed his story when I had convinced him we were not members of the gay rights movement in France; I then told him the meal had better be good because like Marie Antoinette his head may just fall into a nearby bread basket. After the pleasantries had been finalized we tucked into our starter which had been precariously brought to us by a rather disgruntled waiter who looked as if he had just said goodbye to a handsome tip.

After visiting the *Bureau de Change* on Deck seven, I decided to give Lynette my rendition of Rod Stewart's song, "Sailing" as we negotiated the steps of the staircase leading up to Deck nine. The ship was rolling from side to side when we attempted to make our way to the *"Le Derby"*, where the waiters have as much charm as a rattle snake and make you feel as welcome as a fart in an astronaut suit.

Continuing to take one step left and two steps right we eventually arrived at the bar without injury. Following an altercation with a French barman when he tried to give me a lesson on how to pronounce a small bottle of *'Cellier des Dauphins' Cotes de Rhone* red wine, I retaliated by reducing his ego to zero naught point-blank sod all by telling him *his* English wasn't all that special and then I told him to bugger off and not to be so impertinent. He began his retribution and vindictiveness by visiting our table to remove the drinks menu and give me a look that could frighten children; for Lynette and me, the entertainment had only just begun when I said to him:

'You're in the wrong job, mate; you should be up there on the dance floor supervising those unruly kids.'

'Tell me, Chris, why are you so unfriendly towards the crew.' Lynette asked with caution knowing I would say something derogatory to substantiate my feelings.

'It is quite simple, Lynette, the French were deliberately put on this earth to mess people about and if you're not sure about this ask, Sir Winston Churchill.'

'Why do you keep on introducing me to dead people, Christopher,' she said, reminding me of her extraordinary oratory skills which were not dissimilar to his. 'How can I ask someone a question if they're no longer on this planet? And sometimes I think you're not on this planet, Chris.' she added.

'Well, you only have to read thirty-six volumes of his literary works to find out why, Lynette.' I said, and once again giving her the chance to expand her brain with my infinite knowledge. 'He could have written thirty-seven; however, during the war years there was this guy from France who continually banged on his bedroom door during the blitz asking him for shelter and to seek sanctuary.'

'That guy wouldn't be Charles what's his name would it?'

'No, Lynette, like me, Prince Charles wasn't born until nineteen forty-eight and he was just a twinkle in his father's eye.'

'I wasn't referring to Prince Charles, you ignoramus; it's not often you get things right but you're wrong again. And why do you dislike the French so much, Christopher; what have they done to deserve this kind of treatment?'

'Well, again, it's quite simple; how can one begin to like a nation who have great difficulty in liking themselves, and furthermore, everything they do is either synthetic, cosmetic or camouflage; they pick on something bad and then they play on it.'

'Have you ever tried to join the Diplomatic Service, Chris? The Russian

Embassy in Moscow would have a field day with you.'

'Would you like another drink?' another friendly waiter asked hovering around our table similar to a vulture.

'Go away and bring me a drinks menu, preferably one in Braille.' I said.

*

Five-thirty am; the following morning

It would seem the ship had dispensed with its rocking and rolling Lynette and I had to endure throughout the night and was now sailing in much calmer waters off the coast of Normandy, France. The bright spotlights inside our cabin were automatically switched on at five-thirty and compulsory classical music began to play softly in the background to alert all passengers it was time to scramble from their beds and go to one of the ship's restaurants for breakfast.

Our continental breakfast, of course was personally delivered to our suite by Marcel Godard which consisted of a pot of coffee, two glasses of orange juice, a couple of *croissants* and miniscule pots of *confiture*; jam, marmalade and butter. It was when Lynette and I vacated our cabin to supplement our mediocre breakfast in the "*Riva Bella*" Self Service restaurant with bacon and egg sandwiches, Marcel Marceau Godard held out his hand to say goodbye.

'How much did you give Marcel for a tip, Chris?'

'What tip, Lynette.' I replied, cringing with embarrassment.

'Do you know, Christopher, you really are the pits.' she inferred as I struggled to find ten Francs inside my purse.

It was when I was munching away on a squidgy bacon and egg sandwich that could only have been described as a gooey mess I overheard a descriptive conversation on the next table, saying how someone had tried to purchase pastries, cakes, sandwiches and soft drinks from the "*Salon de Thé*", the ship's coffee shop on Deck nine only to be told they had been cleaned out during the night by a flotilla of pirates from the North of England. One lady passenger partially quoted a song "The Liverpool Lullaby" which had been made famous by our best known television and radio celebrity, the late Cilla Black OBE, and begins:

> "Oh, they are such mucky kids
> Dirty as dustbin lids
> One day there'll be an almighty splash
> When the ship runs out of 'bangers and mash'
> But it will soon be *'Over Lord'*
> When Brittany Ferries chucks them overboard"

Lynette and I disembarked at six-thirty allowing a French *l'Atelier de Nettoyage*, a cleaning company to take presidential steps up the gangway before they charged on-board with their paraphernalia; brushes, buckets, mops, Ajax triple action window shine and an assortment of other cleaning materials to maintain the cleanliness of the ship during its next voyage across the English Channel. I had no idea at this point that after Lynette and I had walked through passport control in Ouistreham, a shiny black Mercedes Benz limousine, courtesy of Messrs Thomas Cook Travel Agents, France, would be waiting in the car park to take us on a nine mile journey to the *A La Gare*, the railway station in Caen.

It was dark when the ship's disembarkation procedure was finalized but then as we were being driven along the main road passed the Second World War memorial commemorating the D-Day landings on the sixth June 1944, and in particular the brave and courageous airborne assault by British parachutists on Pegasus Bridge that morning, the sun came up as we approached the slip-road to Bayeux. "Rule Britannia, marmalade and jam, five Chinese crackers up your asshole, bang, bang, bang, bang, bang!" I patriotically sang to myself when Lynette and I were sitting down comfortably on individual soft leather seats in a car which wouldn't have been out of place at the motor racing circuit at Silverstone. Another poem written by our family friend, Major Robert Bingham MBE sprang to mind which goes:

> "Pegasus Bridge"
>
> It was on a Bridge at midnight
> Throwing snowballs at the moon

The devils dropped down from out of the sky
Some to live and some to die
We think of those men in 'Hoarsa Glider'
Paving their way as a Path-finder
They shot at Mars from forty paces
They were the angels with dirty faces

'How is it, Christopher, that the German army who were securing Pegasus Bridge were throwing snowballs at the moon in June?' she asked, after I had received the poem inside a birthday card from Robert when he joined his local Territorial Army regiment.

'It was because it was a cold night and they had nothing else better to do but gaze up and look at the stars; a French local thought it was his lucky day when the Germans were caught with their pants down.

We pulled up outside the railway station at seven thirty-five precisely. Our friendly taxi driver held out his hand for me to shake and it was then I suddenly realized I had to do the tip thing after he had driven us crazily along the nine mile stretch of road, arriving at the railway station in record-breaking time.

The train for Paris which had to come from Cherbourg was scheduled to arrive at the *A La Gare* in Caen at seven thirty-six on platform 'D' and, I must say, we were looking forward to the relaxation of the two hours and twenty-one minute journey to, Paris St.Lazare in the comfort of an *SNCF* train.

Chapter Twenty-two

The train to Paris arrived on time obscuring our line of vision when Lynette and I stood up from a bench seat inside a shelter constructed predominantly from glass. I can remember it was bitterly cold waiting for the train from *Cherbourg* as we gazed over the platform to see a huge concrete jungle; a massive building-site to the rear of the station. I can also recall, the tall inanimate cranes used to hoist long planks of wood, ceiling blocks, window sashes and PVC frames before being put into position by nine-to-five monkey see, monkey do workers from Latvia, the Czech Republic and Poland, and apart from a rope swaying merrily in a slight breeze, a bedraggled cat and the odd glimpse of a security guy doing his rounds wearing a Balmoral tartan dressing gown, the area was devoid of any life until the following Tuesday.

Lynette and I just about managed to clamber up the two iron steps to gain access into one of the first-class compartments of the train. I was beginning to think I had missed my vocation and become a Heathrow baggage handler when I literally relieved Lynette of two elegant expandable bags on wheels, a vanity case, a small integral travel bag and a collapsible beer trolley from the platform.

If that wasn't enough, the lethal automatic double doors in the corridor seemed to have a life of their own, opening and closing at the slightest movement of the train and he or she who hesitates would undoubtedly lose when going through a device similar to two, side-on *Madame Guillotines* and one could easily be transformed into a cheese and pickle sandwich; if the automatic double doors don't succeed in killing you then heavy trolley bags systematically sliding out from the luggage rack will.

The atmosphere inside the compartment was warm in contrast to the freezing cold outside but then, it was still early in the morning and *Caen* wasn't unique in having to suffer vaporous climates similar to Siberia at that time of year.

The seating arrangement was cosy sitting next to Lynette by a window where she could feel at home watching the cows in the fields eating their breakfast; "On yonder hill, there stood a cow, I turned around she's no there now".

I said to Lynette: 'Have you noticed something?' to which she replied: 'Have I noticed what, Chris?'

'Just hear the whisper of the raindrops flowing down against the window; some of them looking like transparent beads of glass, they are the same everywhere.' I poetically explained to her.

'You didn't say that when we stayed in that bloody awful hotel in Weymouth when the windows in our bedroom wouldn't close properly during that torrential storm.'

Each of the seats has a table in front to allow the passengers to read the complementary copy of a French glossy magazine with enough propaganda and sleaze contained on every page to bang the President, Jacques Chirac up for the rest of his life.

The two hours and twenty-one minute train journey which conveyed Lynette and me to *La Gare St.Lazare*, Paris, called into the cathedral town of *Lisieux*, famous for its *Basilica* dedicated to Saint Theresa, and just a few miles further down the track, our second last stop, the picturesque town of *Bernay*, renowned for its cheese, wine, beer, cockerels, speckled hens and well-fed drunken ducks. *Evreux Normandie*, a town on the periphery of Paris and famous for its motorcar manufacturing industry was the last station we pulled into before Paris and where they have railway timetables scrolled in graffiti all along the walls.

It was when Lynette and I were taking a well deserved nap an *SNCF* ticket inspector knocked gently on the table to wake us up. The man with the bag was wearing a dark grey uniform and a peak cap similar to a Hammersmith milkman and waited patiently to either pierce our ears or to punch a hole into the middle of our ticket with an implement that looked like a heavy-duty industrial stapling gun.

The next interruption was a man in white pushing a trolley down the aisle; how he ever passed through the centre of those intrepid automatic doors was way beyond my imagination.

The wheels on his portable '*Salon de Thé*' squeaked as they rolled along slowly in time with the movement of the train. The aromatic smell of freshly made Brazilian Espresso coffee was permeating all around the compartment, and together with triangular plastic boxes containing crabstick, plastic sausages, and chicken, turkey or ham sandwiches, it gave Lynette and I something to savour having bought two large coffees, *café au lait* with milk and sugar and a couple of well-burnt *croissants* which were like eating rubber tyres and the puff-pastry depositing crumbs on to the table because of an absence of essential paper towels.

The bill for this rather extravagant early morning taste of French first-class cuisine had been greatly reduced when the man with the trolley explained in pigeon English that the microwave in the kitchen had exploded that morning after the train's departure from *Cherbourg* due to excessive use and we would have to make do with eating the *croissants* cold. The refreshment trolley had taken on a new lease of life when it lost its squeak after one of the wheels fell off during the attendants walk-about down the centre of the train, and this was when I said to Lynette:

'Do you know, my dear, the French weren't blessed with much on top; they were at the back of the queue when the brains were handed out, and as for Sacha Distel; he was so good- looking he was downright ugly.'

'Here we go again, Chris, having another jibe at the French; I don't know why you bothered to take a holiday in France with your outrageous temperament.'

As we were pulling out of *Lisieux* an elegant middle-aged woman who reeked of money sat down adjacent to us and offered to give Lynette and me one of her personalized silk handkerchiefs in exchange for the train's free magazine which was only good for lighting fires and wrapping fish; that sort of thing. She had the expensive and exclusive *Galeries Lafayette Coupole Main Store* on *Boulevard Haussmann* stamped all over her; even the fragrance of Coco Chanel which Lynette had managed to detect led us to assume she was probably someone famous. The initials in the corner of the dainty handkerchief had *Franklin Gothic Medium* letters **BB** printed in gold and it was when I saw a fur stole hanging up by the side of the window we realized later it could have been Brigitte Bardot and one of her stuffed cats. The lady with the blonde bouffant, hair which could only have been styled by Jean-Paul Gaultier or Vidal Sassoon themselves wore a Christian Dior green coat, green skirt, and green shoes; she had placed her green Iceberg (fashion house) handbag directly in front of her on the table and *Madame* gave us the impression she had just emerged from a greenhouse or indeed the 'White House'. Her stunning modernity, refinement and sensuous elegance became more evident when she lifted her Gucci sunglasses away from her beautiful dark eyes, placing them on top of her head in holiday-type fashion. I watched, mesmerized, as she flicked through the magazine, turning each page with a finger which looked as though it had been in many pies; her sparkling diamond ring reflected like a prism in the window. The lady, giving me the impression she wasn't at all impressed with the contents inside the magazine, proceeded to take out a mother of pearl compact from her handbag to apply more powder and rouge to her cheeks and extra pink gloss to paint her charismatic and pouting lips. On her wrist I noticed a ladies diamond encrusted Constellation OMEGA watch and from where I was sitting the time was so easy to read; it was a quarter past eight precisely. From the screen to the streets and then on to a train, Lynette and I thought it possible she was Brigitte Bardot; the French movie star and singer we British people all loved and admired.

'Do you know, Chris, and this is truly amazing,' Lynette said later when we were drinking our coffee in the hotel's tropical conservatory. 'I once saw Jimmy Saville in Boscombe High Street, but then again, it could have been a blond-haired chimpanzee that had escaped from Longleat Safari Park.' she added.

'Well, it could have been neither of them, I replied, giving her a lesson in zoology combined with a mental guided tour of the natural history museum in London.

'This is a lovely silk handkerchief, Christopher; it looks and feels like velvet and must have cost a fortune,' Lynette said, continuously running her hand over the top. 'She must be Bridget Bardot, who else?'

'With those initials, I didn't think she is called Bill Bailey, Burt Bacharach, Benazir Bhutto or Basil Brush,' I said to her, chuckling. 'And I will now tell you a story, Lynette that will make you feel so happy being married to such an intelligent man. When I was at Oxford University I rubbed shoulders with the Tibetan religious leader, the Dali Lama, who put me in touch with a few important spiritual vibrations.'

'I bet, Christopher; did they include slipping on a banana skin in Sainsbury's and calling the entire French population, frogs?'

Continuing my quest to find out more about the lady on the train with the contrived straggly strands of hair which covered her ears and wouldn't have been out of place on top of a seaside donkey in Boscombe, I said to Lynette:

'Do you know how to hire a donkey?'

No, Christopher, I don't, but I'm sure you're going to tell me.' she so wantingly asked.

'By turning a screw underneath the saddle.' I replied.

'Oh that was really funny, very funny, Christopher, but promise me you won't give up your daytime job to become a comedian.'

The train pulled into Paris *St.Lazare* station at nine fifty-seven precisely. The lady in green wrapped her mink stole around her shoulders placing a pillbox hat askew on the top of her head before pulling down a dark see-through polka dot veil which looked like it had just caught chicken pox or a bad case of German measles.

Lynette and I once again thanked the walking diamond mine for her kindness for giving us one of her personalized handkerchiefs and after we had said our goodbyes in a language even Katie Boyle wouldn't have been able to understand, the lady then proceeded to get up and walk towards the automatic double doors which opened primarily and to literally let the cat out from a bag.

It was two days later when Lynette and I were watching the news on TF1, the French television media programme in our salubrious hotel bedroom we learned who the lady was. She was called, *Madame* Beatrice Ben-Gurion, the wife of a leading French politician, who was trying his best to persuade the French administration to metaphorically dismantle the Eiffel Tower in Paris and then put it back up in Tel Aviv, Israel. *Monsieur* Benjamin Ben-Gurion, her husband and the man with the golden gob in the Government became even more infamous when he took a back-hander from a local construction company to keep up with his wife's obsession for fur coats, silk handkerchiefs and OMEGA watches.

I asked Lynette: 'I wonder who the handkerchief belonged to; him or her?'

'Well, that was the end of that little adventure.' I said to Lynette, as we swiftly followed Brigitte Bardot along the platform heading towards a wide open barrier that allowed us to walk into the busy concourse; stark and barren, devoid of anything remotely resembling a convivial reception area, except for a pathetic attempt with an arrangement of tables and chairs where one, if so inclined, could have a cup of coffee, tea and a ham and cheese baguette sandwich. This was *St.Lazare* station, Paris; a lot of to do about nothing, and our intention was to get out of it as quickly as possible.

We were met at the barrier by a man holding a small chalk board with our name, Mr & Mrs Travis written on it. It was Joe Taxi, the chauffeur, specially seconded by Thomas Cook Travel to take us to our hotel; '*L'Experience Burmais*' conveniently situated on *Boulevard de la Madeleine* and in close proximity to the *Galeries Lafayette* on *Boulevard Haussmann*.

Our luggage, it seemed, was far in excess of the permitted handling arrangement and when we arrived at the hotel, the driver of the taxi demanded that we pay extra for the weight being put on to his tyres. When I told him to go and boil his head and argue the point with Thomas Cook, he went away chuntering to himself, waving his arms around similar to the rotary blades on a wind farm.

'Well, that was fun, wasn't it Lynette, we have only been in Paris fifteen minutes and I'm in trouble already.'

'Listen, Chris,' Lynette said as we stood in the doorway of the hotel with our luggage, trying to avoid the splashes of soapy water which was being caused by a woman cleaning the windows. 'Just please try and make our holiday in France a happy one without causing any aggravation.'

'I'll try, Lynette, but I'm not promising anything.' I replied just as the automatic glass double doors opened to let us in to the lobby and reception area.

Having been told by a German receptionist with an hour-glass figure similar to Lilly-Marlene Dietrich, that we had checked-in too soon and our room wouldn't be available until two that afternoon, I threatened her with extreme violence by offering to spank her bottom; well, in my dreams, I thought. The receptionist immediately changed her mind after goose-stepping in to see the manager when I gave her a generous piece of my duty-free *Toblerone* chocolate, large enough to trap one of her Panzer tanks.

The interior of the Burmese hotel had a very pronounced tropical ambiance and when Lynette and I were sitting in the conservatory drinking our coffee I glanced up to see the biggest aspidistra in the world, growing by the minute underneath a multi-coloured Art-deco glass dome. A huge rubber plant next to an erratic African blue parrot perched inside a cage gave me the idea we were going to spend the next seven days inside a menagerie. I was half-expecting David Attenborough to pop his head up from around a palm plant which had obviously started its days in the depths of a jungle or rain forest in Burma.

'Where are the bananas, Lynette?' I asked, looking around to see a serene stone Buddha sitting cross-legged on a pedestal by the side of a pond with water gushing out from his mouth.

'They are right behind you, Christopher, in a bowl on the next table but be careful, I don't want to call a private ambulance for you just yet.'

'I wish that bloody parrot would stop squawking; it's giving me a headache,' I said to her, trying to hear myself speak. 'Did you know, Lynette, that during World War Two, the British Army *Chindits* Battalions who were based in Burma and Malaya were issued with machetes to dispense with the intertwining overgrowth in the jungle and to dispose of Japanese soldiers and unwanted parrots?'

'What has that got to do with this hotel?' Lynette asked curiously.

'Just turn yourself around and you will see why.' I replied, looking at a prowl of nips sitting around a table drinking Twinings Earl Grey tea by appointment to Her Majesty Queen Elizabeth II; 'Hannibal, our beloved Burmese cat, would feel at home in this hotel.'

Our hotel room on the fifth and top floor had the usual amenities, telephone, television, radio, and hairdryer in the bathroom and emergency escape instructions in case of fire, but alas, no tea and coffee facilities which Lynette and I seem to enjoy first thing in the morning. There were two tall glass window doors leading out on to a terrace where we had a good panoramic view of the city; the *Eiffel Tower* across the River Seine being the most prominent feature.

It was a beautiful sunny morning and the trees, especially the cherry and apple ones were in bloom as we gazed over the shoulder-high eighteenth century wrought iron balustrade to one floor below a typical Georgian roof.

Our double size wooden bed looked as though it had seen better days and had probably been subjected to plenty of action during and after the Napoleonic wars; however, Marie Antoinette was nowhere in sight having been stoned out of her head and guillotined by the Partisans of Paris during the French Revolution.

'Do you know, Lynette, that highly polished mahogany headboard could be worth a great deal of money.' I pointed out when I looked at a motive in the centre with the initials NB surrounded by carved laurel leaves. 'It would be far better resting on the top of a bonfire along with the rest of the junk his predecessors churned out.'

'Here we go again; having another go at the French,' Lynette said, sighing. 'And if it wasn't for the French we wouldn't have that lovely clock on the mantelpiece at home, would we?' she went on.

'Well, Auntie Gertrude's clock was made by Napoleon the Third; he was good at making clocks he was, and do you know, he made so many clocks he couldn't give them away.'

'Now you are talking rubbish, Christopher; Auntie Gertrude's clock and the two matching candlesticks had an estimated value of eighteen-hundred pounds.' she said, continuing with her Antiques Road Show.

'No doubt I had better rummage around inside the garage to find those marble candlesticks.'

Lynette then proceeded to say: 'Come on, let's go and explore the town, Chris, before the hotel's representative from a Thomas Cook's travel agent shows up this afternoon.'

'That's a good idea, Lynette, and if he or she thinks we are going to pay for the extra weight in Joe Baxi's taxi, they will have another think coming.'

Chapter Twenty-three

We had a quick wash and brush-up in a bathroom, which looked like it had been used by members of the Roman senate, was covered in blue and green mosaic tiles, and above the shower I thought I could see Brigitte-Helen Boullard carrying a water pitcher on one of her bare shoulders.

We made our way down in the lift to the reception area where Heidi Schmidt, the hotel's blonde-haired German receptionist was still busy jack-booting around looking for someone to whip into shape behind the desk. Her pigtails were like intertwining strands of multi-coloured Laura Ashley curtain rope, tied together on top of her head resembling a plastic souvenir shop Gretchen sitting on a Bavarian cuckoo clock swing.

'Would there be a possibility I could have one of your street maps of Paris.' I asked, trying desperately to lure Heidi away from the mirror which she continually used to check her beauty spot just to see that it hadn't fallen off.

'What do you call a seat belt in German?' I asked Lynette after Heidi had pointed her long scratchy fingernails towards a stand where maps and informative leaflets were displayed.

'Is this another one of your stupid jokes, Chris?' she said, obviously wondering what my answer was going to be.

As we both stood by the stand I could see her brain working overtime and this was when I said:

'It is called a "*klunken-klicken fraulein-schtrappen*".

'Ha Ha very funny, Christopher; have you got anymore like that?' she wantingly asked. 'Last night you gave me a lipstick that resembled a vibrator and now you are talking about a strap-on; it's a wonder you didn't ask me to bark in the cabin.

'As a matter of fact I have, my dearest; what do you call a German windscreen wiper?'

'Don't tell me, it's a "*flippen-floppen washen-wipen*" she replied.

'Tell me, Lynette, how did you know that?'

'You will leave scrappy bits of paper lying around all over the house, Chris; it's bad enough having one comedienne in our family never mind two.

'This leaflet and street map seems to be okay, Lynette;' pointedly ignoring her comments, 'it gives you information about some of the places you can visit at your leisure.'

'I suppose the courier will no doubt inform us of the various excursions to places of interest; I like the look of the *Palais de Versailles*, that will be fun, won't it?' Lynette said, knowing what I would say.

'Yes, it will and did you know, Lynette, there are moves afoot to ban walking sticks and Zimmer frames inside the palace because of them damaging the floor and furniture.'

'No, I didn't know that, Chris, so you had better leave your collapsible beer trolley in our room.'

'I wonder what will be on the menu for this evening's meal, Lynette; probably stuffed monkey or stewed parrot served up with sesame seeds and dried banana skins I have no doubt, because earlier, I saw a common squirrel monkey reaching from its cage in an attempt to steal an apple from one of the tables in the conservatory.

'Whatever it is, Chris, I'm sure it will be very nice.' Lynette said pointing to the main door and reminding me it was time we ventured out into that crocodile city to find somewhere to eat.

The food that evening looked like nineteenth century untreated brown leather travel bags containing a Malay Curry; two wooden skewers were used to ensure the parched banana leaf parcels were closed and to maintain the heat inside. An entire lamb shank, slow-cooked and served in a rich *Massaman* sauce was an alternative to this remarkable fete of culinary expertise, so rich and beautifully tender. I opted for the charred sacks of curry and Lynette the lamb shank; both dishes served up with plain boiled rice, dried coconut and sauté potatoes. A full bottle of Italian *Chianti Melini* wine was brought to our table by Tonino Omassoli, one of the hotel's over-friendly waiters whose father just happened to be the Mayor of Catania in Sicily. I later said to Lynette, that when we leave for Bournemouth next week we had better give him a good tip or else we and our luggage may just end up floating in the River Seine.

The standard lamp transformer wine bottle which was delivered to our table had interwoven strands of raffia wrapped around its base to make a multi-coloured basket and after I had explained that they were to prevent stains going on to decorative tablecloths, Lynette said to me: 'Don't you mean Mafia baskets, Christopher?'

'Keep the noise down, Lynette,' I said in a very low tone of voice. 'We don't want to give those Italian guests from Milano on the next table the wrong impression.' There were at least six tables pushed together to accommodate the Italian guests who had obviously just arrived in a state of the art bus which we had seen parked in the courtyard of the hotel for most of the afternoon.

'Don't worry, Chris, they won't be able to understand a single word we say.' Lynette, in her infinite wisdom led me to believe before one of them came over to our table and said: 'We know more English than you think.' Well, it sounded like that anyway.

'*Joyeuses pâques!*' '*Buona Pasqua!*' Happy Easter, but don't break any eggs.' I said to Benito Mussolini, the bald-headed priest from *Milano*.

'And a Happy Easter to you both.' he said, giving us the impression he knew just about everything and knew very little when he tried to impress us by saying there is a park nearby where we can play a game called, *boulangerie*.

I said to him: 'don't you mean *boules?*' and this was when I explained to him that a *boulangerie* is a French word for bakery.

Following a swift apology the priest gave Lynette and me the opportunity to receive a blessed benediction before he sat down to resume eating his meal.

We were also entertained by a table full of gay Germans who were deliberately put into a corner by the management out of arms reach of the British contingent; a coach-load of bricklayers from Newcastle-upon-Tyne. The gay Bavarian slap-dancing team from Munich seemed to me like a bunch of wooden Pinocchios wearing tight-fitting leather gear; their bulbous red noses protruding out from underneath their green Tyrolean hats sporting straggly blue and red feathers. It would have been like integrating a platoon of paratroopers with a crowd of budgie fanciers.

After taking our lives into our hands twice that day, negotiating the busy traffic in *Boulevard de la Madeleine*, and then later on in the restaurant, Lynette and I stumbled across a large *brassiere*, a café and bar close to the *Opera Garnier* on *Boulevard des Capucines*.

The *brassiere* was called '*Le Grande Café Para dais*', with tables and chairs outside on a wooden terrace and underneath a green canopy promoting *Stella Artois* beer.

A typical Parisian waiter who was dressed in a pair of shiny black trousers, white shirt, bow tie, waistcoat and an apron, appeared on to the terrace twirling a circular tin tray which looked as if it was about to take off from his middle finger.

Following the usual *bonjour*, the waiter said he was from Stockport in Cheshire and there was no need for us to struggle with the French language because it was difficult for him too, having to speak several languages and to remember a few choice words when German visitors begin to bang on the tables and make irritating noises when they want to be served.

He secured his tip well in advance when he told us his name was Joe Hoyle and had been working as a waiter in France for over two years. Joe asked us if we would like a menu or to take the *plat de jour*, the set meal of the day: consisting of a starter: *soupe* à l'oignon, French onion soup served with *Emmental* cheese and *baguette blanche croutons*; small round pieces of bread; the main course: *hache parmintier*, *salad avec frites*; cottage pie, salad and chips. He convinced us that the main course would be extra special because the chef had worked in Dorchester and then after explaining to me it was in the town and not the prestigious hotel in London I began to wonder about my sense of hearing; later, I blamed it on the traffic which was excessive and overwhelmingly noisy.

I ordered two large gin and tonics and thought this would be a civilized way to begin our adventure in this strange and foreign land where they pee in the street and chuck cannon balls around in the park.

Joe asked if we would like some *gateaux* with our drinks. I thought this to be rather strange behaviour eating cake before we ordered our meal and especially coming from a waiter from the North of England who would much prefer to eat his dessert following a fish and chip supper. He explained quite eloquently that in France *gateaux* were an assortment of microscopic nibbles and came from a United Biscuit factory in Lyon and not a 'Coco Pop' *patisserie* in the Black Forest. Joseph also told us that prior to working as a waiter in Paris he had a catering job in Hamburg selling one metre long hot dog sausages to football spectators; he reluctantly went on to tell us that when he returned to his tiny flat in the notorious red light area, he removed slithers of tomato ketchup, mayonnaise and mustard which had run down his arms when his boss, Herr Schneider, tried to make a quick turnover in profit during half-time. I thought to myself who can believe that story but then he proceeded to show me a photograph of the longest sausage in the world, long and large enough to be entered into the Guinness Book of Records, without the relish.

Lynette and I had two more gin and tonics before leaving the establishment and Joe, our congenial host and waiter, a handsome tip of ten francs. He asked if we would be coming back to the bar later as it was a *"Jazzitudes"* evening and there would be lots of French people in attendance to blow trumpets and to sing the *"Marseilles"*, the French National Anthem.

'Well, that will be fun, won't it, Chris?'

'It sounds bloody disgusting to me, Lynette; will Jacques Chirac be coming?'

The time on my recently acquired holiday *Swatch* watch was ten minutes to three when Lynette and I walked into the reception of the '*L'Experience Burmais*' hotel to wait for the representative from Messrs Thomas Cook Travel to arrive. The 'rep' was a young woman called Pascale Duval and was already sitting comfortably in a rattan chair with her shapely legs crossed and displaying stocking-clad thighs which extenuated her hour-glass figure.

'Did you know, Lynette, the Chinese put fleas into wrist watches before they sell them to prospective customers?'

'And why do they do that, Chris, please pray tell me.'

'It's because when the customers put the timepieces up to their ears, they can hear them ticking.'

'Honestly, Christopher, I have never heard so much rubbish in all my life.'

'Well, you never said that, Lynette, when I bought you your replica *Longines* watch from Hong Kong.'

'Replica, replica; what are you talking about? You said you bought it in a prestigious and exclusive jewellery shop in Causeway Bay, Hong Kong.'

'I did and I'm only joking with you.' I said, trying to lower her stress thermometer to a more acceptable level.

'You will have your little joke, won't you, Chris. Well, I will tell you that I bought your birthday present; your so-called Swiss *Swatch* watch from a stall in Salisbury market.'

'Well, that will explain why I have to replace the battery every week.'

'*Bonjour* and Good afternoon, *Monsieur* and *Madame* Travis,' *Mademoiselle* Pascale Duval said as she got up from the colonial type of chair to shake our hands. 'Haven't I seen you both somewhere before?' she added. 'I have just returned from London and I could swear I have seen your photograph in a newspaper.'

I put her mind at rest when I said it must have been someone who looked like me, putting a hand in front of my beard to disguise my enigmatic profile.

'Well, first of all I will show you our Thomas Cook brochure explaining our wide range of excursions and places to visit during your stay in Paris. These inexpensive tours can be booked at once and I recommend that tomorrow evening you visit the irresistible international triumph; the LIDO on the *Champs-Elysées* where you can both have either a Dinner and Show or Champagne and Show. When I was at *Saint Germain* Convent School in Paris, I wanted to be a 'bluebell girl',' she went on to explain. 'I didn't quite fulfil the criteria as I am only five feet two inches tall.'

'Ah, but you make up for it on top, love.' I explained in my usual eloquent way. 'You should be thankful for small *mercie boucoups*.'

'I know a man who works at the LIDO and he will be able to arrange a table next to the stage,' Pascale said, raising her eyebrows in surprise, proceeding to show me a leaflet depicting a lady cavorting with a string of artificial bananas wrapped around her waist. 'You will both have a better view from where you are sitting.' she added, giving me the impression I was going to be in for a good night's entertainment.

'Christopher, behave yourself, you are old enough to be her father.' Lynette said, whispering in my ear after I had clocked a glimpse of Pascal's French knickers.

'I had my boobs super-inflated at the Doctor Maynard clinic in *rue St Claire*, the road adjoining *Boulevard Haussmann*,' Pascale said to Lynette putting a hand on one of her knees. 'I can introduce you to him *Madame* Travis when the three of us go to the *Galeries Lafayette* on Thursday morning.'

'You certainly will not.' Lynette said, getting ready to up-sticks and leave her company.

My mind was working overtime thinking that this was her way of us traipsing around the cosmetics department in order to buy Pascale an expensive bottle of French perfume instead of giving her a handsome tip and afterwards allowing *Mademoiselle* Fifi to acquire a commission on a surgical operation in a Parisian silicon valley to get rid of my wife's laughter lines.

'*Mademoiselle* Schmidt, the hotel's receptionist had her boobs made larger at the same place and she hasn't looked back.' Pascale told us secretively.

'From where I am sitting it would seem she can't look back because they are so big.' I said, cupping my hands as if they were holding two mounds of undulating flesh. 'And does this Doctor Maynard remove unwanted tattoos from people's bums, *Mademoiselle*?'

'For Pete's sake, Chris, give it a rest; you are so embarrassing.' Lynette said, and this was when I saw *Fraulein* Schmidt checking herself in the mirror behind the reception desk just to make sure her massive protrusions were pointing in the right direction, preferably towards me.

'I recommend that on Monday morning after the *Tour de Eiffel* you go and visit the *L'Eglise de Sacre Coeur*, Church of the Sacred Heart, the Cathedral in *Montmartre*,' Pascale suggested and following on with: 'And on Tuesday, I further suggest after *Notre Dame*, we all go to the *Château de Versailles*, I will be your courier on the bus next week.' she added.

'It is possible, that on Monday morning, Mister Travis will need to go and visit a Cathedral.' Lynette said to her.

'If you do decide to visit *Versailles*, you will be sitting in seats numbered twenty-two and twenty-three,' Pascale took delight in telling us. 'The driver of the bus has a raffle amongst the passengers at no extra charge and one of those two seats almost invariably has the pleasure of winning a magnum of *Laurent-Perrier Champagne*.' and I have suddenly remembered where I have seen you before, sir; you are the two people who won the lottery in London.'

'I work on the premise, Lynette, there is no such thing as a free lunch and it doesn't necessarily follow that if you scratch my back and I scratch yours, you get what you want and then end up with a big disappointment.' I said to the woman who knows absolutely everything.

'You haven't scratched my back in years,' Lynette said with a bigger grin on her face than a heavily made-up circus clown. 'Just give her the money, Christopher and shut up.' she said, sounding like Wilfred Pickles on the ancient television quiz show "Take your Pick".

'You sound like Wilfred Pickles, Lynette.'

'Oh, we're back to Wilson Picket again, are we?' she so said.

After reminding her that Wilson Picket is black and after parting with eight hundred and fifty French Francs for the excursions, a cognac and a miniscule cup of espresso coffee for Pascale, Lynette and I said farewell and adieu to her; well at least for the time being but this was until we saw her again the following evening in the LIDO, a half-dressed 'Snow White' wearing a white see-through costume, and performing coquettishly on ice with her line of dwarfs, one of them was 'Grumpy' who looked remarkably like the coach driver. She was creating a real spectacle of herself; "exoticness" personified, obliging the Parisian and foreign fascination with semi-nude entertainment.

'Do you know, Lynette, I have often wondered why my mum, dad and I had trouble trying to adjust the colour on our black and white television set.'

'Again, you have an answer to everything, haven't you, Christopher?'

'Well, I might.'

Chapter Twenty-four

The following Tuesday 25th April 2000

The Lido de Paris, boasting traditional Moulin Rouge style cabaret and exotic shows, was exciting on Sunday evening and came up to my expectations, especially when we saw Pascale Duval ice skating on stage with the seven dwarfs singing: "Hi Ho...., Hi Ho....., it's off to work we go, with a shovel and a spade, she's about to get laid, Hi Ho, Hi Ho, Hi Ho, Hi Ho" etc, well, it looked and sounded like that from where I was sitting. Lynette had told me at least six times during the various performances to put my eyes back into their sockets; the long-legged dancers, accentuated by six-inch high-heeled shoes, showed off their bare boobs and wore what looked like an arrangement of multi-coloured Robert Dias feather dusters, irresistible to say the least. I had the pleasure to remind myself after one of them looked in my direction to give me a wink of an eye; you know, the one's that seem to last forever and that this was going to be an evening to remember. It was during the interval we ate Scotch *smokies*; thinly sliced red salmon, gateaux and drank Champagne by the bucket-full courtesy of the management because it would seem word had been bandied around that Lynette and I were loaded and I knew one of the performers intimately. It was while I was tucking into my fourth *vol-au-vent*, small explosive puff pastries filled with chicken supreme and truffle sauce exclusively designed by the LIDO's Master Chef, Philippe Laoroix, my wife said:

'I am going to write to the French Tourist Board about the extreme exhibitionism that is going on here; it is in bad taste.'

When she had finished with her unnecessary threats to close the place down, Pascale Duval came over to our table and asked if we were enjoying the show. Naturally, Lynette replied by saying that it was very enjoyable and she wouldn't have missed it for the world.

Sitting there with my mouth wide open, trying to comprehend why Lynette had taken it upon herself to adopt a two-faced attitude, I suddenly saw Heidi Schmidt jack-booting on the stage wearing tight-fitting leather gear, black fishnet stockings and a gay boy hat; she appeared to be emulating a sadistic female member of The Third Reich, erotically going through the motions of giving someone plenty of *Deutsch Marks* with what seemed to be a rather long bull-whip.

'Would you like one of our tee-shirts?' Pascale asked, to which I replied: 'Yes, that would be great and I will treasure it for the rest of my life.'

'What do you mean, treasure it, you are supposed to wear it.' Lynette said, snatching the sexy red and blue shirt out of my hands to check the size to the upper part of her body.

'Listen,' Pascale said. 'I will give you both a tee-shirt, just to save any arguments you may have between yourselves, but don't tell anyone because they'll all want one.'

The next to arrive on the scene was the Lido's *pièce de résistance* in stage entertainment; the rude, irresistible iconic French can-can girls dressed in different shades of pastel coloured frilly dresses which looked like artificial pink, green, yellow and blue carnations. These high-kicking black stocking dancers gave me a headache when they began to scream loudly at the audience; the naughtiness building up each time they bent down to show me their long legs and French cami-knickers.

At eleven the cabaret came to an end and after I had signed a few autographs to substantiate my authority for Lynette and I to sit at the best table in the house, we made our way out into the street where a taxi was waiting to take us back to the hotel.

Yesterday began with us taking breakfast in the restaurant and because we were the famous couple who had just won the lottery we had the pleasure of making sure our friendly Sicilian waiter, Tonino Omassoli, behaved himself in a manner to which we, British tourists, so rightly deserved.

Our breakfast was interrupted by Foster and Isla McGregor, the intrepid travellers from North Berwick; Scotland's answer to Mister and Missus Strange, who would insist in telling us how much they had saved since being in France and where we could find plenty of bargains in Paris. It was during the afternoon after seeing Foster play poker opposite his wife in front of a mirror and endless board games away from the bar, I named them Fosdyke and Isla McScrabble. It was Isla who was in charge of the duty-free whisky bottles which were surreptitiously hidden away inside her handbag only to appear as and when necessary to replenish their hob-knob tumbler glasses.

'The Scots did the world a grave injustice when they introduced whisky into their staple diet.' I said to Lynette as I watched the last droplets of 'Famous Grouse Whisky' trickle into his glass. 'Tight-fisted weenies wearing kilts, I call them.'

'You don't say that when you're taking a wee dram in the Queens, and, you don't say no to 'Walker's Highland shortbread', do you, Chris?'

'Well, that's different, Lynette, but I did silence Andy Stewart when I sat on one of his records.'

'Have you never heard of rapprochement, Chris?'

'Does that come with batteries, Lynette?'

'Rapprochement is re-establishment of friendly relations.' she was quick to point out as if she had just returned from an assertiveness, power and endearment course.

'You won't be saying that if they decided to go it alone and break into Europe; the Glaswegians have broken into everywhere else, so why not Europe?'

'I'm only trying to shake off the shackles of the archetype, Christopher.'

Fosdyke was heavily into poetry and even more so after he had consumed a few more wee drams of whisky from his wife's mobile dispensing unit. I can recall him giving us a rendition of: "A wee in the Dee" penned by a person who should be in jail for trying to recruit Scottish misfits into their wee Highland police forces. The poem went something like this:

'A wee in the Dee'

A *wee* Scottish lassie had a *wee* tartan tie
And a *wee* tartan haggis hanging *fray* the thigh
A *wee* Highland safety pin protruded through her nose
On that bonny lassie *we oot* any clothes

On a Saturday night after a *wee* beer
She weed a *wee wee* by the banks of the weir
Up came a wee bobby on a *wee* mountain bike
And he said to the lassie *will ye* go for a hike
We you...ze, said the lassie this must be a joke
I'd sooner *ma wee haggis* or stiff some *maer* coke
To the station they went *we nae maer adieu*
He said to the lassie *tis awa tae* the loo
It took a *wee* while *tae get oar* the *wee* shock
And *tae nae maer go oot wee oot* any frock
Now the *wee* Scottish lassie wears a wee chequered hat
And a *wee* chequered scarf *tis* good for a laugh
Na maer the *wee* safety pin protruding through her nose
On that poor *wee* lassie *wee oot* any clothes

After the poem had fallen upon deaf ears I decided to give Fosdyke one of mine which goes:

'The Grouse'

There once was a bird that sat on a thistle
Pricked its arse and made it whistle

'I don't think that was in the least bit funny.' Fosdyke said to me in *Jockanese.*

'Neither was yours and don't give up your daytime job.' I rapidly replied.

'Certainly not until I retire from the North Berwick Police Constabulary next year.' he said, with a wicked twinkle in his eye.

'You know, I am considered to be one of the best poker players in the Force.' Fosdyke told me after I had clocked a couple of Aces which had fallen out of his sleeve on to the floor.

'So this is why we can't find a policeman whenever we want one; they are all in the bloody tea room playing poker.' I seriously replied.

He asked us where we had been and what culinary delights had we eaten for dinner during our leisurely trip around *Montmartre*. I said to him: 'where we come from it is called luncheon; you call it truncheon.'

'*Agh, ye canna fool me,*' Fosdyke said, in a language no one south of Hadrian's Wall could understand. 'I did ne cam oar on the last banana boat.' he added.

'Well, maybe you didn't, but your half litre bottles of duty-free Famous Grouse whisky did!'

'Isla and I took to the waters this morning and had a *wee* swim in the *wee* indoor pool; have you been for a *wee* dip yet?' Fosdyke asked, becoming increasingly fascinated by my handsome luminous *Casio* divers watch.

'No,' I replied. 'It is because you may have gone into the waters as a *wee* McGregor and *cam oot* a *wee* Campbell.'

'What do mean by that remark?' Isla asked, checking her casual shoes for the slightest bit of dirt.

'History tells me that when you enter the pool wearing a pair of red tartan shorts, they may come out looking a whiter shade of pale, and rumour has it that one couldn't get in through the hotel bar door last night because of tartan-clad '*Jockstraps*' dressed in kilts blocking the entrance; I heard they all *cam oot fray* the same tin.' I sarcastically remarked.

'History, laddie, is time out-of-date, and we are flying back to Aberdeen tomorrow just in time to see our brand new Scandinavian log cabin being built in a nearby forest glen.' Fosdyke had to mention.

'Well make sure it is well treated, Foster, because you don't want it falling into dilapidation, do you?' I said, knowing the nearest Scandinavian log cabin I was going to see was the tool shed in the back garden of number forty-six Queens Park Avenue, Bournemouth.

'Dilapidation' is that supposed to be a pun or a joke?' he asked, giving me time to think of a reasonable reply.

'No, No, I just thought I'd mention it because Lynette and I continually had to replace our wooden fencing due to the absence of creosote; I don't suppose you have a B&Q where you live, Foster.'

'It will be already treated with wood preservative; it is part of the deal'

Isla quickly interrupted.

'We thought our fencing was until it fell down.' I quickly put in. 'And, I wouldn't go talking about wood preservatives around here, Isla, because the French may think you are on the game.'

'You mean, like Scrabble?' Isla asked naively, behaving in a way similar to a gook.

'Where we live in North Berwick we have a barbeque in our front garden, twenty-six takeaways, five restaurants and two of the biggest fish and chip shops in Scotland.' Fosdyke told me, nodding his head like a donkey, hoping I wouldn't challenge his mathematical exaggerations about having two hundred and sixty-one gnomes in his back garden.

'You must have a very big front garden, Foster, and do you know, when Lynette and I got up this morning we stepped out on to our balcony and could see in the distance a large vinegar bottle from one of your fish and chip shops; it stands three hundred and one metres high.'

'*Agh*, I can easily fit it into the garage which is at the bottom of our two mile long driveway.' Fosdyke said bringing our amicable relationship to a close after asking him if he believed in the Loch Ness Monster.

'I wouldn't say yes, and I wouldn't say no, but thousands of people have seen the *beastie*, including policemen, councillors and pillars of the community.' he emphasized.

'Well, I would suggest you take a little more water with your whisky because it seems to me Loch Ness is just another ruse to accommodate more wealthy American tourists.'

'When I was a young girl participating in the Brighton carnival; I was one of the humps on the back of the Loch Ness Monster.' Lynette interestingly informed me.

'I bet you enjoyed that,' I said, laughing loudly. 'I suppose Charlie, your boyfriend was quite happy to be one of the "triple-humpers" underneath the blanket.' I went on to say.

Our trip to the *L'Eglise de Sacre Coeur* began with us joining a group of tourists in *Quai Branly* to do the *Tour de Eiffel* thing before stepping on-board a glass-top river-boat to take in picturesque scenes on both sides of the River Seine.

Lynette and I had decided not to ascend to the top of the *Eiffel Tower* having done it all before and elected to sit in the garden instead savouring *deux boules*, two scoops of pistachio ice cream delicately placed inside a cornet.

After the last of the frustrated tourists had abseiled down the outside of the tower we all made our way towards the '*Batobus*'; the River-boat shuttle service. The commentary on board was a Multi-lingual system, broadcasted in several languages, including *Jockanese* and from where Lynette and I were sitting on the top of this floating fish tank we had excellent panoramic views of the *Notre Dame* Cathedral, the *Hotel-de-Ville* and the *Louvre*. A bus was waiting by a quayside to take us to the church where we were blessed on the steps by a Parisian beggar who profited by selling us two bookmarks depicting the Madonna and Child; the wording on the reverse is in French and Lynette and I are still trying to figure out just what it is saying; probably take care of your wallet or handbag or something like that.

Following an interesting tour of the cathedral and afterwards, looking down from a height, taking in the awe-inspiring magnificent views of sleepy Paris, suddenly, it was time for lunch. A typical French bistro, *Le Café Rouge* was to be our place to eat, along a cobbled street and situated on a corner *in Rue St.Vincent*, oozing Parisian chic from every cobble, floorboard and poster. The blue and white overhead canopy was very *Provence* as we approached the restaurant with its basic tables and chairs on the pavement. The bistro, situated next to a *Creamerie*, a store which sold French and Turkish wines along with different types of local and Mediterranean cheeses became a talking point later when we discovered it was owned by an Armenian businessman who took great Turkish delight in displaying sweetmeats and almond cakes in his window. We learned from the Portuguese waitress that he also owned a kebab house directly in front of the main entrance to *Montmartre Cemetery*, and to add insult to injury, rumour has it that a French crooner called, Maurice Chevalier went into the takeaway to buy one of those ever-popular *doner kebabs* with hot chilli sauce just before he died.

The restaurant's young waitress was called Lena Ortiz and went into great detail describing her family and friends she had just left behind in a tiny fishing village on the outskirts of Lisbon. Lena was about to become married to a French artist called, Jean-Paul Bardoulet, a Parisian whom she had met in a bar when he was touring around Spain and Portugal.

After the formalities had been concluded, we ordered our food which consisted of a three-course French feast: the starter was *escargot*, snails in garlic, they taste like shit but you can live on them, or *soupe à l'oignon*, French onion soup with gooey *Emmental* cheese and croutons; the main course, *moules Marnier*, mussels aplenty or pan-seared halibut served with fennel and cream. The dessert menu was most definitely to be explored and not to be missed with ten different flavours of ice cream including alcohols, *Calvados* and *Cointreau*, enough to have one rocking in Sneakers that belong to Keith Richards. There was enough bread on the table to feed the ducks in Saint James Park in London, and we were constantly asked by Lena if we would like more with our soup and to soak up the garlic and cream from around the bottom of our square porcelain main course plates.

The hides of March had long since been and gone, the high winds and rain that followed the snow were a thing of the past and had been replaced by a warm and pleasant climate.

Lynette and I were sitting in the shade underneath an apple blossom tree; the white flakes of petals covering the ground below us. We sipped and savoured the *Courvoisier* brandy from special edition Napoleon Bonaparte goldfish bowls which had a gold rim around the edge and a laurel leaf motif printed on the side.

The bells from the cathedral were ringing out loudly in my ears, mournfully heralding another funeral. I came to the conclusion that by the solemn looks on people's faces as they walked around Montmartre, they weren't happy unless they were about to die. Some of the elderly men and women who passed by us were dressed in black and it appeared they couldn't wait to arrive at the church to join in with other mourners and to participate in their own death rehearsals. At low point, I was about to get up from my chair and shout "Good morning Vietnam" but then, one had to think about waking people up in this sleepy part of town.

Looking across the street we could see an *Artisan Chocolatier*, a chocolate manufacturing industry which doubled up as a tea shop selling out-of-date Easter eggs, bunnies, things on sticks and chocolate liqueurs that teetotallers' could get pissed on the silver paper.

The time was two o'clock and more knells of bells began to ring in our ears; this was the hour we said our goodbyes to Lena, wishing her all the very best on her very special day. She thanked us for our custom and instead of receiving a free hot fudge sundae on presentation of a coupon which was part of a tourist information leaflet inadvertently left on the table of the river-boat by Lynette; Lena presented us with us the bulbous Napoleon Bonaparte balloon glasses to take home with us.

We made our way to the car park behind the cathedral to join the coach and the holy-willies; priest groupies and prospective funeral directors who just couldn't wait for the river-boat to arrive at the quayside to take them back to the *brassieres* on the *Champs-Elysées* in order to replenish their alcoholic deficiencies with exotic French booze.

I overheard one Jewish tourist saying on-board the boat that the French had a damn nerve displaying a sign above the door to a synagogue saying that entry wasn't free unless they bought something from their holocaust souvenir shop. This reminded me of Michael Winner's collection of sick Hymie jokes; one of which goes something like this: 'Why are those numbers tattooed on your arm?' Hymie inquisitively asked his father. 'They are the numbers to the combination lock on the safe deposit box underneath the bed.' he replied.

Lynette and I arrived back at the hotel shortly after four, just in time for our afternoon cup of Lipton's Earl Grey tea, small triangular sandwiches and a quarter slab of *Breton* cake; a type of *Madeira* cake made with butter.

We failed to creep past and avoid Fosdyke and Isla McScrabble who were still playing their silly board games in the hotel's "Jasmine" lounge bar next to the reception. I called it banana land because of the excessive amounts of over-the-top plastic oranges, lemons and bananas that were growing in abundance around the bar which could have been designed by the hotel monkey. Lynette passed a rather impertinent comment when she said I should stay away from the bar area because reminiscent of Sainsburys supermarket I could trip over a banana and end up paying exorbitant fees in a French hospital. I told her not to get too excited because we are now fully paid-up members of BUPA, and if push comes to shove she could always arrange for an air ambulance to take me back to Bournemouth.

'Oh, you'll be going back on your own, will you Chris?' she said, with a wicked smile. 'I could volunteer to be a dancer in The *Folies Bergère*, and that will be fun, won't it?'

'With your classic lines accentuated by the fuller figure, I don't think so, Lynette.'

'You would never have said that before we were married, Christopher, I had an hour glass figure then.'

'I know, and in those days I was frightened of having a Hells Angel wrapping a chain around my head.'

'There was nothing wrong with Charlie Payne; he was just a bit careless with boxes of matches.'

'A bit careless with boxes of matches; he set fire to your father's shed and burnt it down to the ground when he was told to go out into the garden one evening to smoke his cigarette.'

'Yes, well that was a long time ago, he's got his own business in Brighton now according to my mum; he's a tattooist and an ear-piercing expert.'

'Well, that could explain why you have that monstrosity emblazoned on your backside, Lynette, and here's me thinking he sold fire extinguishers.'

'Charlie is a real artist and puts things into places where other artists cannot reach.'

'I bet he does, Lynette, and would this include putting studs and ring-pulls into people's noses and padlocks into their.....'

'Christopher, stop it, just stop it, you're being vulgar.' she said and before I had the opportunity to ask her whether he was into belly buttons.

I later rendered one of my better jokes, aptly told for the moment and at no extra charge.

'A man went into see a gay tattooist and asked did he do butterflies? And the tattooist said no, but I do bees. Later that evening the man's wife said to him 'who the hell is Bob?'

'I suppose you think that was funny.' Lynette said putting me in a death row queue once again.

'Not as funny as you riding around Brighton on the back of a seven-fifty cc Harley Davidson motorcycle wearing jeans with more holes in them than a full round of *Emmental* cheese.

'They were expensive designer Levi jeans, Chris, I bought them from McQueen's, the exclusive fashion boutique in Brighton.'

'Well, if I had been you, Lynette, I would have taken them back to the shop and asked for a refund.'

'That's the trouble with you, Christopher; you don't have any imagination or parental control.'

'What do you mean by that remark?' I asked in readiness for her next attempt to rip my guts out.

'It's time your daughter, Victoria, bought a pair of jeans from McQueen's in Bournemouth; they looked as though they had been slashed with a razor and you didn't say anything derogatory to her, did you?'

'Well, she is young.' I replied.

'And, I wasn't entirely a 'Granny Much' either, was I, Chris? And if it wasn't for that kind of inspiration we wouldn't have the shop, would we?'

'Are you talking about 'Lynette Travis Ladies Fashions' in Boscombe High Street or 'McQueen's' in Old Christchurch Road, Bournemouth?'

*

And so this was Tuesday, another day nearer towards me going home on Saturday to see the big match between Bournemouth and Leeds United at AFC Bournemouth Goldsands Stadium and I couldn't wait to take a bite out of one of their freshly-baked Cornish pasties at half-time; the smell being enough to have the referee call for extra time.

The fosdyke saga had pleasantly come to an end and Foster and Isla McGregor by now were probably sitting by the fire in their brand new

Scandinavian log cabin playing Scrabble or counting the Thomas Cook travellers cheques they had not used during their holiday in France. 'How did she manage to set fire to their kitchen in North Berwick? Lynette asked, shrugging her shoulders in disbelief.

'It was something to do with Isla the dragon sticking her fiery tongue out.' I replied.

The coach arrived shortly after breakfast to take us on excursion visits to the twelfth century *Cathédrale, Notre Dame de Paris*, the Cathedral in the centre of Paris and the *Château de Versailles*, eleven miles south west of the city.

There was a gathering of Japanese guests in the lobby waiting to see Pascale Duval, 'Clip-board Annie', before they boarded the coach to buy a curried to death Pot Noodle which was on special offer after they had found the knives, forks and spoons difficult to use during breakfast.

'*Bonjour* Mister and Mrs Travis,' Mademoiselle Duval said as Lynette and I approached the door. 'You will be sitting in the centre of the bus because when passengers insist on smoking camel shit, pungent French Galois cigarettes, Japanese tourists, who I place over a wheel, usually throw up and make a mess. Oh, and by the way, sexy tee shirts!' she added, making everyone on-board feel envious of her presentation of the garments during our visit to the LIDO.

The bus had disappeared to a car park in *île-de-France* near the Cathedral so there was no way of escaping from the Japanese tourists who were staring up towards the belfry waiting for Quasimodo, '*The Hunch-back of Notre Dame*', to swing down from the rafters to chase after Esmeralda. There was an incident in the conservatory the previous evening when one of them bowed so low he hit his head on an extremely large goldfish in a pond and had to be assisted back to his room; up until then I didn't realize that I was so important.

The weather had suddenly changed and dark clouds began to appear overhead as Lynette and I walked through the side entrance to gain access to observe one of the finest examples of French gothic architecture. A balding Japanese tourist guide who was standing at the doorway trying to flog his brightly coloured Oriental type umbrellas to worried passengers lest they got their hair wet, shouted:

'*Aso!*, *le metio*, the weather is very inclement. I have very special umbelella for very special lain.'

I chuckled underneath my breath after saying to Lynette:

'*Aso!*, *la Notre Dame* Cathedral, very special hotel in Paris, ah, but not as special as Lynette Travis from *Bligh ton*.'

A Japanese tourist who appeared to be creeping up my backside said:

'I can understand English you know.'

After I had replied by saying, 'Well, bully for you,' and refrained from blasphemy in one of God's holy churches, he disappeared into a priest hole to commit suicide.

'If wit was shit, he'd be constipated.' I muttered to myself as Lynette fumbled around inside her shoulder bag to find a packet of tissues, and this was when we were accosted by another escapee from the Land of the rising Sun. Looking like he had just signed the Japanese surrender he said that he liked *Bligh ton*. I replied by telling him that Lynette's mother and father live in Brighton and we visit them regularly. 'No, no,' he said, 'Enid Blighton, very good lighter.'

The coach driver reappeared looking as grumpy as ever and I said to Lynette: 'He and Snow White had better get their skates on because it looks like we are in for a storm and we don't want to get our newly acquired tee-shirts wet; do we?'

For once in my life she agreed with me and so we made a dash for the coach which was waiting outside the main entrance to the *Hotel de Ville*, the town hall.

I noticed we were sitting in seats numbered twenty-two and twenty-three on the starboard side of the forty-six seater bus with a chemical lavatory downstairs and a pot noodle station in the centre directly in front of us. As predicted by *Mademoiselle* Fifi, Lynette and I later won the prize draw when 'Grumpy', the pint-sized coach driver invited a Japanese linguistic expert to delve into a small *Galeries Lafayette* carrier bag and pick out our winning seat number.

'Aso! Ladies and Gentlemen, and the winning number is going to be twenty-flee.'

'Fixed it was, bloody well fixed!' one Welsh passenger shouted from one of the rear seats before giving us his rendition of, "Wellies in the Valleys"; the words sounding like sheep dipping or something unmentionable which could have up-tipped the balance of the lambing season.

'Instead of the *Laurent-Perrier* Champagne, we could have been presented with a cardboard crate of *Stella Artois* beer,' Lynette said, whispering in my ear. 'then you could have brought your Brittany Ferries collapsible beer trolley.

We arrived at the *Château de Versailles* at approximately eleven forty-five, just in time to see a re-enactment of the Sun King, Louis XIV of France and his missus, Marie Antoinette, being carted off to be decapitated by the partisans of Paris and, eating *spaghetti bolognaise* with lashings of tomato ketchup fifteen minutes after the event had taken place, made no difference to my appetite. Lynette and I were greeted inside the massive entrance courtyard by an equestrian statue of Louis XIV himself, looking none the worse after being weather-beaten for more than two hundred years.

The Palais de Versailles, in my opinion, was a big motel with its formal garden, the largest aquatic swimming pool in North West Europe, ideal for topless sunbathing, jet-skiing, paragliding, that sort of thing. Prevailing wind and rain was now the order of the day as we paraded through the Hall of Mirrors, commonly known as the *Galerie des Glaces*, and is the largest room in the Palace overlooking Versailles Park. The principle feature of the Hall is the seventeen mirror-clad arches that reflect the seventeen arcaded windows which overlook the gardens. The Grand Canal and the walks and avenues we had to miss because of the somewhat inclement weather and so the only other avenue we had to consider was to go back inside the Palace and listen to a string quartet playing Mozart's "Serenade for thirteen Wind Instruments". I thought this to be nigh impossible until I was subjected later to a rather unpleasant smell reminiscent to a plateful of *Spaghetti Bolognaise Napolitana*.

The rain had suddenly stopped and I found myself gazing into a fountain in the formal garden, seeing a dazzling reflection of my face on top of the water accentuated by a brilliant prism created by the sun. "Three coins in a fountain, which one should the fountain bless, three coins in a fountain, each one brings you happiness".

'Tell me Chris, what are you thinking?' Lynette asked sympathetically.

'I'm thinking what a lucky man I am having such a beautiful lady wife and two wonderful grown up children.'

'Ah, that was nice, Christopher, and here's me thinking you didn't really care.' she said, rubbing her hand up and down my back instead of a knife. 'Come on, let's go back to the hotel and put the kettle on and make ourselves a nice cup of tea.' Lynette added with a smile.

Chapter Twenty-five

Wednesday morning – the following day

Our leisurely day began at seven-thirty when Lynette and I went down to take breakfast in a small alcove belonging to the hotel's main restaurant.

My *Casio* diver's watch which is waterproof down to a depth of one-hundred metres began to ring in my ears informing me it was seven o'clock precisely and time to get out of bed. In a tired state I inadvertently forgot to remove the timepiece from my wrist before getting into bed the night before and it was when the melodious jingle interacted with a buzzing vibration, I fell on to the floor leaving Lynette to sleep peacefully in my wake.

We were greeted that morning by Karen Fontaine, a tall black Senegalese waitress who possessed as much warmth as dry-ice and a backbone similar to an emaciated tiger-king prawn. The first altercation I had with her was when I placed a basket of sliced *baguette*, bread in the centre of our table and like a stick insect she pounced over and nicked the basket and transferred it on to another table giving me the impression she patronized and favoured the Belgium Congolese element rather than seeing to my necessary breakfast requirements. They were temporarily being housed in one of the hotel's broom cupboards because of an overloaded migrant boat capsizing in the Atlantic Ocean during a compulsory on-board fire drill. I immediately got up from my chair and quickly snaffled it back before telling the six-foot two-inch praying mantis she was very lucky not to be carrying a water pitcher around on top of her head and to have a steady job working in such a prestigious hotel in the centre of Paris; parts of which would definitely make her feel at home. After I had inspected my fruit salad and cornflakes for locusts, deadly black tarantula spiders and monkeys with extremely long arms, I proceeded to bring back to life a pineapple which looked like it had been refrigerated to death for weeks inside a maritime storage container. The Brazilian espresso coffee was delivered to our table by my favourite waitress, who by the way, had unfortunately escaped from being kidnapped by stray East African elephant poachers in February of the same year and the coffee tasted reminiscently of *'Tate & Lyle'* treacle. There was a small ceramic spoon which one used to stir the contents of the miniscule ceramic cup and saucer which were made in Stoke on Trent, and a fine chain was attached to the pottery just in case one of the African guests had an idea to remove it from the hotel's kitchen inventory.

'Enjoy your breakfast.' *Mambo* said, giving me a look that could turn the milk sour in my cereal bowl.

I said to Lynette, the woman has a sense of humour and should be promoted to head cheer leader.

'Will you be staying here for lunch mister?' Mambo asked impertinently. 'It is *Monsieur* Omassolis' day off, and I am going to be your waitress for the remainder of the day.'

'Not if we can help it.' I said to her in no uncertain terms. 'We may decide to go to McDonalds instead and take in a burger or two; you never know, Lynette, you could end up with a cuddly toy.'

'I should be so lucky, Christopher,' she yawned. 'And, after last night's performance I most certainly will need one.'

'Well, it was a heavy day, wasn't it Lynette? Traipsing around the grounds of the *Palais de Versailles*; it was exhausting to say the least.'

'That is little excuse for you snoring like a proverbial water hog all night long.' she added, continuing to show me her pink tonsils at the back of her throat.

'What have you decided we are going to do today, Lynette? I am sure you will have had it all worked out.'

'I thought we would have a look at a few estate agents to get an idea of the prices of property because the currency exchange rate is very good at the moment.' she said, knowing I had no choice but to go along with her.

'I hope this is not going to be one of those days when I will be run off my feet because I would sooner stay inside the hotel talking to the parrot or *Mademoiselle* Fontaine, who, as you know has as much charm as a Senegalese black cobra.'

'You don't like Karen, do you, Chris?' Lynette asked, divulging Karin's proper Christian name and making it sound like black magic.

'No, I bloody well don't, and Voodoo is an excellent name to call her, and before you order a hot chocolate my dear, just think of the repercussions.'

'What repercussions?'

'Well, you may just end up in a cooking pot, you know, one of those big black cauldrons pigmies have constantly on the boil in the jungle.'

'Do you know, Christopher Miles Travis, you really take the biscuit.'

'Sometimes I think we would be much better off buying a packet of biscuits.' I replied.

'Anyway, Karin is not a pigmy; she is at least five feet ten inches tall.' Lynette said, describing her height in an imperial size.

'We should be into metric conversion by now, Lynette, and you of all people should know this when you buy garments for the dress shop.'

'Okay, Mister Know-It-All, how big a packet of biscuits do you want?' Lynette asked.

'Oh, a half pound packet of Ginger Nuts should be sufficient.' I suggested.

'You are in France, Chris; not bloody Sainsbury's!'

After I had metaphorically realized that the price to pay for Lynette and me to become too friendly with a Zulu warrior was to have an assegai, a deadly spear poked in the centre of our backs, we both got up from our high-back rattan chairs and walked out of the restaurant.

We both returned to our eyrie on the fifth floor to find Sophie Talbot, the young and ambitious chambermaid making a quick exit from the room having systematically cleaned it in record-breaking time. The television had been switched on and a deep impression in the *chaise longue* was in evidence where she had been lounging, watching my favourite episode of Mr Bean, the one when he becomes caught out in the public swimming baths minus his costume. Nevertheless, things were to our liking, and apart from a piece of duty free *Toblerone* being broken off at one end and supplying us with more than enough sachets of shampoo and shower gel to last Lynette, myself and the girls until Christmas, I suppose it was her way of securing a tip when we vacated the room.

In contrast to the previous day when we overheard a French person in *Versailles* complain that it was raining dogs and cats and she was going to report the severe weather conditions to *Monsieur* Thomas Cook in the hope he would give her a refund, Wednesday morning was sunny and warm. Taking into account that the average French brain works in reverse to anyone else's and that an educated monkey could sit in the House of Representatives in Paris without taking extended lunch breaks in the *LIDO* on the *Champs Elysées* or the *Folies Bergère* in *rue Richer*.

Lynette and I were leaning over the balcony pleasantly watching the busy traffic going by and listening to the distinctive deafening noise of sirens which seemed to be coming from police vehicles, fire engines and ambulances, guaranteed to make an arrest, put one's fire out, or put you into a private hospital, *tout suite*; immediately, but not before you have agreed to pay for their services.

These so-called emergency services have the audacity to visit your home every Christmas to try and flog you one of their calendars and it is during the festive season one finds it necessary to hide behind one's curtains because *le facteur*, the postman plays his bagpipes underneath your window and then bangs loudly on the front door. *Madame* Grandin, a sweet elderly French lady, who became one of our neighbours told us she peeps out from behind her curtains to watch the delivery of publicity, junk mail, government-related letters; the postman, hoping she would eventually open the door and buy one of his poor quality upside down *Bureau de la Poste* calendars to help pay for his next visit to the pub.

We continued to observe the magnificent view of Paris from the balcony and to appreciate the French architecture surrounding the hotel. The early morning heat haze and grey mist hovering in the grounds of the park, engulfing the *Eiffel Tower* at its base seemed to be anxiously waiting for tourists to arrive to have their pockets picked or their handbags snatched as they waited to make a slow descent inside a crowded lift.

'There's only one way up and one way down.' I heard one American tourist say to his wife. 'It will take us five minutes to reach the top and an hour and a quarter to get down and by that time we will have missed the bus.'

'Don't worry Vernon; there's a Hop on, Hop off red bus every ten minutes and we sure as hell don't wanna go to Disneyland Paris tomorrow because I've had enough of spending this Mickey Mouse money and besides we have been to Orlando six times already.'

It was nine o'clock when we ventured out into the busy street, Boulevard de la Madeleine, where if one isn't careful of one's distance between the pavement and the road one could receive a *gratuit*, a free shampoo and set, courtesy of Paris Borough Council. We made our way towards *Boulevard Haussmann* passing by *Place de L'Opéra* and the *Opéra Garnier*, a grand building of historical theatrical importance. Lynette and I also walked by the entrances to the *Galeries Lafayette*, the store *Mademoiselle* Fifi suggested we should visit the following day providing our bank accounts were in a healthy state of credibility. We came up against a line of off-roaders, the Anglo Tibetan *Hari Krishna* lot, banging bongo drums, tinkling bells as they jived along the pavement to the late George Harrison's repetitive chant which goes:

> *"Hari Krishna, Hari Krishna*
> *Hari Rama*, have a banana"

I can recall there was a bonehead playing a miniature piano, a sort of mobile harmonium that needed to be tuned at the first octave and it was supported by a leather strap slung around his neck; he fell into the gutter after being sprayed by a water canon especially designed to remove religious sects from the pavements and slippery walkways of Paris.

Another hindrance as we walked along *Boulevard Haussmann* was a couple of street buskers playing an accordion and tambourine. It is of great significance and importance to tell you that the music *"La vie en rose"* popularised by the French singer Edith Piaf, continued to play after the accordion player on stilts had taken his hands off the keyboard to look inside a straw boater before he visited the local benefit office to top-up the shortfall of coins inside the hat. The accordion player after turning up the sound on two stereophonic loud speakers inside his portable squeezebox continued with the song writers, Hal David and Albert

Hammonds song "To all the girls I've loved before" popularised by Julio Iglesias and Willie Nelson; I thought this to be somewhat impossible because the girls would have to be at least seven feet two inches tall for the fraudster to have done this. The tambourine man whose stature was adjusted when he altered the position of his backside to give it a slap became embarrassed when an amorous miniature poodle removed the shine from the back of his trousers and left a pool of water around his buckled patent leather shoes.

Lynette and I decided it was time we found a brassiere where we could take in a little of some much-needed sustenance, namely, a strong non-decaffeinated *espresso* coffee or 'Red Bull' energy drink before having to continue with the pleasurable experience of stepping out on to the pavement.

It was when the waiter, an odd looking fellow with a well-groomed handlebar moustache, brought us our drinks I saw Helen Hesketh, alias *Mademoiselle* Brigitte-Helen Boullard walking along the pavement on the opposite side of the road and heading speedily away from the estate agents '*Circa Habitat*'. From where we were sitting I concluded she was on a very important *Immobilier* mission because of the brisk way she sped along the street and I could see quite clearly a white plastic mobile phone, the size of a wardrobe pressed up against her ear.

I immediately searched for my sunglasses inside my small shoulder bag and then hard-pressed them over my tired eyes; the three-D effect I had been experiencing was caused either by over indulgence the previous evening or the excessive volume of glucose contained inside a slender blue, silver and red lettered tin. Lynette asked me why I had put on the spectacles in a dark corner of a shaded patio to which I replied: 'it is because I don't want to be recognised as the chap who has just won the football pools.'

'I suppose there is some logic in that, Christopher, but you could have at least removed the 'Cost Cutters' label before you put them on.' she pointed out.

Helen Hesketh had now disappeared out of sight, venturing on an endless journey, hopefully away from the planet forever.

The waiter, looking every inch like the character on a Pringle tube had a temperament equal to a taut spring and became irate when I paid the bill with pounds sterling. He became even more elasticised when I told him that the rate of exchange was worth more than the French Franc and I was fed up with his Mickey Mouse money.

I mentioned to Lynette that I was thinking about visiting a *coiffure*, a unisex hair salon which was situated next door to the brassiere. My salt and pepper beard had become unruly, requiring the assistance of an electric trimmer and after I had made a suggestion to sport a number-one haircut to look incognito, she said: 'over my dead body.'

After I had said to her 'If you want', she proceeded to get up from her seat in an attempt to leave the establishment without saying goodbye.

My intentions to have a quick make-over had fallen on stony ground and when I was struggling to catch up with Lynette to join in with her power-walking exercise I realized, like Helen Hesketh, *my* days on this planet could be numbered too when the woman, the carbuncle on the backside of humanity headed towards me; the greying hairs which still remained on the top of my head were now standing on end as shivers of total discomfort ran down my spine.

Helen Hesketh, still talking to her mobile phone passed by quickly without noticing I was heading in her direction. With my head bowed I was trying to look like the invisible man as I hot-footed along *Boulevard Haussmann* with gusto, the jewellers and prestigious *Cartier* watch shop situated on a corner just waiting to be robbed.

The Gods were indeed on my side that morning but this ended when Lynette asked me why my nose was bleeding.

My story continues with us having lunch outside a quaint little bistro in *rue Londres*, London Road, and called 'The Mariner' where we ate *Moules avec frites*, mussels and chips served in a rich garlic sauce. Freshly sliced *baguette* was aplenty and creamery butter was placed resplendent on the table just in case a foreign tourist had forgotten what it was or indeed what it tasted like. I ordered a bottle of *rosé*, hoping this would wake up the mussels and counteract the nervousness which was still lying dormant within my stomach.

For dessert, we chose the *Plat de Camembert*, cheese and biscuits and along with a large café crème, a cup of coffee with single cream; this became one of our better lunch outings when we were presented with a couple of red flannelette rugby bar towels in the guise of two scarves.

'I wonder what the McScrabbles are doing right now.' I said to Lynette as she rose from her seat to visit the toilet. 'I bet he's still playing poker in the station or trying to sell a police calendar which is fast running out of date.' I added.

When Lynette finally returned from the ladies and I had called off the French RS Search and Rescue party from going to look for her I then continued with my enquiries.

'And, why did Isla McScrabble keep on referring to the *Mull of Kintyre* as being her island? Has she bought it or something?' I asked.

'She said she bought it in metaphor.' Lynette informed me.

'Which supermarket is that Lynette? I was always led to believe Paul McCartney had bought it from Sainsburys.'

At precisely two o'clock we stumbled across an estate agent, '*Cabinet Olivier*', situated in *rue St Clair*, whose window displayed an extensive range of properties of town houses, apartments, small holdings and dilapidated cow sheds; prices ranging from sixty thousand French Francs to well over three-quarters of a million. Lynette and I discussed with amazement the French real estate market for all it was worth and we came to the conclusion that the value seemed to be very reasonable in comparison to Great Britain.

The estate agents had been closed for lunch but they were opened again later by a female member of staff called *Madame* Sylvie Briere, one of those bizarre Gothic types with a medieval appearance and exuded a familiar mustiness which gave me the impression the smell had been lingering on her clothes since the days of King Arthur after she had spent a few hours sitting around his table smoking cannabis.

Madame Briere turned the key twice to unlock the door and this was when she turned on the overhead fluorescent lights to illuminate the neat and tidy office. She spoke to us in English having clocked Lynette sliding a couple of free *Cabinet Olivier Immobilier* estate agent magazines into a green Marks and Spencer carrier bag; the periodicals in the stand looking somewhat dishevelled sustained from the heavy rain the previous day.

From where we were standing we could see that the establishment had just been cleaned by the *Atelier de Nettoyage enterprise*, a Parisian cleaning company, because the coconut welcoming mat had been placed in an upright position by the door to inform the manager of their Wednesday visit. Needless to say, the mat was still in the same position when we later left the premises; 'that's where it was put and that's where it stays until told otherwise', I told myself, being all too familiar by this time with the French temperament. *Madame* Briere told us in no uncertain terms that when the boss, Patrice Cavalier and Valerie Kennie, the supervisor eventually appear from the pub we are not to speak in English because it would mean he would have to pay her extra money for special language skills.

'I know an English woman, who works for an estate agent just down the road from here,' *Madame* Briere was kind enough to tell us. 'She works freelance for '*Circa Habitat*' and sells properties to British people; the ones that are on their books for a long time or they cannot handle because they are falling into disrepair. Would you like me to give her a ring so you can arrange a rendezvous?'

'That would be a good idea.' Lynette said enthusiastically until I quickly took it upon myself to change their minds and say no.

Having convinced myself that French people are all bent and don't do anything for nothing and everyone seemed to be into back-handers and know each other, the inevitable happened.

'Would you be interested in one of my properties? The house belonged to my grandmother, *Madame* Odette Roullier before she died and now it belongs to me.' Briere genuinely told us. It is situated in Méridon, a small town to the south of Caen and it will be ideal for you to use as a *pied*-à-*terre* because it is very close to the coast. If you are sufficiently interested, I will take you there tomorrow and show you around.'

'Oh, we can't do that.' Lynette quickly replied. 'Our Thomas Cook representative *Mademoiselle* Duval is taking us on a conducted tour around the *Galeries Lafayette* in the morning.'

'That would be Pascale, she is a friend of the family and she introduces some of her less fortunate clients to my brother, Doctor Bertrand Maynard who has a cosmetic surgery next door to the *Immobilier*.'

I said to Lynette later, 'I told you these people are related in some way and what do you bet *Madame* Briere paid a visit to her brother's surgery to have her boobs transferred on to her backside.'

'Don't be so guttural, Chris, how many more times have I got to tell you she is only doing her job.'

'Her job, her job, get out of it, Lynette, and unlike snow-white Pascale, I bet she doubles up as a stand for someone to park their bicycle at weekends.'

At this point, *Mademoiselle* Valérie Kennie, the tart of a supervisor walked into the office followed by the manager *Monsieur* Patrice Cavalier, a greasy sleaze bag from down town *St. Denis*. Cavalier mentioned something about the dormant door mat being moved back into its original position by *Madame* Briere who immediately got up from behind her desk to place it down on the floor with the 'Welcome' sign facing outwards and towards the street.

We were presented with one of *Madame* Briere's business cards and in turn gave her one of mine. She was sufficiently impressed with my academic title and she just couldn't wait to contact me later on my mobile phone to arrange that all too important rendezvous.

Chapter Twenty-six

Thursday morning – the following day

The day dawned with me opening the balcony door to stretch my limbs. The morning mist was in evidence once again as I looked over to the park and saw the *Eiffel Tower* engulfed with a tranquil dreariness devoid of any sign of life. And when I gazed into the street below I could see a *boulangerie*, a baker's shop, which had been busy throughout the night producing hundreds of *baguettes*; loaves of bread stretching to one-hundred metres long; croissants, a type of blown-up puff pastry similar to marine crustations and *les pain au raisin*; glazed circular doughnut cakes shaped like a defused Catherine wheel and large enough to satisfy a ravenous battalion of *French Foreign Legionnaires*. A *PMU* licensed betting office with its green flashing sign began to intrigue me when I saw people continually going into the integral *tabac*, the tobacconist, to habitually collect their daily dosage of inhalants; narcotic substances not dissimilar to camel shit. Adjoining the *PMU* was another pulsating sign which had been positioned high above the door to a *pharmacie*, a local chemist and drug store. Ironically, the signs are in the shape of a Cross and when they are illuminated, prospective corpses instantaneously know where to go for advice before ending up in the local cemetery.

It was then, my mobile phone went off on the small bedside table and incidentally, the sound of 'Waltzing Matilda' didn't go down too well with Lynette after suffering Paul Hogan in the late-night film "Crocodile Dundee" the previous evening; the dialogue was all in French and I couldn't understand one single word of it. Lynette had been asleep for most of the night and me, for at least a couple of hours thinking of Helen Hesketh and how she keeps following me around; Southport, Bournemouth and now Paris; wherever next I began to think?

The last person I wanted to speak to at that time of the morning was *Madame* Sylvie Briere who made it her business to inform us that she was sorry to be phoning so early and would I accept her apologies. After conveying to her that I could still see the moon shining through the bedroom window, she continued on with the conversation. She informed me that *Mademoiselle* Pascale Duval wouldn't be able to show us around the *Galeries Lafayette* that morning and would we like to go to *Méridon* and visit the house?

Shouting through the keyhole of the bathroom door I deliberated and conferred with Lynette who I could see was firmly ensconced pampering the mounds of her unwanted flesh, and from the confines of the Roman Baths I heard the response sounding like a pissed-off, Sir Paul McCartney saying "yea, yea; yea".

'I can see I have called at a bad time.' Briere said and purveying to me she had been listening in to the noise booming in the background.

Madame Briere and I made arrangements to meet in the lobby after breakfast and that morning I phoned the super efficient room service facility to have our food brought up to the fifth floor before the moon made a second appearance through our bedroom window. I was in no mood to be in a breakfast-room sitting amongst another coach load of tourists who had arrived during the early hours of the morning from Toulouse; the 'Hinge and Bracket', the ear-piercing racket bellowing out from the hotel car park was similar to Napoleon's retreat from Moscow. I had lost several hours of sleep that night and having to suffer our Sicilian waiter and Karin Fontaine, the Senegalese waitress straight from an African jungle, was just too much for me to handle.

Our cold Continental breakfast arrived after the third telephone call was made to my friendly *Bavarian* temptress, 'Miss Whiplash', Heidi Schmidt in reception; she seemed to be in a more amicable frame of mind that morning having gone through the motion of whipping a few dwarfs back into shape from a dizzy height at the LIDO the previous evening.

The freshly squeezed orange juice made from an extract of concentrated sherbet was disgusting and the blended Brazilian coffee which looked as though it had just been brought from an oil refinery in *Azerbaijan* was equally disgusting. The torpedo-like bread rolls, similar to high-explosive sub aqua-marine projectiles may have had something to do with the sinking of the Royal Navy battleship, HMS Hood during the Second World War, were stale and the small pot of *confiture le Primeur fraises*, a so-called superior jam which had never seen a strawberry in its life was crying out to be thrown into a waste paper bin underneath a folding green baize card table. The two two-minute boiled eggs were cold and had I asked for them to be cooked for at least two hours at the crack of dawn they would still have arrived in a refrigerated state.

'The coffee is delicious, Chris, isn't it?' Lynette said, going on the offensive, contradicting and altering my digestion. 'And as for the triangular shaped '*Laughing Cow*' processed cheese slices, they were simply wonderful and out of this world.' she made comment.

'Yes, I noticed the similarity on the packaging; a couple of horns and a ring-pull attached to its nose.'

'Oh, you will have your silly little jokes, won't you, Christopher?'

'Yes, it is part of my nature to be funny; it seems to run in the family.'

'Well, you could have fooled me, Chris.'

'You will see what I mean, Lynette, when the gob-on-a-stick, *Mademoiselle* Pascale Briere turns up at the hotel in less than a quarter of an hour to drive us crazy along the A3 motorway towards Méridon.'

'Do you think we should take some sandwiches with us, Chris?'

'This isn't going to be a picnic, believe me, Lynette and we are all going to be in metaphor, for another D - DAY and possibly another 'Longest Day' in Normandy. Do you realize that on the morning of the 6th June 1944, there was an Armada of ships and landing craft heading towards the beaches at *Ouistreham?*'

'You mean it was a bit like Bournemouth during the Isle of Wight sailing regatta.' she impertinently replied and again, reducing my wealth of historical knowledge by a hundred percent.

'Yes, you could say that, Lynette, however the British, French, Canadian and American soldiers who were involved in *Le débarquement de Normandie*, the Normandy landings weren't exactly wearing "Kiss me Quick" hats, eating candyfloss or savouring ice cream cornets when they landed.'

'Oh, how awful; that's pretty bad luck.' she replied, putting on a mock 'Sloane' accent which wouldn't have convinced the South Western Gas Board.

'Why are you talking like that, Lynette?' I asked, puzzled by her crass remarks. 'You do realize if it wasn't for the likes of your father wading through the water in *Ouistreham* that morning, you wouldn't be alive today to come out with those statements.'

'My dad was only a lance corporal in the Pay Corps, Christopher, and he inadvertently fell into the water from the tail-board of the last landing craft to hit the beach. It was only after the lucky ones had made it ashore and the town secured by the French and Canadian liberation forces he was allowed to eat his corned beef breakfast.'

'He told me he was so proud to receive all those Second World War medals, Lynette.'

'Yes, but he tells me and my mum they are far too big to put into parking metres.'

'But, your father sustained quite a few war wounds when he was running towards the sand dunes.'

'I know, but if you call being bitten by a rather vicious and rabid stray German Doberman Pincer that had escaped from the *'Grand Bunker'* and was possibly going back to *Caen* to join his mates, then yes, you are absolutely correct.'

'We had a bunker at the back of our house in Queens Park Avenue.' I explained to Lynette, attaching little importance to the conversation. 'It was used to store coal.' I hastened to add.

'Not that kind of bunker, Chris, it was a concrete tower, the only one of its kind used by the German army as an artillery range-finding post in *Ouistreham.*'

'Oh, I know the type, built to last, full of rusty iron rods and a bugger to destroy.' I said.

We said our goodbyes to Sophie Talbot, our super-efficient chamber maid who supplied us with immaculately clean white towels which were placed neatly on the end of the bed the previous day with a decorative arrangement of small plastic *'Wash and Go'* shampoo bottles, sachets of *'Nivea'* shower gel and miniscule tablets of fragrant *'Oil of Ulay'* toilet soap. Personalized mules and complementary dressing gowns sporting the hotels motif were left in the bathroom just in case we forgot where we were staying and, if that wasn't enough, note paper, envelopes and sepia coloured postcards depicting the *Eiffel Tower* and the *Folies Bergère* were lying resplendent on an old mahogany writing desk; the photograph taken during the Grand Exposition at the turn of the century looked familiar, including the pigeons and all these items of memorabilia were meant to impress our friends, relatives and colleagues back home. It was of no significant importance to tell you that a brand-new half kilo box of Duty-Free shop 'Bassett's Liquorice Allsorts' had disappeared from the surface of the dressing table and like the *'Toblerone'* chocolate bar, I had to resign myself to the fact it was another case of unexplained displaced item phenomena; the transposition and transportation promulgated by the distinctive black box growing a pair of legs to enable it to walk out through the bedroom door without me noticing.

Lynette and I, after depositing our breakfast debris in the hallway on the fifth floor, proceeded to take the lift down to the reception area where *Fraulein* Schmidt was reaching up behind the desk to replace a light bulb which had exploded immediately she came on duty, and with her arms outstretched she was giving us the impression that someone important from *'The Third Reich'* could have been present in the lobby.

'Good morning, Mister and Missus Travis.' Heidi said, before adjusting her blouse to enable everyone to see inside.

'Good morning, *Mademoiselle* Schmidt,' I replied as Lynette bumbled around a revolving leaflet stand. 'Has someone been keeping you up?' I asked when her mouth became wide open to show me a glimpse of her tonsils.

'It was very late when I went to bed last evening and I can't stop yawning.' she said, allowing me to glance down inside her massive undulating cleavage which babbled uncontrollably like the ripples from a pebble in a freshwater brook.

'Yes, I understand, Heidi because I can still see your stage makeup and silver glitter behind the back of your ears.' I said after pointing my observations out to her.

'How do you know I have another job working at the LIDO?' she inquisitively asked.

'It was last Sunday, my wife and I visited the LIDO and I had the pleasure of seeing you performing on the stage. I got the impression you enjoyed having a whip-round and a Champagne piss-up afterwards.' I forwardly added, thinking my luck was going to be in that evening.

'Tell me, Mister Travis is that a gun in your pocket or you are just pleased to see me?' quoting the Hollywood stage actress, May West. 'And are you a voyeur or just a dirty old man?' she became keen to find out.

'Yes.' I replied speedily.

'Yes, you are a voyeur; yes, you are a dirty old man or yes you are both, Mister Travis?'

'Oh, yes, Heidi and please call me Christopher, it is less formal.' I insisted.

'Do you say yes to everything, Mister Travis? Here take a look at those.' Heidi said, giving me a couple of signed black and white glossy photographs of her sitting on a high stool half-naked.

'Oh, yes.'

When Lynette returned from her merry-go-round thing she said, 'what are you doing looking at those obscene photographs of the receptionist?'

I said; 'You never said anything on Sunday evening, did you, especially when you clocked a bearded dwarf on stage wearing nothing except for a pair of 'Y' fronts.'

'Well, small people do that sort of thing.' Lynette said, helping me with my education. 'And what was different, he was sporting a long white beard, not a short triangular black one.' she said convincingly.

'Lynette Bakewell, you are disgusting; bloody disgusting.' I said to her ashamedly. 'Did you know, Lynette, and this is truly amazing; before we were married the only Bakewell I knew came in the form of a tart.'

'Well, you should have told me earlier, Chris because I would have taken great pleasure in baking you one and shoving it right up your backside.'

Suddenly, it was time to go when *Madame* Sylvie Briere made her grand entrance into the hall via the front door. She was looking very much the part of an estate agent with portfolio; you can always tell a real-estate person by the serious look upon their faces as they go about their business trying to sell property with enough camouflage on walls, doors and window frames to hide the rising damp, dry rot and woodworm problem inside Buckingham Palace.

I can remember there were two gay Greek Cypriots trying to attract my attention before I attempted to make a quick getaway through an additional revolving door which would have been much better situated in the fun house on Blackpool's Pleasure Beach; I can also recall, one had to put it into a spin and go around at least twice before diving out into the forecourt from a precarious and awkward narrow exit. The two pretty boys, both sporting broken noses and a Trojan smile must have thought I was one of them because when I felt a sudden breeze filtering in through an open fly in my Levi jeans, I was given a strange look of appreciation by one of the 'grease balls' holding a multi-coloured shoulder bag.

'*Bonjour*, and Good morning, Mister and Missus Travis; all is well and all is good?' *Madame* Briere said, preventing my escape towards the whirly gig of a door. 'It is a beautiful day also; the sun is shining and it will be nice for me to take you and Missus Travis to *Méridon* and also to see the French countryside.' she added.

'Yes, I am really looking forward to that,' I said, tongue in cheek. 'I believe those wind farms are quite spectacular; hundreds of propellers going around in unison generating just enough electricity to power a kiddies '*Hornby 00*' guage train set.'

'Now, Mister Travis, you will only begin to fully understand and appreciate the French people until we are moving at speed along the N13 *autoroute* and heading towards the industrialized town of *Caen* in *Normandie*.'

'I have heard all about your motorways.' I said to Sylvie. 'And did you know *Madame* Briere that in the United Kingdom of Great Britain and Northern Ireland, if one careers into the back of a vehicle they are responsible for the damage? But, here in France, it is the reverse; the person driving in front is the one who gets the blame.'

'It is true, accidents do happen in France, but they are very rare, Mister Travis, but should one occur, we have excellent emergency rescue services to deal with the problem.' she emphasised.

'I was once in the '*Red Cross*' *Madame* Briere,' Lynette had to put in.

'Yea, yea, yea,' I said to her, knowing the repertoire by heart.

'I once became an expert with a triangular bandage when a 'Royalist' cavalier serving with the 'Sealed Knot' was accidently stabbed with a poleaxe belonging to one of Oliver Cromwell's 'Roundhead' soldiers during a re-enactment of the battle of Cuckfield, near Crawley in Sussex.'

'Yes, I've heard it all before Lynette; you were also quick in making beds in those days but, not so quick in getting out of them.'

'Don't pay any attention to my husband, *Madame* Briere because he will have his little jokes, won't you dear?' Lynette said to both of us and at the same time pushing me gently to one side giving me the impression she had become angry and was going to beat me up later.

In the hotel's forecourt there was a metallic blue Peugeot 206, open-top waiting to take us on a mystery tour to a citadel the size of a *Bureaux de la Poste*; a French Post Office microscopic metropolitan postage stamp. It may be of interest to note that with the exception of a few academic people like myself, hardly anyone knew where the place was until the Second World War when it was used as an escape route; a thoroughfare for German tanks and Gestapo retreating to Belgium in August nineteen forty-four. Prior to this, the crypt and the Anglo Saxon catacombs of Saint Agatha, the citadel's cathedral, were used to bury Crusaders, mercenaries, The Order of the Knights Templar and The Knights of Saint John of Jerusalem who, on their way back to England fell foul of robbers and agents of the bankrupt King Philip IV, hell bent in taking their spoils of war.

For ten minutes we were stuck behind groupies of an out-of-tune marching band, bum majorettes and baton twirlers as we crept slowly along *Boulevard de la Madeleine*, heading towards the N13 motorway. The ageing baton-twirling tarts continually dropping their knickers and wands in the street were being supervised by what seemed to be the largest woman in Paris after giving me another glimpse of cellulite when one of the baton twirlers fell from the top of a human pyramid. The tinkling tones of the xylophone and the thumping *Um-Pa-Pa Band* noises emanating from a huge brass tuba purporting to be a python wrapped around a musician's waist to this day still reverberates in my ears.

I glanced over to my right and couldn't believe my eyes when I saw Helen Hesketh's silver-grey Porsche 911 sports car with its distinctive personal number plate HSK 151X, blatantly parked outside of '*Circa Habitat*', the *immobilier*, estate agents, on *Boulevard Haussmann*. I immediately donned my genuine *Raymond Bann* Polaroid sunglasses as if I was about to be dropped off outside the venue of the *Cannes* Film Festival and looking inconspicuous like Sean Connery himself proceeded to disappear down the front of the back seat lest Hesketh should suddenly appear on to the pavement from inside her office.

'Tell me, Chris, why is your mouth wide open? Anyone would think you hadn't seen a British registered Porsche before.' Lynette so naively asked.

It was ten-thirty when we finally made it to the start of the N13 *autoroute*. This is the country where one can't bang on a set of drums because of neighbour complaints and one can't play a guitar because the electricity output is inadequate and, if one has a barbecue, one is only allowed one once a month and then one has to eat *boudin blanc* and côt*e de boeuf*, white pudding and rib of beef inside because of the smoke wafting into the garden next door. It is also of interest to any would-be buyer of French property, not to send up any pyrotechnics; rockets and projectiles, especially during *fête de Noël*, Christmas time, and the feast of *St Sylvestre*, New Years Eve, because they may bring down an air force '*Mirage*' jet fighter aircraft or an Air France 'Boeing 747-400', or on a more serious note, the American 'Air Force One'.

Madame Briere told us the French people are like *Escargot*, snails; they carry their houses on their backs and are always on the move.

'Good for the estate agent business and I suppose, it is a bit like the prostitutes who walk along the *Cours de la Reine*, the Queen's promenade, on the north side of the River *Seine*,' I put in; 'they carry mattresses on their backs just in case they meet a fella.' I leave no stone unturned.

'Why is it, Chris that every time you go past this neck of the woods you always wear those sunglasses you bought in Salisbury market?' Lynette asked, trying to destroy my moment of designer accessory ware pleasure.

Chapter Twenty-seven

No 27 *rue Mortain*, the afternoon of the same day

It was just after two when we arrived at the house in *Méridon* after the town's gate-keeper had checked our credentials at the portcullis to allow us to gain access into his medieval citadel and before raising the drawbridge and kindling the fires which illuminated the darkened walls at night.

Apart from a modern '*Carrefour Express*' supermarket and a store which sold computers, wide-screen television sets and modems to enable one to watch an ageing, *imitator, humorist, actor, singer, composer* and *sleep-inducement expert*, Patrick Sébastien, presenting his show "*Le plus Grand Cabaret du monde*", the largest cabaret in the world, broadcast live on Saturday evenings, there was nothing one could relate to in the twenty-first century. It was Shirley and Dino, the popular French comedy double-act who later captivated my imagination when I realized they were not dead after all and about as funny as a broken leg; she looking every inch like the nineteen-fifties singer, Alma Cogan and he, looking like Mister Punch of the Judy fame, had a nose sharp enough to open a tin of Sainsbury's baked beans. The magician took first prize when his pigeons rapidly flew off, escaping from the long sleeves of his jacket up to the roof, never to return again after they had listened to Sébastien, boring the pants off his audience and trying to flog another book written by Bernadette Chirac. Seated at Sébastien's table were celebrities, each with a gob the size of the Dartford Tunnel trying to impress the audience and the viewers before watching a fire-eating act, a couple of pyromaniacs who were hell-bent in trying to set fire to the entire building by what seemed to be a gallon of petrol. Petula Clarke was the only sane person at the table when she fell asleep after being accused of being British and to produce documentary evidence of her credibility. Petula was woken up by the irritating sound of a fire bell which not only silenced her snoring but put an end to Sébastien's biggest cabaret in the world; the tall drinks which were placed in front of everyone at the table would have made little impact because of them being artificial and possibly designed by the man himself.

'Do you think you could pass me *les cacahuètes*, Patrick?' Petula asked, in perfect French.

'*Comment, pardon;* you what?' Sebastian replied frowning, as if he didn't know the French word for peanuts.

'The ready salted peanuts.' Petula said, waving a silk Union Jack handkerchief in front of her face after everyone, except for Sébastien, had vacated the building. 'Tell me Patrick why is it you are not standing outside with your captive audience?' she added.

'It is because I'm waiting to go on stage to take part in the grand finale and get everyone to join in with the audience participation; I want them all to get going.'

'Well, from where I am sitting you will be on your own because they all will be fighting to get inside your toilet.'

This was just one of the spectacular shows Lynette and I had to painstakingly contribute paying to the French Television Licensing Authorities in the *Trésor Publique*, the town's Inland Revenue office, situated conveniently in the next street. Another fodder for the masses television programme was called "*Super Nannie*", where a woman, employed by a French corrective training centre, would try to impress viewers with her extensive knowledge of whipping into shape hyperactive and unruly children; she would have been far better chucking those insufferable Liverpudlian *Scouse* gits overboard from the Brittany Ferries ship, *Normandie*, sailing from Portsmouth to *Caen*.

The three story semi-detached town house had wooden shutters and a pebbled glass-fronted door secured by a decorative design of wrought iron on the outside. The elderly lady, *Madame* Christine-Patricia Grandin, an *ancien professeur*, a retired school teacher living next door in the adjoining house had a blue door and a shiny brass letter box to let people know she was from a middle-class background and to inform any stray dogs not to urinate on her door step.

The large eighteenth century house to the right, set well back from the road and heavily fortified by an automatic metal gate was built on the site of an ancient Roman villa around AD two-hundred to accommodate legionnaires who used Normandy as a balsa wood springboard to hop over to Britain for the weekend; a functioning stone well, a secret garden and a two-metres wide crumbling Anglo Saxon wall leading down to the blocked-off catacombs of the cathedral, St Agatha, built in the year ten-fifty three, could be found to the rear. From a back bedroom window, Lynette and I could see the family's brown and white European cat permanently on guard duty in their not-so-secret garden; it was if it knew what was down there and ward off any would-be adventurer not to trespass into its lair.

Madame et *Monsieur* Goddard, our not too friendly next door neighbours made it perfectly clear at our first meeting that they would much prefer to keep themselves to themselves and not to go digging into the past because our houses are listed buildings and just in case we had designs on turning them into a gaming centre or a Sainsbury's supermarket, to forget it.

Sylvie opened the door and then proceeded to open the shutters from the inside.

We were entering into a house which possessed an atmosphere and little did we know that one day we would realize we had been living amongst the dead. One could imagine sitting in front of a grand log fire during cold and damp winter's evenings; flames flickering wildly causing sinister shadows to dart randomly around the room.

The lounge lead to an open archway where a purpose-built kitchen could be seen giving a sense of spaciousness and taste and this gave Lynette and I the impression that *Madam*e Roulier, Sylvie's grandmother, must have been a typically French country cook; those old culinary delights now being replaced by beef burgers and chips. Everything was included in the price; fridge-freezer, electric oven, washing machine, dish washer and a ghost from Temple Bar Gateway, London trying to make its way up from the cellar in order to find a decent cup of tea.

There were stairs leading up to the first floor and a bathroom and toilet was situated to one-side next to the kitchen; a recent addition to the house was a sky-light which illuminated the bottom rungs of the ornate wooden banister.

At the top of the staircase was a landing leading to a front bedroom and a door to the rear was used to gain access to a large outside terrace with high bamboo fencing on three sides.

A winding staircase was used to go up to the second floor where two bedrooms looked out to the front and rear of the house. The building, because of its very high ceilings was large, large enough to command a good view into the gardens across the road which is where, on the eastern side, one can gain access to the cathedral by way of a side door and sculptured gargoyles, ghouls, dragons and funny looking bogeymen can be seen looking down from the church in order to befriend and keep company a convicted dead witch hanging from the eves.

The main entrance to the cathedral is situated in *Place Drakkar*, the market square to the west and was named after a Viking long ship which sailed along the River Seine in the ninth century AD; *Méridon* wasn't to be the same ever again, apparently.

In an alcove in the kitchen was a heavy wooden door that was opened by Sylvie to allow Lynette and I to climb down a rickety old wooden set of stairs into *la cave*, a split-level cellar where the boiler and an additional cold storage cabinet was situated. The area at the bottom of the stairs had been used many years ago to cook food and a dysfunctional late nineteenth-century cast-iron fire place became the focus of our attention when we learned it had been made in Paris. The floor was Romanesque, lots of orange and blue mosaic tiles and had bricks made from terracotta placed together to form a sort of road which lead to the older and lower part of the cellar, several feet beneath the road. I can remember, the crudely built Anglo Saxon wall to the left, facing the eves; it was wet and damp to the touch and had been standing for eleven-hundred years; so we were told by a leading historian in the town. However, the Goddard's house next door had a different story to tell and I have a theory that the Roman emperor, Julius Caesar, used the bricks and mortar in their *la cave* as a prelude to building Hadrian's Wall in Britain.

Situated to one side of the cellar and underneath the stairs were two huge stone boulders, both with dusty black plastic hessian laid over the top. This was indeed peculiar, to say the least, and it was Sylvie, who later told me that the ground had been used by stone masons when they built the cathedral and the stone rock formations were probably superfluous to their requirements. It was three months later I managed to lever and roll the heavy boulders away from a couple of holes in the floor to discover two stairways leading down into the catacombs.

The temperature down in *la cave* was cold and had started to effect my blood circulation; a certain chill ran down my spine when I momentarily glanced up to see a half-finished stone gargoyle leaning forward against *Madame* Grandin's adjoining wall; what seemed to be a medieval apprentice piece looked as if it was laughing in my direction before I made my way back up the stairs into the kitchen. An old mahogany barometer which was hanging on the wall gave me the impression I wasn't wanted there because one of the two dials had suddenly become nervous and kept switching from hot to cold and the other alternated rapidly between winter and an extremely hot summer.

From the steps of the cellar I could hear Lynette talking to Victoria on her mobile: 'I want, it, I want it, I want it!' For a moment I thought she was talking to one of her old boyfriends until I heard her mention my daughter's name.

'You must be bloody well desperate, that's all I can say, Lynette.'

'Ah, but it's a lovely house, Christopher; I can just imagine us both sitting outside on that beautiful terrace, underneath a parasol drinking iced tea and gin and tonics, and that will be fun, won't it?'

'Yea, fun, real fun, and don't forget the peanuts.' I reminded her.

'Tell me, *Madame* Briere,' Lynette asked Sylvie. 'How much do you want for this property?'

'Er... six hundred thousand French Francs.' Sylvie replied, finding it difficult to get the words out from the sides of her mouth which now looked similar to *Coco* the clown. 'And, under the circumstances, I think it's a good deal for you both.' she added.

'What circumstances?' I asked enquiringly.

'Well, for a start, you won't be dealing with an estate agent and also you will be using my *notaire* in Méridon, the family solicitor in the main Square.' Sylvie was quick to put in.

She made it perfectly clear that if you scratch my back I'll drive your bloody 'E' Type Jaguar.

'And how long before we can move in?' Lynette asked, cautiously.

'Just as soon as the *notaire*, *Madame* Emilie Le Breton is in possession of the deposit, the completed mandate and a cheque for the balance has been handed over to her; the entire transaction should take only a couple of weeks. First of all I want to show you around the town of *Méridon*; here is where I was born,' Sylvie continued. 'And this is where I hope to end my days.' she said, looking up to an empty space in the church belfry dominating the city's main Square, emblematic of *Meridon's* medieval power; her words being enough to bring a tear to a glass eye.

'How long will all this take?' I asked, wanting desperately to get back to Paris as soon as possible to relax and enjoy our last night on the town.

'Oh, not long, about half-an-hour at the very most and then we can go and have a cup of coffee and a sandwich at my favourite café '*Le Chocolate Bar*' in *Place Drakkar*.

'And this is where I went to school, and this is where I met my husband, Charles, and this is where...' she went on, and on, and on; I was half-expecting Michael Aspel to appear at any moment with another red book in his hand. 'And this is the railway station, but sadly it has lots of sad memories attached to it, in particular, during the war when trainloads of deportees passed through here on their way to the concentration camps.'

I had to remind Sylvie that it was getting late and we had a long journey ahead of us when she would insist on telling Lynette and me about a seventy-five year-old Jewish man, *Monsieur* Jacques Mayer who owns a book shop in *Méridon* town centre and how he managed to escape from the German occupation forces in nineteen forty-three. Sylvie also showed us a bronze memorial set firmly at an angle in the grounds of the station telling the story of a man called *Monsieur* James Cohen, who was fatally wounded, losing his life trying to escape from the German occupation forces in *Méridon*.

This was a classic case of *déjà vu* having dreamt about their existence some weeks ago and thought it truly amazing how an accident in Sainsburys could possibly have introduced all of this interesting stuff into my brain.

It was two weeks later and I couldn't wait to return to *Méridon* to pay Monsieur Mayer a visit in his bookshop on the pretext of having my dad's old railway pocket watch fixed.

Lynette and I gave *Madame* Le Breton of *les notaires*, the solicitors, Le Breton *et* Silverman the deposit for the house and asked her to keep in touch. She replied by saying that the notary still have long arms and deep pockets, and perhaps this would account for the photograph of her son on the wall wearing a blue velvet skull cap trimmed with gold and a decorative shawl similar to a tea towel wrapped around his shoulders at his *bar mitzvah*.

The coffee and salad sandwich was great at the '*Bar Au Chocolat*', sitting outside underneath a parasol admiring the different coloured cobbles and paving stones embedded into the grounds of the Square.

The highlight of the afternoon was when we observed a brown and white cockerel meandering around aimlessly underneath the next table; it had somehow managed to escape from the town's livestock market which takes place every Thursday morning. Lynette and I didn't know what bird flu was until we eventually moved into the house and witnessed hundreds of chickens, geese, turkeys and cockerels being transported to the market; it was not unusual to see the fattest of pigs being led by a farmer into the Square to save on petrol; and then having to watch it slowly roasting on a rotisserie before being made into a ham sandwich was just too much for me to digest. A dancing bear, muzzled and tethered by a white plastic '*Bricomarche*' garden chain became another feature of the town's entertainment programme.

There wasn't a hot chocolate in sight and like the black singer, Errol Brown, I too can believe in miracles but that was until I saw a Senegalese street hawker wearing at least half-a-dozen Stetsons on his head; I suppose it could have been worse had he brought his mates along with him.

I remarked to Sylvie: 'I bet his name is Charlie; there're all called Charlie.' hoping she would take me up on my wager.

'My husband is called Charlie.' Sylvie replied giving me the idea she didn't appreciate my extensive knowledge of the African peoples.

'Ah, but he's not black.' I said to her, not knowing that he was.

'He was when I woke up this morning.' she said looking away. 'And because of your supercilious and crass remarks, Mister Travis, sometimes I wish my name was Ella Fitzgerald.' she added.

'Supercilious, that's a big word.' I said to her, thinking she was just showing off in the English language. 'I know a big word, Madame Briere,' I said confidently.

'And what word would that be?'

'Ice cream;'

'Ice cream; that's two words, Mister Travis.' she said, correcting me for the second time that afternoon.

'Well, how come your husband was born in *Méridon?*' I politely asked.

'His ancestors came over to *Normandie* on a Viking long ship wearing leopard skins.' Sylvie said jokingly.

'Ah, that explains everything.' I said.

'Just shut up, Christopher, you are beginning to get on my nerves.' Lynette said, just when I thought I was beginning to understand the Norman mentality; a cold, callous and cruel race of people, hell-bent on causing mischief and making troubles derived from the Viking Norsemen. The Normans retain a powerful sense of separate identity and still grind their bloody axes; many raddled with shit try to convince the world that the city of *Caen* is the capital of the United Kingdom of Great Britain and Northern Ireland.

Lynette later changed her tune when she said that evil flourishes here in *Meridon* and wanted out at the earliest opportunity.

In normal circumstances the carillon of bells in the belfry marked the quarter hour, however, that afternoon they were silenced by a knell of a bell heralding a funeral; at this low point I thought the town had never looked better looking back.

Madame Briere delivered us to our hotel just in time for afternoon tea. She said goodbye, bestowing hundreds of kisses on both sides of our cheeks and then wished us *bon voyage* and a safe journey back to our home in "England's green and pleasant land".

Heidi Hi, my favourite Bavarian 'Puss in boots' was behind the reception desk waiting to give us the key to our room and emphasised that when we depart the following day we were not to forget to put it into the box provided. There was no way we could take it with us because it weighed a ton, resembling a cast-iron pear similar to the ball on the end of an old-fashioned lavatory chain. It was then I realized German women do have a sense of humour if they thought I could possibly walk out from the hotel with that thing bulging out from inside my trouser pocket prior to being accosted in the street.

Our evening continued with us visiting an Italian restaurant, '*Giovanni's*' in *Boulevard Londres*, where the atmosphere and service was superb sitting outside in a shady corner watching the world go by. Suddenly, I burst out into song and without hesitation and any one hearing I began to sing the revamped version of the song "That's Amore" which was sung by Dean Martin. After the second basket bottle of *Chianti Melini* was brought to our table I began the rendition:

> "When the moon hits your eye like a bigga pizza pie
> That's Amore, That's Amore
> When the pizza is brown and the chef turns around and says bella
> Mozzarella, Isabella, lucky fella
> When the stars in the sky begin to twinkle in your eye
> That's Amore
> And when the weather is a fine and you've had too much wine
> You're in love
> But you know it's a dream when you buy an ice cream, say Senora
> And when the food tastes like shit and you can't live on it
> That's Amore, Amore, have some more eh?"

"Tell me, Chris, why are you muttering to yourself?' Lynette asked concernedly. 'Are you ill?' she added.

It was then I decided to give her my rendition of another one of Dean Martin's songs called: "Somewhere along the Way"; this time singing loudly so everyone in local proximity could hear:

"I walked along the avenue and somehow I would pray
That someday soon I hoped to find you
Somewhere along the way"

'Was this when you were going, or coming back from the pub, Christopher?'

Chapter Twenty-eight

Breakfast time, the following morning

Waking up with a hangover was bad enough but having to suffer the stresses and strains of *Mademoiselle* Karen Fontaine, our Senegalese stick insect of a waitress during the course of our breakfast at *'Tiffany's'* was just too much.

'Will Mister and Missus Travis be dining with us this evening?' *Mademoiselle* Fontaine asked with a look that could frighten children; we have something special for you to eat tonight.'

'Don't tell me the Malaysian chef has chosen roast iguana and chips for my wife and I to sample and test his culinary skills, but fortunately, we are leaving for Great Britain this evening and we would much prefer to throw up over the side of a Brittany Ferry on the French side of the English Channel.'

'As a matter of fact the chef is cooking *gigot de aneau*, roast leg of lamb, Jersey new potatoes, French haricot beans and it will all be served with a small jug of mint sauce and gravy, but only on request.' she said, trying to entice Lynette and me to stay for another day in the hotel when she said the gravy came out from a brown cardboard packet and was called *Bisto*. *Mademoiselle* Fontaine told me in confidence that as part of the Friday night's entertainment programme there is a Siamese belly dancing act in the conservatory.

I informed Fontaine that I went to a cinema in Bournemouth to see an Indian film but had to leave during the interval because of a sore neck caused by a scantily dressed principle belly-dancer who would insist on shaking her head from side-to side; the fact that half-way down the building a fire door was wide open but bore no significance to my problem.

'You never told me about this, Christopher; is this going to be another one of your "Fantasy Island" stories?' Lynette asked with a puzzled look on her face.

'It could have been worse had I been sitting on the back row next to one of your old boyfriends, Sinbad, punch bag, Jaffrey; it seems, he has since made a commendable breakthrough by playing the part of a British policeman and wearing a dark blue turban wrapped around his head, which is in total contrast to when he was hanging around outside strip club doorways in London.'

'I suppose you think that's very funny.' she replied giving me one of her more dirty looks.

'Tell me *Mademoiselle* Fontaine,' I asked, looking into the whites of her eyes that resembled two boiled guinea fowl eggs. 'Before you became a waitress in Paris, what was your occupation in Senegal?'

'A nursery school teacher.' she replied smugly.

'You mean one of those pretend persons who give kids a sedative in the guise of a cod-liver oil tablet to send them to sleep at three o'clock in the afternoon?'

'No, it isn't like that at all Mister Travis; we usually give the children a bang on the head with a large carved-out wooden spoon, similar to the one the tourists buy in a Senegalese market.'

'It's a pity Esther Rantzen is not a guest in this hotel listening to your ideas of how to induce forced insomnia into those poor innocent-looking children because she would really love you.'

'Who is this Esther Ransom, is she gay?' Fontaine asked with a phony expression on her face and thinking perhaps it was her lucky day.

'No, of course not, she is a well-known television presenter in Britain, but latterly has become a saviour to thousands of mentally-abused children in the United Kingdom who need her help and support.'

'Ah, well, you can't win them all.' Fontaine made clear before mentioning that she was gay, a lesbian, always on the lookout and on the pull.

'Well you needn't look in my direction because I am spoken for.' I said, in no uncertain terms.

'I usually go to gay-friendly bars on Saturday evenings; one in particular is called 'Mega-Bitches'.' she told us and before I said tactfully: 'Well that sounds appropriate.'

'Oh, super, that's really super; are we going to eat our breakfast now or are we not, Chris?' Lynette asked, sounding like a female version of the late Russell Harty, the television presenter and chat show host who had a condition known only to myself and the gay community.

'You're not on the turn as well, are you Lynette?' I asked.

'Christopher, just shut up and eat your breakfast, you are beginning to get on my nerves again.'

'Did I tell you about Sir Walter Raleigh, Lynette, when he presented a rolled-up tobacco leaf to Queen Elizabeth the First of England? She said, what do you suppose I do with that, put it into my ears?' He said: 'No, your majesty, you put it in your mouth and set fire to it. It is of little wonder why she had his head chopped off.'

'Christopher, how many more times do I have to tell you?'

'Well, Queen Victoria was on cannabis; it is no wonder why she tried to set the world on fire after threatening it with extreme violence; "Rule Britannia" and all that.' I said, breaking the silence so I could continue with my historical recollections.

'She only used cannabis for medicinal purposes.' Lynette replied, sounding extremely patriotic towards the Royal Family.

'And so did Mick Jagger.'

'I am British, and I am proud to be British.' Lynette said giving me the impression she was on something.

'And so was Sir Walter Raleigh until he went to the scaffold and rumour has it Her Majesty, Queen Elizabeth the First was never the same again after he gave her a banana.'

'What are you saying, Chris? Sir Walter Raleigh was on something, and like you, he was into bananas.'

'Well, he might.' I replied, before I quietly sang the 'British National Anthem' to Lynette: "Send her victorious, happy and glorious, long to reign over us, God Save our Queen."

'I wouldn't advise sending the Queen, Victoria's because they are probably destined for the washing machine as we speak.' Lynette said, transforming herself into a comedy role compatible to Joan Rivers.

'And did you know, Lynette, that Queen Elizabeth the First of England had to undergo chemotherapy and radiology treatment after consuming a rotten Mexican avocado pear and then became as bald as a coot?'

'You mean to say she wasn't a 'Ginger Minger' after all?' Lynette said disappointedly.

Our clever and intellectual conversation nearly came to an end when *Senor* Tonino Omassoli, made an appearance at the table to say goodbye; the sole purpose of his visit, to collect a well-deserved tip for looking after our welfare and showing us where the local doctor's surgery was situated just in case Lynette and I suffered the aftermath of eating contaminated Senegalese tiger king prawns.

We vacated our room at midday leaving three of my coveted Oxford University ties, including a bow tie, a stack of handkerchiefs and my favourite pair of black Lycra underpants in the drawer of the dressing table; a crisp white drip-dry shirt which I have worn since the nineteen-sixties was inadvertently left behind by Lynette. Fortunately, our chamber maid, *Mademoiselle* Sophie Talbot, after checking each of the drawers for discarded Liquorice Allsorts, made it her business to hand the items to the hotel's room service in reception. After being charged an arm and a leg for postage and packing, I received the clothes within a few days after our return home to Bournemouth.

I can recall Lynette and me sitting in the hotel's foyer waiting for the taxi to arrive to take us to the railway station. We were desperately hoping the driver from Thomas Cook, who possessed as much charm as a rattlesnake would be having a day off and that there may be a possibility a more user-friendly alternative would arrive; preferably an English person with charm and a sense-of-humour. We were appropriately dressed for the traverse journey across the English Channel looking like two fishermen depicted on the top of a Sainsburys sardine tin; a yellow waterproof jacket, a matching sowester and drawstring which completed the rather unnecessary nautical dressage arrangement. A pair of tight fitting 'Y fronts', underpants which could have enveloped 'Grumpy', the dwarf became more of an embarrassment when I rummaged around in the market to find a size suitable to contain my private parts. In the vernacular I said to Lynette: 'Gone are the days when one could go to a shop and buy underwear, small, medium and large; now it's small, medium, large, extra large, extra extra large or to be labelled a proverbial fat bastard.'

She would insist on buying all this bloody stuff from a market in Paris and she said it would come in handy when we return to France in a couple of weeks' time. I made it quite clear to her that unless we were to cross the Channel on a trawler, life boat or a yacht called: *'Morning Cloud'*, travelling at a great speed of knots into the Solent, this type of gear and equipment would only appeal to the ex-Prime Minister, the Right Honourable Sir Edward Heath.

After she said that the late Edward Heath used to be a band leader I began to gesticulate with a finger, slowly making circles around my temple similar to the whirly thing on a lap-top computer. I immediately got up from one of the rattan chairs when I fortuitously saw a black limousine pulling up outside.

It was the same Thomas Cook people collector that had brought us here the previous Saturday and by some strange metamorphosis he was all sweetness and light when I gave him a twenty franc tip for his expertise in delivering Lynette and I to *St.Lazare*, without any altercation. His command of the English language had miraculously improved during our short break in Paris and he forwardly gave me his business card just in case we wanted his services again. *Monsieur* Jean-Claude Le Floch, alias Joe Taxi, informed me that his relationship with *Mademoiselle* Pascale Duval was purely plutonic when he drove her home at midnight from the *LIDO* the previous evening. Snow White told him to forget the charge for transporting the extra trolley bag and that her office in *Boulevard Saint Martin* would make up the shortfall in his revenue.

The *Paris, Caen, Cherbourg SNCF* train began its journey from *St.Lazare* at precisely fourteen ten, calling at *Evreux Normandie, Bernay, Lisieux* and finally arriving in *Caen* at sixteen-nineteen. I can recall the weather being somewhat inclement; the incessant rain hitting the windows and the damp atmospheric pressure generated by the heaters inside one of the older First-Class compartments reminiscent of the nineteen-forty-five classic film "Brief Encounter", starring Trevor Howard and Celia Johnson. We had the pleasure of sitting next to two Benedictine nuns, a bishop and a *'hoodie'*; a Franciscan monk wearing brown vestments complete with a knotted rope and '*Clarke's*' leather sandals. It was when I saw one of the nuns wearing a pair of '*Philips*' turbo acoustic ear-plugs leading out from a Sony Walkman and then proceeding to read a copy of an '*Hello*' glossy magazine, I said to Lynette that the offertory boxes in the Catholic church must be doing very well especially when they could all afford to travel in a First-Class compartment. Most of them got off the train in *Lisieux*, that is all except one, Friar Tuck, who literally was tied up in knots when his rope became stuck in the sliding door; he probably missed his bowl of porridge that afternoon as the train slowly moved off from *Lisieux* to its next stop in *Caen*.

I asked Lynette: 'Do you get the feeling you've been here before?' as I looked out of the window to see Saint Therese's basilica towering one hundred and ninety-three metres high and reminiscent of *Paris's Sacré Coeur*.

'Do you mean in a former life?' she replied.

'No, No, Lynette,' I said, before reminding her it was once last Saturday morning and twice yesterday afternoon we had the pleasure of seeing it in all of its splendour and how could she ever forget a building of such magnitude.

'I don't look at buildings that remind me of vast crematoriums and have a huge forecourt to enable forty-six seater *Reise buses* to park after travelling all the way from Hamburg in the North East of Germany.' she was adamant to tell me.

'Well, I suppose they have got to go somewhere for their holidays and *Lisieux* seems to me the ideal place to return to after unintentionally buggering off in the August of nineteen forty-four to receive a second and third good hiding by the British, American and Canadian armoured divisions in the *Falaise* pocket of North Eastern France and the *Ardennes* region of Belgium.'

'Would you like to have one of my biscuits?' the monk asked, leaning forward to offer me an *Aldi* '*Smart Cookie*' that looked as though they were suffering from another case of German measles.

'Are they Friar Tuc biscuits?' I replied.

The worst case scenario occurred when he spoke with a German accent and said he had spent several years growing potatoes in a monastery in Carmarthenshire; the product being hand-cooked and eventually ending up on the shelves of a Supermarket in Düsseldorf.

'Were they salt and vinegar or cheese and chive flavour?' I asked, taking the conversation away from him calling me a heathen or something less patronising.

When he said they were hedgehog flavoured, had a small blue bag of salt inside the packet and one had to be aware of the deadly Welsh spiky bits, I knew then he was taking the piss.

The train, as predicted, pulled into *Caen* railway station at precisely sixteen-nineteen where a two point three litre shiny black Mercedes Benz limousine courtesy of Messrs Thomas Cook had been waiting for several hours to take us to the Ferry Port in *Ouistreham*. As I had suspected, it was the same French Formula one racing driver, Alain Prost who delivered us to *A La Gare*, the railway station in *Caen* the previous week and by some strange miracle we were so lucky to be alive. The driver, who gave me the impression he needed to go somewhere in a hurry, held what seemed to be a torn-off piece of brown cardboard which had our name written on it in bold letters. After telling him that our name was Travis and not *Traversée*, and he possessed a memory equal to the size of a pea, *Monsieur* Bertrand Provost said: 'This has reminded me, I must go to the toilet before we move off.'

'You see, Lynette these people are cowards, non-confrontational, lacking in any sense of humour and have an affinity with lavatories, and when they can't find one or refuse to pay the entrance fee, they do it in the streets in full view of everyone.'

'When you've got to go, you've got to go; you can't interfere with nature.' she replied, knowing that it wasn't such a good idea to enlighten her with a new set of observations.

On the Brittany Ferries ship *'Duc de Normandie'* we had the pleasure of listening to a country and western entertainer called Barry Vaughn Rogers, a *wanabe* cowboy from Bradford who would insist on playing a semi-acoustic guitar badly and possessed a voice that sounded like it was coming from the bottom of a bucket. We later called him Clint Eastwood because his shirt collar kept riding up from inside the back of a red velvet jacket when he sang the song popularized by Neil Diamond called, "Sweet Caroline" to an audience who were asleep, pissed or just tone deaf. I said to Lynette: 'He looks like Clint Westwood, doesn't he?'

'Don't you mean Clint Eastwood.' she replied.

'No, my dear,' I said, focussing my spectacles on the end of my nose to see more clearly.

'He's a *Paki* and he is coming from an entirely new direction.' I said, trying to imitate my smooth-talking adversary, Raman Patel.

'I can't see him holding a raffle and trying to get rid of a Brittany Ferries trolley bag at this time of night can you Chris? He may think he's back in a Bradford market.'

'I wouldn't have thought so, Lynette because there is no one on-board who is in a fit state to check the numbers.'

I can remember standing at the bar trying to break through a line of English truck drivers and a multitude of weekend biker-likers' from Stoke-on-Trent who had somehow managed to travel back to *Ouistreham* from *Marseilles* without incident. The French bar manager who was more of a hindrance than a help was about to send for the ship's Sergeant at Arms to throw me in the brink after I jokingly threatened to spray him with a soda siphon when he reduced my confidence to minus zero.

'Here we go again' I muttered to myself; 'another French smart arse; another centrally heated Viking; another wolf in sheep's clothing telling me how to pronounce a packet of dry-roasted peanuts and trying to humour these people is like pushing an upright piano in a marching band.'

The following morning we were met by Victoria and Barbara at Portsmouth's International Ferry Terminal. I said to Victoria: 'Who is that sitting in the back seat of the Volkswagen?' she replied by saying, it was her new boyfriend, Umberto Zaveroni.

'Oh, you mean the other half of the double act, Vicky and Umberto.' I said cheekily.

'How did you know that, dad?' she asked, inquisitively.

'That's what dreams are made of,' I emphasised, 'and anything that effects my pocket I will know all about it, especially when you're about to leave college to become a comedienne.'

'How was France, dad?' Barbara chirped in.

'Well, it was still there last night, but only just.' I replied regretfully.

Chapter Twenty-nine

Spring Bank Holiday, Monday 29th and Tuesday 30th May 2000.

It was four weeks later during the British Spring Bank holiday we returned to France by Brittany Ferries via Portsmouth, sailing to *Caen*, *Ouistreham* during the afternoon of Monday the twenty-ninth May 2000. Lynette and I made a decision to take the car after agreeing it was in good mechanical order to travel on French roads and the auto-route which was to take us to the City of *Méridon* where evil flourishes and goodness is an expensive commodity to find, especially on the shelves of a *Champion* supermarket.

The journey from Bournemouth to Portsmouth was horrendous when Lynette pointed towards a cow in a field as I drove the car steadily along the M27 motorway towards Eastleigh in Hampshire. She, revamping one of my best attempts to entertain the public and to render, the Poet Laureate, Andrew Motion redundant and out of business, asked:

> "On yonder hill, there stood a banana
> Was it Helen or Margarita Sultana?"

I was instantly mortified with her rendition of "The disappearing Cow" and wanted to know just who she was referring to?'

Lynette explained I had been doing a great deal of talking in my sleep of late and put it down to too much lead in my pencil. I said to her: 'it's no use having lead in your pencil if you've no-one to write to.'

'These pillows do a lot of talking, Chris and you had better beware because you may have to bring one along with you to a divorce court.'

'Well, thank you for that, Lynette; I need you like a hole in the head.'

'Don't mention it.' she replied, looking out of the side window to see the similarity between her and a wild 'Hampshire Hog' scavenging around in the New Forest. 'You're welcome.' she added.

'I'm welcome to do what?' I asked, wondering who the hell she was talking to.'

'You can poke anyone you like, Chris, but not in my bed.'

I emphatically explained to Lynette that the king-size double bed in

Number forty-six Queens Park Avenue belonged to us both and not exclusively to her and, furthermore, I was not in a position to poke anyone except the fire in our not so new house in *Méridon*. And, when I said I could always revert back to a single bed, Lynette, for some inexplicable reason, became somewhat erratic when she tried to improve on my ingenious suggestion by saying:

'You had better behave yourself in *Méridon*, Christopher, because you may just end up sitting on top of the coals.'

The sky was blue, the atmosphere was blue, but everything was beginning to go grey all around me,

The remainder of the journey was in complete silence after I had told her to shut up and rattle her cage somewhere else as I continued to drive along a stretch of motorway on the outskirts of Fareham.

We travelled over to France again on the *Normandie*, and from the moment I drove on to the vehicle deck I came under the care of the crew. I had to switch off the alarm, my ignition and headlights; apply my handbrake and place the vehicle in first gear or 'park'. I then had to lock the car doors because the Company cannot accept liability or be held responsible in the event of the car being either lost or stolen, and if that wasn't enough we had to make a note of the position of the vehicle just in case I forgot where it was parked. I broke the ice when I said to Lynette: 'who the hell would want to steal a bright yellow Volkswagen Estate from a Brittany Ferry when it is sailing sixty nautical miles out to sea.'

'The 'Frogs', they would nick the shirt of your back; that's what you would say, wouldn't you Christopher?'

Lynette and I made our way up from the garage to the reception area on Deck seven and then climbed two precipitous flights of stairs to '*Le Derby*', the lounge bar where the musical entertainment was in full swing.

'Oh, no.' I said to Lynette, removing my sunglasses from inside my jacket pocket to avoid recognition.

'What is it, Chris?' she replied reluctantly.

'It's that bloody bar manager; he's been given a transfer onto this ship and to make matters worse we will have to be subjected to the ship's disc jockey, Peter Harmony from Preston and the local transvestite, Gloria

Fontana from Tipton in Staffordshire and, if I play my cards right, I could win another collapsible trolley to replace the one which was confiscated by a *gendarme* after colliding into a chest-of-drawers whilst walking through 'The Hall of Mirrors' in the *Château de Versailles.'*

It was around seven-thirty, French time, when we docked at *Ouistreham*. The car was still parked in the ship's garage and not lying at the bottom of the English Channel where a Dover sole could swim freely through one of the windows I had inadvertently left open to allow some much-needed fresh air to enter into the vehicle whilst travelling through Porchester, that afternoon.

I pointed the car in the general direction of *Méridon* and put my foot down on the accelerator pedal to maximise the speed in fourth gear along the N13 *Autoroute*. Keeping to the right was easy, no articulated trucks to bully you off the road and no bandy-legged 'Lycra-likers', dangerous cyclists, pepper-potting their way through the traffic wearing safety helmets that look like aerodynamic pencil sharpeners and tight-fitting shorts which could only be described as bloody disgusting.

Even the breed of cattle in the fields looked different; the French *Charolais*, white in appearance and not your regular black and white Friesian variety, that we in our own country have learned to live with. The white coat with dark brown spots, "glasses" or dark rings around the eyes, a wide forehead and a well developed chest; these are the main characteristics of the Norman cow, the result of interbreeding somewhere between Crawley and Brighton.

There comes a time when ones first impression of a town begins to decline after spending a night in a hotel which had been built in the year ten forty-seven when *Guillaume*, 'William the Conqueror' founded *Normandie*.

Lynette and I located a car park in *Avenue St-Germain-de-Livet*, in close proximity to the hotel which was called: *'Le Maison des Donjons'*, and appropriately, the police station was situated next to the parking area just in case one decides to put a *Groat*; an historic English medieval silver coin, worth four pence, into a solar-generated metre instead of half-a-dozen French *Centimes*. It was no use trying to do a runner because the draw-bridge was about to be pulled up over the moat and any attempt to cross the river would mean instant removal from this earth. A rope which was attached to a wooden ladder and submerged in the water was used during The Second World War to enable the French Resistance Movement and the Jews of *Méridon* to escape into the surrounding countryside. Almost invariably, the ladder would be pulled up from the water by the *Gestapo* and those who tried to run back to their hiding places were instantly shot; their brown leather suitcases punctured with several rounds of nine-millimetre ammunition. I said to Lynette with tears in my eyes: 'it's a nice place this innit; what this town needs is Freddy Mercury or the Andrews Sisters to liven things up around here because there is more life inside the *rue morgue*.'

'Tell me Christopher, what is the difference between a Biker-liker and a Lycra-liker?' Lynette asked, adding to her confusion when she attempted to figure out how the parking metre worked.

'Well it is quite simple, Lynette; Biker-likers are likened to one of your ex-motorcycle friends from Brighton and Lycra-likers are exhibitionists and tarts who like to sit on the back of them.'

'I can see it's going to be the end of another one of those days.' Lynette replied, shaking her head like a '*Bollywood*' go-go dancer.

'And do you know what Micro-lighters are, Lynette?'

'Go on, enlighten me because you are going to tell me anyway.' she said, looking up at nothing in particular.

'Well, a Micro-lighter is someone who takes to the skies from Thruxton in a powered hand glider on Sunday afternoons and prevents me from having a kip in my back garden.'

'Oh, suddenly it's your back garden, is it? she said, questioning the true ownership of number forty-six Queens Park Avenue, Bournemouth.

I remember that afternoon all too well, Lynette and I wearing genuine Chinese army surplus khaki shorts, the type that drape four-inches below the knees and have a red star sewn on to the back pocket. I can also remember us wearing the same headgear; olive green Australian outback hats which had an elasticised cord and leather toggle to secure them; our outfits were not complete without Lynette's navy blue day bag and me with a black leather holdall securely wrapped around my bum, I must have looked like your regular Volkswagen dipstick and Lynette, successfully imitating a regular Tasmanian Sheila.

I can recall a middle-aged man driving what seemed to be a brand-new San Marino Red Honda Accord Coupe out from the car park. I could tell by his extremely sharp features, accentuated by a nose which could instantaneously open up a tin of Sainsbury's baked beans that he wasn't French, and then I came to the conclusion he was from somewhere between the *Golan Heights* and *Tel Aviv*. After he had automatically wound the window down he asked us if we knew of his tailoring shop in *Méridon* to which I replied: 'I have come over here to buy a house, not a bloody suit.' The Jew drop drove off in disgust, giving me the impression he wasn't happy with my manner and would have to find another British couple to annoy and enhance his business empire. Lynette and I learned from a waiter several months later that during the war, the tailors shop had been frequented by German officers when their tunics needed to be decorated with an additional medal ribbon; whatever happened to the tailors after they had done this remains a mystery.

I said to Lynette: 'A four-by-two driving a Japanese car, whatever next?'

She inquisitively asked me what a four-by-two was, to which I replied: 'It is a length of timber, four inches wide and two inches deep, also it is a piece of cotton wadding, four inches wide and two inches long which was popular with the British army 'Red Coats' to shove down the barrels of their muskets.'

'I must admit, Christopher, you are very knowledgeable but what has all this got to do with him?'

My explanation to her was simple; the man was as thick as a plank and his complexion looked similar to a Jaffa orange. I then stood to one side and left her to vacantly ponder over my response to her ongoing series of questions.

At nine o'clock it was time for us to eat and to have some liquid refreshment, namely a large gin and tonic with ice and lemon to quench Lynette's thirst, and a well deserved glass of *Calvados* brandy for frustrated little me. We sat down at a table inside the hotel's *brasserie* where the atmosphere was like sitting over a wheel on the top deck of a smoky Hants and Dorset double-decker bus. I can remember at one point, having to put some pressure on to Lynette to go outside into the street because of the inhalation of toxic fumes emanating from *Gauloises* cigarettes and pipe tobacco; the smell reminiscent to farmyard compost.

It all seemed to be going well until we ordered our meal. The busty Rumanian waitress who was called, Lyudmila Lenska, looked as if she would be far better entertaining guests down inside *les donjons*, the dungeons rather than serving the *Plat de jour*, the meal of the day to the public. The set menu consisted of *Toulouse* sausages, eggs and chips, and for the desert, a *Normandie Pom D'or gateaux*, a slice of golden apple tart served with *crème frais*; the white stuff that evaporates by magic in front of your very eyes. The only alternative to this culinary expertise was to choose the *a la Carte*, a small menu consisting of *les Cuisses de Grenouile*, frogs legs; *les tripes*, a disgusting oven-proof pot of slowly simmered ribbons of tripe, diced carrots and onions, and to add to this gastronomic voyage of discovery, the restaurant had *boeuf bourguignon* with *Penne Rigata* on their menu; a microscopic dish of cubed braised steak with pasta; both these dishes served along with a French governmental health warning.

We elected to have the *boeuf bourguignon* which seemed to have been cooked in red wine to create rich-tasting gravy; the type of sick-making stuff your granny wouldn't approve of.

Two strawberry ice-cream sundaes which looked as though they had been prepared on Sunday were brought to our table by Lyudmila, the lustrous Eastern-bloc country waitress with chains tattooed around her ankles, a snake coiled around the top of her arm and a spider crawling up the nape of her back; I began to wonder that evening where the monkeys could possibly be hiding.

Suddenly I had the urge to visit the lavatory which was down a steep spiral staircase similar to a helter-skelter on a funfair. I had the idea that *Guillaume*, the young William of *Normandie* may have used these cellars to go to the toilet before going into battle against Henry the First of France in the year, ten forty-seven because of a red piss-potty engraved with two yellow leopards printed on its base hanging up on one of the walls; I can recall it being made in China and an excellent item to take to the BBC 1 television programme, "The Antique Road Show" or 'The Great Antique Hunt", especially when Jilly Goolden, the controversial wine critic, journalist and presenter wants to go to the ladies powder room to blow herself up. I can also remember there were heavy wooden doors with old wrought-iron handles and latches, some ancient and some modern to mix the past with the present. The *la cave*, the cellar, was a labyrinth of tunnels, hewn out of solid rock, local lime stone which had been primitively transported from a nearby quarry. It was difficult to find the entrance to the gentleman's room because all the doors looked alike, apart from what looked like a top hat painted high in the centre and one could easily end up inside one of the dungeons. I had the presence of mind to metaphorically take pot luck and recite the old nursery rhyme, selection and counting game which goes:

> "Eeny, Meeny, Miny, Moe,
> Sit the baby on the po
> When it's done wipe its bum
> Eeny, Meeny, Miny, Moe"

I remembered being taught at Grammar school, the logic and doctrine laid down with authority to describe the word dogmatism; the ancient Roman army would select every fourth man and put him to the sword to find the perpetrators of descent and mutiny amongst its ranks.

And when it was all finished and the blood ran freely into the gutters of Rome, there would be cheers from the spectators and twenty-five legionnaires made ready to make up the numbers in the century; it sounds a bit like cricket but a little more dangerous. It is amazing how you can still remember events which happened a long time ago having been hit several times in the chest with a piece of chalk thrown by an irate and frustrated schoolmaster who found it difficult to locate the boy making faces behind his back.

Fortuitously, I found what I was looking for; a gentleman's cloak room that was undergoing a course of redecoration and it wasn't long before the *Calva*, commonly known as *Calvados*, the ordinary rough apple brandy produced in *Pays d'Auge*, began to take its toll, making me feel tired and drowsy. It was there; in solitary confinement I fell asleep and began to dream of bizarre things.

In my dream I pointed to one of the doors in the cellar and turned a large circular handle which squeaked noisily.............

I pushed the creaking door forward, hoping to find a wash basin, hand-dryer, a separate urinal and a walk-in lavatory, but instead I was confronted by a haze of dusty cobwebs, tarantula spiders, rats as big as cats, a cage with two manic chimpanzees, a growling grizzly bear shackled to a hay-strewn floor, and what looked like a fifteen-foot brown and white python coiled and asleep on top of a black wooden coffin; its outside diameter larger than domestic drainpipe. There were frogs dismembered at the waist hanging down from a washing line; their muscular legs waiting to be dropped into the vat of the hotel's deep-fat fryer.

This is what nightmares are made of, I thought to myself, when the two monkeys began to jump up and down, rattling the bars of the cage violently in front of me; the python now awake and beginning to slither slowly away from the coffin lid, heading towards the ground. The bear was now foaming at the mouth and showing me his blood-stained teeth giving me the impression it had rabies and couldn't wait to return to the "Come Dancing" sessions in the Market Square. Who was in the coffin? And was the python part of Lyudmila's extra mural activities down in the dungeons? I wasn't going to stay to find out.

Paradoxically, when I woke up, the urge to use the toilet had worn off and I rapidly made my way out from "The House of Dracula" in *la Cave* and proceeded to climb what seemed to be a never-ending spiral of stairs back to the restaurant; I could have sworn I heard Tarzan hollering in the background.

'Which lunatic is running the asylum?' I thought to myself.

'Chris, what have you been doing down there? You have gone white and your hair is covered in dust; you look like Hannibal.'

Completely out of breath, I said to Lynette: 'Don't be so silly, I don't look like the cat.'

'I didn't mean Hannibal back home, I mean Hannibal Smith from the film "RAIDERS of the Lost Arc". Just, what have you been doing down there, Chris, because I need to go to the toilet myself.' she added.

'No, don't go down there, Lynette, the stairs are very dangerous.'

'It's that tart of a waitress; she's down there isn't she?' Lynette asked, looking around to see if Lyudmila was in evidence inside the restaurant.

'No, don't go down there, Lynette; the place is filthy.'

She, having refused to take my advice, got up from the table and went down the spiral stairs resembling a fan of playing cards spread out by a magician.

Lynette returned ten minutes later and said to me that the ladies powder room was so clean and aesthetically pleasing she could stay there all night, sleeping on the *Chaise longue*, a comfortable red velvet sofa bed situated next to a non-user friendly Italian hand-dryer that roars like a lion when activated and tries to bite your hand off.

'I wouldn't advise you to do that, dear, because of the menagerie next door.'

'What menagerie, Christopher, are you going off your trolley?'

'Trolley, trolley, which trolley do you mean?'

'The trolley, that's inside your head, Christopher.'

'I think you had better go and put some more money in the parking metre, Lynette, we don't want any traffic wardens, reminiscent of *Bayeux Bogeymen*, a bunch of badly dyed ragamuffins sporting noses which look like solidified peeled bananas pointing in a southerly direction and completely obscuring the lower part of their ugly faces sticking their idea of a summons underneath the windscreen wiper of our car, especially during the first night staying in this wonderful country. On your return, would you call into the Turkish take-away and buy a couple of *doner kebabs*?'

In my mind I appropriately began to sing "I'm Your Boogie Man" written and sung by Harry Casey of KC AND THE SUNSHINE BAND.

"I'm your bogie man, that's what I am
I'm here to do whatever I can
Be it early morning, late afternoon
Or at midnight, oh it's never too soon
To put a sticker on your van
I'm your regular bogie man, uh-huh"

It was at this point, Lyudmila; our friendly Slavonic waitress asked if everything was okay. I replied, saying: 'Of course, everything is just fine, the food was excellent; the ambiance quite pleasant and can you recommend a good hairdressers' salon.'

Chapter Thirty

Les Notaires; the solicitor's office, eleven o'clock the following morning

I can remember Lynette and I were sitting in the reception area waiting for *Madame* Brier to arrive from Paris.

'Tell me Chris, why is it that people always seem to do crosswords and play Sudoku when they are waiting for someone, or something to happen?'

'Well, there is a simple answer to your question, Lynette and this is truly amazing. The Viking women in the ninth century played *rune stones*, a kind of Scandinavian domino game, as they waited for their men to return home after wreaking havoc here in Northern France; however, the Roman Empire, five hundred years earlier, developed Gaul stones because of eating too many *Hamburgers, Berliner* and *Frankfurter* sausages and drinking far too much *Löwenbräu* in the *Bier kellers* of Northwest Europe and, meanwhile, the Chinese *Mah-jong,* a game with different hieroglyphic characters depicting dragons and fat moustachioed little men fishing on the end of a wooden jetty in Peking, carried on regardless. And, we British, played bingo, ate fish and chips and got merrily sloshed while waiting to see a barrister or lawyer prior to a divorce case in sunny Bournemouth; does this answer your question, my dear?'

'Here we go again, you will have your little joke, won't you, Christopher?'

'I'm not joking, Lynette.'

'I do wish I could speak French fluently, Chris.' Lynette said with a sigh.

It was then I explained to her that the French language was totally illogical, complicated and designed by Latin monks who had fallen out with the Pope.

'So,' Lynette said as if she had just discovered the meaning of life, 'this explains why their dictionary is so small in comparison to ours.'

I reminded her of the time I took up a German correspondence course and it was supposed to help me become fluent in three months, but after two years of hard study I abandoned it because I didn't know the difference between a sausage and a banana; that was the *würst* scenario.

'Was this why you had an accident in Sainsburys?' Lynette asked quickly, folding her arms and then looking up to towards the ceiling to admire the decoration.

'Ah, but you didn't complain about the compensation, did you, my dearest.' I said, rubbing my hands knowing I had won the first round in a succession of arguments.

Waiting for Sylvie Briere to arrive was similar to watching paint dry as I munched away through a second packet of Crawford's ginger biscuits having been offered a *tres joli*, a decoratively pleasing and debatable colourful arrangement of flowers for breakfast; most people eat eggs, bacon, fried bread, tomatoes and Heinz baked beans to break their fast, but we get a Continental breakfast of bloody flowers that have probably been frequented this very morning by the hotel's cat.

Lynette and I were like two bats in a bricked-up belfry; totally blind, with no one to help us because the *Notaries*, *Madame* Emilie Le Breton hadn't arrived and *Madame* Briere apparently was caught up in a traffic hold-up somewhere along the N13 *Autoroute*, between *Evreux* and *Bernay*.

It was midday when the secretary postponed the meeting until two-thirty that afternoon; the excuse being, *Madame* Le Breton had another engagement in *Caen*.

'Has it escaped your notice, you never get any word of apology from the frogs.'

'They're busy people, Christopher.'

'That is no bloody excuse and the next person I hear saying the word *pardon*, I will personally kick in the balls.'

'But, *Madame* Briere's secretary, *Mademoiselle* Sophie-Anne Moine hasn't got any balls, Chris.'

'Judging by her distinctive Parisian tone of voice, I rather suspect she has.'

'And, did you see that pink rubbery thing she had on the end of her pencil?' Lynette asked with embarrassment.

I said they are called rubbers, my dear; you can buy them from a shop in Bournemouth but for the time being they are out of stock because of increasing demand.

Lynette suggested we go for lunch because she had taken more than enough of my witticisms that morning and furthermore, threatened me with extreme violence if I continued to be in competition with my daughter.

We shook hands with *Mademoiselle* Moine, and I said assertively to her we would return early at two o'clock sharp that afternoon to complete on the sale of number twenty-seven *rue Mortain*.

'All this kissing and shaking hands is a total waste of time.' I had to remind Lynette again after the secretary had quickly shown us the door and for me to fall down an extremely dangerous concrete step leading down into the street. 'Maybe, the step was designed intentionally to prevent clients coming back to interrupt *Mademoiselle* Moine filing her nails.' I continued to say when I picked myself up, brushed myself down to start all over again. For a moment, I thought I was sitting on my backside in sunny Bournemouth but, then I should have been so lucky when *Madame* Briere appeared with her husband who looked remarkably like Sir Trevor McDonald OBE.

'Would you like to join us for lunch?' Sylvie Briere asked without any word of apology passing by her red painted lips.

'No, *Monsieur Dame*, Lynette and I are not hungry at the moment; it may have something to do with your *Notaire* taking leave of absence and your good self turning up late.'

'Oh, well, maybe another time.' she said and behaving like nothing had happened.

'We will see you at two o'clock this afternoon, *Madame* Briere.' Lynette said to her and not to her husband.

'But, the meeting isn't until two-thirty.' Briere unnecessarily reiterated.

'We will nevertheless see you at two in the *Notaires* office.'

Lynette and I ventured off down the street and into the Square where the last remnants of debris were being clinically swept up from the morning market. We found a place to eat in a tree-lined street called, *Avenue Saint Anne*, a cosy spot with tables and chairs outside its *restaurant* cum *Bistro* called, *Hotel Du Vin Bistro*.

The waiter became aware we were not French when I began to read a copy of the British *'Times'* newspaper, an expensive rarity in France and poorly printed in Belgium. I can remember the music playing in the background which reminded me of the days when I was a teenager hanging about the rock and roll dives in Bournemouth.

'Those were the days,' I said to Lynette as we listened to the singer and songwriter, Johnny Ray, melodiously singing: "Who's Sorry Now" as we ate our roast breast of *Barbary duck, roasted figs* and *Grand Marnier jus*, under the shade of an apple blossom tree.

'I can also remember wearing black leather winkle-picker shoes, fluorescent socks, drainpipe trousers and a sky-blue Marty Wilde shirt. I can also recall going to the Winter Gardens' ballroom in Bournemouth where I could stand in the wings combing the grease in my hair as I waited for the right girl to come along.'

'What has changed, Christopher?'

'I became an expert dancer and was able to twirl my partner around, toss her up in the air, slide her under my legs and then throw her over my back.' I explained before Lynette stopped me from getting up to do a demonstration.

'You wouldn't be able to do that sort of thing now, Chris; you could give yourself a hernia. I can remember Slim Whitfield; he was a good singer in the fifties.' Lynette so wrongly put in.

'Don't you mean, Slim Whitman and not David Whitfield, Lynette?'

'It was such a long time ago I have a problem trying to remember. I know, Chris;' Lynette said, recalling her favourite tune. 'it was Frank Ifield; he was good, he was.'

'You mean that blond-haired six-foot two, eyes are blue, Ouchy, couchie, couchie-pooh Australian, who constantly had problems with the elastic in his underpants; you seem to have an affinity with these high-pitched pantaloons, don't you, Lynette?'

It was at this high point, in the vernaculars, I decided to give Lynette my rendition of one of Frank's famous songs; revamped for this occasion and is called: "I remember You".

"I remember UYU"

"I remember UHU
This was the glue that made my dreams come true
All those years ago
I can remember too, an 'Airfix' kit
And bits that stick to the top of your fingers
I remember too, an aeroplane
A Hawker Hurricane I built to scale
Had a Swastika emblazoned on its tail
Another one that couldn't fly and put onto a stand
Firmly secured by an elastic band
And I can remember too my Auntie Mabel
Giving me hell at the kitchen table
She said, here's five bob and buy some glue
And then come back and eat your stew
When my life is through
And the angels ask me to recall
The thrill of it all, then I will tell them
I remember UHU"

'Yes well, that was very entertaining, Chris; could we now please get on with our meal.' she said.

I began to cry into my onions when we were attacked by a low-flying *Mirage* jet fighter aircraft from a French air force base situated two miles south of Méridon. The pilot must have broken the sound barrier because of a loud bang, a sonic boom when it flew over the restaurant causing one of my figs to take-off from my plate and land on the next table. A Serbian refugee who had travelled all the way from Bosnia to search for a better life was somewhat relieved when he realized he wasn't a target, or the sky raining figs.

It was exactly one o'clock when the bells from the Cathedral began to take their toll, ringing loudly in my ears to herald another funeral and to lessen the population of Méridon. 'Bing bong! Bong bing! Clang! Clang;

the noise was enough to drive one insane and I knew then, how Johnny Ray eventually became totally deaf.

I ordered another one of those *Les Trappe monk's* beers which can get you drunk within seconds when drank from a chalice that may have looked like the Holy Grail; it is of small wonder why the *Franciscan* order of monks seek sanctuary and lock themselves inside the local monastery because half the inmates wouldn't be in a fit state to venture out. And as for the *Carmelite* order of nuns from the Abbey; they are known to produce small bottles of medicine, *Molotov Cocktails*, wrapped in twisted brown paper, a *Cross* between the German pick-me-up '*Underberg*' and their highly explosive concoction called in France, '*eau des Carmes*' and in Germany, '*Karmelitergeist*', literally translates as the Carmelite ghost, a disgusting type of liqueur guaranteed to blow one's brains out.

Our well burnt *crème brulées* arrived at the table as ordered; they looked as if they had been attacked by a high octane Butane gas blow lamp and then suddenly it was time to go, leaving the pigeons to eat the crumbs left over from the basket of sliced *artisan baguette* breads and to dip their beaks into the local hand-churned *Normandi*e butter.

Sister Monica, a *Carmelite* nun and a local pain in the arse popped up as if she had just come out from nowhere, rattling and rolling her tin fiercely in front of my face to show she was very much in charge of things in the town and the mayor had no say in her highway robbery activities. I had the presence of mind to tell her to bugger off but then I thought we have to live here, remember, and I didn't want to end up on a church black list. It was after I had put a ten Franc note into the church coffers, Sister Monica told us her maiden name before she became engaged to God; she was called Doris Haughton and came from Aintree near Liverpool and then added she would die for a plateful of *Scouse*. I said: 'Lynette could make you some and that would bring your mortality problem to a close, wouldn't it?' She made no comment on an offer she really couldn't refuse; needless to say, the sales of French dark sexy chocolate sold in the nearby *Champion* supermarket had increased dramatically since her arrival. Sister Monica told us she worked for the Coal Board in Crosby but that was until she was made redundant, by the then Prime Minister, Margaret

Thatcher and it was interesting to learn that Miss Doris Haughton had never looked back.

Méridon's quarter-covered wooden market had all but disappeared; a small caravan selling sausages, chips and a variety of *crepes*, pancakes was all that was left from the morning's attempt to sell produce to the public at over-the-top prices equal to the supermarket; however, it wasn't exactly Shrove Tuesday, and to make a pancake which has a layer of brown stuff called, *Nutella*, spread thickly around it's circumference, was not aesthetically pleasing especially when the caravan was parked outside the ecclesiastical quarter of the church.

The mansions, brick buildings and half-timbered wattle and daub *Normandie* houses which were miraculously left intact during the allied bombings in June nineteen forty-four could be seen all around us; I was half-expecting the swash buckling three musketeers, Athos, Porthos and D'artagnan to appear at any moment, but that was until little miss know-it-all, Lynette, corrected me by saying there were four of them and he was called, Aramis.

Méridon, this is the place Lynette will be so happy to visit for at least six months every year for the rest of her life; a non-functional, soulless place without a McDonalds, Kentucky Fried Chicken or a pub that dispenses real ale, but however, there is a cinema, 'The Plaza' nearby, showing a Hollywood blockbuster film called "The Wizard of Oz" starring the child actress, Judy Garland.

My stomach became upset when I saw *Monsieur* Jacques Mayer cleaning the inside of his windows of the antique bookshop in *Place Drakkar*; his long grey beard drooping down, tapering to a point, and on top of his balding head he wore a skull cap which reminded me of one of Charles Dickens's characters in the classic, "Oliver Twist". 'I must call in to see him soon.' I muttered to myself as I walked a few paces behind Lynette, giving me the impression she couldn't wait to injure herself on that awful step.

According to my *Casio*, perpetual time and date watch, it was exactly two when Lynette and I walked into the reception room of the *Notaires'* office. *Madame* Sylvie Briere was there waiting for us to arrive and I commented to Lynette that all this British assertiveness is beginning to pay off when I learned she had been seated cross-legged for at least thirty minutes in the waiting room after contracting piles from sitting outside on a cold step.

'Why is it, Chris, the church bells and the clocks in Northern France always ring and chime two minutes late?'

'The bells are used primarily to summon people to church Lynette, and the chimes from their clocks are not for you to argue over the difference between Greenwich and local meantime.'

'Well, how is it, the clock above the reception desk is on time but, paradoxically, two minutes slow?' Lynette asked, looking at a huge round black plastic timepiece that one can usually see inside a hospital.

'This is because when the time was changed at the end of March, it wasn't done correctly, but on the other hand, my interpretation of all this is because the *frogs* want to be different to the rest of the world.'

'You know, Christopher, sometimes you come out with the biggest load of garbage I have ever heard in my life and if you continue to persecute the entire French population, I'm not going to speak to you ever again.'

'Just at what time will this moment of silence commence, Lynette, because then we can all have a modicum of peace and quiet.'

'Now, seems to be the right time Christopher.'

'The *"froggies"* cannot abide waiting, Lynette, and it is because of my indignant and intolerant attitude towards them, *Madame* Briere is an exception to their rule.'

'You are only confirming what I have known for years, Christopher, that you have an attitude problem.' she just about managed to put in.

It was two thirty-two when *Madame* La Breton opened the door to her office from the inside and quickly poked her head out like a mongoose to see if we were there and hadn't defaulted on the completion by going to the cinema.

Following the archaic ritual of having to listen to *Madame* Le Breton, dictating word-for-word from what seemed to be hundreds of documents relating to the deeds of the house, Lynette and I after signing and initialling each page were handed the keys.

The *notaire* desperately wanted to know when we planned to return to England and after I informed her we were going back to Portsmouth on the Friday evening, she asked me to arrange an appointment to see her on Thursday morning regarding the testament. I wanted to know what she was talking about and it wasn't long before it occurred to me that it was an ongoing '*Last Will and Testament*', which if signed, would have left me penniless.

Chapter Thirty-one

La P'tite Livre Magazin': 'The Little Bookshop' in *Place Drakkar*, the same afternoon.

I had just about had enough of *Madame* Le Breton explaining how I could be in a position to be ripped-off every year by her and *Madame* Weismann, her legal partner in crime, for the remainder of my life, and furthermore, Lynette could kill me and still benefit from my estate which would automatically be inherited by my two daughters, Victoria and Barbara. These ancient, archaic and out-of-date French laws were designed to make the average male participant in a marriage totally worthless; it is of little wonder why there are so many gamblers today and yesterday who dispensed with all their money before divorcing their wives to get married once or twice again to rich and ugly aristocratic women in France.

So, here we were again, happy as can be, all good fun and jolly good company, sitting outside the *'Bar Au Chocolat'* in *Place Drakkar*.

'Do you know, Lynette,' I said, perusing quickly through the menu. 'I could murder a large *café crème*; a big cup of coffee with *Crème Frisch* and sugar.'

'And, do you know, Christopher, this is the second time this afternoon I have heard the word, murder and to tell you the truth I'm beginning to get sick and tired of it all.'

'Yes, you are right as usual, my dear.' I replied with a sigh. 'You know who profits from all of this; it is the solicitors and the directors of the casinos.'

'I can't fathom out how the French seem to operate.' Lynette said without surprise.

'Now, you are beginning to understand and realize, Lynette that the brain of a Frenchman is different to most human beings and whatever they do they start from the back and slowly work their way to the front; they have been known to put up a mast and then build a boat around it.'

'You do talk twaddle, Christopher.' she had to put in, and when I gave another example of my better observations from life's highway, she said:

'I can see this is going to be another one of those days.'

'Now, you see those people walking across the road on the zebra crossing, Lynette, they walk diagonally and not in a straight line, cutting other pedestrians off in their wake.'

'They are German tourists, Chris, they have just got off a coach from Minden.' she said, after I noticed an eighty year-old man goose-stepping over the black and white strips of wet paint in the road leaving a trail of white foot prints all around the town.

'Well, Lynette, I suppose, "the road to hell is paved with good intentions".' quoting the late Riesa Gorbachev, the wife of ex-Russian president Mikhail when I saw Sister Monica assaulting the group with an empty tin; it was probably her way of showing her anger and the way down the straight and narrow-minded path of righteousness after they had bombed the shit out of the Liverpudlian people during The Second World War.

'You're always going on about the bloody war, Chris, why don't you give it a rest?'

'I wish I could, my dear, but you see, the church in *Sainte-Mère-Eglise*, still has an American paratrooper hanging down from its clock tower and the Hollywood actor, Red Buttons, would be horrified and not at all pleased to learn he had been up there since the sixth June nineteen forty-four.'

'Ah, poor thing, he must be feeling cold.' Lynette said, until I told her he was only up there on a temporary basis to attract German tourists and that the French cut him down on Tuesday evenings prior to choir practise.

'Well, that's alright then.' she said convincingly putting on her mock Sloane accent once again after I allowed her to profit from my extensive range of military knowledge.

'Tell me Lynette is that *Madame* Le Breton and *Madame* Sylvie Briere I see going into Ismailia's Jewish Antique Jewellers' across the Square?'

'Yes, I do believe it is, Christopher, and I suppose there are no prizes for guessing who will be paying for another string of cultured pearls to hang around Le Breton's pretty little brass neck.'

'You see, my dear, you give these people sixpence at the beginning of the week and then it is changed by some kind of strange metamorphosis into a shilling by the week's end.'

'We are into decimalization these days, Chris, haven't you noticed?'

'I am talking metaphorically, Lynette, and I have calculated these sums of money today would amount to several pounds sterling.'

'This sounds very much like you, Chris when you come home from 'The Queens' with all those tins of lager after winning the pub quiz.'

'Ah, that's a point, Lynette; what is green and lives at the bottom of the ocean?'

'I haven't a bloody clue, Christopher, and could you please ask the waiter if he could bring me my pot of Lipton's tea because we have a ferry to catch on Friday.'

When I said it was Moby Frog she quickly got up from the chair and hit me with her suede navy blue day bag.

'The reason why the waiter is taking so long delivering our order is because we are English and the French people who have just sat down get served *tout de suite*; at once, if not immediately.'

'Well how is it, Chris, they are speaking in an accent which sounds very much like Irish and seem to be from somewhere between Belfast and Londonderry?'

'How was I to know they are from the Republic of Ireland?' I said, before trying to make myself invisible by wearing my black Polaroid sunglasses, complete with string to look like your regular IRA man.

'Belfast and Londonderry are situated in Northern Ireland, Chris; you should know that being so clever and telling everyone you are a citizen of the world.'

'Did you know, Lynette, the French language is back to front and unlike the British and your more logical European languages....for instance, a 'walkie-talkie' is a 'talkie walkie', a 'lap-top' is a 'top-lap' and when it is raining they say: 'it is raining dogs and cats'; how can one comprehend that?'

'Everyone has their own way of saying things, Christopher; the French people are not so unique in expressing themselves.'

'I can remember, my dear, one of your ex-boyfriends, Isaac Green saying he sends his *Yids* to *schulle* and had a habit of saying *schedule* instead of *schedule*; I thought this to be a load of *skit* if you ask me.'

'You've always got to have the last say, Chris, haven't you, and even at our wedding, you asked the vicar to hurry up because AFC Bournemouth was playing away to West Bromwich Albion and the match was being televised and shown in The Queens that afternoon.'

'Well, it was a great day all the same, Lynette, wasn't it?'

'It was our bleeding wedding day, Chris, remember?'

'I didn't mean our wedding Lynette; I meant Bournemouth winning three-one.'

It was at this point I moved the entire canteen of cutlery to one side of the table lest one of the sharper pieces may have been seen by Lynette to be the ideal implement to kill me.

'And, did you know - '

'- what's this, Chris; another did you know?' she interrupted.

'- that one of France's leading exports is the singer and jazz guitarist, Sacha Distel; well that was until he was abducted by Burt Bacharach and Dianne Warwick; he isn't quite the same after all those raindrops falling on his head. Our contribution in Europe, Lynette is the singer, songwriter, Joe Cocker, the guy from Sheffield who now lives in France and always sounds as though he has a frog down his throat.'

'You know, Christopher, one of these days you are going to get your comeuppance when you'll be hit by a massive thunder bolt from heaven and that will probably put paid to your sarcastic remarks.'

'Well, I hope the person who despatched it has good eye-sight and is able to penetrate AFC Bournemouth Goldsands Stadium.'

'You needn't worry, Chris, he's got telescopic eye-sight and from a dizzy height he can spot meat pies, toilet rolls, sausage rolls and half-eaten weenies being thrown onto the pitch.'

'Don't look now Lynette, but can you see *Madame* Silverman going into Ismailia's Jewellery shop; do you think they are having a 'bring and buy' sale this afternoon?'

'How on earth can I see if I cannot look?' she replied looking at her watch and tapping lightly on the table to attract the waiter's attention.

'And also did you see that rare honeycomb pattern diamond bracelet in eighteen carat two-tone gold *Madame* Briere was wearing this afternoon?' I asked.

Lynette explained to me that it belonged to her grandmother, the late *Madame* Odette Roulier and was made by *Cartier* in Paris during the First World War and its estimated value is around eighteen thousand dollars. I made comment that if the German army had found it underneath her mattress it could now be lying in someone's jewellery box in Bavaria. I carried on improving Lynette's gemmology knowledge by saying that I had seen a similar bracelet in the window of *H Samuel* in Boscombe High Street; it was in the January sale and was a bargain at fifty quid. She then asked the obvious question: 'if you were so impressed with it why on earth didn't you go in and buy the dammed thing?'

I explained to her that one evening after a hard day's lecturing at the University I passed by the shop on my way to the pub, I was then caught up in a lengthy discussion with Councillor Bennett regarding the exorbitant prices the brewery were charging for a pint of real ale and a packet of cheese and onion flavoured crisps; she, with no apparent reason went ballistic and said: 'Next, you will be telling me, Christopher the price of ascending in Bournemouth's static hot air balloon is going up, and it's all due to inflation.'

At last the waiter came with my *café crème* and a pot of Lipton's Earl Grey tea and the original *Lotus Speculoos* ginger biscuits for Lynette. He said: '*Je suis très désolé*, but why do you British people call us frogs?'

It was at this point Lynette and I looked at each other and said in unison: 'I don't know!'

I was in a frame of mind to refer the waiter's enquiries to the *Mick*s sitting at the next table but declined because of violent repercussions and instantaneously began to think about my mortality and quality of life. This was the first time I had seen *Guinness* being served in a fifty centilitre *Heineken* glass and I hoped it was probably the last.

'Why is it Lynette, that when one strays over border controls in Europe, people have a certain disdain for foreigners, in particular, the

English and call you names like Beefeaters, Insular monkeys and a race of people that come from the last hostile country in the northern hemisphere?'

'It's because of the football hooligan element, Chris.' she replied, pouring more aromatic grey stuff into her cup and at the same time accentuating her little finger up towards the sky. 'You can't really blame them when you insist on throwing meat pies and sausage rolls at the referee during a World Cup match in Monaco, can you?' she added.

'Ah, that Prince Rainier doesn't stand any messing he locks them up and throws away the keys.' I put in after once witnessing an England football supporter being handcuffed and arrested by a policewoman outside the casino in Monte Carlo.'

As I was scraping the last remnants of *Crème Frais* from around the inside of an old ceramic *Ovalitine* mug which had probably been nicked from the Savoy Hotel during the blitz on London in September nineteen forty and then transported over to France by General de Gaulle himself in June nineteen forty-four, I saw *Monsieur* Jacques Mayer in his shop stacking shelves with old books.

A priest who looked as if he had escaped rapidly from a confessional box in the cathedral was heading speedily towards us as we were about to pay, we were to learn later he had visited *Madame* Silverman to find out who had bought the house in *rue Mortain*. I said to, Lynette; 'these people are the worst kind, come on let's get the hell out of here and we can take a look inside the Antique bookshop across the Square because you never know the owner may know something about the house.'

'Okay.' she said, bringing our afternoon tea party to an abrupt close.

The old-fashioned door bell melodiously tinkled ting-a-ling as we entered the shop. *Monsieur* Jacques Mayer who was sitting at a table counting out his money became curious when I introduced myself to him and asked if he could mend my father's old cog and wheel railway pocket watch because it had stopped during the hours of darkness on Tuesday the seventh of December, nineteen forty-three. Jacques Mayer rose to his feet slowly from a rickety old chair, bending forward to stare at me closely from several inches away from a now perspiring face as if he was looking at fish through the glass of an aquarium. With poppy-eyes and mouth agape, he asked in English what was I doing here in *Méridon* and how did I know that he had been hiding from the German Gestapo before he became an assistant, and subsequently the owner of an antique bookshop in the centre of town and that he was a watchmaker and horologer from *Cherbourg*.

Lynette, after seeking permission from *Monsieur* Mayer, who was now nodding like your proverbial donkey, began perusing through old history books which were about to be put away on to his top shelf and out of arm's reach of any would-be gold diggers dropping into his shop to delve into Méridon's bizarre past.

"If you go down in the woods today, the teddy bears will have a picnic". *Monsieur* Mayer said to me in metaphor; giving me advice and a warning not to go rummaging around beneath the floor of the *la cave* of number twenty-seven *rue Mortain*. The warning later was to take on the form of a threat from the clergy, the town hall and the local Masonic lodge who tried their best to run Lynette and myself out of town.

I wanted desperately to know what he meant by the caution and it quickly dawned on me that Jacques Mayer knew who and what was to be found lying in the catacombs of Saint Agatha; Anglo Saxon artefacts, namely, broad swords, shields and priceless jewellery. Furthermore, I was sure there was the ultimate find, the discovery of the treasure, paradoxically belonging to 'The Knights Templar' which had disappeared without trace for nearly seven-hundred years and remained a mystery until I found it on Sunday, the eighteenth of June of this year. I also knew who had been buried down there since October 1307; for instance, there were members belonging to the Order of the Knights of St John of Jerusalem, *Roger de Charney*, *Edwin of Charnock*, *Charles Blanche* of *Burgundy* and fellow Temple mercenaries who were put to the sword by agents of King Philip IV the fair in the same month.

It was during the following week Lynette and I witnessed a mysterious fire, an act of someone's God, causing the cobbles and paving stones in the main Square to subside and give way allowing grey smoke to ascend between each one. The inferno which raged for two days had cremated the bones of the dead, turned rubies, sapphires, amethyst, opal and jade into multi-coloured glass; gold and silver jewellery into worthless unidentifiable pieces of molten metal and this was how the spoils of war destined for the International Monitory Fund, based in Temple Bar London was destroyed. Interestingly, we were to learn from our next door neighbour, *Madame* Grandin, that a middle-aged Russian couple, a man and a woman had been snooping around in *rue Mortain* enquiring as to who owned the house and what did she know about the catacombs that lay beneath; It would seem I had found what they were looking for and had it not been for the extremely low price they paid for the purchase of our property, they would have hot-footed back to Moscow.

'Hey, look at this Chris.' Lynette called out with an element of surprise as she glossed over the pages of an early twentieth century book which had been attacked by mildew. 'It's our house in *rue Mortain*,' she added. 'And the sepia photograph must have been taken with one of those old-fashioned cameras which are primed with gun powder and explode in front of your very eyes.'

I immediately took the book away from Lynette's possession and proceeded to turn the pages, discovering more knowledge about the cathedral, its history and more importantly, acquiring a mental geophysical map of its grounds.

Lynette and I said goodbye to *Monsieur* Jacques Mayer and thanked him for his friendly attitude towards us and after apologising for the impromptu visit we left his shop wondering if he had the presence of mind to inform the authorities of our unwanted presence.

*

'Buxom Books' bookshop, Winton Road Bournemouth - Wednesday 24th August 2000

I can recall visiting Bournemouth's bizarre bookshop, 'Buxom books' the day after we finally returned home from France. I remember reading through a book called the Last Battle of the Crusades written by Tim Pickles and the assistant asking me if he could be of any assistance. I said to him, politely: 'it is about time you got someone to re-write your history books because time has no meaning and history is time out of date.'

'You're not from the University by any chance, are you?' he asked.

'No, no, whatever gave you that idea.' I said, tongue in cheek. Nevertheless, I bought the book and left the shop.

The same morning I had the urge to go to the pub, taking Lynette, Victoria and Barbara with me to make up the numbers for the absentee regulars. The landlord and landlady, Percy and Doreen Stables, Pauline Hodge the waitress and Councillor Frederick Bennett were all positioned in their usual places waiting for the lunchtime rush to begin. The place became animated when we walked into the lounge and this was when Bennett said:

'It's good to see you again, Christopher after all this time; it must be at least six months.'

'Three months actually,' I corrected him.

'However, Christopher,' Councillor Bennett continued in his pontificating way, no different than he'd been when I first met the man, 'what I'm trying to convey to you, young man, is why don't you join us.'

'What are you trying to say, Frederick?'

'The Lodge, man, the Lodge!'

'Frederick.'

'Yes, Christopher.'

'Piss off, just piss off.'

It was then Vicky put her five eggs in with one of her jokes.

'Who's thin, dad; sings and works for MI6?'

'I haven't a clue, Vicky.' I said, watching a sad Frederick Bennett drinking alone at the bar.

'It's 'Boney M', dad.' she replied laughing at her own joke.

'Who the hell is 'Boney M'?' I asked, thinking it was something a butcher would give to his dog.

'Oh, dad you're so boring.'

> "By the rivers of Babylon, there we sat down
> Ye-eah we wept, when we remembered Zion."

An afterthought...

The French president, Jacques Chirac, apologised to the world in 1995 concerning France's involvement in the deportation of thousands of Jewish people to the concentration camps in Poland during WW2, orchestrated primarily by the Vichy Government who were irreproachable under strict orders from 'The Third Reich'.

History nowadays is created at a speed which leaves us all breathless and it is time out-of-date; falling rapidly away into endless depths devoid of any logic or meaning.

I, as the sole author of this book have attempted to catch up a little with events leading up to and including a brief survey of The Second World War. It is my fervent hope that history will never be repeated and no comparable novels will ever be written in the future.

Other titles by Michael Alty:

The Guildford Boys – ISBN 978 1 84549 428 5

The Ghost of Latchford Hall – ISBN 978 1 84540 528 2

The Bells of Saint Clements – ISBN 978 1 84549 620 3

Published by arima Publishing.